MY CARPET OF THE RAINBOWS

SHRINI PAL ZAHEER

ISBN:	Hardcover	978-1-4828-1711-9
	Softcover	978-1-4828-1710-2
	Ebook	978-1-4828-1709-6

This is a work of fiction.
The names, characters are all fictional.
Any resemblance to any person, living or dead is entirely coincidental.
Liberties have been taken with the location of some places like hospitals, beaches etc.

To order additional copies of this book, contact
Partridge India
000 800 10062 62
www.partridgepublishing.com/india
orders.india@partridgepublishing.com

CONTENTS

Book 1
. . . From Home

Book 2
For a Shelter . . .

Book-3
To a Refuge?

To,

Mishtu and Zaheer.

You are my world.

ACKNOWLEDGEMENTS

*Leslie, for inspiring me.
*My mother, for her support.
*Pablo Neruda for the title of the book.

BOOK 1

I

The Rift

I WAS WAITING for the supreme sunrise at the Tiger Hill. But before my eyes could witness the rainbow grandeur, my ears had picked up some cloudy words.

'The sight is just beautiful. Divine. The more I see it the more I like it.' the woman said.

'But you are even more beautiful.' the man said, staring at the woman. And the sky of Darjeeling got sore in front of my eyes. I witnessed a swollen red round wound, bleeding, suppurating over the white heavenly height of Kanchenjunga. Never before had the sunrise at Tiger Hill presented such a ghastly scene for me. Through the natural blind of the foliage of a larch tree I saw them and listened to them, and was almost blind with disbelief. He was my father, and she was, no, not my mother, but Sheila Aunty, my best friend Joy's aunt. Joy's father had a brother, Ramesh. Sheila Aunty was his wife. Her eyes were hidden behind a pair of sunglasses and the divine sight of a rising sun over a snow-smothered peak was getting reflected on the glossy black glasses like two miniatures. Without looking into the eyes of somebody, without sinking into the depth of its liquid charm, how could one gauge somebody's beauty! That too, my father! I could clearly see his profile from here. His small Mongolian nose, the prominent jaw line, the wide forehead, so familiar to me for all these fourteen years of my life, looked so different! As if he was wearing a mask with a strange expression! We had so many Tibetan masks in our curio shop. Some of their curious lines and curves appeared to have been added to Father's face.

I turned my back towards the mask, cloudy sunglasses and the so-called 'beautiful, divine' sight: The sunrise over Tiger Hill Any avid tourist would find his tour of India incomplete without viewing this spectacle. For me, it had been a common sight.

I was born around fourteen and a half years ago, in 1981, in Darjeeling, the beauty spot of the Himalayas, with the grandeur of Kanchenjunga in the background. Tiger Hill is a place about eleven kilometres away from downtown, but a must for the tourists to experience how the white mystery of the Kanchenjunga absorbs the colourful glory of the new-born sun. On a clear sky this sunrise is a wonderful sight. To be caged in your camera. To be framed in your memory. On a cloudy day, however, the unlucky would miss the transformation of the solid white solitude into a melting colourful radiance. Today there was no cloud in the sky, although it was the end of the rainy season here, and most of the time the clouds would linger and one would be walking in clouds, towards clouds, with eyes full of clouds. And my heart prayed aloud for a cloud to blind the sun, and blot out the radiance of the snow-clad peak! Had I not always seen in that spectacular spectrum the colourful loving eyes of my mother? Yes, my mother, with her gentle movements, warm cuddles and a serene green soul, like that of Darjeeling. The Kanchenjunga of our home.

Our home was in proper Darjeeling, by the road climbing up towards the Mall. It was just five minutes' walk to that Chowrasta, or that. flat heart of Darjeeling amongst all its curves, all ups and downs. It was a home. It was a shop. It was a love drop, from the melting icicle of the enormous Darjeeling roof. There were only three of us there. Three moving pieces and numerous peacefully static pieces, the antiques and curios in the showcases and shelves of the Curio Corner, our shop, adjacent to our house. The house was pretty old, the home was not, and the shop was a place where time did not exist. The house and the shop were my father's ancestral property, inherited from his mother's side. The mysterious shop, where time did not exist, the ceiling was low, the light was never enough at any time of the day. Sunlight was restricted through the blinds and the neon lights were regulated to make the curios even more curious and the antiques even more ancient.

Every time I entered the shop, the rest of the world ceased to exist for me, unless some customer came with some worldly affair of selling and buying. Just as when one enters the Planetarium, and after the lights go off the whole universe starts moving around you, with blinking stars, dashing comets or mystic Milky Way, this shop opened up a timeless, space-less canvas around me wrapping me up in· an enraptured existence. Standing there I knew there was no yesterday, there is no today and there will be no tomorrow.

The smell inside the room was weird, like some primitive cave or under the deep-sea trench. The old exquisite clinking chandeliers, the deadly carved grandeur of the dead wood, the stony statues with life juxtaposed on death, or death on life, the Tibetan bells of various sizes with curious clanging clappers to ring the time in and time out, and some big paintings with a fossilised feast for your eyes were all so known and yet so unknown to me like the network of my own consciousness. Time and space both vied with each other not for coexistence but for non-existence. Although most of the items were Tibetan and Nepalese, we had Victorian rose-stained glass lamps too, some exquisite Japanese and Chinese Cloisonné vases, a German Grandfather clock, book-shaped Bhutanese lime boxes, Sikkimese dragon jewellery, a few rare pieces of jewellery of the Mughal and Rajasthani rajas, and some ethnic jewellery of the Himalayan tribes of India.

Even as a very young child I used to hang around the shop. The curious rare artworks were forbidden toys for me. I had heard from my grandma, who had been staying with us till her death last year, that, my four-year-old ambition had been to touch a large peacock blue chandelier. It had been too high for me. Father used to make me stand on his strong shoulders and even then it had been out of my reach. Like the sky of Darjeeling. Even standing on the greatest height of the Himalayas, could one touch it?

Chandeliers show that even light should be served beautifully. I had a craze for beauty even at such a young age. I used to cry when I could not touch it. So, one day my mom who never knew how to lose out on something, had stood on a stool and held me up high. The blue grandeur was within my reach. I caught hold of some dangling decorative prisms and pulled hard. The small delicate prism broke and a fine sliver got stuck in the even more delicate skin of my hand. Everybody had been surprised that I did not cry and did not let that broken piece go from my hand. The peacock blue got a violet tinge with drops of my eager blood. My father came, saw it and hurled his wallet away through the door of the shop. It was foggy and raining and it got lost along with his whole day's earnings. The antiques of the shop silently looked at his antics. They had been used to it for such a long time.

'Are you angry because you won't be able to sell it off?' Mom had asked him.

'Yes, but more so because you have hurt her. You are pampering her. Giving her impossible things, she can never get. Now, she has hurt 'her hand. Later, it will hurt somewhere else, and will hurt much more when she grows up.'

'I'm teaching her to reach for the unattainable and not to retreat in fear of pain.'

Next, both of them had said sorry to each other and attended to my wound. My father had brought that broken chandelier to my room and hung it there from the old ceiling.

Even now it was there in my room, serving me intoxicating light in hundreds of colourful goblets. Instead of candles we had fitted some fancy bulbs. I didn't remember this episode, obviously, but my grandma had repeatedly narrated it for me. Father's antics had been very common at home. But for the first time an antique had been brought from the shop to the house, to our home, only because he was too much fond of me. He was very fond of his shop too, of his *antiques and antics*. I was in awe of both of them.

'Hey, Lucie, why didn't you wake me up?' Joy came running uphill. His eyes were still reddish, might not have had enough sleep at night. His face was a bit swollen and that added some extra charm to his natural good looks. We had come to their home or hotel-cum-home over the weekend. Joy was my closest friend. Just two years older than me and now ready to enter college after the higher secondary exam. He had been there at my home, at my shop, in healthy sunshine, in sickly snowfall. He had a home there, just by the side of our home. They had had a shop there too. Just by the side of our shop. Twin home-cum-shop buildings.

I could recall it all. Twin families with the flavour of love, the leaves of youth and the buds of childhood. Meena Aunty, Naresh Uncle, Joy and his sister Polly, almost six years younger than him. The only difference was in the articles in the shops. There were no antiques in their shop. Rather, it was anti-antique, in the sense that, very modern electrical appliances and novelty items were sold in that shop. The items mostly had MADE IN NEPAL or MADE IN CHINA or MADE IN JAPAN embossed on them. The imported indulgence. Camera, portable TV, walkman, headphone, calculator, clocks and watches with uncommon features and facilities and all such very sophisticated items. Two shops, side by side, the ironic TV tower by the side of the decorated spire of the church. Two parallel tracks: rail and road. The wheezing racing car by the side of the huffing-puffing vintage toy train.

But the homes behind the shops were replicas of each other. Mom and Meena Aunty were great friends. And so were Joy and I. The men were not so close. One used to go to Nepal and the border of China to get more modern and more fascinating items. The other used to go to palaces and places where 'timepieces' were auctioned or sold.

I went with Father many a time. I liked the bidding. The calling of the auctioneer always used to fascinate me. As a child I used to imagine myself at the top of Kanchenjunga with a huge snowman I had made out of snow. I would start calling the bids. Once, twice, many times and at the end, when it was finalised, I would look back to see the snowman had all melted away. The gavel would slip through my loosened grip, shattering my dream, perhaps.

Joy came very close to me, so close that I could feel the warmth of his existence heating up the freezing cold air of the dawn.

'Look at your hair, Joy.' I was about to run my fingers through them to give a combing effect but my hand stopped in the air. Mom would not like it. Touching a grown-up boy without any reason. I tore off a dull leaf from the chestnut tree to divert the movement of my hand and had a full view of this grown-up boy who had grown up with me. He had grown even taller, I thought. I had seen him around a month ago. But Mom told me that now changes in both of us would be very fast. Yes, every time I saw him, after he had left their old home, I noticed changes in him. His voice had got hoarse, his upper lip had a bluish line of a faint moustache. Today, I saw a five o'clock shadow on his chin and noticed his Adam's apple had grown so big and prominent. Mom said he was going to be a man. Even I had changed so much over the last two years. Not grown very tall, but my breasts had been growing bigger and prominent. I had to wear a bra to stop them from bouncing while running and I had to be careful now, on some days, as I was now growing up to be a woman. My thick black hair had grown quite long, touching the hips. Joy threw a cursory glance towards the rising sun and at the glowing and glimmering grandeur of Kanchenjunga. Turning towards me he smiled, showering all the radiance on me.

'Where is Polly? Won't she come to see the sunrise?'

'You know her. She does the things always in the easiest way they can be done. Getting the best by doing the least. That lazybones would rather enjoy it from the bedside window, lying on her back. She has got her bed near the window just facing the east. Anyway, pretty boring sight by now for us, everyday seeing the same thing, for the last two years.' He remarked casually.

'But Joyee, every sunrise is not the same, I have found it so very different every time.' Of course, I didn't mention the difference I had observed today. I had a very small mouth. Quite conspicuous and most of the time I could speak out only half or even less of what I wanted to speak.

'You are as crazy as always, grow up and you will know,' he said with the seriousness of an adult. Then, his eyes twinkled· with childish naughtiness. 'I shall show you something else, really interesting.' He grabbed my hand and took me towards another corner of the hill, away from the crowd.

We came near the edge of the peak from where one could have a bird's eye view of Darjeeling town. The morning mist had blurred the vision. Yet, Joy pointed his finger at a greenish spot in that hazy landscape.

'Can you see, that tea garden over there, near the Happy Valley Garden? It is going tobe mine. I think, later in the day Papa will take all of you to visit it.'

Tea garden! I wondered. 'How come, Joyee-?'But before I could finish my question, talkative Joy answered, 'Well, my grandpa, my mother's father, has made a will the other day, and it seems that I am going to inherit it after I grow up. Sounds great, doesn't it?'

To me it sounded rather incredible. This Joy, a small boy, whose cowlick I used to pull till a few days ago, would grow up to be the owner of a tea garden and control a hell of a lot of people under him, just as we saw in the movies! How would he look then and how would he talk? A big head, a lacquered cowlick and a pair of tea-coloured eyeballs. I would hardly know them. Rocky Tiger Hill as if turned into a green patch, bristling with tea leaves and buds. Two leaves and a bud. So unique: 'They coexist in order to exist.' The air around me filled with the enticing aroma of Darjeeling tea.

I would always like to remember Joy, as a boy I had known for all these years. But Joy, my friend of everyday happenings, my childhood companion of all deeds and the chief sharer of all our mischief had been away from my everyday life for the last two years. The twin homes had become history now. One of the Siamese twins had been operated away from the other. At present, they were living their separate lives. One at the old place, the other on the Tiger Hill. And now they had new family members, Ramesh Uncle, Sheila Aunty and their one-and-a-half-year-old daughter. Ramesh Uncle was a civil engineer. He had gone to Saudi Arabia long ago. He had been there for seven years. In between he had got married. Around two years ago, they had come back to India and Darjeeling, and had brought a pair of large scissors to cut the threads of the kites Joy and I had been flying. The kites had got lost somewhere beyond Kanchenjunga. Over the rainbow. I was holding the black and white thread even now. And dreaming about walking on the carpet of the rainbows in search of the kites.

Ramesh Uncle and Sheila Aunty had come back loaded. For Ramesh Uncle, *his purse had become his personality*. He purchased a piece of land on Tiger Hill. They had their cottage built there and one ugly morning they had put down the shutter of the shop, locked the door of the home and left for their new home with a plan to build a hotel there shortly. The peak of Kanchenjunga had got lost in the pea-souper. I had been left all alone in a half-dark world of antiques and antics. I missed him badly during our music lessons, comic sessions, and mostly for meaningless activities and talking sessions. They were now leaky, airless, flat balloons, plain pieces of amoeba-shaped plastics. He might not miss me that much as he had a little sister, Polly, who was, very young though, around eleven. Also he had his niece Manasi, Aunty Sheila and Ramesh Uncle's one and-a-half-year-old daughter. They also had this hotel 'Sunrise', with many tourists and their many activities. So, it was never loneliness for him, never lack of company, never dusting the ancient dirt off the inanimate antiques, or facing the animated antics and wondering about the enormous enigma called life!

We had been meeting at intervals, no doubt, but a part of my home had been missing. *'A portion of the earth has been pulled out of its body. They are still related by the gravitational force, they are still moving together. And with them moving a dividing distance. The space is mysterious.'* We had been trying to keep our old days alive by arranging family picnics, get-togethers and outings. Today, our coming here was one of such reuniting plans. Meena Aunty and Naresh Uncle had come to our house two days ago and invited us to their new hotel, opened recently at the top of Tiger Hill. We had reached just half an hour ago. Mom had gone inside the hotel to meet Joy's family. Father and I had been waiting to see the sunrise. Sheila Aunty had joined us shortly. Father had asked me to go to the hotel and call the others as the sun would be out shortly. I had started for the hotel but the small crowd gathered on the peak had shouted, 'There, there it is.'

I had stopped and come back a little to see the glorious spot on the rainbow-coloured sky and dream-coloured Kanchenjunga, perhaps a snowy shadow of the evasive Everest, at a dreamy distance. But instead, I had come across the clouded goggles and heard the even cloudier words, and for the first time, the divine sunrise seen at terrestrial Tiger Hill turned into some discoloured dismay for me. Presently with Joy and his joyful smile by my side, I began to feel better. I was listening to him, as always.

'Hey kids, what are you doing there?' We looked back to see that our moms were coming towards us. My mom was looking great in a pale silver sari. Her tall poplar body moved uphill with natural grace. She was very tall. Taller than my father, by two inches. My father was short, only five feet four. They were called the odd couple. Her oval face with a pointed chin was looking gorgeous in the soft light of the baby morning. Meena Aunty had grown fat. She was panting a bit after walking uphill. I hadn't seen her for over two months. Two days ago when they had come to invite us, I had been away to attend my lessons at a coaching centre.

'How was the sunrise today, Lucie?' Mom asked me. 'Could you see it clearly or were there any clouds?' Her eyes were very clear I could see, like a dream of last night you could recall in the morning' with all details. I didn't want to cast a shadow of cloud over them. Also, I did not feel it was correct to say anything in front of so many people. I also had a faint doubt that maybe Father had been kidding although that would be quite unlikely of him. I just informed Mom that it had been a clear sunrise.

Meena Aunty hugged me affectionately and said to Mom, 'Now, she has grown up, Eva. She is looking so pretty. And my,. my, look at her complexion! She is getting fairer day by day.'

'What fair! I would say she is not dark,' Mom said.

She never considered me fair, although all the others used to call me pretty fair and she herself used to call me fondly 'my orchid' at times. Orchid is a fair flower, or is it pale? The reason of her dissatisfaction was that, Mom used to compare me with herself And Mom was as fair as a shining white cloud. She had English blood in her veins. Her Goan grandfather had married her English grandmother when India had been under the British rule and Goa under the Portuguese. She had got that touch of English fairness. I had not. I had an Indian complexion, typical Indian, fair or whatever one may call it. In fact, everything was Indian about me. My hair—dark, and my eyes too.

When I used to stand in front of the mirror, especially of late, as nature had started adorning me with changes, I would see a long-necked Indian girl with two heavy eyelids, hiding half of the two large wondering eyes. They are a bit peculiar. The lower edges of my eyes were not as much curved, as they should be. They were almost straight. Next, I'd see a small mouth. Extra small. Not thin. My lips looked full, moderately fleshy, but the width was almost as much as my thin nose. Pouted. Then there were a few spiralling curls along my hairline. My hair was inclined to curls, but these were crisp curls, like mahogany shavings. Flouncing on my forehead, and cutting off its width for a better show. Father used to call them 'tender tendrils' affectionately. This would be all about my simple face. In fact it was so simple that Joy would draw my caricature with a· few strokes. Two semicircles, one small straight line in between and one tiny dot just below that. He would not take the pain to outline the face; instead, he would encircle it with a few whorls, suggesting my curls. And that shabby geometric mishmash would be me!

I smiled to myself as I heard Meena Aunty speak.

'But she should put on a little more weight. Don't go for this slim trim fad. Too slim and too fat both are bad if you ask me. And why don't you braid her hair? They are now so long and thick. If you don't take care of them now itself they will start falling off like mine.'

Meena Aunty was scrutinising me with her extraordinary large eyes. Then, she fondly pinched my lips and kissed the hand with which she had pinched them. This is a common Bengali way of fondling an older child. But in most of the cases, people would lightly pinch or touch the cheek and kiss the hand with which they had pinched it. In my case it would be usually my lips, as everybody would say that I had the smallest and cutest lips in the world. As for me I didn't like it much. Such a small mouth with a natural whistling pout! As if the words would get hurt squeezing out of them. Joy would tease me, 'God does not want you to talk much.' Yes by nature, I used to talk less. So did my mom and to some extent my father too. So, I was not sure if I could blame it all on my small mouth. Only my thoughts and dreams and secrets used to remain refrigerated within me, Kanchenjunga's snowline, out of anybody's reach. Nobody had ever scaled it. Neither did I want anybody to do it. Today's conversation between Father and Sheila Aunty would also remain there like the frozen hawk in the mountaineering museum.

I started thinking over the conversation once more. Something disturbed me thoroughly. My father. The change in him! Yes, it was there. This time he had pulled the shutter and locked the door of our Curio Corner without any grumbling. He had left his antiques without his antics. How? And why? The shop was my father's obsession, and session after session he could spend with those antiques, even when there were not many customers. He and my grandma used to keep the showcases real showy. Every now and then Father would give a facelift to his shop, he would meet suppliers and read literature to get more and more items for his shop. He knew history very well and would tell the customers about each item briefly but interestingly. Usually, my father would not take a break for months, as he always remained too busy with his antique' shop. Mom and I would badger him to go to *Mirik* or *Kurseong* over the weekend but he would not, telling us how much loss it would cause to his business and finally he would give in, with a lot of grumbling and a series of terms and conditions. Whenever he was angry he would sit in the shop the whole day without coming home for food. Mom would not dare go there lest he create a scene in front of the customers. She would send me or my grandma to request him to come and have his meals.

'Do you want me to take my shop to another rented room away from home? Don't disturb me, I'm busy.'

And he would be busy calculating his accounts or would give a hot and hasty order to the Gurkha boy who worked in our shop. *The antiques and the antics*—that was him.

However this time, when Meena Aunty and Naresh Uncle had come to our house and invited us over to their new hotel, he had agreed without any sign of protest whatsoever. The formal inauguration had been done around two months ago by some VIP, and we had attended the function. They had requested us to stay with them that night but Father did not agree. Mom had to come back reluctantly. So had I. One sunrise, to be seen together with Joy, had been missed. This time surprisingly there was not a whit of protest from his side! It was wonderful, but made us wonder about his sudden change of mood. His mood had been unpredictable no doubt, most of the time but this time it had been almost shocking. It had been a pleasant shock and so locking our house and shop we had come to enjoy the weekend with Joy & company.

Mom and I, of course, used to visit Tiger Hill every now and then. Guests and visitors and friends would keep on invading this tourist place all through the year and we had to oblige them by taking them to all the unique places while my father would take care of his antiques and antics. This tourist spot was the zingy thing for the tourists. And now it was a visiting spot for us too, as Joy's family, our second, extended home had been shifted here. With their new venture 'Sunrise', Uncles Naresh and Ramesh were expecting good business. The business seemed to be picking up nicely.

In fact, Naresh Uncle had offered my father a partnership and asked him to join them in the motel business. My father would have had to sell off his business and house and invest the money in this new business. From the mystery of history to the limited geography of the three-storeyed floating population. No, he had not agreed to it. Our home had, experienced a blizzard of arguments. Mom had wanted my father to take up the new motel business. Reason? It would deal in life, apart from earning more profit, and home would be so much more than a shop full of dead antiques. Mom had liked it more as her family had been in the same business in Goa. Mom's parents used to run a hotel *'Casa no Duna'* (A house on a sand hill) on the sandy golden beach of Goa. But my father had not wanted to part with his own business. Neither had my grandma, who had been alive at that time. I remembered some of their arguments.

'You have already spent more than fifteen years of your life in this shop. Why don't you try something new?' Mom had said.

'What is wrong with this shop? It has been with our family for the last three generations. Fed us. And now I should get fed up with this? Think about Mummy, how she would feel about it.' Father had tried to explain.

'You are not doing very well, of late.'

'For that matter I am trying to add something new and working on that. But only because a few bucks are less in my cash box I can't back off. You should rather buck me up and we'll sail through the bad times.'

'I am bucking you up but not the way you want it. I am asking for a change. Why are you people so resistant to change?' And here Mom had overstepped the edge of the ridge and fallen on a rift valley.

'You think you Christians are the only people who changed the world! We Hindus are all backward? Change, change and change!' Father had clenched his fist and banged on the table. Antics to protect his antiques . . . and then a landslide on the mountain pass—'How would you like it if I wanted to change you, this home, this family? Would your Christian adventurism like to venture on it? Tell me.'

Yes, it had been a mixed marriage. My father was a Hindu. His Nepali mother and Bengali father both were Hindu. Yet, it was an unconventional marriage. Two persons from two ethnic communities. In Bengal and generally in India, a marriage would be usually between two people of the same caste and the same community.

Mom was a Christian. Goan Christian. Grandma used to worship Lokesvara, Pashupatinath and my father, although not a religious man used to celebrate all major religious festivals in a festive way. He would never go to temples or perform the formal 'formulaic' rituals, as he would name them. However, he had never objected to Mom's going to the Church or celebrating Christmas in a religious way. We used to have the sparkling star on the Christmas tree and the quivering flames on the Diwali lamps. Mother had a cross around her neck and Father had a sacred thread across his torso. My grandfather had been a Hindu Bengali Brahmin. And perhaps he had believed in the power of the sacred thread before threading his way through the underground uncertainty of the Naxalbari movement: An attempt at an armed revolution fuelled by the China backed communists in West Bengal, now,—a page of history. *Soaked in blood. Burdened with blunders. Blurred with the tears of my grandma and many other grandmas.* Nobody knew what had actually happened to my grandfather. My grandma had tried her best through all known sources to trace him out. Then after a long time, one morning the sky over Kanchenjunga had not got the vermilion touch of a loving sunrise. The parting of my grandma had remained shrouded under clouds ever since. But inside the four walls of ours there had never been any religious clouds.

In my school, of course, many of my classmates and seniors used to ask me about my religion. Even one of my teachers in my primary school had once asked me, 'How can you worship Hindu gods when your mother has had beef and you are born of her! You are committing a sin.' Now, I knew that the target of those words had been more sinned against than sinned. That's why Mom had immediately taken me away from that school and got me admitted into a Christian Missionary School.

At home, we never had beef and Mom would have it only when she would go to Goa. Father had never objected to it nor had she ever asked Father to have it. I had never tasted it because meat itself had not been my favourite. I liked eggs and fish. So did Father. But I had a cross pendant hanging from a chain around my neck. Mom used to say it would protect me from any bad influences. I had a Buddhist *Gau* too, on my arm. My grandma gave it to me as a lucky talisman. I used to go to various churches with my mom and temples with my grandma. Mom also used to visit the temples sometimes. We used to speak mostly in English at home, because my mom didn't know Bengali well. So, our family was considered by most of the people as semi-Christian.

'What is my religion Mom?' I had asked her once, when I was very young, just nine years old.

'What do you think it is?' She had wanted me to explore.

'Can't I be both Hindu and Christian? Is it illegal like bigamy?' Mom had smiled at my question. And Father laughed.

'You may not be anything and still you may love God. Some big men prescribed some ways to serve God and be nearer to Him. Common people followed them. You may follow your own,' Mom said.

And Father dropped a clanger. 'God is but an imagination of men. Imagination of an ideal Superpower. Different groups of people in different parts of the world and at different times imagined Him differently, so there are different religions.'

Father's communist father had left many diaries and write-ups and perhaps a red throbbing vein in my father. Maybe he had told him the same thing when he had been a child. Father's idea had confused me then and haunted me later. 'God created man in reality, or man created God through his imagination, in a dream?' I excavated the answer in myself I created my god in my dream. And my dream became my god.

I wish everybody had his own god. His very own. He should worship Him in his own way. Just as one dreams one's own dreams, and relishes them his own way. Can't God be personal? Impersonally personal? Why should there be some solid mechanical machinery to reach out to the abstract of all abstracts? What if we don't have any religion and bear our own god with us, our own way? Not to be inherited like a property but to be absorbed like the air. In my own heart.

Once I had revealed this idea to Joy, a thirteen-year-old Joy. At that time, he had not accepted it at all. 'There will be no fun. How can all of us celebrate Diwali, Durga Puja together then?'

'But you don't celebrate Christmas. We don't celebrate Eid. There are always some people left out.'

'They have their own group.' Joy just could not comprehend and smiled it off. 'You and your crazy ideas, Lucie. Why can't you think like others?'

I just couldn't. I wished everybody had his own god, so that he could feel Him his own way and not through the edicts of others. Why nobody understands God is not to be felt in a vicarious way. Isn't it degrading Him? Why should there be a Hindu, Muslim or Christian way of feeling God?

However, I had heard the argument about the Christian and the Hindu, for the first time in the four walls of our home, that day. I could not recall any other argument on this line so far. A few years ago there had been a long agitation, for a separate Gorkhaland: of the Gorkhas, by the Gorkhas, for the Gorkhas. There had been strikes, demonstrations, frequent lathi charges and occasional firing. Our business had started suffering. The number of tourists had been falling, day-by-day. I had got curious. The curiosity of a six-year-old girl.

'Daddy, do we have to go away? What is this new Gorkhaland they want? Will it be a fairyland?'

Father had sneered, 'All such land, be it here or in Bihar or in Punjab, would be a ghetto.'

The word ghetto had sounded unfamiliar, but rang in my ear. 'Ghetto? What is a ghetto? Some kind of ghost?'

'Ghetto means a place where people of one community stay together. Hitler made it for the Jews. Now, people want to make it for themselves.' He had spoken more to Mom than to me. His tone—acrid. 'They are turning this world into a zoo. Each species in its own cage.'

'Who will visit them?'

'Nobody, each one will look at the others till one day out of boredom, they will break the cages. 'He paused and said, *'Mixing and mingling is what has made this world. Think of air, water, soil. They are all mixtures—strange and grand. Life is a mixture . . .'*

Father would go on. And I would go on with my thoughts. I had thought of a life, where reality and dreams were blended. I had been thinking ever since.

The argument about the Hindu and the Christian had not prolonged any further. Mom always used to be cool and in control of the situation. She had said in an apologetic tone, 'I didn't mean anything about the Christian or the Hindu. Don't imagine things. If you don't want to take any risk and make the best of an opportunity, don't do it. But you may regret it later.'

'I will not,' Father had said, 'can't you see, going there means leaving my own proprietary business, where I can do anything I like. There it would be another story. I'll be the weakest partner. And Ramesh—no, I just can't bear that man you know.'

And he had not gone to join the lucrative business of a motel at Tiger Hill and avoided the company of Ramesh Uncle.

Ramesh Uncle. A man fast balding in his mid-thirties. He was the kind of person whose unkind coldness stung much more than the snowy winter wind of Darjeeling. He had a round face with a bristling moustache. His ash-coloured eyes always reminded me of two flat coins. Yes, he had coins in his eyes, in his pockets, and maybe all his body and mind were stuffed with coins, Indian, foreign. He was a human piggy bank. He used to laugh very little, and when he did, it was just a jingle of coins. He was not only involved in· many kinds of business, he used to lend money to people, including friend and foe in their hour of need, and take it back with high interest.

But this piggy bank had a hole in the bottom,—the attraction of the lush racecourse of Darjeeling, the highest racecourse in the world and the racing ground in Calcutta, lavishly decorated and fiercely crowded. With a binocular slung around his neck he would frequent the fancied fences during the racing season. He would take Sheila Aunty with him as she was supposed to be lucky. Joy once went with him but that day the hole in the piggy bank grew bigger, so next time very rudely he refused to take him. He had never taken him again. Joy had not liked it and told me about his ill feelings. However the gallop brought Ramesh Uncle gallons of fortune and he remained steeped in pleasure. The pleasure had been punctured when the daughter had been born, and not a son.

Sheila Aunty had earned an 'unlucky' tag. I still remember the day vividly. When we went to see the newborn baby, Ramesh Uncle could not suppress his frustration and Sheila Aunty could not suppress her tears because of his reaction.

It was just after Durga Puja. I asked my family, *'Did the Himalaya get frustrated the same way when Devi Durga was born? How does every one worship her then?'* In the Bengali mythology, Durga, the mightiest goddess of all was the daughter of Himalaya, the king of the mountains. My grandma felt scandalised.

'Don't you talk like that about the gods. It is outrageous.' My grandma shared a home with my grandfather, but not his ideals. Her Kanchenjunga was pointed towards her Lokesvara, and her ocean depth was inscribed with a belief that my grandfather's misfortune was due to his atheism.

'Did you cry when I was born?'

Mom held me in her arms and Father kissed me. They comforted me.

'Darling Orchid, you are the pupil of our eyes.' I was, no doubt. But Manasi was considered a loss and in order to compensate the 'loss' Ramesh Uncle marched avariciously towards a few more millions and not towards the new millennium, ushering new ideas. 'To the millennium, to the millions was his motto. *A coin-eyed cunning man.*

Although Naresh Uncle was his brother and had the same type of round face, bristly moustache and receding hairline, his eyes were very different! No coin, but affection was coiled in his dark brown eyes. He always used to bring me beautiful toys whenever he went to Nepal, Bhutan or any such place. He used to show me the novel electrical items and explain their usage elaborately. When Joy and I would fight over something he would mostly be on my side and try to tell Joy that he should allow me to have my way as I was younger than him. He was a huge figure, tall, robust and strong, unlike my father. When I was five or six years old he used to carry Joy and me on his broad shoulders, as broad and strong as the rock used by the students of mountaineering. Along with a strong body he also had a strong mind, always cheerful, always witty. If Ramesh Uncle was a piggy bank, Naresh Uncle was a fountain of jokes and anecdotes. *Like that hilly fountain of Darjeeling whose water is always warm, even in freezing winter.*

'There comes your "Mister" Meena Aunty's words addressed to Mom stirred me from my reverie. 'You must look after his health, he is growing thinner.' I looked back to seeFather walking towards us. His thin legs were moving slowly and his eyes were as if looking through us. Was he thinking about his antiques, I wondered. There was no Sheila Aunty with him. Nor around him. I started thinking that whatever I had heard or overheard might be having no overtones. He had been joking for a change. Otherwise, why was Sheila Aunty not with him now. The maples, the poplars, the larches around sighed a deep breath of relief, rustling their leaves, blowing my wisps of hair, and blowing away my doubts.

'How did you enjoy the sunrise Biren-da?' she asked him.

'Marvellous.' He gave a ready-made reply, as mechanical as the answering machine on a telephone. And he was blinking fast, which usually he did when he was uneasy. 'Have you seen Sheila by the way?' Meena Aunty asked it to all of us it seemed, but Father replied hurriedly, 'I saw her going that way.' He pointed at some shady corner of the hill with a lot of trees spreading out their leafy branches.

'Maybe she has gone to catch some butterflies. She has strange hobbies and interests,' Joy said, as talkative as always. Meena Aunty only smiled and said,

'Okay. Let's go in. Breakfast is waiting for us. She will come back soon I think.'

We all went back together to the hotel, where Uncles Naresh and Ramesh were busy attending to the customers. Naresh Uncle came from behind the reception counter, all smiles, 'Welcome brother, welcome.' He hugged Father, as he would always do when they met after an interval. They both looked happy. Ramesh Uncle smiled dryly. Coins flashed in his eyes.

We went to their big dining hall. Some of the hotel customers were already there. We went to a very big table and all of us sat, except Ramesh Uncle, who remained busy with work. And Sheila Aunty joined us just when breakfast was being served. She was not wearing those goggles now. Her eyes looked very restless and her high cheekbones were shining as if she was sweating. She was wearing a heavy overcoat and must have walked uphill very fast, I thought. Polly, the eleven-year-old sister of Joy asked her, 'Were you jogging Aunty? You are panting.'

'No, dear, I walked quite fast,' she said, and settled on a chair by me. A strong perfume stifled my senses. Her long varnished nails, her well-set long brownish hair, her mascara-coated long eyelashes all gave her the looks of a heroine. She was beautiful, Father was right, but she was definitely not more beautiful than the sunrise at the Tiger Hill. And obviously not more beautiful than Mom. A rhododendron arrogance pitted against the magnolia magnificence.

'Why don't you call Ramesh, Sheila? Let him come for fifteen minutes. Bishu can look after the place during that time,' Meena Aunty said. Bishu was the caretaker of the hotel, an employee of theirs.

'He won't come, I know very well and I don't want to waste my energy and patience on this.' Sheila Aunty's voice sounded as bitter as a badly brewed cup of tea.

'Ramu will keep clear of this place. He may have to laugh if he comes here. He will get hurt if he laughs much.' Naresh Uncle said in a humorous but loving tone showing affectionate indulgence of an elder brother to his over serious sibling.

'Sometimes, I wonder Naresh *da* that you are brothers!' Mom said.

'Just after my marriage I felt the same way, Eva.' Meena Aunty said 'while taking a bite of a crisp toast. Everybody had started breakfast by now.

'But when will he have his breakfast?'

Mom enquired. 'He will get his plate there and have it there,' Meena Aunty replied and started preparing a plate to be sent to him.

'Don't worry about his breakfast, I think his fast has already been broken. Maybe two or three times.' Naresh Uncle was again in a jocular mood, 'He tastes all the dishes before they are served to the customers. And if there is any fall in quality, the poor chef will have a very bad time.'

'But it is required. This dedicated attitude makes one business more successful than another,' Mom said in a serious tone and immediately Sheila Aunty's voice twanged.

'Yes, he is a very successful businessman. But don't you have any topic to talk about other than making fun of him?' She pulled back her chair and almost stormed off the room like the gusty chilly winds of a Darjeeling winter.

'Listen Sheila, I didn't mean it, Sister.' Naresh Uncle went behind her with an apologetic attitude.

The tallest poplar of the Darjeeling forest, bent and arched by the gust of a stormy wind. There was an uneasy silence where the only sound was of crisp potato chips being chewed. Joy was never very fond of his uncle and aunty. He looked at me and made a silent sign to imply it had been good riddance. But Meena Aunty was feeling embarrassed, 'She has suffered a lot, you know. Poor thing. I don't blame her. Every woman wants a normal husband who cares and shares. He takes her for granted. That too just after three years of their marriage!'

She was speaking in a low voice to Mom so that the children could not hear, but although my mouth was small, I had very sharp ears and could hear it all. Joy was busyhelping Polly with her pizza. And soon Naresh Uncle came back, flanked by Sheila Aunty and Ramesh Uncle. They were clinging to his left and right arms.

'See, I have got two birds by throwing only one stone of a joke. Good performance dear Sheila. Sometimes, you must overact, I mean overreact like that, and only then our serious brother will take you seriously.' He made both of them sit side by side and with the exaggerated humbleness of a waiter said, 'May I now serve you breakfast, madam and monsieur?' Everybody started laughing. Even Ramesh Uncle smiled and said, 'Enough Dada. Let me finish quickly. The fishermen are about to come. Yesterday the fish they supplied was not fresh. Some customers complained. I have to talk to them about this and recover the penalty.'

Along with the smell of rotten fish, the sound of jingling coins filled my senses. I did not enjoy my breakfast very much. I could not even play footsie with Joy, as in our early childhood days. The distance in space was a few inches, but the distance created by time was impassable. Mom warned me very specifically not to play footsie with anybody anymore as I was growing up to be a woman. And no good woman played footsie, she told me. Yet just to divert my mind from the business talks going on over the cup of tea at the breakfast table, I looked down to glance at Joy's trouser-covered legs (nowadays he hardly wore shorts), and that was not prohibited by any standards. But my eyes got fixed on a woman's legs playing footsie under the table. Sheila Aunty's with my father's. I looked at their faces and saw that they were sipping piping hot tea with a cool composure. I closed my eyes. *Ghoom*. The highest railway station of the world. The breathtaking Batasia loop. The spiralling railway track from the *Ghoom* station waltzing down to Darjeeling town. The two parallel rails of the track diverged. A wide distance unfolded in between. My toy train got derailed.

I excused myself and came out of the room. Breakfast was already over. The adults were having tea. We, children did not have tea, so I had no problem leaving the table. Joy and Polly also came after me.

'Anything wrong Lucie? Are you feeling sick? Your face is very pale.' Joy was worried as usual. He was affectionate, like his parents. I looked down and shook my head to indicate no. But he held my chin up and smiled.

'Look at you. Your small mouth has got even smaller!' Yes, my small mouth hurt me. I could not speak out anything. Not even to Joy. I slowly pushed his hand away. Mom taught me not to touch any boy or get touched by· him unless it is very much required. Like you are falling and need somebody's help. Or some boy needs your help in some similar situation. Only touching hands would be okay.

'And what about Joy?' I had asked her with daisy simplicity in my eyes. Twelve years old, I had experienced just a couple of 'red litter' days. That would be a few months after Joy's family had left their old home and our neighbourhood.

'Joy is also a boy.' Mom's cool eyes had rested on mine.

'But I have always touched him.'

'You were a child then. You used to run around topless when you were seven years old, can you do it now?' Mom had asked, looking at the growing heaviness around my chest. She had not explained further. I had got the drift, and hardly drifted from the path directed by her. With Joy it used to be difficult, however. So often my raised hand stopped before a friendly, and oh-so-usual pat. Or before arranging his tie or dishevelled hair, as it had happened this morning. Sometimes, I felt, maybe, it was better that Joy's family had gone, as he could never have been so close as he used to be. *More than space, time had created the chasm between us.*

Time, which life is made of, changes so many things.

'Something wrong, Lucie?' Joy was still staring at me. I shook my head with a faint smile. And deep inside I felt something was wrong somewhere. The blue stretching sky, impaled on the snowy· sharp summit of Kanchenjunga bled and spread a colourless emptiness in front of my eyes.

'Look at the clouds,' Polly shouted. All of a sudden a sharp chilly wind started blowing. And the clouds invaded the sky. An approaching storm. Now, all around us were only the clouds, only the wind, only the drops of rain, only black and white and grey. Colours were blown away by the storm.

Our outing was spoiled. We could not see the cascading mountain falls and had to be satisfied with the boring sight of the rain trickling down the windowpanes. Meena Aunty and Sheila Aunty got busy in showing Mom their newly acquired dresses and jewellery. They called me to see them too. Somehow, I never liked those things. Joy, Polly and I started playing video games and our fathers sat in front of the bigger TV, watching programmes and discussing politics. I did not want to continue playing with video games for a long time. Neither did Joy. We were growing up. To be man and woman. The toys and these games could not interest us anymore. We left the joysticks and guns and game with Polly and went upstairs to the balcony. Raindrops came slanting and covered us with cold kisses and the clouds touched us subtly. We enjoyed it like we had always done in our childhood. We stretched our hands and played with the raindrops falling on our palms. But the wind was very strong. Soon we had to run away. We entered Joy's room. We were half wet and shivering.

'You must change,' Joy suggested. He went to our suite and got my bag. Then, he left the room allowing me to change. I was never before alone in grown-up Joy's room. Last couple of times when I had come here he had shown me the room and we had spent a few minutes together. Today after changing my clothes I looked around the room. One corner was filled with the usual posters of sportsmen. One portion of the wall was covered with a beautiful curtain. I thought that might be a door leading to a balcony and so I pulled the curtain. But to my utter surprise, I saw some big close-ups and revealing posters of models and heroines pasted on the wall. A shocking discovery behind the innocent cover. Quickly, I covered them up again. I came out of the room and saw him coming. Somehow, I could not look into his eyes. *He knows all about a woman's body,* I thought, and nervously felt that the tea coloured eyes were throwing an X-ray look towards me. My limbs twitched. Almost the way they had that night when overnight I had grown up.

II

Growing Up, Growing Gap

THIS ONE WAS an olive green among the deciduous forest of memories. Grandma was still alive. I had just entered my teens. Joy's family had shifted to Tiger Hill around a year ago. It was winter vacation for us.

The Season's first snow had decked up the maple leaves with a soft white whispering glow. Icy cold wind had kissed the window-panes warmly and left their mark all over. This was a lean season for the tourists. So Father had closed the shop a bit early. I had been busy the whole day in finishing a painting, and couldn't go to the shop although I wanted to. I had always wanted to go to the shop alone, at night after it was closed and Father had left to be with Mom or his antics. By then Grandma would have retired to bed. I would come in through the backdoor on the pretext of cleaning the items and shelves. But I never dusted very seriously. When the hand of time had adorned them with its adorable dirt and grease, my hand was too insignificant to remove them, I always thought. Sometimes, I used to stop our attendant Gorkha boy from vigorously rubbing a *Phurba* or the *Shams*. However, I did not allow them to be shop-soiled either. Lightly dusting them one by one gave me an opportunity to see the item closely, read its details and memorise them. I had already outgrown my toying days and wanted to grow up with these items. Or did they ever grow up?

I did not know. But I certainly grew up. I knew that some new items had arrived the previous day. Grandma was asleep, Mom and Dad were watching TV in their bedroom. I unbolted the backdoor and slipped into my unique world. I switched the light on. Away from the showcases, near a corner a few wrapped-up articles were kept. Father had not got time to unpack. I took them out one by one. One magnificent bronze *stupa*, a pair of *tsampa* bowls, one antique *torma* stand, a few Tibetan *chang* pots, two beautifully carved cylindrical holders of scrolls, one Victorian rose-stained glass lamp and a few jewellery items of the Bhil tribe of Rajasthan. I kept them all on the lowest shelf of the showcase. They would have to be listed, and tagged before display for the public, I knew.

While stacking them I noticed a long and flat packed item kept against the wall. *Can't be a tanka. Must be a Western painting*, I thought. Eagerly I unwrapped it. When I was carefully tearing off the last wrapper, hardly did I imagine that I was going to unveil my youth, and my childhood would be shelved along with the antiques hereafter. The inevitable did happen. I knew it happened to everybody one day or the other, for me it was the moment. I just looked at him, and with a start crossed my arms over my breast, little realizing that I was fully clad. I forgot that those eyes were painted eyes. I was in Adam's garden. And my Adam was looking at me straight from the frame, so lively, so lovely. A devastatingly handsome figure, most probably of a knight from the Middle Ages. Perfection personified. *An enchanting charm to which one could only succumb.* For a long time I stood there facing him and memorising each and every line of his charm. Then I covered the portrait, switched the light off, and went out on the road, without asking anybody's permission. The freezing breeze hugged me, the snow shower kissed my hair, my fingers, my face. I was still warm. Standing on an empty road, I looked up to the expanding space and I did not feel lonely. Overnight, I had grown up and no one was aware of it.

'Hey buddy, where are you?' Joy waved his hand in front of my eyes as though to break my trance. His bare arms showed hair all over. I had never noticed this before. In my memory a picture of the soft skinned, stem like arms of a boy, was inscribed. Yes, I had spotted the changes only in his face so far. And maybe the height. The change in his voice. Growth had embellished him all over. Today, when I was trying to avoid his X-ray eyes, an alien panorama burst upon my view. Alien yet aligned with my teens. When had I seen those highland shoulders? They used to be wobbling branches on which I stood up sometimes, in my early childhood to reach out to something high. Look at that vast expanse. Was it the same reedy chest I used to slap, while playing hide and seek? And those thin and weak legs, when had they acquired the muscular strength?

'What's the matter Luchi, you look lost!'

Joy used to tease me by calling me, 'Luchi,' which is the name of a Bengali dish. I was not in a mood of retaliation by calling him, 'Toy, toy train'. He was no more a toy train at the moment. He had outgrown the narrow track. Growing fast. A speeding Toyota. I wished to call him Toyota. At the moment, however, neither my small mouth nor my large eyes wanted to confront him. I just ran past him and went straight to the room where Mom and the aunties were talking. He stood there with a baffled look.

The rain and storm subsided near about lunchtime. I went out in the open. Nature was washed clean. The green looked greener, the roads looked cleaner, and the blue of the sky was bleached. Joy and Polly soon joined me.

'Why did you run away? Just to listen to the idle gossip?'

'Mom never gossips.'

'If not gossip, they talk about clothes and jewellery. And the latest fashions. At the most, TV serials. That's all.'

'Shut up. How dare you talk like that about the elders!'

'Am I wrong?' He was laughing, Women don't have too many things to discuss. You bet, after a few years you will also be the same. An idle, gossiping, jolly woman.' He was in his usual teasing mood and was smiling mischievously.

'And yet, you men will discuss and think mostly about women,' I retorted. With my small mouth, however, I could not say that even his manly curiosity at this point was all about women, in spite of their limitations. I had discovered it already. However that awkward feeling about the X-ray look had subsided considerably. After all, all the pictures were of pretty Darjeeling butterflies, grown-up women celebrating their youth, while I was just out of my chrysalis. With my Knight? I glanced at Joy. The square face with the tea-brown eyes, the wide mouth with a charming wide smile. I recalled the face of my Adam, my Knight. A line by line, feature by feature, expression by expression scrutiny. They did not match. I could not figure out why the disagreement disturbed me.

We were called to get ready for the outing. We packed some dry food quickly and started in the spacious jeep of Naresh Uncle. Ramesh Uncle, as usual, could not come with us. He had to remain at the hotel to look after the business. Sheila Aunty was about to come, but she got an urgent call at the last moment from her uncle's house.

He had been hospitalised and she would have to rush to see him. They stayed a few kilometres away from Darjeeling. She told us that she would not come back that night, if the condition of her uncle so demanded. My windowpane, blurred with water vapour, was wiped clean. Again, we were together. We, the twin families. Just seven of us. Without any coin-jingling piggybank or black-goggled glamour amongst us. As it used to be in the pre-Ramesh Uncle era. We visited the tea garden, Joy would soon own. We took a cable car ride on the ropeway. But no, everything was not the same. There was no rolling down the slope together with Joy, as we used to do some three or four years ago. Polly alone did it today. I only gathered some mountain flowers in my hand, filled my eyes with the rain-fed greenery, and hoisted a sinuous happiness up there, in the billowing blue sky.

I saw Mom and Father walking hand in hand, talking and laughing happily. Naresh Uncle put some wild flower in Meena Aunty's hair, at which she showered him with mock anger. Joy was carrying the video camera and I had my own small camera for still photographs. Meena Aunty had gifted it to me when I entered my teens. That was my thirteenth birthday. Thirteen. Unlucky number. Teenage starts with an unlucky number. Is it because of this, that it is full of unknown pains and unnamed aches? I had wondered many a time. Joy was carrying one binocular too. Earlier, Naresh Uncle used to carry it. We used to take it from him, and fight as to who would see through it first and then putting our heads close together both of us would see through it simultaneously, one with the left eye, the other with the right. We could not see clearly this way, but had the satisfaction of seeing or not seeing things together. Today, Joy saw a colourful bird through the binocular and gave it to me, 'See, it is beautiful, isn't it?' he asked. I agreed with him. But this was not beautiful. *This growing up. This growing gap. Between two growing persons.*

Maybe Joy also felt the same way. He bit his nails and again I had to control my advancing hand to restrain him from this bad habit. Instead, I had to restrain myself He had always had this bad habit, an incorrigible habit. He bit his nail, spat it off and asked me, 'Do you go to the skating rink now?'

So many snowy soft pictures glided into my memory.

We used to go to the Gymkhana club. During the winter the skating rink used to be open. I loved skating. Specially, figure skating. The smooth gliding flowery movement on the ice was like a whisper of a dream to me. My god! We used to skate together. In the early days when we were just seven and nine years old and had tied the skates for the first time, we could move only by holding and supporting each other. And even then we used to fall so often. It was like divided we fall, even united we fall. And falling was fun. Slowly, we learnt to glide on the ice. Joy did not enjoy figure skating. He liked speed skating. Speed skating is only movement. Movement and forward movement, like time. There is no backward nostalgic turn like the Batasia loop, there is no spiralling like your consciousness, there is no butterfly flow like your dream. On the rough surface of life this is probably the smoothest dream ride. The whole world whirls around you. Fast and flowing. Mom changed the proverb for me, 'Lucie, life is not a skating rink. You can't glide that smooth on the path of life.' Yes, you cannot. So, we grow up and grow old. Along the rough edge.

'Do you go for skating?' Joy repeated his question again. 'Rarely. What about you?'

'No time, boy, class twelve. Study, study and study. School and coaching classes, and private tutors. Dozens of them with hundreds of possible exam questions. More difficult than climbing the Mount Everest.'

'Better attempt climbing Everest then.'

'Would you accompany me, Bachendri Pal?' Joy said jokingly, flashing his tea-flavoured eyes. As though, if I accompanied him, he could climb the ever-highest Everest! I smiled and kept quiet.

Joy asked again, 'Do you skate alone? How much have you picked up by now? Can you jump without falling?'

'Oh Joyee. I wish you'd come and see. Make some time this winter.'

'I will. But I've forgotten how to skate, I think. Last three years I haven't been at the rinks. Mummy curtailed my outdoor activities so much before the class ten exam, you remember?' Of course I remembered clearly.

'You girls are lucky that way. Not much bothered about your career.'

Here, he expressed the most commonly held belief about a girl from the Indian middle class. Even in the last decade of the twentieth century. More than eighty per cent of Indian women are housewives and for them their face is their fate. The average Indian does not care much for the figure. He does care for the other figure· though, the fatter the better. More than ninety per cent marriages are arranged ones, and the fat round figure is more indispensable than the seven rounds around the fire. Even for an ugly face this fat figure would be the saving grace. By law it is banned, by custom it is fanned. This is a dowry-fanatic nation. These are not my words. I have read these in my grandfather's diary. Mom had explained them to me (they were written in English). That was when she had told me that I must have a career, outside of marriage. Father had remarked lightly that I would inherit the shop and that would be my career. Mom had not agreed.

I too did not agree with Joy.

'This is not fair Joyee. Studies are equally important for me. But I love figure skating while you don't.'

'Bet I don't, a feminine sport, my dear.'

'Feminine! My foot.' I was angry. 'Who are more masculine than Grinkov or Christopher Dean?' I was small-mouthed no doubt, but not a mush mouth.

'Hey, how much do you know about this masculine thing? You cutie "kidult"!' His tone was normal and jovial, typically Joy-like. But I could not figure out why I got flustered. The sunrise of Tiger Hill coloured my face.

'Dada, Lucie-di, come. We are packing up.' Polly came running. She liked the company of elder women more and used to stick around them. She came and started pulling me.

'Come quickly. Mummy is saying we should not be late, we have to go to some other places, you know.'

Joy jumped down from the big protruding boulder we were sitting on and ran. I was about to chase him, when I remembered Mom asked me not to run fast. *The soft hills bounce and it hurts.* I started walking. The small toy train allowed the swift Joy-Toyota to speed by along the parallel road track.

Polly walked with me and asked me a peculiar question.

'Lucie-*di*, what does "rendezvous" mean?' She pronounced it as 'randadjvus'.

'I don't get you.'

'Even you don't know? Dada always says you know English so well.'

'Can you spell it?'

'No.' She shook her head. Then took out a small chit from the pocket of her worsted jeans. A few letters were scribbled on it: RENDEZVOUS AT ELEVEN AT HILL VIEW COFFEE SHOP. Hill View was the name of a very famous hotel, where there was an excellent restaurant. The scribbling looked very familiar. But it had been written in a hurry and most probably at the time of writing the chit had not been kept on some smooth surface. Yet, they kept blinking at me familiarly. I tried to recognise the handwriting, when Polly's impatient voice rang out, 'Don't you get it?'

'Where did you get it?' I asked her.

'Near the porch of our house. This morning. Do you know what it means?' Her round red face radiated expectation.

'Yeah. It means somebody has asked to meet somebody at that place and time.'

'Why don't they simply write "meet at so and so place"? Why such a difficult word?'

'Because it is not a common meeting. It is special.'

'You mean between a boy and a girl? Without the knowledge of others?' She winked.

'Maybe,' I answered in a serious tone. Polly was a precocious child. Particularly in matters relating to boys and girls she had much insight. She used to move around with many young boys who came to stay in their hotel. Meena Aunty was quite disturbed about her and that's why she would always accompany Polly wherever she went. She did not allow her to go with Joy either, lest she did something silly with his friends. Polly's agate eyes twinkled.

'Good word to learn. Difficult but useful. You really know English pretty well.'

'This is a French word.'

'French! My god you know that too!' My small mouth did not allow me any further lexical explanation. But she spoke. With a mischievous flash in her eyes.

'Who has written this and to whom? Do you have any idea Lucie-*di*? Is it from Dada to you? Or for me? Maybe some boy . . .'

'You are too young dear.' I interrupted. 'And this is definitely not Joy's handwriting. Why should he write to me, he'd just ask.' My embarrassment honked. I had a full view of this pony-tailed premature wonder, and wondered: *Just the other day she used to play peek-a-boo and today it is pick a boy! So fast!*

Time passed fast. The great outing was soon over. After the great outing, we had a grand dinner specially thrown in our honour. At the dinner table along with the sumptuous dishes Naresh Uncle served us lots of delightful jokes. Clinks of plates and pots mingled with our choral laughter. We ate and drank and had fun. Everything was so normal and jolly that I forgot the clouded goggles and the colourless sunrise. The playing feet faded away. The dangling doubt fell off like the dry leaf from the deciduous trees in the fall.

It was surely a joke. Father was capable of cracking jokes at times. And those feet under the table might not be his. I might have made a mistake, I thought. But Polly's chit spoiled my mood. However when Joy pinched my nose for spilling salt and spoiling his bowl of *rasgulla*, (a Bengali sweet dish) I looked at him and rediscovered my snowball man. As cool, as simple. Not the sunny knight. As we were all pretty tired we retired to our respective bedroom just after dinner, bidding each other 'good night'.

But the night did not turn out to be so good, at least for our family, or to be precise, for me and my mom. We were given a beautiful suite. I had a broad soft sofa to sleep on. The bedroom of Mom and Father was quite spacious and the whole suite was nicely furnished with expensive teak furniture. But my adoring eyes stopped on the teak face of Father. I looked at his marble-eyes and understood that he was not in a good mood. I slowly escaped to my own room, dropped on the soft sofa and got ready to hear the bass.

'We must leave tomorrow morning just after the sunrise,' it said. The merry air full of fun, frolic, and frothy delight, which had been ringing around us, was suddenly forced out, leaving a vacuum of uneasiness. A power cut imposed on a Diwali night. For a few seconds or minutes, none of us could say anything.

Finally Mom asked, 'Why? Is something wrong?'

'Well, not exactly, but I have to go.' He wouldn't explain as usual.

'But try to understand,' Mom pleaded, 'Meena has made some programme for tomorrow, we are going to Mirik for boating and picnic. Wasn't our original plan to go back on Monday morning?'

'This morning after coming here I saw an ad in the newspaper about some important auction, day after tomorrow. I have to attend it.'

'We are going back day after tomorrow in the morning.'

'But I must go and get some idea about the things to be auctioned tomorrow itself. I have to talk to some of the agents. I just can't stay.' His well-defined jaw-line looked determined. Mom's upturned nose rose higher too.

'I can't go back tomorrow. This time, we are meeting after so many days. I need a break from the daily chores. I also need to do some shopping.'

'Yes. Only concerned about your needs. Never concerned about our shop. Never. Even after all these fifteen years. It's a pity.' I could hear Father sigh. Mother's apathetic attitude towards the shop had always hurt him badly. For Mom the shop was a dead thing. Beautiful but carrying the memory of a buried past, like a tomb. Mom was fond of life. Life in splashing waves, life in rolling wheels, life in flapping wings. She just co-existed with the shop, while Father existed to cohere.

'Sometimes, I wish I could be an antique or a curio.' A chaffed wound was laid bare.

Father answered, 'Here, I put my foot down. I'm going back tomorrow.' I heard a noise. Father had hurled something on the floor.

I was eavesdropping all along, sitting quietly in my room. I felt it necessary to enter now.

'What's going on Mom, won't you sleep?'

'We have to go back tomorrow, Lucie. Your father can't stay. No Mirik, no shopping, no new clothes for you. Okay?' Mom's voice was dry ice.

I went very near to Father, threw my arms around his neck, looked straight into his marble eyes and said in a pleading tone, 'Please, Daddy, please let's stay tomorrow. Please.' My small mouth could not say more but my semicircular eyes spoke the rest. 'I don't have company, don't have much fun. At least one more day let me play with abandon.' Most of the time it had worked. It worked wonders today also. The marble softened into wax and a soft flame flickered.

'Okay, if you insist . . . you stay. Both of you. Let me go back alone. I just can't wait. You come back day after tomorrow morning, as it was originally decided.'

'Are you sure you are saying this from the heart and not just pretending . . .' Mom was still doubtful, but I jumped at the suggestion.

'Oh Mom, please . . . Daddy has agreed. Let's go to bed, we've to get up early in the morning.' Next, we and our differences got buried under warm, quilted darkness for the night.

Nobody missed Daddy much the next day. Sheila Aunty did not come back that day and rang up to tell that she would come back only in the evening. Her uncle was recovering from a mild heart attack, she informed us. She was missed a few times by Meena Aunty during shopping as she depended heavily on her remarkable ability to judge the quality of things and to gain from bargaining over the smuggled goods. At the end of the day however, we came home with lots of bags and packets full of things and our minds satisfied with the nice trip. In fact, my mom and Meena Aunty's chemistry used to work so well that when they were together nothing could go wrong. When we had been neighbours, others used to take them for sisters. So, it was little wonder that this time also everything went so well, barring the bargaining of course which was somebody else's field. But even when they felt slightly cheated they just chattered the uneasiness off their minds. Meena Aunty was a gem of a person. Although she was very rich and purchased much more than we did with our limited resources, she made things easy for us by emphatically telling us, now and then, that she was shopping for two families, her own and that of her brother-in-law. Naresh Uncle took care of the children. Polly and Manasi.

When we came back it was already late evening. I was tired but after dinner, Joy took me to the terrace. It was a moonlit night. The mystic splendour of Kanchenjunga seemed so close to us, as if, by stretching a hand through the darkness I could touch it. The snow-clad peak under the moonlight looked like a huge silver antique, which had lost its shining glaze but acquired the depth and mystery of time. I would have liked to handle it just as I did the antiques in my father's shop. But instead of a dull, cold, lifeless metallic touch, I felt something soft and warm. It was Joy's hand. He was asking me what I was holding in my fist.

'Out with it. You can't hide anything from me,' he was smiling. His tea-coloured eyes were now coffee-dark in this semi-darkness with a doubly stronger effect.

'Not hiding. A surprise for you.'

'Surprise! Well, let me see.' In our earlier days there would· have been a mock scuffle over the possession of the surprise, but we were growing up and throwing away all childishness. So, he just tapped slowly on my closed fist and I opened it slowly without much ado.

It was a small pocket torch, as sleek and smart as Joy himself. Its light could be regulated to different degrees, from dim to very bright, depending on your need. I bought it today for him at the market on the way to Mirik. Joy started examining it, made the light dim, then brighter, then further brighter and when it was the brightest he just focused it straight on my eyes.

We had a hearty laugh and Joy said, 'That was my gift for you, I didn't go to Mirik to buy something.'

'Do you have to give me some awful gift always?'

'You call light an awful gift! Madam, that is the source of life.'

We would have gone on like this with our meaningless childish chirping, but Sheila Aunty came up, combing her long shining hair. That meant she had come back. Till dinner time she had not been there. She didn't notice us, it seemed. She sauntered across to the other side of the terrace, very much lost in thought.

'Hi Aunty, is everything okay with your uncle?' Joy asked.

She was startled and looked towards us, smiled, and said, 'Oh—, he's all right now.' Then, the high cheekbones shone even higher, like some barren Himalayan peaks. In a peculiar tone she asked, 'It's pretty late. What on earth are you two doing here?'

'Seeing *Kanchenjunga* in a full moon night, what else?' Pat came Joy's reply, 'You've also come for the same, haven't you?' She did not reply and kept on combing out the tangles in her hair and then I saw it. Just then. That chunky antique bracelet on her bony wrist. It was from our shop, unmistakably it was. So many times I had cleaned it, clattered it, and clasped it in my hands! It was exquisite. I was told that it belonged to Noor Jahan, when she was in Bengal, as the wife of Sher-Afghan, long before her marriage to Jahangir. Father used to tell me stories about many of his antiques. Stories of history? Or were they his stories just to light up my imagination? To deepen my dreams? This was one of· the items about which he had related a few fairy tales. The bracelet was magnificently crafted on a heavy plate of silver and inlaid with semiprecious stones. Even in this half-darkness, the stones were blinking like the memories of history. I had always imagined the course of its journey from the glamorous, brilliant, hands of the ruler's consort to the insensitive, coin dealing hands of the merchants to its finally landing up in our shop. But now, I just could not guess how it got from our wooden shelf to this wooden wrist.

I could not help asking, 'Oh my! Aunty, where did you get this bracelet from?'

I was not sure but I thought she was startled. The next moment she echoed a clattering laughter, 'Why, you like it?'

'Yes, but I mean, this was in our shop.' I put it very straight.

The china-clay eyes shone in the darkness. Did I see some fine cracks in it? A gust of cold wind blew making the tall maples bow and scrape. Sheila Aunty turned away from us and said, 'I didn't know that. Today when I went down to my uncle's place, my cousin's wife gave it to me. I haven't had the least idea where she got it from.'

'I know, it must be from our shop-'

Joy interrupted my excitement. 'Let's go to bed Lucie, it is getting late.' His face looked a bit strange to me. Strangely serious. When did I last see him this serious? Just before the secondary exams perhaps. We climbed down the stairs, said 'goodnight' to each other and went to bed.

Mom was already fast asleep, so I could not share the excitement about the bracelet with her either. But I knew Mom would not be able to recognise the bracelet. She hardly stepped into the antique anarchy. She was fond of living things and hated the old and dead. If she was asked to choose between the museum and. the zoo, for a visit, she would always opt for the zoo, no matter how good the museum was.

Sometimes, I wondered how she married my father. *Some butterflies do live on wooden sap.* I tried to imagine how it could have happened. A little I had heard from my grandma, my mother's mother, who had been in Goa running her own hotel business. I had heard a lot from my grand aunt, my grandmother's sister. My mom, Eva Pinto was a beauty from Goa, with a sand-coloured body and surf-coloured eyes. And her heart had the fathomless depth of the sea in which one could always anchor, whenever needed, just as I always did when I hurt too much. My mom was my great emotional anchor. How she, from the sultry sea level got attached to the highlands of North Bengal was an intriguing story. Some portions I had heard, the rest was supplemented by my imagination.

It was a summer vacation, around sixteen years ago. A twenty-one-year-old beauty travelled all the way from Goa to Darjeeling. Her friends were with her. They were in high spirits in the highlands until Eva Pinto lost her handbag one foggy evening containing all her money, shopped valuables, return ticket, etc. They were all feeling very low. Next day while they were moving along the Mall, a pair of marble eyes followed them. The group was addressed finally, 'Excuse me, has anyone of you lost your handbag?'

'How do you know?' The timid wave surged up in expectation.

'Well, listen, yesterday someone forgot a handbag in my shop. When I opened it I found a group photo where all of you are-'

'Eureka, Eva,' one of her friends was stoked. 'It must be that group photo we got taken yesterday morning.'

'Where is the bag?' All were very eager.

'There, in my shop,' he said. 'Will you please come in?' The shop Curio Corner got flooded with undulating sea waves and perhaps washed away the stony, ancient sombreness, at least for quite some time. The marble got softened to wax and a flame of love was kindled. There was a thanksgiving dinner. It was followed by a return dinner, arranged by the shop owner's beautiful and hospitable Nepali mother. She had married a Bengali man who had later got involved with the Naxalbari movement, led some operations, remained underground for some months and never resurfaced. As if, mother Earth took him back to her womb, like the Sita episode of the Ramayana. Father had been about fifteen years old at the time Grandpadisappeared. Grandma had been allowed to run her family shop along with her father. Her other sister had already been married and settled in Nepal. Her two brothers had fled to Nepal to avoid the iron grip of the police who had been suspicious of every young man at that time, especially anyone connected to a Naxalite family. The brothers had stayed there and decided not to come back to India even after the Naxalite storm had subsided. Grandma's father had died a few years later leaving the shop to the mother and the son. Grandma was a good storyteller and had told Eva the story of her life in bits and pieces during her numerous visits to the shop, sometimes with some of her friends, sometimes alone.

The wild Goan wave somehow got fond of beating against the highland stone, maybe, to wear it off. After a fortnight when the wave went back to the sea, it was never the same. Nor did the stone remain unaffected. It started rolling between Darjeeling and. Goa, and unlike a rolling stone it did gather moss all over, moss and messages, and finally gathered the sea lass in marriage. The new story started which was now history, an invisible antique piece in the Curio Corner. I still didn't understand why she had loved him or why he had loved her. Grandma said 'Love is blind' and perhaps that was the reason, or it was just beyond my understanding at this age. I also didn't quite get it when my spinster granny, my maternal grandma's spinster sister said, *'Love is blind, is only a half-truth. Love ends as blindly as it starts. It is a blindfolded journey at both the ends, in-between light and lightning as long as it lasts.'*

Next morning after an early breakfast with Joy's family, without Sheila Aunty who apparently had a headache and could not come down, we started for Darjeeling. Joy came with us. In fact, he had to go to his junior college in Darjeeling, so he dropped us at our place. All through the journey, which lasted roughly half an hour, he kept on bantering and I forgot to tell Mom about the Noor Jahan bracelet. When his car went out of sight we went into our small house, adjacent to our Curio Corner. Father was in the shop already, talking to a customer. I changed quickly and went to the shop as I wanted to make sure before telling Mom about the bracelet. Besides, I had to see my knight. After two days. There was hardly any time for Mom too. She got busy in the kitchen. She used to give private tuition to some schoolgirls, which gave her the satisfaction of doing some worthwhile work. In fact, being a Goan she knew English pretty well and young schoolgirls used to come to learn spoken English in her tuition classes. Mom had even wanted to work in a school but Father had never wanted her to go out to work. Interestingly his mother, who had died last year, had never objected to her daughter-in-law's wish to work as a teacher in some girls' school. But she had never interfered in their life. So things had continued as my father wanted and the wild wave had been stilled and sealed in an oyster shell to decorate my father's 'Home Corner'.

Without disturbing Mom, I entered the shop. I looked at my Adam. He looked back at me. Father did not notice me as he was going through his accounts book. I looked up at the shelf and yes, I was right, it was not there. I was very happy that Father could sell at least one very expensive piece. He was always unhappy about not getting genuine customers for his costly pieces. Most of the people were interested in buying trinkets and small statues and less costly Tibetan ethnic items like silver censers or *tsampa* bowls. Their curio value was not much. Also the profit from them was very less. I was just going to congratulate my father about the grand and unusual success, when Father got up and looked at me. He seemed to be quite pleased to see me.

'Good that you've come here, just sit for some time. I have to meet a supplier, will be back in half an hour.'

The suppliers were those who supplied curio and antique items to Father, important persons for his business. This was nothing new. Many a time I was asked to stay in the shop for a short period. I knew almost all the items, their price list was in the drawer. Small items I could sell. For bigger items I used to request the customers to wait while I showed them various other items to keep them busy and to get some, more items sold. Although because of my small mouth I was not an ideal salesperson, I could somehow guess the taste of a customer and show him the items of his interest. Till last year Grandma had been there and she had worked along with my father, but after her death my father did not get my mother's support for running the shop. So, he had to take my help now and then. I could not possibly replace Grandma, not at this age at least. I just tried to do my best to help my father, to help the business, which, according to my grandma, would eventually be run by me. Mom never wanted me to pin my future on dealing with dead articles, however beautiful they might be. She wanted me to develop my painting talent and would look gloomy if I took too much interest in the shop. I never wanted to hurt her, I loved her most among all living things. She cradled my sentiments all the time.

I remembered the problem I had faced with the portrait of my knight. I had been infatuated with the portrait and had all my teen dreams centred around it. The episode would be like this . . . . I started spending night after night ill the shop with that portrait. I used to dream myself on the horseback behind that fairy-tale figure. Like every common teenage girl I started suffering from a *Cinderella syndrome*. I did not talk about it to anybody, not even to Mom, nor to Joy. I feared they would laugh at my esoteric feelings. It was my very own secret pleasure. I did not want anyone to share it. It was all mine. However Mom somehow got wind of it. One day when I was looking at the old ceiling of our room, lying down straight on my back, and imagining that most charming face slowly closing in to kiss me, as in the films, and closed my eyes to take a dip into the delicious darkness, Mom awakened me.

'What's it Lucie? Something wrong?' Mom's eyes were microscopic. I woke up from the trance and only shook my head.

'Are you seeing any boy? Or have you taken a fancy to anyone?' I blushed heavily. The morning sun unveiled the mist over Kanchenjunga. My eyelashes drooped and my breathing got faster. I could not look into Mom's eyes. But she hugged me and kissed my hair. The anticipating anchor.

'It is a great feeling, isn't it?' She was trying to make me speak out. However, my small mouth did not let out anything.

Not for long could I keep it a secret. One day I heard Father was asking Grandma to send some pictures to one address. I enquired with Grandma. One rich foreigner had chosen three pictures. And yes, that portrait was also one of them. My Adam would soon have to go. I had crested the mountain of desire and now I started sliding down, crashing to reality. But I did not know how to tell anybody. How to express my feelings. It might be taken as nonsense. And that would hurt me more. My dream, my Adam, my feelings, all were as real as the blue span of the sky. But who else would feel that way? The ice had started melting. And it could not be kept secret from Mom.

'Why were you crying last night?' Mom asked me next morning. Tears welled up in my eyes, although I knew Mom hated tears. Her mind was a seasoned snowfield.

'You know tears are strangers to my eyes. Why are you making friends with them? Don't cry and tell me your problem.'

'Mom, they are taking that portrait. Please, don't allow them.' I sobbed badly while speaking out my secret. Mom went inside the shop, saw the picture, and came out smiling.

'Don't worry, I'll tell your father.' She comforted me. I could always depend on that solid anchor. But there was a problem. The antique had to be sold. Father had already promised to give the portrait to the man. Now he just could not go back on his word. He did not care much for money. But it would damage his image as well as that of his shop. Damage to a dreaming heart would be less serious compared to it, although he always related to my dreams very dearly. Besides, my small mouth was to blame.

'Why didn't she say it earlier that she wanted to keep it? I wouldn't have displayed it. Now, it's too late.' He was quite logical, no doubt. Grandma tried to comfort the by assuring that an even better portrait would be brought from Nepal. Or maybe a very rare *tanka*. She could not exactly realise my feelings.

The only person, who did, remained calm and thoughtful. She did not comfort me.

'If a thing has got to go, it has gotta go. You can't keep your beautiful dream alive in the morning, can you?' She told me, yet I had a feeling that somewhere deep inside she was thinking of a way out. That was my mom. First, she called a photographer and got a large snap of the portrait. It was not so lively. However, it was better to have half a loaf than none and I tried very hard to comfort myself with that. Mom also advised me not to go to the shop for a few days in order to get used to the feeling of not seeing 'him'. I kept the snap under the pillow and felt the warmth touching me through the layers of foam. Following Mom's advice, I exercised mentally to stop thinking about the real portrait; when it was packed, when it was despatched to the esteemed customer.

After a few days, I returned from school to discover the portrait hanging on the wall of the shop. Yes, the same one. The same charm, the same looks. Instantly I was on top of Kanchenjunga. And I touched the sky. After the first few minutes of wild snowboarding, my mind settled' to pose a logical question.

'How did you get it back?'

The three happy faces looked at each other. I could read some secret code signal in the blinking of their eyes. I could not decode it.

'He gave it back to us at my request.' Father was smiling. Grandma too.

'That is a fib,' Mom said softly. And then she explained how she engaged one painter of repute to make a replica of the picture.

'It must have been very costly, Mom.' I felt a slight guilt.

'Not costlier than this smile of yours, dear.' Mom cuddled me and Father kissed me.

However, they never told me clearly if this one was the original painting or the one sold to the customer. Knowing Father and his honest nature, I could imagine the truth. But I also knew Mom and her insistence and intelligence. She might have kept the original one for me without even Father's knowledge. She was invincible: the Kanchenjunga of our home.

'May I see those statuettes, please?' A customer's voice brought me back to today's world. I did a little bit of selling till my father came in. He was almost out of breath.

'Are you okay Daddy?'

'Oh yes,' he said, but the marble eyes were lost in thought. I had never seen him like this. When I gave him an account of the last hour's business, he did riot seem to be listening carefully. Closing the accounts book, he told me, 'Thanks and now you may go.'

'Let me be here for some more time.'

'No Lucie, you go inside. When required I shall call you.' Saying this, he picked up the receiver and started dialling.

I just wanted to tell him about the bracelet and longed to linger. 'Please Daddy, a few more minutes.'

'For heaven's sake. Don't disturb me,' he said angrily and banged the receiver down without making any call. The antiques and the antics, I had to leave them behind for the time being. I could not tell him about the bracelet. Neither could I tell Mom, who asked me to prepare some soup and went out hurriedly to take a friend of hers, a spinster teacher in our school, to see a doctor: This lady stayed alone and depended heavily on Mom. After an early lunch, I had to go to my private tutor. I was preparing for my secondary exam, which was just a few months away. I decided to congratulate Father at dinner time when all three of us would be together.

Just before dinner a storm broke out. Not the snowy storm alarming the stability of Kanchenjunga, but the storm inside our four walls. I was studying in my room, and I didn't know when Father had closed the shop and come in. Our dinner time was around nine at night. But much before that Mom called me. I went into their room. I saw Mom sitting on the bed with all the packets we had bought from the marketplace near Mirik. Father was sitting on a deck chair.

'Lucie darling, show your father what we have brought for him,' Mom said to me.

We started showing him the dresses and items we had bought. The marble was cold. The nice blue T-shirt we bought for him got a half nod. He stretched his body loosely on the chair till we showed him all, exquisite showpieces made of glass and silver, one imported gold watch for me, a few novel electronics items.

After seeing all, he sat up straight, looked straight into Mom's eyes and said, 'You've spent a lot, I see. Why did you try to compete with them?'

'What do you mean?' Mom did not like it, 'I never competed with anybody, I spent the minimum.'

'I didn't mean to upset you, only you must know that this year I am not doing well.' Father got up, went near the heater and made the heat a bit low. And I opened the window wide and invited the storm.

'But Daddy, the Noor Jahan bracelet must have fetched quite a good profit!' My small mouth indulged in a big blunder.

'What are you talking about?' Mom asked.

'Yes Mom, we should congratulate Daddy, finally he could sell that expensive beauty.'

'How do you know?' Father asked.

'I saw it on Sheila Aunty's wrist yesterday.' I hardly noticed the uneasy calm in the room and continued, 'Did you know that you were selling it to Sheila Aunty's cousin?' Father did not answer. Neither did he look at me.

To convince them I had to say again, 'Sheila Aunty told me—' I trailed off as I looked at Mom. Not two surf-coloured ripples, but two iceberg eyes . . . and my words froze on my lips.

Nobody spoke for a few seconds. With an unknown uneasiness creeping into my mind, I looked at Father. The marble white was now bone pale. Mom asked me to go down and lay the table for dinner. I went out of the reach of the storm. After fifteen minutes Father flew down the stairs and flung open the backdoor of the shop and rushed into it. He slammed the door behind him. The antics would be now buried in the antiques. Another door was slammed upstairs. Mother had locked the bedroom.

Mom did not come down at all. I went up and knocked at the door after some time.

'Have your dinner, Lucie, and go to bed. I'm not feeling well. Goodnight.' she spoke from inside. I followed her instruction and went to bed early. But I was not able to sleep. I looked at the sky through the windowpane; a splinter of a moon in the clouds. A splinter in my conscience. The bracelet was cutting deep into my mind. My sleepless eyes could now also see the playing feet, the discoloured sunrise, and the shady goggles. I thought about Mom, I thought about Father. A deep chasm and the rope bridge across it snapped and hanging hopelessly in the air. I got up from bed. I could see the night pulsating on the blinking blob of a firefly. As silently as the snow fell on Kanchenjunga, I went to the back door of the shop, pushed it soundlessly, it was not locked from inside. I entered the shop. I saw Father had dozed off sitting on the chair.

His head was hanging on his left shoulder. I stroked his hair, dusting the anger and anguish off this living curio.

'Come and sleep in my room, Father,' I murmured. He opened his eyes. Two marble eyes embossed with a dream. Or a nightmare? They looked like a pair of antiques. Two *dzi* beads bereft of charm. I repeated, 'Come· and sleep in my room, Father.' I held his arm and tried to make him stand. He did not protest. Slowly, he stood up and walked to my room. He lay down on my bed. I covered him with my blanket and watched two marble eyes slipping down deep into the stream of sleep consciousness.

After making sure that he was fast asleep, I slowly entered the shop again. My lively knight's empire at the dead of night. I cast my first glance towards the portrait as I always used to do. Now, it had a SOLD tag on it. Father said that this would serve both the purposes, nobody would buy it and at the same time it would give an impression that the business was running well. However, tonight I had not come here to share the dream of youth with him. *Tonight I have to do something real. Tonight I have to keep my eyes open,* I told myself On the other nights I would close my eyes in front of the portrait and feel the feathery touch of the darkness. And the goose pimples. And the pimples would burst into brilliant stars. The vision of darkness.

I didn't know who had defined darkness as want of light.

It is not. It is just another stream of consciousness. Darkness is my darling. Why do we close our eyes when we listen to some beautiful music? In all movies why do I see lovers close their eyes while their lips melt over each other's? Why did Lord Buddha close his eyes to reach and acquire the ultimate knowledge? Darkness is not only in the silent graveyard, darkness is in every cell of a living entity. In light we see, in darkness we feel. Darkness fills us with that, which we fail to see in the light.

But tonight I had come here more to see, and maybe, less to feel. I went near Father's desk and pulled out the drawer. The accounts book, the stock register in their hardbound outfit looked well composed. Many a time we had pestered Father to buy a computer. Many shops nowadays are furnished with this one invariable work-piece. But Father said that among the antiques it would look odd. Among the curios it would be a curiosity. And this was one time we heard him joke, 'Lucie will get some antique computer sometime in future when she will run this shop. Let her work on that.' One of the rare moments when Father cracked a joke.

I opened the accounts book, went through the recent entries on the receipt side for the last few days. Father and mainly my grandmother taught me how to check and maintain an accounts book. So I understood, not as an expert would do, but pretty well. I couldn't see any entry of selling that bracelet and noting down the amount received for it. I checked again the accounts which I had seen earlier, expecting that there might have been an oversight on my part. But searching thoroughly through the last one month's entries I failed to find that particular entry. It could not have been sold before one month, in fact even around fifteen days ago, I had seen it, dusted it, I could clearly recall. I suddenly felt as if a cloud had entered the room, being filtered through the transparency of the windowpane. Not to shower a few icy drops on us, but to be blended with my consciousness. I tried to get rid of it. Perhaps, Father had forgotten to note it down. Sometimes, he did note things in another rough book and copy them afterwards. But this time the entries were updated till today. Then?

I looked up into the stock register. The page, where the Noor Jahan bracelet was entered could be found out easily. And what did I see? Instead of the date of sale and corresponding cash memo number against the entry, there was an asterisk with a capital letter S. The asterisk! The star! The twinkle, twinkle little star started flashing towards me, flashing and flushing out all my wit. Yet, I pulled myself together and from a hidden place took out a duplicate key of the cash drawer. There was the cash-memo book. I took the memo book out and there was no duplicate bill voucher in it, showing the sale of the bracelet. My hand shook, and the key fell on the ground, shattering the still silence of the night. More shaken was my mind. Did somebody shoplift it? Stole it without Father's knowledge? That innocent-looking *Gurkha* boy, who cleaned and attended our shop and home? He had been so trustworthy all along! Why did Father not mention any theft when I told him about the sale? Then, I remembered the bone-pale eyes, I remembered the storm in the bedroom. The nostalgic smell of the beeswax polish of the door of our shop grew stifling. All the beautiful Tibetan silver censers emitted a pathetic smell of a burning future. A deep chasm developed in the *Teesta* Valley and chased me out 'of my invaluable world. My timeless, darling darkness flamed up in the *Newari* and silver butter lamps and I closed my eyes to be buried in it, to be carried away by it, far, far away from these awry happenings.

'What on earth are you doing here?' I had to open my eyes to see Mom standing near the back door. Mom's eyes were red. Starry eyes. Stars get red when their light dies away. That asterisk was still very blue, popping out of the book and slowly changing its colours and shape to be the brightest and nearest star rising right over *Kanchenjunga.*

'*You are even more beautiful.*' I recollected those pale words discolouring the sunrise on Tiger Hill!

Mom came near the desk, had a glance at the books, took up the cash-memo book, leafed through it.

'It is not sold,' I whispered. Mom's eye fell on the asterisk. The starlight was stilled. Two etched carnelians were showcased. I had never felt her so lifeless. She closed the book, kept back all the things where they used to be with unusual meticulous care.

I helped her. Nobody uttered a single word, neither did we look at each other, yet as *'darkness reveals more'*, we talked volumes to each other in the sealed silence. Tears welled up in my eyes. I suddenly felt there was no roof over my head, the endless Darjeeling sky with cloud and· rain and mist was hanging above my head, moving away farther and farther upwards. Mom hugged me, kissed me on my wet eyes and took me with her. I spent the night with her in their bedroom.

III

The Fire

NEXT MORNING I got up pretty late, and still managed to go to the school. But when the school was over, I didn't feel the urge to return home. Was there a home any more for me? I started walking very slowly, along the ups and downs of Darjeeling roads.

It was a pleasant afternoon, the roads were wet after a short shower. Some tourists were going with their baggage loaded on the backs of small local boys. Barefoot and barely dressed, they were dragging their existence uphill with their backs bent, knees bent and heads lowered. Instead of going towards home, I took the road towards the Mall. The Mall would be always crowded, mainly with tourists and also with the local people who could feel the evenness of the earth only here. Otherwise, Darjeeling is out and out hilly, curvy. You have to walk upwards or downwards. I passed the rows of shops and restaurants, I saw the tourists enjoying horse riding, I passed some foreign hikers with rucksacks on their backs.

Finally I reached the Mall and took a deep breath. A tea-picker woman passed, carrying a child piggyback. The child waved at me. Perhaps, I was the only one who was alone there. I had never come here alone before. I was allowed to be alone. My school uniform spoke aloud. So, no photographers asked for instant snaps or any horse keeper trotted around. I kept my schoolbag on one of the benches meant for the tourists to enjoy the surrounding view, and went near the edge of the Mall. I stood against the railing and looked down, not to enjoy the scenery but to rest my eyes looking for emptiness.

The vast rocky expanse of the Himalayas, the green grandeur, the bodiless white clouds were all as profound as they had always been. The happiness of the touring crowds moving around was profuse as usual. The sunny trot of the mules and horses, the antique smell of the unwashed wool of the horse drivers' clothes, the fresh smell of the horse poops, were all just the same. Only something different had happened to me. Why?

God is a sadist. I remembered a line from my grandfather's diary. *Either there is no God or if He exists, He is a great sadist.* My grandfather had written this, perhaps on one of his worst days. His dear comrade had been brutally tortured with a hot iron rod forced through his anus. He had succumbed to death later and it was proclaimed that he had been killed in an encounter. I read about Tiananmen Square. I read about many young comrades of my grandfather in his diary. To me there was no difference. The same budding desire to bring dreams to reality. The same bleeding wound. But I could not agree with my grandfather. My God is not a sadist. My god cried with me. I closed my eyes to feel him. The dream of a childhood. Holding one hand of Mom and one of Father, I swung. My childhood swung. In between them. The soft cushion of my dreams slowly soothed me. *I was in the arms of my god. My dream. I was alone and I was safe.*

I was not allowed to be alone for very long. A friendly touch on my shoulder and I turned back to see Joy standing in front of me. My senses got filled with the aroma of Darjeeling tea. There were bubbles of surprise in the tea-coloured eyes.

'Hey, what are you doing here? Attending to the guests? Where are they? In one of those shops?'

I could not but feel amused at his series of questions. Yes, the cup of tea was full and flavoured as usual. Everything was the same as usual, and it hardly mattered if the roof of one obscure 'Curio-Corner home' had vanished into the blue.

'I've come here alone, what about you?'

'Alone! Are you kidding?' He was about to laugh, when his tea-coloured eyes caught sight of tiny dry lips, pale cheeks and lightless eyes, which silenced him. Some boys came towards us, calling Joy to go back with them. They were his classmates; some of them knew' me and said 'hello'. It seemed that they had come here to make some purchases, and also to have some snacks and fun in one of the restaurants. But Joy changed his plan. 'Will you guys please excuse me? I have to go to Lucie's house, her father has called me, there is something urgent.'

Why did he tell such a white lie and so smartly? I couldn't understand. But that is the way the tea boils, the aroma spreads and the taste stimulates.

We sat on the bench after the others had left. It was nothing new for his friends, as they who knew about the closeness of our families. But, for the first time I was not feeling close to Joy, for some obscure reason. When he asked me what was wrong, I could not answer. I cursed my small mouth.

He didn't ask twice, but held my hand and said, 'Let's go and have some ice cream.'

He knew I was very fond of ice creams. I followed him silently. Yes, Joy had grown up, no doubt. We entered a restaurant, and preferred to sit in the open air, rather than within the four walls. We sat at a small table for two. Joy asked me how my studies were going on as, my school leaving exam was not very far off I answered casually. We did not laugh, we did not gossip, we did not even squabble, yet we were together. It was so strange. And something even stranger was waiting for us. It came with the cups of ice cream.

When the waiter came with the tray in hand, my eyes caught sight of them, far behind the waiter, near the entrance of the restaurant. My eyes stopped blinking, and reflected my inner pain. So, Joy looked back. We saw them, my father and Sheila Aunty walking side by side, shoulder touching shoulder, eyes lighting up eyes. Her long hair was flying in the fondling north wind and flowing over Father's face. Father's dear face crossed out. A flat face on a *tanka*. The stones of the Noor Jahan bracelet winked at me scornfully. They did not see us and went inside the restaurant, hand in hand. My ice cream melted in the cup. I could not lift my eyes and look at Joy.

'Let's go and talk to them,' he said in quite a normal voice.

'Should we?' A flush was creeping up my neck.

'Why not?' Joy got up and went inside. I didn't go. I just could not. I kept on looking at the melting ice cream. Joy came back shortly with a grave face, sat quietly for a few moments then asked, 'Does Aunty know about it?'

Ice cracked on the Himalayan peak. It melted and melted. Darjeeling clouds crowded and covered and protected one more Shakuntala from the curious public eyes. When we reached Joy's car we were half drenched.

The driver was located and Joy dropped me at my house, but did not come in.

Next day when I came back from school, I saw Meena Aunty sitting with Mom in the living room. I didn't mean to eavesdrop but I could hear a few words. MeenaAunty said, 'I tried my best to bring her back to her senses, but she won't listen.'

'You can't inject sense into anybody, particularly in such a delicate matter.'

Mom said very calmly, as if discussing a third person's problem. *'The sea is vast and the sea is calm and the beach is so aloof.'* As I entered the room Meena Aunty asked Mom if she could take me with her for a few days. But Mom didn't agree, neither did I want it at heart, because I wanted to be with Mom, even within the collapsing four walls without any roof It would be better to get buried there with Mom rather than leave her alone and then live all alone. Meena Aunty also suggested to Mom if we could go to Goa for a few days for a change. But Father would not go, we knew, especially after Grandma's death it was just not possible for him. Meena Aunty went back to the sunrise, to colour, to life. And left us in a house full of antiques including an antique home, sold to time.

Father behaved quite normally with me. But everyday I could hear or overhear some argument going on between him and Mom. I could not hear the words clearly but some confused noise. Mom never shouted, neither did I ever hear her weeping. Time was limping and I was afraid that any moment it might stop.

That day when I was assisting Father in listing the newly arrived items I saw Sheila Aunty enter the shop. I started a countdown to the zero hour. Father asked me to go inside. I went out but could not help looking through a chink in the wooden planks of the door and eavesdropping. Mom would have scolded me for this, but I was not a sea oyster, protected in the shell of aloofness. I wanted to witness the destruction, the shipwreck, how one by one the parts would fall apart.

'Well, so what have you decided?' Sheila Aunty asked Father. Her high cheekbones looked rocky and barren. 'Don't you know how difficult it is to decide?'

'Yes I do, but it is getting pretty difficult for me at home.' Sheila Aunty's long shiny· hair was getting unruly in the strong cold wind.

'What's wrong now?' Father asked.

'Now they are planning to send me to Dubai again with Ramesh.'

'Dubai! But you have left it forever.' Father came from behind the table near Sheila Aunty. 'Ramesh does not have any job there anymore.' His voice was full of worry.

'Yea, but he is trying for one, or maybe they just want him to take me out for a tour of a couple of months, and they think, you know . . . out of sight is out of mind.' Aunty grinned and shook her head, 'The old, foolish creeps, never think of life beyond their domestic limit.' She was cynical.

'But what should we do?'

'Let's get out of here. Let's go to Calcutta.'

'That's next to impossible.' An echoing bong of the Tibetan monastery filled the air. 'I can't leave my shop. And think about Lucie.' The bass got mingled with the prayer of the Tibetan monks, deep and sombre. I knew Father loved his shop, his antiques, and me. He wouldn't leave them. He would pick up the beads of the broken rosary and in place of the missing low roof of a small house, the manifold decorative overhanging roofs of a pagoda would spread out.

'But you have to leave the shop. Even otherwise this shop does not bring much. Sell it off come to Calcutta with me, take Lucie with you, I like her.' Sheila Aunty was insisting now, 'I told you my sister and brother-in-law are influential·, they have a flourishing business in Calcutta, they will help us.'

'Will they? Won't they object to our-'

'Oh come on, don't think so low about them. They don't have silly moral values.'

She sounded quite determined. 'Make up your mind, dear, please.'

Father looked like a helpless antique statue.

'Give me some time, Sheila, please, give me some time.' Going back into the womb of time the antiques were begging to start as the new, shining, untouched pieces again.

I heard some noise behind me and looked back. Mom slapped me hard on the face. I went to my room. *Mom, the avalanche is approaching, can't you hear the rumbling?* I wanted to tell her but could not. Mom wiped off two drops of tears rolling down my cheek. We both went into the living room. Mom was knitting something. Her hands were working pretty fast. Plain and purl. Plain and purl. Did she drop a stitch there? But she did not stop. There were no bubbles in her surf-coloured eyes.

She looked straight at me, asked, 'So, when are they planning to split? Or do we have to?' I was startled and stared at the straight lines and curves on Mom's face. The face,—knitted in plain and purl. I knew I could not count the waves on the sea. I told Mom in a nutshell, what I had heard. But my small mouth did not say anything about the sunrise-conversation and the playing-footsie story. Mom remained silent for some time and then told me, 'Bring the knight's portrait to your room, you never know when the shop might be sold.' There was not even a cloudy touch to her clear tone. Following her advice I went into the shop after Sheila Aunty had left and brought the portrait to my room. Father was looking out vacantly towards the foggy sky and did not even notice my presence.

At night Mom went into the shop. Nowadays, Father would carry on sitting in the shop till very late, with or without reasons. Of course today there was some reason. In the morning, Father and I had gone to a nearby king's palace, where an auction of old items had been held. We came back a bit late and empty-handed. Father had not bid at all. It seemed he had not been much interested in the auction. And interestingly Mom had looked after the shop, when we had been away, one of the rare occasions. First Mom showed Father the whole day's accounts and then I heard her asking Father directly, 'Do you want us to go to Goa?'

'I never said so. Did I? And what about Lucie? She can't go with you.'

'Yes, she can. She is now old enough. You can ask her,' Mom said boldly.

Poor Father, he could again repeat the same answer,' Just give me some time, will you?'

He had always dealt with time, time which was carved in each pattern of the antiques and added extra value to it, and there he was now standing as an antique to be auctioned to Mom or Sheila Aunty, whoever could give more time.

'I want you to decide quickly, and I won't force you for anything. But Lucie will be with me,' Mom said with all the rockiness of the Himalayas and left the shop with Father and his time behind.

'Of course she won't. She is a part of my life, my shop. You can't take her away from me.' Father threw these words towards the door which closed with a bang behind Mother. He flung a shell paperweight down on the floor. Antics and antiques and a few broken pieces of colourless helplessness. I stood rooted to the place. I had sucked the sap of life from my mother's womb, from my father's home, from this old family shop. Now all of a sudden, I was just turned into an item, like the one in the king's palace, and Father and Mom were fighting it out there, bidding for me.

Joy came to meet me the next day. He asked me to go out and get some fresh air to feel better. Mom permitted. We went to the Rangeet Valley Ropeway, one of the longest passenger ropeways in Asia which takes one to the river valley of Rangeet, a beautiful fishing spot. In the car, Joy started with his jokes which failed to cheer me up. We reached the cable-car station but instead of getting into the cable car and having a thrilling thirty-minute joyride over the foaming tea bushes and frothing Rangeet, we went away from the cable car station and the touring crowd and sat under a pensive pine. Joy told me that the situation in their house was also very tense but he told me not to worry as Ramesh Uncle would be taking Sheila Aunty to Dubai soon. Everyone at home was trying their best to bring her to her senses, even her uncle and her cousins were dead against this involvement. So, she wouldn't get any shelter in their house.

'Do you really think everything will be just the same as it was before?' I asked Joy. He slowly removed the wisp of hair touching my eyelashes backwards and said, 'Hope' for the best.' He was also very sure that once Sheila Aunty went out of here, there would be a cloudless sunrise over Tiger Hill and we would enjoy it, all of us together, as we were used to before their entry into our 'joint family'. Joy was very quiet today, quite unlike him, but somehow I liked him this way no less. Tea was weak, but addiction was not.

We had to start back early as it had started drizzling. In the car Joy told me that he would be going on an educational trip with his college mates and teachers away from Darjeeling for a week.

'By the time I come back, I believe everything will be all right, don't worry as uncle has already booked tickets for Calcutta and from there they'll fly to Dubai.'

When we got down from the car near our shop we could see them standing near the lamp post. My ears caught a few words my father was saying, 'Please don't ask me to leave my shop, please. We shall think of some other way out.' I did not know if Joy could hear it but he got into the car hurriedly, and the car rolled down the hilly slope and went out of sight. It would be out of sight till the end of the study tour, but not out of my mind!

And so Joy was gone for a few days and I started counting the days when Sheila Aunty and Ramesh Uncle would go to Calcutta. I told Mom about it. But nobody told anything to Father. The days were smouldering cigarette stubs on a pale ashtray called life. One flicker and lots of smoke and piles of ashes. We did not have to wait long. Just three days after Joy's departure, through my room window I saw Sheila Aunty approaching our house. In fact, she went into the shop. Mom was sitting by my side, knitting. I did not know if she had seen her, but her hand started moving very fast. Plain and purl. Plain and purl. A dropped stitch. A ravelling rhythm. I was solving some maths problem, and closed the notebook. Soon we heard footsteps. They came into the room. Father asked me to go out but Mom did not allow. 'Let her face the reality,' she said.

'I am very sorry, Eva, I've never meant to hurt you, but sometimes things go beyond your control, you see . . .' Sheila Aunty was faltering. Her bone-china eyes were avoiding Mom's eyes, as if, they would break if they clashed. Father was standing behind, as still as one of his antique pieces.

'Just what are you getting at Sheila, stop beating around the bush, come to the point.' Mom's voice was as cold as the Darjeeling winter. The coldness left the two figures frozen, who were already half sunk in uncertainty.

'Well, I think I have got the drift.' Mom was only doing all the talking without the slightest tremor in her voice. 'We are going away, the stage is left to you Sheila.' Mom even smiled.

The old Grandfather clock started ticking.

'No, she didn't mean that exactly.' Father was looking for words lost among the crevasses.

Sheila Aunty found them, 'Oh yes, I meant to say that we are going.' Snow glistened on her high cheekbones and the words got wet, 'Let us put an end to all these torments.' Her last words thrust me into the Rangeet Valley cable car, all alone, stuck midway and dangling over the echoless hollow depth.

'So you are going, are you? Leaving your shop?' A deep gong rang out to resound a deep disbelief Mom was looking straight at Father.

Father avoided her eyes, looked at the dishevelled hair of Sheila Aunty and said, 'I don't know. Just allow her to crash at our house tonight. She doesn't like to go back to that torture. It is already late evening, we'll see tomorrow.'

'She is most welcome.' Finally some bitter froth oozed out of Mom's mouth.

But Sheila Aunty sounded a bit nervous, 'Oh, no, Biren, they can very well come and find me out here. Let's get out of here.'

'But where?' Father almost shouted, 'Where on earth? At this hour? The Road to Siliguri is not safe now, you know very well.' His fingers ran impulsively through his hair. He almost scratched his scalp. Father would be leaving the antiques behind, but would the antics leave him?

'Why don't we go to a hotel?' Sheila Aunty suggested.

Yes, Darjeeling is a city of hotels, beautiful, comfortable, luxurious hotels. But are they good enough to allure us out of home? I thought.

Just at that time the telephone rang. We had a parallel connection at home. Mom went and picked it up. 'Yes, it's me, Eva speaking.'

'Yes, Meena, what's wrong? You seem to be excited.' Then, she listened for a few seconds, with her eyes fixed on Sheila Aunty. Again, I saw a faint smile on her lips.

'No, she has not come here. Not today.'

'Yes I am sure. Yea.'

'Well, he is here at the moment. He went out earlier. I can't tell where.'

'She hasn't gone to her uncle's place either? Oh don't worry Meena, Darjeeling is full of hotels. She might have taken shelter in one of them.' Mom put down the receiver and looked at them.

They were speechless for a few moments, then, Sheila Aunty said, 'Thank you very much, Eva, you are great.'

'You may save it for some other time, Sheila, I think,' Mom said but I didn't get why she had told a lie to Meena Aunty, her best friend and that too on such a serious matter. I wanted to say Mom you were wrong. It could be the best opportunity to get rid of her, but my small lips did not utter a thing.

'Well, now I think we should go, all of us can't stay here, even for one night.' Mom announced, 'And don't worry, we won't go to a hotel, we have got other places to stay in,' Mom said to Father.

'What do you mean by 'we'? Lucie can't leave home,' Father said. The word 'home' sounded so strange. Like dry Ice.

'Yes, Lucie should be with us.' Sheila Aunty also got vocal. With pain I heard Mom agree to that, too easily. But I did not.

'No, I shall go with Mom,' I almost cried. Father came to hug me, to comfort me but before he could do that, Mom had held my hand and pulled me away from him.

'I shall talk to her and convince her, don't worry, she will be here.' Mom was turning out to be a complete puzzle for me and for those two adults too, I believe.

Mom took me to a corner of the next room and almost whispered, 'Don't cry, darling, set an alarm on your wristwatch for four o'clock tomorrow morning. Keep it under your pillow. I shall be waiting for you just outside the door.'

She patted me on the head, kissed my hair and slowly went out. When my cheek touched hers, it was hot and I could even feel the rippling rush of blood through the wildly vibrating nerves. Yes, I could touch the extra soft skin of the oyster through its hard and tough shell. Mom put on her long overcoat and went out without looking back even once. Through my tears I saw my room, Mom's knitting, antique chandeliers, the eyes of my knight, Father's unshaven chin, all jumbled up and confused, juxtaposed with their liquefied shape and the long, grave, grey night sobbed with me, confined in this antique sarcophagus. Father stroked my hair mumbling something, Sheila Aunty kept on pouring out words, kind or unkind, and I just couldn't get the meaning of any of them. Only the rumbling of an approaching avalanche deafened me. Darjeeling means the abode of the thunderbolt. For our home, it proved no misnomer.

Somehow, I was counting on Mom's words and waiting for the dawn. Sheila Aunty was sharing the room with me. Both of us kept awake till very late, tossing and turning, in our respective beds. I kept the watch near my pillow with the alarm set. The sweet beeps wouldn't disturb others but would wake me up. Even if Sheila Aunty woke up, I knew I could run away easily. I held the watch tightly in my fist. I would bolt the door from outside and run away with Mom, beyond Sheila Aunty's reach. With my subconscious self eagerly waiting for the beeps, I fell asleep, I couldn't tell exactly when.

I got up with an uncanny feeling soon, even before the alarm rang,. I looked into the watch, with a pencil torch. It was 3.34 a.m. Sheila Aunty was sleeping. Her sculpted breasts were rising up at regular intervals to the tune of her soft breathing. There was some strange smell in the air. Some strange sound. Or was I half asleep? With my tormented senses was I just imagining things? I could not understand but with my eyes wide open I just tried to interpret the strangeness of the feeling. Did I hear some stealthy footsteps on the passage in between the home and the shop? Was it Father? I didn't like to go out and see his dark, fossilised face. He must go back to his room before my alarm beeps, I thought. I heard some faint squeak of a door hinge. Is Father working in the shop? I wondered. After a few minutes of silent suspense, I felt I was smelling smoke. Yes, I was almost certain it was smoke, and it was almost the same type of smell which I would get on the Darjeeling road, in the shivering winter, where small hill boys and folks would sit surrounding a fire with crackling woods, and croon a low hilly tune.

Yes, something was crackling, it seemed. But who would light the old fireplace in our living room? We never used it except on some rare occasion of electricity failure in the cold winter. Why had Father lit it today? Would he burn away all the past memories of this house with me and Mom? Burning! Yes my senses got alarmed. Something was' burning. Not the dead logs we used to burn during our bonfire parties with school friends or family parties where cracking of jokes, cackles of amusement and the crackling of wood would mingle together. *What was burning then? Should I go out and see?*

What if Father sees me? How can I escape with Mom if Father is awake? I had all these disturbing thoughts. But the air was getting smoky. I even felt like coughing. But I controlled myself, lest Sheila Aunty should get up. Yet, it was choking.

I got up slowly. I tiptoed to the door and opened it with the least possible sound. The night was vibrating with the dead darkness and stiff silence and yes, there was a lot of stifling smoke. I had to cover my nose with my hand. A controlled cough came out of my choking lungs, shaking the dead silence of the night. I caught the sight of a shadowy figure as it glided through the passage, went near the main door and before I could light the torch, it had vanished. I again wondered if I was dreaming. No, I was not. I went near the back door of the shop, from where strange sounds were coming. I went and saw the door was locked. A new brass padlock. This padlock was not ours. I had never seen this padlock before in our house. So, I had no idea about its key. Through the narrow chinks in the planks of the door, I could clearly see the furious flames. Our shop was on fire.

I was too shocked to think or do anything for a few seconds. Then, I ran to the main entrance to our house. It was not locked. It was ajar. I could clearly remember that I had closed the door at night and had not bolted it, so that Mom could come at dawn, unlock it with her latchkey and take me out. A sudden sunrise burst upon my senses, not as colourful as that on Tiger Hill, but just as revealing. I closed the door and left it unbolted. I went near the shop door again, a strong smell of petrol was floating in the air. Petrol! A small can of petrol we used to keep at a corner of the passage to clean some antiques, could it cause so much fire? I saw the wooden door had caught fire.

Now I rushed up the stairs to my parents' bedroom, where tonight, only Father was sleeping. The room was bolted from inside. I knocked at the door once, twice, and again and again. 'Daddy, Daddy, please open the door. Please, fast, Daddy.' I kept on shouting. Perhaps, he also slept quite late at night, tossing and turning in the bed and so, was fast asleep in the later part of the night. 'What's wrong?' he asked from the other side of the closed door in a heavy, half-sleepy voice.

'Please open the door first,' I pleaded.

After a few seconds he opened the door, he was tying the cord of his dressing gown when I broke the news to him directly.

'Fire, Daddy! There is a fire! Our shop is on fire.' Choked with nervousness, I could hardly utter those words. And Father could hardly believe it.

'Are you serious?' But looking at my pale face he was disturbed, 'Are you sure? Let's see.'

He grabbed my hand and both of us came down hurriedly. Light was on in the passage and we saw Sheila Aunty standing there like a stony statue with a vacant face and a vacant look. She had covered her nose and mouth with her sari and with one hand she just pointed at the shop. The door was half burnt by then and we had to restrain Father from going inside the shop where the devastating fire was reducing all his past, present and future hopes into ashes. Father was delirious, he sniffed the smell of petrol in the air and pushed away Sheila Aunty violently. I saw his eyes spit fire towards her, 'You vile woman, couldn't you do better than this to take me away from here?' Antiques were burnt down but the antics were not. Sheila Aunty's eyes looked like filled up ashtrays. The shocked Victoria Falls with their cascading water frozen midway.

Some neighbours rushed in as the main door was unbolted. They tried to throw water, but it was too late. Somebody rang up the fire brigade, some inquired about Mom. A noisy concert and a Sheila Aunty,—disconcerted. Soon, she woke up from the state of shock and rushed to Father. She was about to fling her arms around his neck, but Father avoided her. There were curious eyes all around. Sheila Aunty could not say much. Her writhing voice could barely manage to eject these words, 'You are wrong. You are terribly wrong.'

'Yes, I was. And I won't be any more.' Father went away from her. *A telescopic distance away.* I saw her enter my room and breaking down in splitting sobs over my bed. That was the last I saw of her. The fire brigade arrived and everyone welcomed them and watched them tackle the fire. I too got busy.

What happened next was just like a story. The fire brigade, the police, the insurance people all came. They worked and talked over the next couple of days. In the meantime there was an imperceptible exit of Sheila Aunty and the silent entrance of Mom. Father was very sure that it was the work of Sheila Aunty, who wanted to take him to Calcutta. She was aware of his obsession for the shop and would go to any lengths to take him away from here.

However, to the police, Father said that it was an accident, the cause of which none of us knew. I told the police that I woke up as I was getting choked and came out, saw the shop was burning and went to call Father. When I was asked if Sheila Aunty had been sleeping when I had got up, I said I hadn't noticed, maybe she had been. They also asked me why my mom had not been present at home that night. I told them as Mom had taught me. She had gone to a friend's house, that spinster schoolteacher of my school. The teacher confirmed the fact too. They also interrogated Mom, and our neighbours. Some routine inquiry over a ruined kingdom, handed over from generation to generation. Father was all shattered. He kept apologising to his dead mother, grandmother and grandfather and other ancestors who had built the shop. He felt very guilty for his middle-age blunder.

The fire might have burnt the shop, but it cooled down the temperature prevailing in our family and Joy's. Mom was again in command. She took control to bring us out of our uncertain future. Father was to get some compensation from the insurance company. But the procedure would take time. It could take maybe months or a year before Father could get some considerable amount. Two three visits to the insurance office gave Father a clear idea about the delay involved in getting the money. So, to rebuild the shop seemed to be pretty difficult.

Mom, then, gave the idea to Father, 'Let's go to Mummy. So many times she has requested us to go and settle down with them. Daddy's days are numbered, you know. With the cancer he is mostly inactive. Let's lend a helping hand to Mummy. You would like it, dear. Hotel business is very interesting and challenging. And after all, I shall finally inherit it. Big brother is a well-settled doctor in Singapore. He'll not come back to run this family business. So, you do have every right over it, as much as I have. So far I have never told you as you were so happy and engrossed in your business. But things have changed since, you know. Right now what could we do here?'

She did not insist, only suggested. Naresh Uncle, Meena Aunty and other well-wishers although were ready to give monetary help for rebuilding the shop, did agree that Mom's idea was a more practical one and the best thing for this couple who had survived a fire and a home wreck. Finally, Father decided to leave Darjeeling and go to Goa, and start afresh.

So, just within a span of a couple of days the hill-river which was about to get lost under the crags and boulders, changed its course dramatically to flow with flair. My toy train at Batasia loop. A dramatic turn and an incredible descent to a decent height, a thousand feet down. We started packing. Meena Aunty often came to help us. It was decided that we would not sell our ancestral property but Naresh Uncle would rent it out to a decent tenant after we had gone, and would even look after it. Ramesh Uncle and Sheila Aunty, with their daughter, had gone, not to Dubai, but to the south to visit temples and probably to thank God for all that had happened and not happened.

All quiet on the Darjeeling slopes. Not quite though. Somewhere the glacier was rolling imperceptibly.

That day was very cloudy. We were busy packing necessary things and disposing the unnecessary ones. Clouds were coming inside frequently, giving damp hugs and cold kisses. It was late afternoon. Joy came into my room like a gust of wind. His shirt was not tucked neatly into his trousers. The parting of his hair was not straight. A cloudy sunrise on Tiger Hill. The blurred face of a distant memory. 'Is it because he is too weary because of the tour?' I asked myself

'When did you come back?' Mom asked him.

'This morning. I am so sorry to hear about the fire.' He stopped and for the first time I saw Joy, the talkative and smart Joy, floundering. He looked at the crates and boxes of various sizes kept ready for transporting to Goa.

'May I have a glass of water?' Joy seemed to be a bit out of breath.

'Can't you see we are busy? Just go and take it in the kitchen. Joyee, don't behave like a guest,' I said. Did I see a little pinkish touch on his cheeks?

'Well, I thought you had packed things . . . .'

'No, the kitchen things will be packed on the last day,' Mom said.

'And when is that? I mean when exactly are you leaving?'

'Day after tomorrow, after lunch at your place. Meena will come up to Siliguri to see us off. There is nobody to look after the hotel, otherwise your father also could accompany us.' Mom explained to him. Joy went out to have water and called me out from there.

'Hey Lucie, the water is very cold. Will you warm it up for me a bit, I have a bad throat today.' Joy and his bad throat. It had always been irritating for us. I went to the kitchen. Joy grabbed my hand the moment I entered there.

'I don't need water. Just let's go out somewhere. I want to talk to you,' he said in a voice quite unknown to me. *Yes, now that we are going to be away from each other, we should sit quietly together and remember all the good and bad things we shared together*, I thought. But why he didn't say it in front of Mom, I wondered.

We took Mom's permission to go out for some time. Joy told her he wanted to give us a farewell present and wanted me to help choose it. Joy also met Father in the room upstairs. And when we were coming down, Joy touched the banisters and said,

'Remember how I used to slide down this handrail?' He smiled, 'And you tried to outdo me once and fell and injured your leg.'

'But what about climbing the stairs in your house? I always used to jump over three steps in one bound. You could never do it,' I retaliated.

By now we were out of the house and both of us looked at the building where Joy's family had once stayed. Just by the side of ours.

Now, some other family was staying there, and though we knew them quite well, it was no more a home for me.

'First you left, and now it is our turn,' I said.

'But we didn't leave Darjeeling.' Joy sounded a bit agitated. It was quite unlike him. Even in his childhood he would hardly get agitated or annoyed, even after a lot of teasing. He was almost a grown-up now, maybe that was why he had changed and was behaving so strangely.

I was going to get into the car parked by the side of the road, when Joy prevented me.

'No car. Let's walk. The Mall is just around the corner. We can purchase something from there.' he said, and so we started walking along the road. The same road where we would have left behind our footprints, tottering small ones to hiking and running bigger ones. Most of them would be side by side.

We were walking slowly, Joy was almost dragging his feet, he was that slow. I was remembering our good old days. Was he too? *Making snowmen, throwing snowballs at each other during our upper Himalayan tours, learning skating together and falling and rolling all over the skating rink, counting the maple leaves meaninglessly, competing with the winding toy train and outrunning each other, jumping together to see who could reach the clapper and ring the bell at the temples, plucking tea buds where it was prohibited and blaming each other when caught.* These soft memories showered down on us like the tender flakes of snow, which covered us completely, and left two memory-clad minds melting in silence.

We reached the Mall without saying anything and then I broke the ice, 'Which shop, Joyee?'

Joy didn't answer, caught hold of my hand tightly and took me to a less crowded corner. We sat on a bench. Joy looked into my eyes and said, 'How can you leave Darjeeling, Lucie? You can't.' The tea-coloured eyes were changing hue and I saw some strong wine filling up his pupils. My eyelids drooped automatically.

'It is not my choice, you see,' I almost whispered.

'Yea, I know.' Joy stood up impatiently and went near the railing. He bent down over it. I went and stood by his side. 'These messy adults! Make a mess of our lives.' He grumbled and then turning towards me asked, 'Do you have to go? Really?'

'Why are you getting so upset Joyee, we shall keep on coming here and you shall also come to Goa.' I tried to comfort him.

'No, I shall never go.' He pouted; just as he used to do as a child.

'Oh Joyee, please take it easy.' I patted his hand.

'How can I? There will be nothing for me in Darjeeling anymore.' He took my left hand in his and started sliding the ring I was wearing on my second finger back and forth. Back and forth.

'I always thought we shall have a home, by the side of the Happy Valley Garden. We shall run the tea estate together,' he said. I was at a loss for words. He was not looking at me. His eyes were fixed on my finger and he was sliding the ring back and forth. I stared at him. The square face with the tea-brown eyes, the wide mouth without the usual, charming, wide smile. I recalled the face of my Adam, my knight. A line by line, feature by feature, expression by expression scrutiny. They did not match. His growing man's body leaned on my lean one and I held it as I would hold my favourite soft toy. *Soft and vulnerable. Making things so much harder for me.* Even for my dream. We had to stand straight up as the figures of our fathers approached at a distance. Joy's soft, sad eyes reflected the snow-clad loneliness of Kanchenjunga. It was so cold, so much cold around me.

When the cool stars shivered in the sky at night, I lay close to Mom, and asked, 'Mom, will we never come back to Darjeeling?'

'No, darling, not for staying,' she said. I saw Joy's eyes blinking in the stars.

'Mom, I have your key which you dropped in the passage that night of the fire,' I whispered. *A sliding door of darkness gaped ajar. The speechless inertia snowballed. A few blind moments. Then, Mom sat up on the bed. Two gracious arms. I got anchored on her soft bird's nest breast.*

'Why did you do this Mom, why?' I asked her.

A patch of moonlight fell on her face. A sculptor-made bust. The idol's lips moved, 'I had to. There was no other way out, dear. A time comes in life when one has to risk everything for better or for worse. I burnt my house, to save my home. And I succeeded.'

Yes, she has saved her home, but poor Mom will never know she has ruined one home, a home of tomorrow, by the side of the Happy Valley Garden, filled with the arrogant aroma of tea, the adolescent fragrance of romance. My mind mused.

'You'll understand when you grow up.' She hugged me with assurance. I felt I was growing up . . . from adolescence to adulthood. With my dream, with my god. The hilly curves of Darjeeling were rolling away into the distance. I closed my eyes to touch the light of darkness and saw my carpet of the rainbows fading . . . . fading and disappearing beyond somewhere.

BOOK 2

I

The Accident

IT WAS AROUND two o'clock on a sunny spring day of 2000. The new century. And a new world suddenly opened up in front of me. 'Over the rainbow'.

There was nobody on that lonely lane of Shantiniketan to witness the accident except for me. An accident. A life crossed the path of death violently and abruptly. A shattered shell bared a shelter less soul. A dreamt reality. I remember it all as if it had happened just yesterday. The time was odd. After midday. The sun was sliding down towards the west, leaving long linear shadows of the rows of trees standing by the side of the lane. It was the fall season for many of the trees in this area. So, the shadows of the bony trees were not shady. I was coming back from a landscape sketching session. I saw a small, about ten-year-old village boy, as skinny as those lane-side trees, with a brown terracotta body, crossing the lane quite leisurely as there was absolutely no traffic on this half tarred, narrow, lonely, rough lane of a small town in West Bengal. His small head was crowned with exuberant black frizzy hair. It looked as if he was a crested wonder. I looked at this unusual sight and wondered if I could do a portrait of him with such a spectacular natural hairstyle. I called him, 'Hey, you, you boy . . .'

The boy turned his face towards me. His vitreous eyes reflecting a bewildered question. Just then. It happened just then. In a flash, emerged a helmeted figure behind him, at the corner of the lane, barrelling along on a motorbike. The boy, the small village child with his black, frizzy natural crown, already half shocked at my call, confusedly stopped, but the motorbike could riot. The helmeted rider braked sharply. His motorbike swerved across the lane to hit against a tree and stop without any apparent damage to the rider or carrier. But he could not avoid the accident. The boy had already been hit. And the air was hit by a sharp screeching sound and a terrified scream. The shining silence of a spring afternoon shattered into pieces and fell wasted with the piles of dry, dead leaves. There were no houses nearby.

Shantiniketan is a place set in the midst of nature with more open rustic and rugged land wrapped in fragrant calmness and less people and concrete structures and their intimidating interference. It is almost a quiet countryside, around 150 km away from Calcutta, the capital of West Bengal. An ashram-like township with a residential university for students, coming from all over the universe. I was a student in the department of Fine Arts, learning painting. I was out to observe the nature of this tableland so that I could serve up its speciality on a colourful canvas. And here the colour spilled, scary scarlet, streaming along the furrow of the broken rough lane. The boy was flung down by the speeding motorbike. His head hit against the rocky pavement. Blood was gushing out.

The canvas, papers and other drawing accessories slipped down from my loosened grip, while I began to stiffen in the grip of some unknown feeling. Do I have to see death from such a short distance? I thought and yet the life in me pushed me towards the boy. I squatted by his side and saw the unconscious skinny face, flailing legs and gasping agony. 'Help, please help.' The words rolled out of my mouth automatically without knowing who I was calling for. But I got the answer immediately in a clear foreign accent, and in a voice as deep as the calmness of this afternoon nature. It was as if some echoing device was inbuilt in the voice. It said,

'Will you look after the boy? I shall come back in a jiffy with a rickshaw.'

The voice vibrated in the shimmering afternoon and the last words were almost lost in the loud vroom of the motorbike. I turned my face round only to see the helmeted figure vanishing with his motorbike at the end of the lane. Barrelling like that! Even after such an accident! What nerve! Or perhaps, he had just escaped! There was no guarantee that he would come back. I had not seen his face. It was all covered under the blackish visor of his crash helmet. The skeleton branches of the barren trees with one or two dangling pallid yellow leaves were getting reflected on it, as if it was the face of death. I could recall only that much. What if he did not come back? He! Yes, it was a man, a man no doubt. The construction of his body and specially his voice, when he spoke, made it very clear that it was a man with a unique voice. But he had gone after hitting this boy down, half-dead, and I had allowed him to go, stupidly, without knowing anything about his identity. A man in the helmet mask with a voice deep and echoing. Even more mysterious than a veiled lady. Even more romantic? But with death sucking out life bit by bit in front of me, romance seemed just a distant blob, near the invisible star of the afternoon, hidden under the shining sunlight. 'Only darkness does not hide a thing, light also does.'

I was feeling wretched for having called the boy. Did he stop short for that? Was I as responsible for the accident as that rash driver? Many a time I had called unknown faces, specially the tribal women with their terrific figures, to capture them on my canvas. Never before had such a thing happened. Had the speed been moderate, nothing would have happened either. Who could have known that in such a calm and balmy afternoon, some motorbike bum would vroom in out of the blue, making it all red! It was his fault, I concluded. Yet, I had a guilt-pricked feeling. It pricked me more for allowing that masked stranger to go. No doubt, there were not many options I did have. I could have gone myself, for calling a rickshaw, but in that case too, the stranger could very well have escaped before my returning back with one. This was a small place and no taxi was available. Bicycles and cycle rickshaws were the main modes of transport. Scooter rickshaws were rare. A few lucky people had their two-wheelers and cars. Rickshaws were available only on the main road. There were some rickshaw stands also. But rickshaws were pretty scarce during this time of the day. This was siesta time for the people of this small countryside-town. Being an ashram, classes would start early in the morning at seven o'clock and be over by one o'clock in the afternoon.

Till four o'clock outdoor activities would remain minimum, except for the rustling of the mango groves, the rippling of the vast corn field, the fluttering of butterflies and the quivering of a cute serenity over this peaceful town, nurtured by nature. Even the small shops, which were just a few, would stall business with their shutters half-down. Inside, there would only be the stealthy movements of mice and the soft breathing sound of the sleeping owner.

Just to think I had come from a place called Darjeeling! A city teeming with tourists and the touring excitement. Shops were open all day long, inviting even the fog and clouds along with the tourists. We had our own shop, a shop of antiques where my father would sit and attend to the customers and his antique pieces the whole day. From His Highness highland of Darjeeling I had come down to His Humbleness plain in Shantiniketan. Alone. Away from my parents who were now in another tourist spot, Goa, Her Majestic Excellency. I had been staying in the girl's hostel here for the last three and a half years or so, playing with my brush, colours and canvas and never before had colour scared me so much. When I watched a blood-soaked scene on the TV, I would press the colour button of the remote to make it black and white in order to avoid the bloody part of it. How I wished I had a natural remote now. Instead, I kept pressing the wound with my palm to stop the flow of blood, while the red was getting darker and darker. He had fallen unconscious. His eyes were half closed and beneath the eyelashes the glassy stare made me shiver. Will he survive?

What about that masked man with a majestic masculine voice? What happened to him? Why wasn't he coming back? I looked anxiously towards the end of the road for his return. Or somebody else, maybe some of my friends. No, it was a rickshaw, it came slowly and stopped by my side.

'Oh my, what a ghastly scene!' the rickshaw driver said.

We both carried the boy to the rickshaw. We laid his thin body on the seat and I sat at a corner holding his injured head in my arms. I had in the meantime, gathered my drawing papers, board, etc. and kept them under a tree, under the weight of some chunks of rocks. Later I shall come and pick them up, I thought. There was hardly any time to lose. I asked the rickshaw driver to take us to the local hospital. It was not a big, well-equipped hospital, but the doctors would take immediate care to save his life. The rickshaw started moving slowly along the bumpy dirt lanes. It was as if I was sitting on a jerking machine and for the next ten to fifteen minutes I would have to. I was wondering at my power of tolerance. My flesh used to creep at the sight of blood, and here I was, sitting with a bleeding head on my lap. The frizzy hair was wet with blood and had almost straightened out. Blood was dripping, drop by drop on my right foot shod in the white sling back and dappling it. I did not cry. Tears were strangers to my eyes. There might be a very few occasions when I welcomed these watery guests. My mom had taught me to treat tears as strangers. So my eyes remained dry but I got too numb to feel anything, to think anything. I forgot about the helmet-clad stranger, the hit-and-escape driver!

I got the boy admitted to the hospital. I had personally known Dr Sen, who was the doctor in charge of the hospital. The boy was taken to the emergency ward. I was told that his condition was serious, as the head injury was severe. However, the doctor told me they would try their best and if necessary he would have to be shifted to the main hospital, about fifteen kilometres away from Shantiniketan. I had to register my name as the boy's escort. And I felt very amused while signing as an escort, as I was still in my teens, turned nineteen just last month to be precise and an accident had promoted me to the post of a responsible escort.

I was hesitating in the beginning, but the doctor explained the formality of the hospital and when I looked at the boy I felt more than pity, a strange empathy. From the clothes and bare feet it was clear that he was from a very poor background. But he also had a life to live in his own way, with a crown of unusual, frizzy, black hair, petal-shaped eyes and perhaps, a lot of perfumed dreams stuffed in them. I did not know his whereabouts, not even his name. I asked them to write his name as 'Keshi' in the official record. Kesh means hair. I told Dr Sen the whole story. I knew him very well, as some time ago when I had viral fever the doctor had treated me with a lot of care and affection. This elderly professional was quite popular in this small area for his excellent behaviour and sincerity, despite his limitations as a doctor. He advised me to go to the local police station and lodge a complaint against the unknown motorcyclist. He also promised to help me in case of any problem, 'I can't go with you right now, leaving my duty. But I know the man who is in charge at the local police station and I shall talk to him on the telephone,' he said.

In a small place, usually all prominent people know each other. But I did not know the police, in fact, I had never even thought of going to a police station. I was shaking a bit within and cursing that irresponsible, inhuman, seen yet unseen, known yet unknown human form. It was so clever of him that he did not show his face. Otherwise, being a man why would he keep his face covered under the crash helmet like a burqa-clad Iranian woman! I thought, and started sweating. Dr Sen was a fatherly figure. He kept his hand on my head and said, 'I understand your feeling, my child. Why don't you go back to the hostel first, freshen up, take some of your friends with you and go to the police station? It will definitely help you.'

'Yes, Doctor Uncle. That man must be punished. I've heard his voice. And I'll definitely recognise it if I hear it again. Please, take care of the boy.'

'I shall do my best. And don't worry, that rash driver will be found out. There are not many motorbikes in this small town and the police has records about all of them. He will be brought to book no doubt,' he said, and went inside the ward.

I walked through the huge halls and long corridors of the hospital, smelling sickness and medicine all over. This was the smell you could only get in hospitals, the shelter for the sick and ailing. I came out of that sick-sheltering centre, feeling a bit sick myself after the shocking incident I had witnessed and the nerve-wrecking experience I was going through. There would be still more—the unpleasant feeling of visiting a police station, a sleepless night with the haunting glassy eyes of the boy, dripping blood on my feet, and the masked masculine motorbike rider. I went near the tube well by the side of the hospital, which provided water to the common people. My white top and blue jeans were smeared with blood. The dark thick stains of blood were slowly drying up. A rickshaw was standing near the hospital, some people had brought a patient in that. I requested the rickshaw driver to pump water for me as it was just impossible to do it myself and wash the red stains from my palms, arms, face and other bare parts of my body. Clothes could not be washed here. I washed the red stains off my arms and face as far as possible. The silty, turbid water in the narrow drain turned reddish, to match with the red earth of Shantiniketan. Only this colour was not loveable. I asked that rickshaw driver if he would take me to the hostel, but he was in fact engaged to wait and take back the people whom he had brought. However, getting a rickshaw here wouldn't be a problem. The rickshaw stand was just a few yards away, on the road, across this stretch of open ground in front of the hospital.

I started walking towards the road. The ground was strewn with dead, dry leaves. Their brittle existence was getting noisily crushed under my shoe. There were quite a few trees standing on the ground. I was passing them, one, by one. As I was feeling uneasy in the bloodstained and soggy clothes, I was looking down while walking to avoid people's inquisitive eyes. Of course, there were not many people around, except for a few hospital staff and a few more people going towards or coming from the hospital.

'Excuse me,' I heard a voice suddenly. Rather I heard 'the voice', the unique voice which had been haunting me all through. It sounded from somewhere behind me, very nearby. I looked around. There, just ten or fifteen feet away from me by the dark flaking trunk of an old leafless tree, he was getting down from his motorbike. With a camcorder hanging around his neck and of course with his crash helmet and lowered visor fully covering the face.

'Do you have a minute?'

The sound came filtered through the visor. It was so unexpected that I could not think. Only my reflexes pulled me towards him. Or was it something else? The urge to unveil a masked mystery? As I went near him, I saw the distorted reflection of my face on his glossy visor. Slowly, he raised the visor uncovering his cheeks, eyes and nose. A window of wonder. I saw a little of his autumn-brown eyelashes, the aquamarine eyes, a pinnacle of a nose and a lot of pinkish white skin. Oh gosh, some foreign student!

And he was the killer driver! Unless the boy died one could not call him so. But he was the killer. I realised it as soon as he took his helmet off, completely off his head. And I got completely off my head, at least for a few immobile moments. The human flesh cast in a die of gracious Grecian perfection. A tall towering arrogance. Trim as time. Strong as passion. A long face with a strong jaw. A slightly projected mythic chin. With a mystic dot on it, a mysterious dimple. A chiselled nose as high as a fragrant desire. A melodious forehead. Two dashing rhythmic eyebrows. Deep aquamarine eyes with overflowing warmth. And a pair of lips with a dreamy droop at one corner and a lilting curve at the other. A soft transparency. But no, he was no anachronism. The unruly silky dishevelled blonde hair added the careless jazzy touch to the classic sonata. And the combination was deadly. In fact, the charm was oppressive.

It was better veiled under the visor. How could simple human eyes· bear such a superhuman sight! Beneath the bloodstained clothes my blood rushed madly through the veins. I could not talk for a few seconds. Neither did I hear anything from the other side. A raven cawed shrill enough to break my trance and with a little hesitation I started, 'Listen, I . . .'

'Would you . . .' He also started simultaneously. Then, both of us stopped simultaneously, willing to give an uninterrupted chance to the other. A few seconds' silence followed. Then again, both of us started together and again stopped simultaneously. The next moment, he shook his head, and broke into a hearty laughter. It vibrated through the quietness of the surroundings. The deadly curve on his upper lip straightened, deep dimple on the chin lost depth and the sunlight-coloured face sucked all the radiance from the spring afternoon. I got infected by his laughter and could not help smiling. It was good to relax after the tense encounter with death and blood and intense repentance for letting the culprit escape. Actually I heaved a sigh of relief as he had now turned up, on his own.

'How is the boy? Can I see him?' He inquired.

'Not right now. Doctors have taken him to the operating theatre.'

'Is he serious?' He was concerned about the boy's condition, no doubt.

'Yes. He has to be operated on.'

While I was talking to him I felt a cool touch of the spring wind on my eyebrows, on my cheeks and hands. I realised that the water had not dried up on my face and hands. Suddenly, I became aware of my miserable appearance. Here I was standing in front of the most handsome man I had ever seen. In all probability I would never see another. And I was in a completely shabby and blemished shape. Automatically, my hand took out the handkerchief from the pocket and I was about to wipe the watery touch off my face, when a strong hand with throbbing blue veins visible through the transparent white skin touched my hand. A subtle feathery touch, with the tip of the fingers, yet it was powerful enough to prevent me from rubbing my cheek with the handkerchief.

'Hold it. Just look at your hanky.' He said with amusement bubbling in the aquarium eyes. It was difficult to take my painter's eyes off that perfect portrait face, but I looked down, literally. So far I was looking up at a face set at a height of six feet plus and now I, only 5'2" tall looked down to my hand and saw a pale pink hanky smeared with dark blood spots. The blood had soaked through my pocket, soiling the hanky. So much blood! The poor boy had lost so much blood! Would he survive? I dropped the hanky on the red soil; the crumpled red hanky looked almost like one of the small red chunks of rock scattered on the rustic barren earth.

'Thank you.' I just managed to say.

'I'd say you are a very brave girl, what's your name . . .'

'Lucie Roy,' I said and forgot to ask his name. As though deep in my heart I believed that no name could befit this perfection. My subconscious realised that anything would be a misnomer for this perfect visual phenomenon. Next, I was expecting a fleshy flashy handshake but he folded his hands in a semi-Indian style and I had to return the compliment. Once more I felt wretched for my soiled appearance on the backdrop of such a lovely red land and in front of such a radiant vision. As he folded his hands I saw a fresh red wound on his left hand. Right below the knuckles. Blood had dried up but it was a big red wound. When he hit the tree he must have scraped his hand badly against the rough and hard tree bark.

'My god! You are hurt!' The words rolled out automatically from my mouth.

'Oh this? Nothing serious,' he said looking at the fresh live wound.

'Why don't you go to the hospital, get it dressed and bandaged?'

'Not required. Just a small scratch. I'll tape it up myself later.' He did not pay any attention to his injury and shrugged off the worry shown by me. Then he looked with gratitude in his eyes and said, Well, Lucie Roy, I think you should freshen up. Where will you go? May I drop you?'

Although the pillion seat appeared more coveted than the throne of a queen, I restrained myself with a lot of effort and quipped, 'Thank you, but I am in no mood to come back here to lie down on a hospital bed!'

He shrugged his shoulder, looked straight into my eyes and laughed again, that vibrant laughter, changing the contour of his face and making it even more charming. The remote sky of Shantiniketan hung down very close, as if to provide a roof over only the two of us, the two strangers. The anxiety, the tension, the bleeding face of a helpless boy seemed too far near the pale moon of the placid afternoon. He waved his hand, covered his face with the helmet, and drove off. The smoke of red dust blurred my vision and before the dust had settled, he had disappeared. Such incorrigible craziness. I trudged along the ground and wondered, he had not thanked me even once.

When I came back to the hostel I got mobbed by the inmates there. Why were my clothes soiled with blood, why was I looking so pale, why was no wound visible on my body. They threw a hundred and one questions to get more details about the incident. My small mouth was in no mood to elaborate. I just gave them a thumbnail sketch of what had happened. Then, I asked my room-mate Deepa to go to the accident spot and bring my things back. After a proper bath and a cup of hot coffee I felt refreshed.

I stretched myself on the bed and was about to stretch my imagination beyond this small hostel room with a piece of sky at my bedside, when a friend of mine entered with two letters received today. One was from Mom, I could recognise it from the handwriting on the envelope. The other one was a sky-blue envelope, with a touch of flowery design on it. It could only be from Joy. He was so predictable, at least, for me. I knew so much about him, maybe more than he knew himself. Joy had been my best friend since my childhood. In the nursery we had trotted to the school together, in the primary we had run to the playground together, in the secondary, we had gone hiking together, and in our college days we would have entered ecstasy together, had not destiny separated us. At present I was here, at Shantiniketan, and he was in London to do his MBA, as his dad had planned for him.

The map of his life had always been well planned, no earthquake, no landslide, changing the face of it. Or maybe there was one, our separation. Had it affected him that much? May be it was a little upsetting tremor he had shaken off while he still believed that a happy villa was waiting for both of us near the Happy Valley Garden, on the lush hilly slopes, among the exuberant leaves and buds, amidst the favourable flavour of Darjeeling tea. He always wrote me letters and no, he did not dream. Joy was not a boy to dream, but he assured me of that home in many ways, though never very directly. I could never visualise it very clearly. The future seemed to have smudged the picture with a little Darjeeling fog and flurries and a lot of worldly uncertainties and worries. Yet it was there. It had always been there. Like the undefined, intangible soul in the perceptible human body.

I always used to get the flavour of strong Darjeeling tea whenever I received Joy's letter. The strong, tantalising aroma of tea. But today the flavour seemed to be very feeble and the alluring smell of the mango blossoms had filled my senses. The mango grove was by the side of my bedroom, yet never before, the smell had invaded the senses this way. Strangely enough, I didn't want to open the letters today. I kept them in the bedside drawer and looked outside the window. Perhaps, I was too tired and exhausted to relish any cup of tea at the moment. I was seeking some time to allow all the incidents of the afternoon to sink into me.

It was past five o'clock and the sky had darkened, branches of the tree and the leaves had darkened even more. The incidents came crowding into my mind, one by one. Was I forgetting something, perhaps; some minute details? I could not remember it till Deepa, my room-mate, chucked a magazine at me and said, 'Where are you, dear? Should I inquire with the police in the lost and found department?'

I was startled and realised clearly what I had forgotten. The police station. Yes, Dr Sen had asked me to go there, and lodge a complaint. And I had forgotten. I had even forgotten to ask the stranger's name, although he had asked mine, I recalled. The intoxicating attraction, the lavish lustiness, the white shining illusion had totally overwhelmed me. A tingling sensation crept up my spine. I had missed the police station and I had missed him again. What would I tell Dr Sen? There was no guarantee I would meet him again. He never assured me that he would come to the hospital in the evening. And I did not know much about him. Only a fascinating face with a deep dimpled chin, a vibrant voice, and a bubble-subtle touch of the finger tips, too subtle to even leave a fingerprint on my hand. But my memory was full of his larger-than-life figure-prints, at least for the moment.

A nudge at my waist woke me up. 'Lost in thought again? What's the matter?' Deepa was standing near me. Her widely set fishing-net eyes were trying to fish out some secret. She was holding a plate in her hand with some snacks in it.

'Here have some,' she almost ordered. Deepa was a sympathetic room-mate.

'Just look at you. You are looking so dry,' she said as the fishing net was rolled up and an affectionate gossamer web was spread. She stroked my long hair and tried to push away some of my curly forelocks falling over my eyes. I had this special feature. Curly forelocks along my hairline. My father affectionately called them 'tender tendrils'. People used to say these curls had beautified my otherwise common face. As did my small pouted lips.

Deepa looked at those lips and said, 'You must have been out today without an umbrella and without even applying that sunscreen lotion. You've got a sunburn. And look at that small mouth of yours. As everybody says, those lips are the smallest and the cutest, one has ever seen. Now just see, they are cracked so badly. Take care of yourself, dear. What will happen to all those dozens of boys who hang around you, if they see you in this condition?'

'It will do them good. Only the sincere one will still stick around.'

'Gone are those days when the inner beauty was more important. Nowadays-'

'Nowadays, *the cover covers up everything*?'

'No. You need both. Appearance and intelligence . . . the woman of substance don't you know?' Deepa was in a mood to give a small lecture, but I stopped her.

'I know your philosophy very well, my dear. Now skip it. I am exhausted.'

'You can afford to be so careless about your looks, because you don't care for any boy here. Broken a couple of hearts too, for that matter. You are doing well with that steady boyfriend of yours from London, aren't you?'

Joy, my boyfriend! Somehow, it sounded very strange to me whenever Deepa called him that. Joy was just Joy. Did I ever take him for a boy? All through my childhood? What was the meaning of gender in these tender days? Only those last few days in Darjeeling had added a new note, a love-toned hue. Just when we had found the forbidden apple, we were forced to depart without sharing a bite. The shadow if the apple hangs between us, without its taste. I smiled faintly.

'You always exaggerate things, Deepa. Nobody has really broken his heart for me.'

'How do you know, you don't allow anybody to approach you that way. You just snub them.

There is always a cold air around you.'

'Imported from London in a sealed envelope you know.' I said with mock seriousness, and both of us laughed. Then, I told her that since I was anxious about the boy I didn't feel hungry. I also made a clean breast of my guilt and told her that I had called out to the boy, confusing him, which might have been a cause for the accident. But Deepa smiled it off.

'You are crazy. In no way you are at fault. It is only that speeding driver. Nobody else. However don't tell anyone about it. People tend to exaggerate.' She spoke in a mature tone and offered the plate.

'If you don't eat, it will in no way help the boy recover.' She averred and also explained, 'Physical weakness begets mental weakness.' Like a caring mother she fed me and made me feel at home.

Home. Yes. At this moment, I was missing my home and my mom specially. But there was no home for me. Although I used to go to my parents in Goa in the summer vacations and during Christmas holidays, I never felt as if it was my home. With a bunch of strangers always around I could never feel the intimacy and the privacy of a home. I never liked crowds. I had been a diffident child and a difficult teenager. Ever since we had left Darjeeling, I felt that I had lost my home.

From Darjeeling we had first gone to the 'home sweet hotel' of our grandparents. I stayed there for a short period. A few months, till I passed my school final exam. After that, following Mom's wish—she had always wanted me to be a painter,—I enrolled for a diploma in painting at the Kalabhavan, the Department of Fine Arts of the Vishva Bharati University of Shantiniketan, one of the best Art schools in India. Mom chose it for another reason. It was in West Bengal, and right from my birth I had been in Bengal. She thought I would feel more at home here. So, I was admitted to the university and stayed in the residential hostel for girls. But this was no home for me, no home for any of us, it was only a shelter for a brief period of our lives.

We stay here, share our lives with each other, but never feel as if it is our own. Never, after reaching the hostel, we feel that this is the end of the journey. It cannot give us the wide gamut and the various shades of feelings which can be unfurled in the folds of a home. If home is a kaleidoscope, our hostel is a paperweight with floral patterns in its transparent body. There was no home for us, we only tried to make ourselves at home.

At the moment, I was missing home and feeling homesick for the old house filled with antiques and antics, lost in the grip of time; or the other one, yet to be built, a villa by the side of the Happy Valley Garden, hidden in the grip of the future. I looked at the stars set in the frame of my bedside window, and recalled the twinkle in Joy's eyes.

In London it would not be evening now, Joy would be busy with his studies. I, had last seen him around two years ago, when he had been leaving for London. From Darjeeling he had come to Calcutta to catch the flight to London, with his family. He had made time to come and meet me at Shantiniketan, just 150km from Calcutta. Without his family.

I relived the moments.

He arrived in the morning and left in the evening. That was our first meeting since we had left Darjeeling. But the soft snow flurries were not to be found on the dusty red rocky soil. We visited the important places together, laughed together, trod on the gritty ribs of barren Khoai, remembered our gliding childhood days on Darjeeling snow. But it was never the same, no way the same. The snowball did not roll and roll to grow bigger and bigger. To sum it up, it was Kanchenjunga without the snowy summit. Of course, we hugged—once. Forgetting Mom's 'no-touch' advice, to give each other a touching farewell gift. But we had hugged so many times in our childhood, that there was hardly anything new, at least for me. That was wip.ter and both of us were wearing thick warm clothes. So, there was not much to feel near the heart. The only difference I felt, was that my chin could no longer reach his shoulder. He had outgrown me. And I had outgrown the Darjeeling delirium. The tea had been getting cooler and cooler and cooler.

I wondered why I had been thinking about Joy. Maybe I was just afraid to think about the present. I wanted to escape from the thought of a damaged terracotta body, a hospital bed with a few dangling bottles of blood and glucose and hope of life. Even more, I felt that I wanted to evade a perfect portrait, the vibrant laughter, and an imperfect police station with the smell of crime. A glaring blunder—yes, I had not asked him his name because I thought perfection could hardly bear any mortally imperfect name. And now my friend Rani came running and informed me that Dr Sen was on the phone. My imperfection will be bluntly bared.

'Dear Lucie, will you please come here immediately. A few policemen have come. We reported on behalf of the hospital. You . . .' I could gauge the urgency in Dr Sen's tone.

'I'm very sorry, Doctor. I couldn't go to the police station. I got late and . . .' I was excellent in keeping a secret but very bad at telling lies. I started groping in my mind for some exclusive excuse. But Dr Sen was a nice man. He relieved me of my uneasiness, 'Doesn't matter. You may come now.'

'How is the boy?'

'I'll tell you. First, you come immediately. They are waiting. I'll speak to your superintendent to permit you. Don't worry. Just be quick.'

I had to rush. My hair was still wet after that late bath. I was wearing a long ankle-length skirt and a loose top. A comfortable outfit but not presentable enough. Yet, I had hardly any time to change. After all, I required to be marked present by the police. Their eyes look for criminals and not for beauty. I just flung the purse across my shoulder, borrowed Rani's moped and set off.

When I reached the hospital, Dr Sen was talking to the police in his chamber. There were three of them, from the local police station. Dr Sen introduced me to them. One was a sub-inspector and the two others were constables. They noted down my name and address and other necessary whereabouts. They also took a brief account of the accident, as I had witnessed it. They wanted to know the exact time of the accident, which I could not supply. I just expressed a tentative idea about the time. When I used to go out for some outdoor session all by myself and without any fixed engagement thereafter, I never wanted to be disturbed by thing, not even by the distracting presence of the watch. I was not wearing it that day.

As they asked me about the man behind the accident, I floundered. The aquamarine waves surged to flood my normal sharpness. A disturbing dilemma.:

'A motorcycle knocked the boy down, that much I saw,' I said with a lot of effort, and did not mention that I did see him afterwards and allowed him to slip by, owing to my weakness for wondrous beauty.

'Deliberately or accidentally?' the SI asked in a grave tone. His dilated egg-white eyes behind the glasses gave me nausea. The smell of smoke almost choked my heart. Our burning shop. Police enquiry, people's curious eyes, burnt and half-burnt corpses of the curio items. The same question had been hurled at me on a foggy morning in Darjeeling after the burning of our shop and house 'Deliberately or accidentally?'

I closed my eyes for a few seconds. Mom's eyes lit up in my memory among all charred curios.

I answered firmly, 'Accident, it was an accident.' The very same words I had uttered around five years ago. And the very same words kept gnawing me when I almost chewed the words out. For Mom then. For a stranger now. The only difference was, this time I was convinced that, I was telling the truth.

'Describe the man as elaborately as you can,' he commanded next. His assistant's hand was ready with the pen and a pad. How would I describe? Would they understand if I say a Michelangelo magnificence, a Rubens-Vinci-exuberance, a Cezanne-enigma, one Dada dimple, two surreal eyes and one super-real existence?

I was pondering over the question and how to answer comprehensively, when to my great delight the sunlight face appeared right at the door of the cabin. The swing door swung back and forth, back and forth. My mind too. The very next moment I desired to be eclipsed, with my dishevelled hair, with my shoddy clothes and shabby appearance. There was one Indian man with him. They came in and to my big relief he did not wish me to show that we had met earlier. But was it really a relief? He didn't even glance at me. A sneaking squeak in the hinges of my pride. I wanted not to look at him, but in the blue synthetic light of the room the aquamarine acquired overflowing excellence and I could all but keep staring at that.

'Hullo Prateek, how are you dear?' Dr Sen's intimate tone made me look at the new man on the scene. An average Bengali man probably in his early thirties. A key chain with keys was jingling in his hand, just like my senses at that time.

'Well Uncle. Something unfortunate has happened I heard. This guest of ours was driving my mo'bike. He has just come here two days ago. Today there was a mishap, he's informed me. So we have come.'

'Well in time I'd say. The police are here.' Doctor said.

The sub-inspector's sadist eyes gleamed behind the specs. He started asking questions when Dr Sen held my hand and made a sign to go out with him. I went out of the chamber and proceeded along the corridor. We came near the operating theatre. He stopped and looked at me.

'Lucie, my child. The boy is serious. It is a serious head injury. We need to operate on him, immediately. We don't know about his family. You have to give consent and sign if you really want him to have the operation. Medicine and all. Quite a big amount involved you know. Of course money won't matter much, now that-'

'Money won't matter Doctor Uncle. I shall arrange somehow. You must try to save him.'

'Oh you don't have to spend I think, now that we know about the driver and specially when he is with the Ganguly family. They are our very close family friends you know.' He spoke with a firm assurance. Then after a few seconds' pause he asked me, 'You don't know Prateek I suppose, do you?' I shook my head.

'He is the bank manager of our local branch here. His father is a retired army man. They have a big bungalow in Purvapally.'

Purvapally or the eastern parish is the name of a locality in Shantiniketan. A posh locality against the rustic backdrop. He kept on talking something about the family which did not reach my ears. A frizzy crown clammy with blood disturbed me. A glassy frown freeze-dried in a spring afternoon haunted me. What if I had not called him suddenly? The thought drove me mad.

'Doctor Uncle, I think we should send him to the District Hospital. Before it is too late.'

I knew that apart from lacking in highly skilled doctors, this small hospital did not have many sophisticated and improved facilities, which might be required in such a serious operation. The District Hospital was about fifteen kilometres away and the boy could be taken there.

'You are right. Although we'll try our best, it would always be better to take him there. In fact, I was just thinking of sending him there. I was only hesitating that nobody from his family . . .'

'Doesn't matter,' I urged. 'Please send him there. Poor boy. He should live his life,' I said without having the least idea about what kind of life he would live. A poor village boy! Two bare feet, one mere existence. Yet, it was a morsel of life and I felt desperate to save it.

Dr Sen looked at his watch and sent for the ambulance.

'I think we can start just now. You just sign a paper that you are sending him to the District Hospital. I'll take care of the rest of the things.'

We came back to his chamber. The SI was scribbling down something. He looked at us and made a sign with the index finger of his left hand, to go near him.

'Was it him? Can you recognise him?' he asked me looking straight into my eyes. I glanced at him. Did I see a faint smile at the corner of his lips? I dropped my eyes as they met his and answered, 'I could not see his face. He was wearing a helmet.'

'How did the mo'bike clunk the boy?' His eyes were fixed on me. Stuck. Fevicol-white eyes. 'Was he driving rashly?'

A motorbike slid along the wall of the well of death. Inside me. I could not look at the stranger. But strangely, I saw his magic face. Inside me. A lie bubbled out of my mouth, 'I . . . I did not notice exactly. Normal speed, must be.' I swallowed a lump. 'I think-'

'She thinks wrongly, officer.' A deep voice cut me short, 'I was driving quite fast. There was hardly anybody on the roads and I did not expect him to be there, in the middle of the road.' He jerked his Greek God head in annoyance, 'Shit!'

I was shell-shocked. So was Dr Sen. A macho mind flexed its muscles through a dreamy masculine body. Mr Prateek Ganguly tried to cover up for him.

'Well, it is about perception officer. The speed you are thinking high, she may think it normal, it happens. It's the way you look at it.' He spoke with some authority in his voice, 'He has already shown you his international licence. He is ready to bear all the medical expenses. I think you should drop the case.'

'The boy is not out of danger yet . . .' The officer adjusted the specs on his big fleshy nose and got up from the chair implying, ' . . . so is the foreigner, therefore.' He thanked Dr Sen. 'Well doctor, I think we have gathered all the necessary facts for our preliminary enquiry. I 'll contact you again. In fact, all of you should remain in town, till we permit you to leave the station. Also keep me informed about the boy's condition.'

'Shit! I've got to go back to Calcutta.' A deep annoyance resounded in the foreigner's voice. 'Can't stay here for more than ten days.'

'That will depend on how the thing goes.' The SI scratched his sweaty nape and advanced to the door. 'Goodnight officer,' Dr Sen said very politely. 'Goodnight.'

The SI adjusted his belt over his bulging stomach and flanked by his two assistants made a grand exit.

An uneasy silence enveloped the atmosphere. Dr Sen sat on the table, Mr Prateek got up from the chair. The fair foreigner took out a wad of notes from his pocket, as fresh and crisp as his appearance. He kept it on the table, in front of the doctor. Dr Sen took out a form from the drawer of his table and handed it over to me, along with a pen. And all this without any sound. A silent movie. You could hear a pin drop. Instead, the pen dropped from my trembling hand. The silence was broken. The blond head bent over and picked the pen for me.

'Thank you,' I said without looking at him. Dr Sen instructed me how to fill in the form. I followed his instructions. Then, he informed Mr Prateek and his friend about my decision of sending the boy to the District Hospital.

'Why? Do you know this boy?' As I shook my head, Mr Prateek looked surprised.

'Has anybody from his family asked you?' He continued to be surprised at my unreasonable decision. I shook my head again and Dr Sen told him that nobody had come so far from the family of the boy.

'Then?' Mr Prateek looked into my eyes. Two coin-coloured eyes. Suddenly I remembered Ramesh Uncle of my Darjeeling days.

'I just want to save his life. So he has to be shifted to the district hospital.'

The rolling coins got fixed on me. I felt like an eighth wonder of the world. But why me? The wonder of the world was very much at hand. The most handsome male figure with a mellifluous voice.

'I'd say it is better for you too. If something happens to the boy you see . . .' Dr Sen suggested the rest with his eyes.

He continued, 'You know very well about our condition here. We can't give him the best.'

'Is it required?' Mr Prateek jingled his words with his keys.

'Oh, his condition is pretty serious. It is a head injury. Multiple-' He could not finish his words as one doctor entered the room and intimated that the ambulance was ready and the boy was being taken on the stretcher. I rushed out of the room. I saw him, lying on the stretcher. Heavily bandaged and unconscious. The oxygen mask was pumping life for the moment. I let out a scream.

'Oh god, is it life or death?'

I spoke to myself, but the words crawled out entangled with the scream. Dr Sen's fatherly arms supported me. The faces of Dr Sen and the two others, who were standing by my side, faded and went out of focus. I remembered the face of death. The only death I had seen in my life at very close quarters was when my grandma had had a heart attack. I recalled . . . They took her unconscious to the hospital. When we went there, it was all over. Her body, her face were all covered with white. *Absolutely white. Ghastly white: an eye without its iris and pupil.*

All of a sudden, I felt possessed.

'I have to go with him to the District Hospital. I have to, Doctor Uncle,' I pleaded. I feared that proper care might not be given to this unknown unidentified piece of life unless I remained present there, as his kin. On the plea that I was too young I was not allowed to go to the hospital, when my own dear grandma had been admitted. I could not save my grandma. Now, I could save this tender life. The life which was in danger partially due to my fault.

'It is not necessary, my child.' Dr Sen tried to reason with me, 'I'll talk to the doctors there, personally. You needn't worry.'

'Let me go with him, doctor.' My eyes did not shed tears but did send the shocking appeal he could not shove away any more. He put his reassuring arm around me and pressed my shoulder. He told the doctor in the room to look after the charge as he had decided to go himself He rang up the District Hospital and informed them. At my request, he also rang up my hostel superintendent to take permission from her for taking me to the District Hospital at this odd hour. He explained it was an emergency and my going there was absolutely necessary.

'In case you need some more . . .' the fairy-tale man came forward and took out not the magic wand but the very real solid wad of notes.

'Don't think it would be necessary, right now,' Dr Sen said, and proceeded to the ambulance with me. The other two followed us. Tension was stencilled on their faces. The stretcher was already inside. One attendant was sitting. We went inside and sat on the opposite side. The ambulance started with its customary honk. The wheels rolled. The attendant got up and went to the door to lock it. But the door was violently pulled open and my fairy-tale man dashed into the vehicle, thrusting aside the attendant. He was thrown off balance for a second. Dr Sen caught him by the hand. He never lost his composure, however. He locked the door safely behind him and sat opposite us.

The attendant sat by him grumbling and mumbling. It was so sudden!

'Do you want to go with us? To the District Hospital?' Dr Sen asked him.

'Yea. I just thought I'd better go.' His deep melodious voice filled the darkness. Perhaps, it filled my sweet darkness too. Nobody said any more, on the way.

We admitted the boy to the hospital. He was taken straightaway to the Operating Theatre. Dr Sen talked to many doctors and officials there. As

Dr Sen was with us we did not have to wait outside. We were taken to a big room with large sofas and divans—the rest room for the doctors. It was—quite comfortable. But discomfort pervaded the mind. For some time Dr Sen talked to a doctor who was sitting in that room. The foreigner went out. I held up a newspaper sedulously in front of my eyes. All the news was stale. I was remembering Dr Sen's words to Mr Prateek and his friend, 'It is better for you too. If something happens to the boy . . .' What could happen to them? I imagined the wonder face with striped shadows of bars on it. The fragmented beauty. A shiver crept up my spine. The big clock of the hospital struck eight. The operation was still going on.

Dr Sen turned towards me as the other doctor left the room.

'Are you feeling okay now?' His eyes were sympathetic. 'Yes Uncle,' I just managed to say. Our third companion walked in.

'Oh come in. I didn't get your name,' Dr Sen said with a tone of familiarity.

'I never told you I suppose.' He looked at me and smiled. His satin-blade lips dangerously carved a deep slit in my heart. A few seconds' throbbing silence. Then, he opened his lips.

'I am Leslie. Leslie Fraser.'

'Well, I'm Dr Subir Sen. This is Miss Lucie Roy. You must have met her at the site of the accident.' He slowly nodded. 'Are you a foreign student here?' Dr Sen asked him.

'Sort of.' He shrugged his shoulders and sat down on the sofa. It seemed he was not much interested in answering too many questions about himself Yet Dr Sen went on, 'You are from . . .'

'The States.'

'How do you know the Gangulys? They are our family friends.'

'My professor is their friend,' he replied, and lit a cigarette. In order to avoid any further question he held the camcorder in front of his eyes, as if to shoot. He was not shooting though. The lens of the camcorder was pointed towards some big display board showing the growth of medical care in the district. Now the Doctor's attention was drawn to the injury on the hand. It was bandaged unprofessionally.

'Are you hurt?' The Doctor's worried voice drew his attention.

'Just a scratch.' He shrugged off the serious tone of the Doctor.

'I think it is bad enough.' I could not help saying. 'Please have a close look at it, Doctor Uncle.'

He brought the camcorder down and let it remain suspended on his broad chest. Then he sneered, 'You Indians worry a lot.' He said without looking at me, 'I'm fine.'

'Let me see how fine you are.' Dr Sen went near him and undid the bandage. The scarlet wound was swollen badly. Dr Sen shook his head seriously and opined that it was to be dressed and bandaged properly. He took Leslie Fraser along with him to do the needful. I sighed and for the first time, cursed my fate for not being a doctor or a nurse, forgetting conveniently my aversion to blood and bloody sights. I went out of the shadow of sickness. The big, vast ground in front of the hospital was almost empty. A few leafless trees were displaying their skeleton presence. I looked up at the sky adorned with the waxing gibbous moon. *I felt gibbous, humped, dwarfed. Life and death and their mysteries all are out of my reach.*

How long I wandered with my thoughts I could not say. Dr Sen touched me lightly on the shoulder and I came back to earth. He informed that the operation was over succesfully.

'Well done Lucie. I really doubt if we could have saved the child there.' Dr Sen affectionately patted me on the back. Then he added, 'Now the only thing left is to inform his family.'

'The police know already and they should take care of it.' Leslie Fraser, who was standing by his side, remarked.

'Well, I wish things were so systematic here. People hardly seem to bother about these poor uneducated people,' Dr Sen said regretfully.

'Uncle, I feel that the holes of the Internet are too big for these small fish to be caught in it.'

Dr Sen gave a hearty laugh. So did our fair companion. In fact, I wanted him to laugh; I wanted to hear the resonance of his voice. And laugh away the lingering tension in our minds. The doctor informed us that the next forty-eight hours would be crucial and· the boy would have to be under intensive care. that Anything might happen during that period.

We were about to start for Shantiniketan immediately. It was nearing ten. Leslie Fraser did not get into the hospital car.

'I'd prefer to walk.'

'Walk? All the way to Shantiniketan?'

'I suppose so.' He shrugged his shoulder.

'It is around fifteen kilometres from here. The roads are deserted at this time.'

'I don't like crowds very much,' he announced in a cold tone, 'and fifteen kilometres is not a big deal. A matter of one and a half hour. Nothing new for me. I go hiking quite often.'

His smooth tone ruffled me. I hadn't ever come across such craziness! As unique as his charm. And he did not sound crazy at all. As if it was his routine activity.

'As you wish, but bad elements, you know . . .' Dr Sen tried to warn him.

'Bad elements!' he laughed again as if there could be nobody worse than him! Well, in that case, take these with you. I'll collect them tomorrow. I have my passport with me and a hundred bucks. That should be enough.'

He took out a stuffed wallet from his pocket and handed it to Dr Sen. He handed over his camcorder too.

'Give me your watch too. You are our guest. I don't want you to be in trouble. And please give a second thought to this wild idea of yours. Come with us in our car.'

He just shook his head in silence, obstinately. Dr Sen arranged one big flashlight for him and we started our return journey.

The road was almost empty. Darkness solidified as some wandering clouds covered the moon. The road lights were very dim. Many of them were not working. The vehicle moved very slowly along the bumpy and rough road. I was dropped near our hostel gate. Rani's moped had to be recovered the next day from the hospital scooter shed.

Life seemed not very easy after the accident. Two images occupied my mind completely. One of life, the other of death. Both were equally strong. A flash of lightning. The light of life or the thunder of death? Deepa and Rani, my two best friends got suspicious.

'Something is wrong with you, Small Mouth, you don't look yourself.'

'Do I look like Miss Deepa then?' I tried to put it aside with a laugh. But it was difficult to deceive Deepa. She had her stupendous and sometimes even stupid logic to overshadow people. She had been a brilliant student of logic in her school days, I had heard, and now she was a bright student of philosophy.

'Your daily routine has changed, I've observed. What's the matter?'

'Nothing, dear. I am fine.'

'You are fine, that's why those two letters are still sealed even though one is from London. You forgetful jerk.'

'Hey you creep, you spy on my things?'

'I didn't open any of them. But this is the sacred duty of a room-mate to remind her friend to open the letter of her boyfriend. Isn't it?'

'Yes, and I have to remind you to meet Nandan. You haven't seen him for the last six hours and seven minutes, so hurry before he is all at sixes and sevens.'

She chased me in mock aggression and I escaped. Both of us had fun. Nandan was a senior student of economics, whom Deepa had been lumbering for quite some time now.

Rani was a student from Bangladesh. She was a student of music. She had came on a scholarship to India. Her real name was a bit of a mouthful: Nazrana, Nazrana Amin, so we used to call her Rani. Rani means 'queen'. She was as beautiful as a queen. As bubbly as a child. I loved children. I loved childhood. I loved the callow youth in her.

'Are you in love?' she asked me directly. The word didn't even knock at my consciousness. I blushed however.

'With whom?' I wondered aloud.

'That I should ask you. Who is the lucky boy?'

'No Rani. You're wrong.'

'People forget things like this when they fall in love.'

'Do they? How many times have you fallen in love dear?'

'Oh no, no. Don't say this. I can't fall in love. I mustn't. My parents won't allow it. Say, if the boy is not Muslim, I'll have to die. I don't want to fall in love to die. That's not worth it.'

'I hope you don't,' I said and thought, I shall also never FALL in love. Love is not a pit or hole to fall into. Love is a big sky. I shall float up into it.

In my memory, at that time two images were floating up. Two aquamarine waves and a few drops of black-red blood. They were intertwined together. Inseparably. I kept on calling Dr Sen. Twice a day. He informed me that the boy's condition had not yet improved. He also informed me that nothing could be found out about the boy or his family. On the third morning, when I rang him up, he was out of station on some urgent work That was the day when we were supposed to know if the boy was out of danger. As I could not get the information, I kept feeling restless. I wanted to ring up the District Hospital to know more about the condition of the boy, but Deepa said it would not help.

'You don't know the ward number, cabin number, do you? They may give you some wrong information about some other patient if you enquire on the phone. You know very well dear, how they all work. You'll be unnecessarily worried.' Deepa and her logic. We were all under its spell. But she was pretty helpful.

'I'd suggest Lucie, it would be better if you were to go there. Today is a holiday. You won't miss any class.' In Shantiniketan, Sunday is a working day. Wednesday is the weekly off 'Just take permission from the superintendent. She is already aware of the incident, rather I'd say accident. I hope she'll allow.' Then in the same breath she continued, 'But I'm sorry. Today, I can't come with you. I'm already tied up. You take Rani with you. Don't go alone.' She rushed off to keep her appointment.

Rani shrank at the very name of the hospital. A shade of pallor shadowed her radiant face.

'Lucie dear, I hate death. I hate hospitals. I'd go with you just anywhere else in the world except a hospital. That smell of the hospital gives me a nausea. Even when my mother was admitted for an appendix operation, I didn't go to see her. Believe me.'

'So, I'll never expect you by the side of my hospital bed, if I fall ill.'

'God forbid dear Lucie, God forbid. Don't you ever say this again.' She planted a warm kiss on my cheek. I did not insist. I decided to go alone. The boy's life was still in danger. That terracotta body, that frizzy crown and those glass-bead-like eyeballs. What if he were to die? My senses became as numb as snakes in hibernation. I could not hear what Rani was talking about, neither could the chime of the large bell at the famous Bell Tower of Shantiniketan reach my ears. I just wanted to go and see him.

Taking permission was not an easy thing. Our superintendent, Madam Banerjee was a nice decent elderly lady. She never used to cover her head with her sari like the many traditional or village women would do. But her mind was veiled, burqa-clad. A stern voice sounded from inside that burqa.

'I don't know what is wrong with you. That night too you were very late, I didn't like it much. Is your going absolutely necessary? In what way can you help that boy? You don't even know him.'

A rage surged inside me. Nobody knows nobody initially. Even madam herself must have slept with a man, her husband, without knowing anything about him. That is the tradition of Indian arranged marriages. I wanted to fling some angry words towards her. A gale. To blow her veil off.

But Mom spoke within me. When you are very angry, don't talk. Don't ever talk. And still better, don't listen. Just don't listen to what the subject of anger is saying. Mom did not tell me what to do instead, but I had my ingenious way. I used to dream. Dreams are the gods, or God is the dream, this world cherishes. I saw the face of the· unconscious boy. J saw his frizzy crown. Without blood. I caressed, I combed his hair. His glass-bead eyes rolled at me and on that I saw the reflection of two aquamarine waves. There was life all over.

I did not hear what she was saying so far, I just pleaded, "Madam, I just feel so much for the poor child. A mere child. You are a mother, you will appreciate.'"

She thought for some time. A soft rustle of the burqa. Two mother's eyes peered through the veil. A mother's heart faintly spoke, 'Well. If you feel so much; it is better that you go, but . . .' the veil was still a veil. 'But your local guardians must give their consent. You bring a letter from them.'

She took up her pen to start her unfinished work but stopped and said, 'You see, I have a big responsibility. I have to be very protective.'

Maybe she was right in her own way. My local guardians were a local family. The head of the family was a cousin of one of our family friends at Darjeeling. Relations between us were just formal. Moreover, their house was pretty far. To go there, convince them, get a consent letter, bring it back to madam . . . Time would not permit me to go to the hospital. I went near the table, without any permission, picked up the phone and started dialling frantically.

'What are you doing?'

'Madam, why the local guardian? I am talking to my real guardians. They will permit me.'

Madam looked dumbfounded. The veil got all dishevelled. Fortunately, I got Mom over the phone immediately. I didn't have to tell her much. She agreed. I gave the receiver to a bewildered superintendent. Mom spoke to her. Madam Banerjee could hardly speak. She was at her wit's end. She hung up the phone when the talk was over and looked at me. A half-hearted nod and I smiled, 'Thank you madam, please charge me for the call in my hostel bill. Bye.' I rushed out of the room, before she could change her mind.

'You must come back before lunch.' I could hear her voice behind me filtering through a black, lightless burqa.

When I reached the main hospital by a local bus jumping and bumping along the narrow, eroded, rough roads and stopping after every ten minutes or so, to stuff more men with bare feet, more women with lice in their hair, more children with running noses and a couple of friendly chicken or goat companions, it was already eleven. The sun was getting hot. I could not get an express bus as the frequency was very less and I did not want to wait. The bus stopped just by the side of the hospital. Today I was in a sari. Outside the ashram campus, away from friends and acquaintances, and particularly in a Bengali village, the sari would be the best thing to wear, I thought. But it proved the other way around. As I was about to alight, my anchal caught the sharp edge of some sharply pointed wooden planks, being carried by a passenger. The anchal is that part of the sari which hangs loosely over the left shoulder like a lesser version of the long, trailing robes of the ancient nobles. Utterly uncontrollable for me. Quite unaware of the fact that my anchal was caught I hurriedly stepped down. Before I knew it I tumbled down the steps of the bus. I fell with a thump on the ground. The flying anchal was torn, shaped like a forked tongue of a snake.

When I got up on my feet, I noticed that the abundant red dust had adorned my sari, my arms and my face most adoringly. My purse had also slipped off my hand and was kissing the red dust. As I bent down to pick it up and take out a hanky to wipe my face, I noticed a masculine hand with long and strong, rajnigandha-stem fingers and blue veins throbbing through the white transparent skin, on my black purse, covered with the red dust. The hand picked up the purse and as I stood straight, I saw in front of me that sunlight-coloured body, that dimpled chin and curved lips. I had to cover my face with the torn anchal. This sun was much more dazzling than the one in the sky. And why, just why was it that every time I stood before him I was a miserable mess! I wanted to brush myself down quickly but everything went wrong. I forgot to take the purse and bring out the hanky, instead wiped my face with the torn anchal with which I had covered my face. But as it was torn, I made a mistake in keeping it back on the shoulder. Half of it was placed on the shoulder while the other half was not, and under the open blue sky, in front of so many people, half of my blouse got uncovered for a few seconds. Soon I gathered myself, my sari, and also my purse from his hand with a mumbling 'thank you'. I could not look into his eyes as I felt terribly embarrassed. I could feel that even without any touch of red dust, my face and ears were red and this red could not be wiped or shaken off with any hanky of this world.

I walked towards the long and broad, giant steps of the hospital. I remained cautious, holding the pleats of the sari in my hand carefully. The sun was bright and I noticed that just by the side of my shadow, a long shadow had also appeared, moving up with me, getting wavy on the flights of steps. The figure behind the shadow had been printed in my memory. A lot of people were climbing up or down casting their corrugated shadows on the steps. I could not stop there. I stopped after reaching the porch, so did the shadow.

'Hi! Want to see the boy? He is okay.' I heard the deep voice and it was more than music to my ears. The voice as well as the news. I turned towards him, and he, towards me. I forgot about my blushing blouse or embarrassed anchal.

'Have you seen him already?' I asked.

'Yea, I did. He is out of danger. But still under special care. Would you' like to see him now?'

'Yes,' I said, 'that was why I'm here. What's his ward number?'

'I'd rather show you.' His sky blue eyes were not overcast today. So, the shade was lighter. The other day they had been. Deep aquamarine. Or was it my brush of imagination?

The boy was kept in a single room. Leslie Fraser told me that the doctors had wanted to keep him in a common ward, but after seeing the condition there, Leslie had asked for a single room and paid for it.

'Oh, that common ward, as you call it! Sickening enough to make normal people sick,' he remarked.

I saw the terracotta body, still unconscious. The eyelids had completely covered the glass-bead pupils. And instead of an uncommon crown of frizzy black hair, a heavy white bandage decorated his head. I uncovered his body, and looked at it. Small hands with smaller fingers, thin legs with slightly cracked heels and toes. There were patches of sticking plasters at various spots on his small body, to cover minor wounds. I felt a disturbing pain looking at the damaged breathing body. Leslie Fraser was standing by my side and repeated the question, that I had involuntarily asked the other day.

'What are you looking at? Life or death?'

'Is he still unconscious?' I asked the nurse ignoring his question.

'Yes, he hasn't regained consciousness so far. That's the biggest worry. This morning he was operated on again and doctors are hopeful that he will come round today.'

I could perceive the receding shadow of death over this hapless piece of humanity. And then, I looked at life, a sun-size life, placed in my orbit out of the blue, across a leaking darkness. Today, he was wearing a cream-coloured T-shirt and a pair of hip-hugging jeans.' His strong and long arms were almost bare. They gave me an idea about the rocky muscles on the terrain of his body. Tall, like my imagination, wide-chested like my fondness, and supple like my nostalgia. My hands miserably missed a brush, a canvas and a few squiggly strokes. An extravaganza of beauty and life, a dream was in front of me against the backdrop of death, cased in this hospital. This man seemed so unrealistically real.

'Would you like to go now?' he asked, causing me to blink after a long time.

'Oh yes, I think I will. How about your wound? Healed?'

He showed me the bandaged hand and shook his head carelessly, 'It was nothing.'

We left the hospital, the shelter for the sick, unknown, helpless, damaged terracotta body sheltered in it. We walked through the long corridors and big halls, crowded with pathetic patients and their kin, white-collared doctors and white-clad nurses. The air was filled with the smell of health and sickness. A very typical smell of a hospital which Rani found nauseating. We came out in the open. Leslie Fraser had come on the same motorcycle. But this time he did not offer me a ride back to Shantiniketan. This time perhaps, I would have accepted his offer. However, he proposed to share' a drink, soft drink of course. There was a small, very small tea shack, with a few bottles of cold drinks, kept in a big icebox, a few jars containing biscuits and toffees, a few packs of cigarettes and bidis, i.e. local cheap Indian cigarettes, betel leaves or *paan* and a few more titbits. The shopkeeper and all the people around, kept on staring at Leslie Fraser, because unlike in Shantiniketan, a foreigner could be quite a rare species in this part of the country. Especially one who was so good looking.

Oppressive heat. Their eyes were scorched. Some small children came closer and looked up with their innocent eyes innocuously wide open. One of them, a four or five-year-old naively touched his leg with his teeny-weeny fingers, perhaps to check if it was as real as their dust and distress-stricken life.

'This tacker is so cute. Is he asking for some money?'

'Oh no.' I stroked the untidy head of that sniffling tacker and caressed his pink cracked cheeks.

'They are curious about you. They hardly see any foreigners here. This is not Shantiniketan.'

He looked around himself. He smiled. And that smile, that one particular curve at the corner of his thin satin-blade lips changed his countenance so much, I felt I had never seen him before.

'Never mind. I'm quite used to it. Anywhere in the world. Even in my own country.' The blazing blue overflowed as if in a blue-blooded superiority, and made me feel blue. The boy was quite conscious about his exquisite exterior, I realised. I had intended to warm up our acquaintance over the bottle of cold drinks, but his words silenced me. The fizz of the coke fizzled out abruptly, leaving the insipid liquid cold and blandly cold.

'Do you stay in Shantiniketan?' His bottle was perhaps still fizzy.

'Yes, in the hostel,' I answered without looking at him.

The conversation did not proceed further. Next, I saw my bus coming in like a saviour. I wanted to depart with a formal goodbye. But he stopped me.

'Can't you take the next bus? I need your help.'

'Yes?' My large eyes asked him.

'Doctors at the hospital wanted some clothes for the boy. I don't know anything here, neither do I know the language very well. If you help me get some clothes . . . ?'

'Yes, that would be necessary if he survived, I thought and blamed myself for not remembering such simple practical necessities of life. I also did not have much idea about the place. Only once had I come here, when one of our hostel girls had got admitted for an appendix operation. So, I thought it would be best to take a rickshaw as the rickshaw driver would know all the important places. But my sari! What about the torn anchal? In the hospital where people went with broken limbs and torn ligaments, torn clothes were not out of the place. But out on the road to a shopping area? Even though it was a small town. I tried to cover up my torn anchal as much as possible. Like the Santhal women of this area, I wrapped the torn anchal around my waist and tucked it inside the petticoat. Now, the torn anchal was hidden, but my bosom was highlighted, the narrow curve of my waist was bared. In brief, my vital statistics were on total display. I was feeling awkward, as like most Bengali girls my 'waves' were high. But I had the glass-bead eyes engraved in my heart and I was ready to do anything to help them.

The rickshaw driver took me to the nearest market, which consisted of two rows of small shops. Leslie Fraser followed the rickshaw on his two-wheeler. We went to a small ready-made garments shop. The shopkeeper got excited. He stood up, welcomed us, ordered coconut water and was kind enough to show us all kinds of expensive clothes. I told him that the customer was me and not my companion. The shopkeeper's face paled like some cheap cloth which lost colour after the first wash. In the meantime the entire crowd outside had gathered near the door of the shop, for window-shopping. There was the most spectacular showpiece they had ever seen or they could ever afford!

First of all, I asked for a 'chunni' which was a kind of long scarf usually worn with a salwar kurta. All my curves got covered with that scarf. I saw Leslie Fraser looking at me with silent amazement and amusement bubbling in his blue eyes which must be carrying too many bikini-clad memories. I was not bothered. Next, I selected three pairs of shirts and pants, ordinary, cotton, suitable for that terracotta complexion and took out money to pay for them, when he objected and insisted that he pay for them. He was almost going to hold my hand to stop me, and every pore of my hand was bursting in anticipation of that intoxicating touch. But I did not allow it to happen.

'Look,' I told him, pointing to the crowd at the door of the shop, 'they are already enjoying the scene.' The rest was said by my eyes. We came out of the shop as the crowd made way for us. I handed the packet over to him and said 'Goodbye' as I decided to wait for the bus at the stop, by the side of the marketplace.

'You are quite a girl. Goodbye.' The black helmet encased the sunny face, and the two-wheeler sped away.

II

Two Strangers

LIFE WENT BACK to its normal routine, and normal speed for the next two days. The classes, the brushes, the colours, the strokes. And the silence devoted to the effort of forgetting an unforgettable fantasy figure. I had wanted to measure the depth of his charm but I was not ready to scale the height of his conceit, to make it even higher. I also had an undercurrent of fear about those glass-bead eyes, the terracotta figure. The third day was a holiday. I went to meet Dr Sen to know if there was any news from the main hospital about the boy regaining consciousness. It was early in the morning, around eight o'clock. The sun was pleasant on the skin, like a child's soft touch. But as I pushed the door of the doctor's chamber, the super brightness—of a blond head blinded all my senses. Never did I except to see him here. His face was towards the doctor. Dr Sen smiled and greeted me, so he turned his face, smiled and we exchanged 'Good morning' a bit mechanically. I had to sit on the chair next to him. There was good news for us. The boy was recovering. He had regained consciousness but had been too feeble to talk for long. So, his identity had not yet been established.

'It beats me,' Dr Sen said, 'it really beats me. Nobody has come to look for the boy. Even the police have not found anything so far. Of course, the police never search very sincerely for such trivial cases. They seem to have other, more important business to attend to.'

'Why don't we put out an alert in the newspaper and radio?' I suggested. The boy seemed to be from a village where TV might not be so common but the newspaper and especially the radio might help. Dr Sen agreed. Then, he looked at Leslie Fraser and said, We may as well start then . . .'

'Are you going to see the boy? You too?' I asked the doctor.

'Oh yes, I have some official work at the hospital. Leslie has to go to make some payment to the hospital, and ensure that he can go back to Calcutta now, so I am taking him with me in my car,' Dr Sen said as he signed a few papers on his table. Then, he raised his eyes in order to avoid looking through the glasses used for short-sightedness, and looked at me straight—the straightforward, farsighted person. 'Do you want to come with us too?'

'Yes, I do,' I just blurted out, without any thought whatsoever. However, Dr Sen appeared pleased.

'Very well.' He stood up, started arranging the things in his briefcase and went on, 'These bus journeys are no good here, on this route. Better you come with me. The only thing is that you may have to wait for sometime there, till I finish my official work. It may take one hour or so. You can wait, can't you? We shall come back before lunch, anyway.'

Suddenly, I remembered my hostel, its boundaries, its regulations. I recalled the veiled heart. I stood up and with some hesitation said, 'I have to inform my hostel superintendent. I can't leave Shantiniketan without taking her permission.'

'Can't you break the rule sometimes, for a change?' A wild drum resounded in the wilderness of the Santhal Pally, the tribal village. I looked at the dashing dimpled chin, the devastating aquamarine depths; I smelt the calamitous cologne, fresh after the morning shave. I lost my word, I lost my world: a limited, well-known place for me. Dr Sen saved the situation.

'Just ring up your superintendent.' He handed the phone to me, 'Explain the situation to her. If required, I shall talk to her.' She was not available. It seemed she had gone to the adjacent town, Bolpur, for some shopping. I was hesitant, but Dr Sen said, 'You may leave a message with your friends, and explain after you return. After all, you are going for a good cause, not to fool around. Of course, this is only a suggestion, the decision is yours.'

He was by then ready with his briefcase. Leslie Fraser also stood up and was ready to go with him. I made myself ready for the forbidden ride out of Shantiniketan, without proper permission.

There was a small garden near the verandah of the hospital, at the back. With the doctor's permission I took some flowers from there. It did not make quite a bouquet, as the flower season was almost over. However the small bunch of flowers and leaves looked cute.

'This is for the poor boy,' I said to the doctor. He looked very pleased.

Our ambassador car started soon. The driver and one official of the hospital were sitting in the front seat. Dr Sen sat between Leslie Fraser and me. The road was rough and rugged and often we found ourselves bouncing on our seats.

'When I first came here I hated the red earth, the dust and heat, the rough roads, everything. It was like the rugged area we used to see in your Hollywood Western movies. Instead of the Red Indians there were the Santhals, the tribe with their excellent physique,' Dr Sen narrated his experience.

Leslie Fraser asked, 'So you don't belong to this area?'

'Difficult to answer. I came from Howrah, a place near Calcutta, by the side of the Ganga, a very green place. But now, I have been here for the last twenty-five years. My wife belongs to this place, my children grew up here. Now, you tell me where I belong.'

'Obviously here,' I said.

'Oh no, he does not. He doesn't seem to love the place. Do you doc, honestly?' Leslie Fraser asked.

'A difficult question again. Love the place! Now I just can't think of any other place to stay.'

I threw a 'you see, I win' glance to our foreigner companion. But he didn't give in.

'Staying at one place for a very long time gives somebody this kind of feeling. This you can't call love.'

'Well young man, like it or not, this is love, Indian style. The more we get used to a thing, the more we love it. For you, it's just the other way, I think. That is also quite fascinating, only it doesn't suit our tropical climate.'

We all laughed together and I liked the doctor more than ever for such frankness, such a sense of humour and the young heart which mixed with young people so easily. However I protested,

'I don't think it is Indian style. Love must be long lasting, or it is no love.'

'Oh dear, it sounds like a sturdy steel cupboard,' Leslie quipped.

'And yours is a silly bubble.'

'Bubbles are not silly, they are just bubbles, meant to be momentary.' He blew the words like bubbles, most casually and caused my bubbles to burst.

Soon, I got lost in the world of bubbles and these words came out of my mouth as I was picturing them in my mind. 'Maybe you are right, they are not silly, they are so perfectly round and transparent, delicate and beautiful. They don't pretend a long existence.'

As I muttered this, the whole galaxy opened in front of my eyes with bubbles floating in nothingness, waiting to burst into nothingness. The strong belief, about a long-lasting love instilled in me like thousands others over the centuries, got a jolt but could not be obliterated.

So the next moment I smiled and said, 'When an entire life is a bubble, love is a bubble, too, no doubt about it.'

Leslie Fraser looked at me, wanted to say something, but he did not or could not say it. Dr Sen diverted our attention towards some rare species of trees found in this area and described their special features. The forbidden ride became a fun ride for me, so different from the everyday routine, I had been on outings with friends and teachers, now and then, for picnics or educational tours. We had enjoyed ourselves, but it was totally different. Boating on the river and surfing on the sea. I closed my eyes and felt the rise and fall of every wave. 'In the light you see, in the darkness you feel.' At the moment, I was full of feelings.

Within forty minutes we reached the hospital. The driver was efficient and the car ran reasonably fast. Time ran even faster. First of all, the three of us went to see the boy. He was sleeping then. He looked almost the same as I had seen him earlier, on the hospital bed. The nurse said he had been sleeping for quite some time and might get up any moment now. The doctor of the main hospital also came in and he and Dr Sen started discussing the boy's condition in medical terms. I was eager to see the boy open his eyes. I had touched the body, I had carried the body, I had had his blood smeared all over me, and now I wanted to see the terracotta body move, corked safely with all valuable blood drops secured inside. We waited in silence for a few seconds. Dr Sen begged our pardon and went away with his senior counterpart to attend to his official duty.

A sick silence prevailed in the room, along with the strong smell of medicine. To inject some health into it I started asking the nurse about the boy, if he had spoken anything about himself The nurse informed me that he had said that his name was Mukul and that he was from the nearby village. But when asked about his parents he had not replied anything, only tears had flowed from his eyes. All the conversations were in Bengali, as the local nurses were not well versed in spoken English. I had to translate them in English for Leslie Fraser. We were soon called to the chamber of the doctor-in-charge. Dr Sen was sitting there. We were offered tea as special guests with him. We spoke about the boy. He would be sent back to the Shantiniketan hospital soon, maybe within a couple of days. Here he could not be kept for long as there was always a rush of patients. He would not require it either. Dr Sen turned to me and said apologetically, 'Sorry, but it will take some time. I don't think it'll be before three. If you want you can go back, my driver will take you and again come back for me.'

'I would like to wait at least till he wakes up,' I said.

'Very well. You may wait if you like and go back with me. I only thought you might get bored in such a healthy and lovely atmosphere. After all, you are not used to it,' he spoke in his usual jovial manner. His senior partner now took charge of the situation and said, Wait a minute. Why will they go back early? If they are interested, they can go and visit the deer park nearby while we work. I shall send a man with them and I think they can take your car and the driver.'

'Oh definitely. Let them. This is a marvellous idea, sir.' Then turning towards me he asked, 'Have you seen it, my dear?'

'Yes, just once, but long ago, just after I came to Shantiniketan. I would like to visit it again. Thank you very much, sir.'

'And for our foreign friend it must be the very first,' our doctor said. 'You are adventurous and love nature. I'm sure you will like it.'

Leslie Fraser got up and smiled, 'I look forward to seeing it and capturing some interesting moments.' He patted his camcorder, his perpetual companion. I stole a glance at his injured hand. It had healed up, leaving a slight purple scar.

Just then the doctor was informed that the boy had woken up. I rushed to his room without waiting for the others. I could hear the faint sound of some footsteps behind me. When I entered the room I saw the boy lying in the same way, only he was blinking, like a blinking Barbie doll. But he was not a Barbie doll, his was a terracotta body with the bead-like eyes of a Barbie doll and long lashes. I went near his bed, very close to him, and called, 'Mukul, how are you feeling?'

He looked at me with questions in his eyes. Question or something else? Dead leaves rustled inside me. Did he recognise me? I tried to avoid the aversion in his eyes. The nurse told him, however, that it was I who had saved his life. The Barbie-doll eyes got some life into them. He wanted to fold his hands in gratitude. But I held the hands, sat on his bed and gave him the flowers. A teardrop fell on my palm. It was warm and I loved it. No more dripping blood or oozing wound. No more bleeding conscience about killing a life. In fact, it was clear from his behaviour that he did not remember my face.

Dr Sen and Leslie Fraser, in the meantime, had reached. Leslie Fraser looked at him, his handiwork, made out of a live terracotta toy. The doctor asked him if he was feeling better and he nodded slowly. He was looking very weak. The terracotta shade was paler. Dr Sen asked us to leave him alone and not to ask any more questions. So, I got up and said, Well Mukul, get well very soon. Then, I shall come and take you home.'

Without having the slightest idea about his home, I said this only to comfort him, to add a shade of hope to that tortured terracotta mind, which must have looked for his dear ones, all these days. We left the room, the boy. His bleeding wound, pleading eyes and flickering life.

'Don't you think the boy may be an orphan?' Leslie Fraser asked me in the car on the way to the deer park. We were on the back seat, the weather was getting warmer, and through the open window of the car the red-hot dusty wind was greeting us warmly.

'What gave you that idea?' I was annoyed.

'He never called for Mummy or Daddy. Did he? A boy of his age would have first of all looked for Mummy, called her,' he said confidently. Yes, there were logic and sense in his thought. Oh boy, he is practical, just like Joy. I thought, It is only me, who thinks and feels in darkness and gets a handful of starry reflections. I looked at him, the boy with Joy's mind and most probably of the same age. The aquamarine blue was however so much deeper than the colour of Darjeeling tea. I gave in and said, 'But he must have somebody.'

'Maybe, and he does not seem to be too fond of them.' His eyes were fixed on the rustic plain as if he was looking into the history of that boy in the shimmering rustic ruggedness. I could see only the mottled barks of trees, a few magpie tails on the barren branches and some black-faced monkeys at every bend of the road.

After a half an hour's journey, we reached the reserved forest area. An enormous iron fence, and on the other side of that, a green and yellow forest had sprung up as one of nature's wonders. On this side of the fence, was the barren red earth with rocks and hillocks and a gritty rough path. We walked down to the big iron gate of the Deer Park. The man who came to show us the reserve forest, talked to the authority and then the big iron gate opened. The squeak of the bolt, the clatter of the chain and the heavy iron lock.

The gate was opening, as if in a slow motion. I had to go through. I had to. I could not stop. There was no going back for me. The gateway was widening to transfer me somewhere else. To a new phase of life, perhaps. I stepped forward in silence.

Inside, yellow and brown foliage and bushes hailed us. The grass below our feet was dull, pale brown and rough and prickly like a middle-aged Red Indian's unshaven chin. Some women were cleaning the dead leaves with long brooms. The time for the public was from 11a.m. to 5 p.m. The doctor's recommendation enabled us to enter early. Not only that, the attendant promised to take us beyond the point where the common public was generally allowed. The forest showered on us, young people, dead leaves in plenty. Dead leaves with their sad yellow hues. Some got stuck on my black hair, some added an unhappy shade to his blond brilliance. Falling season. All will fall one day, on this earth, deep down inside the earth, with no resistance they will give in to the final gravitational pull. Being showered with rustling brittleness all over, my senses were searching for a green relief Even a mirage! Unfortunately, it was no desert. There were bright red flowers on the huge Shimul (silk-cotton) trees, and the Palash (forest fire) trees. But these were not too many in numbers and they were not showering us with flowers. They were flaunting their fiery presence along the decay, like saucy youth among the aging grey. Soon, the man made a sign to stop and pointed his finger towards a spot. I saw them. Some darling deer. It looked as if the forked branches of the leafless trees decorated their temples. In fact, one tiny little black bird sat on the antlers of one and preened. Leslie Fraser's camcorder got active to capture the moment.

The attendant explained about the speciality of each kind. We went further and saw many more varieties. The spotted deer, the sambar, the antelope, the gazelle, the rare black buck. There were no cages, no pens, no barriers between those harmless beauties and us. The man even took us very near to some of them and gave me some grass to offer to one of them. It was a hornless female. She took the grass happily from my hand and looked at me expectantly. The big black eyeballs absorbed all the shining darkness which I used to see, feel and marvel.

'Don't you think these eyes are like that boy's eyes? That Mukul's?' I asked my companion with a childlike excitement as if I had discovered something. He smiled and all of a sudden, in a twinkle of an eye, his rapier like body bent down and sprang up. In his strong grip he was holding a twisting, writhing, spiralling body of a snake. I covered my mouth with my hand. Leslie Fraser was smiling and enjoying. The attendant said that it was a poisonous one and advised my fairer companion not to play with it. He just laughed it off 'I have been in the jungle of Africa. I'm used to it. Don't worry,' he said. Then he asked me, 'Why are you scared of this?'

I could not tell him that the feeling was not exactly related to fear. I just watched in silence, the gaping extra large mouth and an extra large forked tongue waving a victory sign. He came nearer to me and said, 'Just feel how cold and slippery is the body.' But I turned away my face. He smiled and then hurled the long twisting body far, far away, deep into the forest beyond our sight. The colour of wildness shadowed the aquamarine shade and sent a shudder through my heart.

The attendant took us to the other part of the forest. Here we saw peacocks and guinea pigs and rabbits. The attendant picked up a puff of a white rabbit which had been scuttling away swiftly through the heap of fallen leaves. Leslie Fraser took it from his hand. I could feel the palpitations of the little body. In the grip of his strong hand with the throbbing blue veins, the white softness was a shattering shiver. He started fondling that furry bundle, stroked all over its body, and rocked it in his arms. As I watched him doing this I didn't know how and why, my whole body got covered with goose bumps, without anybody stroking it, without anybody even touching it.

'What do you think about his eyes? Like yours?' he asked, coming quite close to me and showing me the rabbit. 'Do you know that it is because we love to rub it, that is why it is called a rabbit,' I told him.

'Why don't you rub it then?' he said and before I could say anything it was in my arms. The attendant also enjoyed it. He was smiling. 'Madam, there are many in this forest, if you want some I can give you.'

'Oh no,' I said, feeling the smooth softness with closed eyes, 'let it enjoy its freedom.' And so I let it go soon. Its touch lingered over my senses. Water flowed out of the cupped palm, leaving a lingering dampness.

The forest was getting denser. So far the shedding brown columns had been at a friendly distance. Here the big trees were thick together. As close as lovers. Many evergreen trees cast their ever-cool shadows. The wild tiny red berries rippled, the soft, sugar-like white neem flowers bubbled in the streaming green. Wings of multicoloured birds mellowed the show. There were black and white ones too. The black-faced monkeys, with creamy white fur, jumped from one branch to the other. Leslie Fraser's camera remained active all through. Then he himself got active. Tossing his head up and throwing his arms up in the air, he declared, 'I feel so wild in the forest.'

He kept down his camcorder and jumped to hold a strong branch, horizontal with the earth like a high bar in the gymnastics event, but not that high. He hung from it and swung to and fro. To and fro. His golden hair covered his more· precious face. Next he took a flip and ended with an· excellent dismount. He threw a blow into the air and laughed. He was having great fun.

I had fun too, and I had one more thing. When Leslie Fraser was doing the flip, something fell just near my feet. I thought it was a dead leaf. But when I looked down, I saw a small box. A sort of a jewellery box. I picked it up without his knowledge and hid it. He was then busy trying to jump from one branch to another, a la Tarzan. The attendant was enjoying his acrobatics thoroughly. 'Why don't you swing a bit?'

'Oh, I'm not used to it,' I said as I sat on a small rock and started picking up some red Palash and shimul flowers, scattered on the ground. There were more deer, more rabbits, some monkeys, so many birds, chirping and cheering over our heads. And then there was this man who got wild in this wilderness. Finally, a little tired, Leslie Fraser came and stood near me by the rock, leaning against a tall silk-cotton tree. The tree had hardly any leaves. It was full of big red heavy flowers. The barren branches with red rapture were etched on the body of the blue. It made quite a picture. And below that, against the mottled bark of the tree stood a youthful dream, my eyes could not shake off. I wanted water and the man went to bring it from the nearby hut of the watchman. Leslie Fraser's hand slowly touched my hair. He started stroking the yellow leaves off carefully, rather than shaking them off. The fingers glided over the dark smooth layer, without disturbing their smoothness, but the lower layer got all ruffled up.

'These dull yellow leaves don't look good on the shiny black,' he said looking at me from the depth of his aquamarine blue.

Then he said, 'I like this place, you know. It is wonderful. The red ground, the red flowers, the calm and the quietness. I am touched by it. In fact, I never expected it to be like this, after the din and bustle of Calcutta.' His deep voice was sinking deeper. After a few seconds' silence he said again, 'I feel like extending my stay here for some more days.'

Yes, he had come here just like the migrant birds we see during this period. They start flying back after the spring is over. Soon all of them will be gone. There will be no wing-prints etched in the blank blue. They will not even leave a trail of smoke behind them, as the flying jets do.

'Are you going back to your country very soon?'

He smiled as if to himself.

'I am going from here, but where, I can't say at the moment. I've not yet made up my mind.' He looked at my face which might have looked a bit puzzled. Well, don't you look at me like that. I am not cracked. I am sort of bitten by a bug, wanderlust. India is the twenty-fourth country I'm visiting in the twenty-fourth year of my life.'

'Don't you have a home?' I asked spontaneously.

'I do. My parents are in the USA at the moment. And mind you, they are not divorced. I spent most of the time with my uncle, my mother's brother.'

'And you left America and visited most of the places with him?'

'Right. But not America. I was born in Hobart, in Australia.'

'So, you are an Australian?'

'Not exactly. Half Spanish. More than half I'd say. My mother is Spanish and I spent most of what I can remember of my life, with my Spanish uncle.'

'And he must have been a great traveller?'

'He sure was. Theirs was a family of sailors. For generations. Rich and adventurous. They had that blue of the deep in their blood. And I have got the blue blood too.' He smiled and looked up, as the only blue patch he could possibly find now, was up in the sky.

'Tell me about your uncle and the sea.'

'My mother was busy with her swimming career. Father with his research. I was sent to Spain to my uncle. Later, when Mom gave up swimming, Father finished his research and my brother was born, I was sent home. But the sea kept calling me. I escaped from home on small canoes, a couple of times with some crazy friends of mine. So, my mother sent me back to Spain. To my uncle again.'

'What about his family?'

'He was not married.'

'Married to the sea I think.'

'Oh yes, you could say that.' He stopped for a few seconds. His aquamarine eyes were getting darker and darker and drifting miles away as he was speaking almost to himself, 'That was the only time I could not accompany him. There was a shipwreck and he did not come back. Don't know . . . why I . . . how come I . . . missed . . . I did not make it . . . didn't go with . . .' Some sea-deep grief crippled his words, 'He left me all he had. What to do . . . I didn't know . . . I didn't know what to do with the legacy.' A few moments of widening silence.

'Sorry. Do you sail around now?' I slowly floated the words after some time.

'No.' He shook' his head violently. 'I hated the sea. It killed him. Well, I tried to hate it. But no, this deep blue sea, it still keeps calling me and I just can't resist its charm.'

'How come you are in such a dry land then? Here everything is red . . .' I said to. bring him back to this earth of reddish reality at the moment. He smiled at my question, a wavy, curvy smile stirring my blood stream, and sensations.

'Good question,' he mused, 'but, that is another story. I came here to assist a professor in her research work. She is my father's colleague. My father is a professor in marine biology.'

'Sorry, I'm getting confused about Australia and America.'

'Should be.' He smiled. 'After my uncle's death I went back to my parents and my brothers. After a gap of nine years. By that time they were settled in America.'

'So you are a research scholar!'

'Scholar! My ass!' His loud words shook the air and the silence. 'Pardon my French' with some difficulty he drew out these last words, noticing my withering look.

'I came here to see a new country. I had heard a lot about it. And for the first time my dad approved of this assignment of mine. He hadn't liked the other jobs I did.'

'Like?'

'Like that of a shipping clerk, a shipmate, an overseer of a tobacco plantation, a volunteer in a forest research group, a member of the civilian contractor's team for providing life-support services in Tuzla, have you heard of it? It is in Bosnia. During the war. Then for some time, a freelance photographer for some god forsaken magazine . . .'

'My god! I can see you don't know what to do with your life?' My interruption was just spontaneous.

'Do you?' Most scornfully he fired the question point-blank at me. It hit me hard and my reply rebounded sharply, 'Why not? I want to have a home where I can share with others whatever I love to do.'

'I see. You have no ambition. It is very easy to have a home. Almost everybody has one.'

'Not the one I told you. It can be in a tent, on a ship, in the sky, anywhere.'

My small mouth did not speak any further. But the big thought lurked inside. The whole world is busy hurling ambitions towards the mountains or the sky or even as high as space, hurting others if they are successful and hurting themselves if they are not. *Hurling and hurting.* I didn't want to be a part of it. I just wanted a shellfish existence with my beloved ones, without being selfish. The hustle and bustle of competition and the rustle of dollars were not as alluring to me as a cosy corner with a quivering candle flame and two giant-size shadows of profiles facing each other and growing larger and larger to outgrow the four walls and fill the whole universe.

He smiled and said, 'I see, you love to dream.'

'What is wrong in dreaming? The whole world has been dreaming, one common dream over the centuries, of God,' Pat came my reply.

I could tell him much more about dreams, my favourite subject, my favourite activity. I chose to say only the extreme one. Dreams are not something absurd, something unreal. They are a part of our real consciousness. Dreams are not worthless either. All the writers and poets and filmmakers and music composers of the world, what have they done but spin their dreams? Even the most realistic writer only dreamt when he wrote his masterpiece, which had never happened in reality. Finally, God. The most common dream all mankind has cherished is the one about the most perfect, most judicious, all powerful Superpower. The dream supreme. That one dream has created and recreated history. Survived through the ages with mankind. That dream has been more than real. Super real. Life would have been a lifeless junk if this one dream had not been dreamt. The sky over this earth would have been as infinitely black and eternally monotonous as over the other lifeless planets.

When I looked at Leslie Fraser, I found his eyes completely dreamless. Wide open. He looked dumbfounded. 'I can't get it. God is a dream? What do you mean by that?'

'I think either we dream about a God or we are nothing but a part of a dream of the very real God. Both ways, you can't deny dreams.'

The killing curve of his lips straightened. Strong taut lines on the face loosened a bit. A soft reflection of a blazing sun on the cold waves of my dream. The hushed air awaited the next rustle of words. They seemed all lost in the black holes of the time galaxy. Finally, after how long I couldn't tell, I stood up as if to trample on the uneasy silence.

'Never mind. Elusive idiotic ideas of mine.' I smiled and felt a bit embarrassed as he stared at me with wonder surfing on the aquamarine waves. I changed the channel and asked him, 'Please, tell me about your work here.' He seemed to have been lost in some thought, and woke up as I talked to him.

After a few seconds' silence he started, 'Yes. Meera, I mean my father's colleague in the university is doing research on some aspect of Oriental philosophy. I am helping her.'

'Philosophy! Why not a marine subject?' I interrupted him again.

He replied with an indulgent smile, and in an intolerant tone, 'Oh no. I can't do that. Dissect something I love. That's my father's field. He doesn't love the sea. He just knows it, not even knows . . . in the real sense. I mean . . . he . . .'

'You mean he just comprehends a phenomenon called the sea.'

'Exactly. You have got it.'

'Well. You're talking about the Indian professor.'

'Yeah. She is an extraordinary woman. Her views of life, ways of doing things are so bold and fascinating. She is working on some project on Indian occultism. I am working for her. Videotaping the interviews, relevant festivals and places. Working on the microfilms of old scriptures, scrolls. But as I told you, basically I wanted to visit a new country, I had heard a lot about. She was looking for an assistant. One day she just asked me if I was willing. I jumped at the idea. And that's it.'

'How long will you be here?'

'Around twelve weeks. After that I'd like to go to the far Southeast. A lot of islands are there. I would love to be on the islands.'

'But you said you'd be in Shantiniketan for ten more days?' Leslie Fraser looked at me through the corner of his eyes, with a semi-smile at the corner of his mouth. I got cornered in an embarrassing uneasiness.

He replied however, 'Yeah, that was the schedule. But this accident . . . It has upset things.' He did not look or sound much upset though. With a naughty smile he asked me, 'How do the oinks work here? Will they let me off with some fine?'

'That'd be fine for you, I believe. Let us hope the boy recovers soon,' I replied reticently. We fell silent as if to pray for the boy.

'If my schedule is upset, Meera will be furious,' he said after some time. 'She has to do so much during our twelve weeks stay in India. Seven weeks are already over.' Then he muttered to himself, 'Now, I've got to tell her about the accident.'

Reading the curiosity written large in my eyes he went on, 'She doesn't know. She is not here. She is in Calcutta. With her kinsfolk. Her daughter by her first husband. Indian husband. Now, she is married to an American.'

'May I know what are the places you've been so far?'

'They were unusual places. Leslie Fraser narrated a few episodes about his visits to unusual places like New Guinea, Nauru, Port Antonio, Djibouti, Malta and some small islands in Cuba. A Bohemian sky expanded over my head and a pagan path unfurled under my feet. Life could be so much more than a home, and a few bundles of emotions. Yet, we turn to a home to get our insecure souls sheltered.

The attendant brought water for us. He took the water without any fear of getting infected by the infamous Indian virus and bacteria, quite unlike most foreigners. I took it too. Then, I saw him take out a pack of cigarettes. The smell of smoke always disgusted me. It reminded me of our burning home. I almost snatched the cigarette from his hand.

'Please, spare these trees and animals this poison.'

The liquid blue solidified. His glare implied, 'I am not used to being ordered by anyone.' One more cigarette he took out from the pack and held between his lips.

'Life without a bit of poison is too dull, isn't it? Why has nature filled poison in the scorpions and snakes?' The distorted words smouldered as he took out the lighter.

I wanted to say that I could hardly imagine any sensible person who would have preferred to be a snake. Instead, I took up his camcorder, offered it to him and pointed at a distance.

'Look. Quick. Mustn't miss.'

He turned to see a fight between two deer. Antlers entangled in antlers. Quite a scene. I had been seeing it for some time, but now pointed it out to put off the smoke. It worked wonderfully. The cigarette slipped off the lips, the lighter got dumped in the pocket. He got busy in recording the movements.

When he finished I asked him suddenly, 'Have you lost something?'

The naughty eyes fished out some extra meaning and smiled. 'Maybe.' He blinked, making my senses blank. The aquamarine fizzed mischievously, 'You don't think you have got it, ha?'

'I am sure I have got it.' I squirted him with the words.

He raised his eyebrows and gave me an incredulous look. And he looked incredulously charming. As if the beauty, the fragrance and the music of the nature around had taken a human shape in him. I lost myself for a few seconds.

'Impossible.' The sky-high word brought me down to the earth. I smiled.

'Here it is.' I opened the fist and held my right palm out in front of him. The small box appeared very big. 'The flip was good but this one slipped out of your pocket.'

An anticlimactic embarrassment. He took the box from me and grinned sheepishly. At his own silly ideas, I guess. He held it between his palms very fondly and stared at it, shaking his head disapprovingly. There was curiosity to see inside. But my civil sophistication prevented me from asking anything. I saw him open the box, maybe to make sure if the thing inside was intact. As he flipped it open a sparkling blue beam brightened his face. I saw the solid aquamarine grandeur. He held it out towards me, 'Look. Grand. Isn't it? Gee, I was going to lose it.' He was talking to that blue diamond ring.

'You should carry it on your finger, rather than in your pocket.'

'But this is not meant for me. Why should I wear it?' His rippling aquamarine flooded me. In my brown study, a white hand appeared. Manicured. Polished nails. The nails scratched me wildly. He closed the box and kept it back in his pocket.

'I pity your girlfriend. She has to deal with a careless man.'

'This is not for my girlfriend,' he said. Very casually. My small mouth remained shut and my eyes opened wide in confusion. He smiled at my bewilderment.

'This is for my wife.' My confusion was cleared but the daylight blurred in front of my eyes. Just for one moment everything got lost in a black hole. Then, I emerged unscathed.

'Doesn't she wear it?'

'She will, when I find her.' He smiled mysteriously.

Then he shook his head and said, 'Well, this is a secret. But you have recovered the ring. You deserve to know. In case I choose my wife all of a sudden, which is very likely, how am I going to propose to her? So, I carry it. You never know when the moment may come!'

This wild unique idea fascinated me just like his ideal appearance. Deep inside me, the Niagara Falls cascaded rapturously. But on the outside, I pursed my lips and commented, 'I wish I hadn't seen it. By this time it would have been on the finger of one of those brainy black-faced beauties! Look.'

I pointed at the monkeys. Blinking blankly at us. Their black, bony, crooked fingers were scratching their body hair. I had him in stitches. I laughed too but more than that, I watched him. Every movement of his body, every curve of his face, every spark of his half-closed eyes. His resounding laughter ruffled the smooth forest air.

It was already eleven, and we saw a few visitors at a distance. Of course, none could come to this place, as it was not allowed for the common public. Yet, I wanted to go. 'Let's go back,' I told him and started towards the exit. He did not advance with me and shouted at the top of his voice from behind,

'Watch out! A snake! Just behind you.'

Instinctively, I was rooted to the ground, clenched my fists tightly and held my breath. After a few seconds he came near me, narrowed his eyes set deep under the two rhythmic, expressive eyebrows. A faint frown emerged on the plateau of his forehead. He was surprised.

'Strange! You didn't jump or scream. Weren't you scared?'

'Yes, I was. But with a snake, jumping doesn't help.' I said and remembered, 'You've got to stay still, as if lifeless, then it does not touch you.'

I stepped forward. 'Well, but I do not think there was a snake anywhere nearby. Was it?'

He smiled sheepishly with a nod and I felt my reaction to his childish prank acted on his Himalayan conceit.

We wanted to avoid the public. Therefore, the attendant took us out through the watchman's shack. A small door, then a vast empty barrenness, scattered thickets, a few trees with flowering leafless branches like dreams not embedded in sleep, and we two, two strangers brought together as if in a dream, through a cruel, real accident.

Our car started the journey back. He was sitting on my right. I looked at his perfect classic profile against the moving rustic backdrop. A Greek gold coin with the head of Alexander, lost and found in the Texas-terrain. I was wondering how under such a classic countenance a wild, unorthodox, unruly mind existed. He turned towards me and said, 'You talk very less, don't you? You didn't tell me anything about yourself.'

I answered Leslie Fraser very briefly, 'Well, I am doing my final year diploma in fine arts here. My parents are in Goa.'

'Goa! I've heard it's a beautiful place.'

'Yes, you'll find your blue seductress all over there.' Both of us laughed.

After reaching the hostel I went straightaway to the superintendent. To answer and apologise to her for this unapproved trip. I just hated to allow the blind veil to spoil the beautiful spell cast on me at the moment. I hesitated at her door. Just then, Rani came running and dragged me away.

'Don't meet her now. She is in a very bad mood,' she almost whispered.

'On account of me?'

'No, dear.' Rani shook her lovely head and her big eyes fluttered with childish mischief, 'Poor madam, her daughter has got married without her knowledge or consent. In the court. She has come to learn of it, today. She is in a terrible state of mind.'

'That means she does not know I was out of station?'

'She has hardly any time to care for anybody here, now.'

'Oh, thank heavens.' I heaved a sigh of relief and started for my room. Rani came along.

'By god! What a girl you are! You didn't even ask who the boy is.'

'Not interested,' I said curtly, as I had hardly any time to think about any other boy. Rani, however, was bursting with excitement.

'The boy is our Ajay Nayak. My classmate. That sitar expert,—professors are pinning a lot of hope on him. That weedy shy fellow.' Rani went on telling me that the boy although very talented and well behaved, belonged to a lower scheduled caste and so Madam Banerjee, a high caste Hindu Brahmin had dissuaded her daughter from having anything to do with him. I knew that already. The daughter was a student of English literature. According to Rani's report the couple formalised their marriage in the court in Bolpur today. The news reached madam quite late. When she rushed there, it was all over. The castellated caste feeling got severely damaged. No damage, however, on the sweet spell. I felt elated. All the words of Rani whistled past my ear.

Rani took offence, 'What's wrong? Cat got your tongue? You maybe a small mouth but at least you can say yes or no to my questions. Tell me, do you agree with me?'

I didn't hear any question at all. So, I shook my head half-heartedly to denote something between yes or no. Rani interpreted it in her own way.

'I knew you would support them. But I don't feel anyone can be happy by hurting their parents. They do so much for their children.'

'Yes, bring them to this earth without taking their permission.' I almost talked to myself and had Rani in stitches.

'You are a dear, you make a mockery of such a serious topic.' she said still laughing.

The veiled velocity was avoided, but I could not get time to take a dip into the green memories of a red-letter day. I had to hurry to the studio; my professor had sent a message for me. This one was a French visiting professor, who used to like my paintings very much. However, today I was called to get a mild scolding from him. The last few days I had not done enough work, and whatever was done, was all messy. Therefore, he asked me to finish one of my works today itself I was exhausted, but somehow my brush got so fond of the canvas today, every stroke breathed love spontaneously. The picture was finished before midnight.

Dr Sen called me over telephone, after three days to tell me that the boy had come back to his hospital and he was doing fine. We had some outdoor assignment and I could go to the hospital only in the evening. Dr Sen said that he would not be there after five; however visiting hours would be up to seven. Along with Deepa, I reached the hospital around six, found out the room and as I entered, I saw Leslie Fraser, with a Japanese student, whom I had seen sometimes on the roads of Shantiniketan, but did not know. In fact, Leslie Fraser was about to go out of the room when I was entering. Somehow this time there was no accident. My brakes were quite reliable and I was never used to go flat out. We said 'Hi' and 'Hello'. Deepa and the Japanese boy knew each other. Shantiniketan was a small place and almost everybody knew everyone else. Except for a few introverts and self-centred creatures like me. Deepa had never seen Leslie Fraser before. Leslie Fraser was new in Shantiniketan. He did not introduce the Japanese boy to me. I had already observed that he was not much for decorum. He never said thanks to me. He was used to taking everything for granted. Nevertheless I introduced him to Deepa and she, forgetting her manners, completely forgot to introduce me to the Japanese boy. I saw her staring at Leslie Fraser. I could not blame her, she had come under the sweeping spell of the perfect specimen. I looked directly at the Japanese boy and said, 'Hello, I'm Lucie Roy.' I offered him my hand and he shook it and said with a cute lisp,

'Hello. I'm Takahashi. Nice to meet you.'

I gave Deepa a nudge to break her trance and pulled her by the arm to the bed. Today, the boy was awake. He was sitting half propped up against three huge pillows. There were not many bloodstains on his bandage, but below the bandage it was the same pale face, and two paler eyes. Yet, for the first time I saw life creeping into his Barbie-doll eyes. He recognised me, folded his hands to express namaskar. Leslie Fraser and his friend were still inside the room.

'Who is he? A film hero. Isn't he?' Mukul asked me quite naively.

'No, I am the villain here, I suppose,' Leslie said smilingly and told him in broken Bengali that he had been driving the motorbike, which had hit him. 'You will be okay young man.' He held Mukul's hands in his own.

'His touch is . . . just like normal!' Mukul's bewildered wise remark made everybody laugh. As if he expected some out-of-the-world touch would enrich his senses with a new feeling altogether. Leslie Fraser did not look embarrassed. He must be quite used to such remarks I concluded.

'He is a white sahib from the other side of the sea?' Mukul asked with his eyes glued to his wonder man.

'Yes, he is,' Deepa told him.

'I have never seen any sahib so close. I've never seen any man so handsome. Not even in the films.'

This small rustic boy did not know any pretensions. He spoke from the depths of his cherubic innocence. As clean as the air at dawn. As clear as the first gush of a mountain stream. Leslie's male friend might not have liked it much. He requested us to excuse him as he had to keep another appointment and both of them departed.

As soon as they left, Deepa gave out a scream, letting her pent-up emotion come out.

'Hey you jerk, Small Mouth, don't let the secrets out of your Lilliputian lips! All the time you told me about this boy, without ever mentioning he is such a hot stuff. This is unpardonable.' She pretended to be furious.

'But I told you, I told you he was handsome.'

'Handsome! Yea, that's quite a handsome description about this absolute dream. Did you want to hide it from me? Why? Have you got something going with him? And that is why madam has been so absent-minded of late? Are you going to betray your childhood love?'

She was going on and on when I stopped her. 'Oh Deepa please. I'll answer your string of questions later. You see, how your yelling has upset the boy.'

In fact, the deer-eyes looked a bit scared now. I had brought some fruits for him today. I gave them to him and he folded his hands. His dark eloquent· eyes thanked me as the green leaves would thank the sun every morning. He looked a bit sad. Maybe because nobody had yet come with a message from his home, in spite of a small ad in the local newspaper and an announcement on the radio. Maybe, Leslie Fraser was correct, he could be an orphan.

Another homeless hopelessness hovering in the emptiness of this strange universe, where the Leslie Frasers outgrow the roof of a home to embrace the infinitely blooming space. Dreams always outgrow reality. Reality can only outlive dreams.

'Wait a few more days, your mother will come to take you.'

Talkative Deepa said without thinking anything, as usual. I saw tears welling up in his deer-eyes. He could not move his head as it may have still been hurting, but he said in a feeble voice, 'She won't. She has gone to the guy upstairs.' His voice choked and the baked terracotta almost melted.

'And what about your father?' Deepa went on crassly.

'Gone. To the foreign country.'

I didn't like to see the terracotta grandeur get reduced to pathetic clammy clay. Before she could say any more, I literally dragged her out of the room.

'This is not the right time to ask. He is in agony. Can't you see? He is too young to suffer this much.'

I peeped through the door and waved at him, which could be translated into: 'Don't worry, everything will be okay. I'll come to see you tomorrow.' And I smiled. My parents used to tell my smile was infectious. I tried to get him infected by it now. Somehow, I knew that the smile I gave was not real; widened lips, shining teeth, credible creases on the skin of the face. Altogether a colourless rainbow. It was not capable of showering, not even sprinkling happiness on a sore mind.

In the hostel, Deepa got busy in illustrating the 'human illusion' as she called Leslie. Some of the girls said that they had been fortunate enough to catch a glimpse of him in Dr Bose's library. One pretty senior girl said that she had talked to him as she, too, was doing research under Dr Bose. Then, when they started describing each part of his body, I felt I was at a post-mortem table. They all wondered why he was not at Hollywood. I wanted to stop the discussion and said a bit philosophically, 'Skip it dear, it is just an illusion.' Some heaved a deep sigh. Rani started pestering me to show her the 'perfect specimen' the very next day. Even the foreign girls got interested. We had a few Nepalese and an Austrian student in our hostel. Other foreigners were mostly housed in the International Students Hostel, half a kilometre away from our hostel. Like Rani there were many Bangladeshis too in our hostel. But we never counted them as foreigners. On this issue, I found them all equally excited. I really wished this boy would be banished to some 'holy wood', to the other side of the curtain, 'where illusion is illustrative, where real and unreal are all juxtaposed'. Deepa, I and a few others flocked around the TV to watch a famous Hollywood movie. Rani never liked English movies. She wouldn't see one. Today also, she reiterated her views.

'I'm not going to see. Their movies are just about eating and drinking. They always eat and drink. Food and wine and beer and what not. They talk and move and quarrel and do whatever else they like to do while eating or drinking. Dining and wining.'

'Why are you whining? Oh gosh! Why do they always nosh!' I quipped. She ignored me completely.

'Always. Eating and drinking. This is almost half of the movie. And during most of the other half, they eat and drink each other's body. I am not joking. You may check out scene by scene to see if I'm right or not. Disgusting. I hate 'em.'

'Said a mouthful, dear, now let us enjoy the movie.' Deepa stopped her bluntly.

We got engrossed in the small screen looking for a face familiar to the one we had just seen.

The next day Deepa informed me, that many girls had visited Dr Bose's private library where Leslie Fraser was supposed to be working. All of them had to consult some books urgently. Books and looks were, of course, consulted, but with what result only God knows. I was busy with my unfinished work, as my final exam was approaching. In the evening, however, I went to see the boy. Rani came with me quite dressed up for going to the hospital. Perhaps, she knew that her nose and nausea would be overshadowed by the sensational sight. Deepa, too, accompanied me, and today Deepa's steady boyfriend Nandan did not let her go alone and came with us. A few more enthusiasts who could not make it to meet Leslie at Dr Bose's library also came with us.

We reached there at the same time as we had gone yesterday. Today, I met him at the porch of the hospital. Leslie Fraser was picking up friends. He was standing there and talking with Takahashi and a dark South African boy, Mark. Mark had been a friend of mine, he had been doing some research work on Tagore's literature for the last three years or so and had been a very popular figure in Shantiniketan because of his good Bengali and his gregarious charm. We were good friends because when we had staged the Shakespeare's Othello, he had acted as Othello while I was Desdemona. After that he would always call me Desdemona. All of us greeted each other. Leslie Fraser asked me, 'Are you going to see the boy?'

'Yes. How is he? You've seen him already, haven't you?'

'When I went there, he was sleeping. The nurse said that he was much better now,' he said.

Nandan wanted to talk to Mark and Takahashi. The others also did not show much interest in seeing the boy. Rani suddenly developed allergy to the smell of a hospital. Deepa asked me to go and see the boy. They would be waiting for me in the open ground in front of the hospital.

I went into the sick room alone. The boy was sleeping. I sat near him and watched the soft movement of his body. I touched his hand,—cold and rough. Life's gift for him. I brought a few colourful picture books for him and a small storybook for very young children in Bengali, in case he could read that much. I gave them to the nurse, who thanked me and said he would enjoy them as he usually felt bored when he was awake.

A common ward might have been better for him; he could spend time with the others. But Leslie Fraser had put him here. He wouldn't go below his standard. Just when I was thinking this, I saw him enter the room.

'Has he got up?' he came near the bed and asked me. 'I brought a box of chocolates for him and just forgot to give it to him.'

The nurse took the box and kept it in the drawer carefully along with my gifts.

'Will you wait till the boy wakes up?' he asked.

'Wish I could. But my friends . . .'

'Yeah, you've got quite a few today. They don't care for the boy, do they?'

'They care for your charm and you know that very well too',—I wanted to say, but could not. Instead I teased him, 'They have a good suggestion for you.'

'For me?' A feigned surprise flickered in his eyes.

'They want you to be in Hollywood.'

'Ah. Hollywood! So many people have suggested the same. But what's the big deal about being an actor? Monkeys and elephants and dogs have acted so brilliantly in so many super hit movies. In one it was just a nine month old baby; in some others a few lifeless dummies like King Kong. They were all superb. What matters is the technical excellence of the crew and the director. They can make anybody or anything act. I don't find anything challenging in acting. It is much more difficult to go surfing, which I can do perfectly well.'

He was speaking not cynically, but in a mockingly serious tone. I enjoyed his point of view and wanted to scale the Everest of his conceit, when he looked straight at me and asked, 'By the way, what do you suggest for me?'

'Couldn't you do something with your unique voice?' I answered without thinking, as in my heart the music of his voice had been echoing right from the first day.

'How do you know I had a whack at singing?'

'You should continue. *The sea is nothing but a symphony.*'

'Yes, it is. But darn it, how did you know?'

'About the symphony of the sea?'

'No. About my singing. I don't think I ever told you about this.'

'Intuition,' I tweeted. His blue eyes got bubbly.

'You like music? Fond of songs?'

'When sound dreams, it is music; when words dream, they make lyrics,' I almost said to myself.

He was going to be critical about me and my dreams, when Mark came in and called us, 'Hey, Desdemona, what's the matter, what's keeping you so long? Come on, let's go. Let the poor fellow rest.'

Turning to Leslie Fraser he said, 'Come on dear handsome man, the girls are getting impatient for you. We have a dinner party at our hostel. Remember? We're getting late for that. And the girls must be going crazy there.'

'Some of them must be waiting for you too,' Leslie Fraser snapped.

'Must be. But look at this crazy girl. She wants to care just for this waif. Hey Ducky, wanna be a sort of Mother Teresa or what? You are far too young for that.'

The word 'waif' stabbed me. I retorted a bit acridly, opening my small mouth wide, 'Mother had also been young some day, Mark. And for the matter of bringing a dead person back to life, you men are undoubtedly inferior to women. Where Orpheus failed, Savitri succeeded.' After all, I may have been small mouthed, but I was definitely not a mush mouth.

'Who is this Savitri?' Leslie Fraser could not follow the allusion.

'Some daring dame from Indian mythology who brought her dead husband back to life. Yeah, she didn't fail like poor Orpheus did. But that's because the God of death was a man, I mean a male figure. So he went a bit soft over a woman, you see.'

Mark laughed at his own joke, without any of us taking part in it. When he stopped sheepishly, I voiced my protest,

'No, my dear Othello, you have falsely murdered the story. Savitri simply outwitted the god of death.'

Mark gave out a hearty laugh this time. Leslie looked bewildered as he could not follow anything without knowing the story.

'Tell me the story, will you?' He kept on looking keenly from one to the other, expecting to hear the full story. None of us was willing to relate it. For me it was my small mouth. And for Mark it was something else.

'I can't tell you the story now. If I get late for the party I am going to be murdered. You can count on it.'

Mark was dating a beautiful girl Miranda who had an NRI father and an English mother. He was referring to her, no doubt. When Mark is in a jovial mood he banters. He did so now, casually,

'Hey Leslie, why on earth do you always move with that camcorder around your neck? Try to impress people? To show you are working on a serious project? Hah, I know you don't have anything in that, other than some spicy shots of some sexy girls.'

Mark winked. Leslie Fraser did not blink for a few seconds. I could not say if it was an angry or an annoyed look. His eyes narrowed. The deep dimple deepened. He took the camcorder in his hand. A feline blink. A feral look. Then in a flash he hurled the camcorder up in the air and threw these words at Mark.

'Why don't you take it then and use it for a better purpose?'

Mark was too shocked to move. But I moved super swiftly and caught it. With a thud I sat heavily on the floor but held the camcorder tightly and safely in my arms, against my breast. Fortunately, the nurse was not in the room at that time.

'Are you nuts? This is a hospital and you behave like this!' Mark came out of his shocked state. 'I was kidding. And you got wild. Thanks to her quick reflexes or else your machine would have been broken into pieces!'

'Hardly matters. Everything is meant to be broken, if not today then tomorrow.'

Leslie's voice was as cool as the blue of his eyes. He even smiled. A saucy, Palash smile. I could not understand how a person could be so ruthlessly unattached to his own possessions. But that was Leslie Fraser.

'This one has to wait for tomorrow. Are you sorry for that?' I said as I handed him the camcorder. His fingers touched my hands. And his eyes soaked up my eyes. Mark came in between us.

'It is hard to outsmart this girl,' Mark said, pinching my nose lightly. 'I hope you're not hurt?'

Then he nudged Leslie impatiently, 'Com'n, let's split. Before you get still worse.'

All three of us came out of the room and joined the others in the open area. We returned, singing songs of Tagore, passing through the mango groves, Palash groves, along the musical lanes. Only Takahashi and Leslie Fraser could not join in our chorus. They clapped with the others to the beat of the songs. This was Shantiniketan, the ashram, the culture, the life with wings. The natural shelter under the infinite sky.

When we came back to our hostel, Deepa, Rani and I shared some heart-to-heart talk. Our dehydrated Rani seemed to be thoroughly moistened.

'It is unbelievable. Just unbelievable. I can't imagine somebody could be so handsome. So fatally handsome.'

Her eyes became dreamy. Not the kind of dream I dream. Hers was a desperate desire with the overstretched neck of a giraffe, to drool over, to decimate by dragging it into reality. My dream does not have tentacles to reach out to something. It is complete in itself Just like my god. My very own god. Very personal like a dream. It cannot be shared like a bed.

Yet man made the mistake of sharing it and named it religion. Religion framed strictures. Dreams have no strictures. Strictures have swords in the hand. Swords thrive on blood and flesh. A dream of the ultimate perfection, power, justice plunges into blood, because they want to drag it out of dreams. They fear dreams are not real. What is real? This wobbling world? This molecular life?

'Hey Lucie, where are you?' Rani hit me with a rolled-up magazine.

'Oh, she is lost in the memory of that prince charming,' Deepa teased.

'Really Lucie, now I can understand why you have been absent-minded all these days. I never thought I'd feel this way ever.' Rani heaved a sigh, 'God, I should not have seen him. Never. Never.'

'Tell us about him, dear, does he talk to you? Friendly?' Deepa asked but Rani did not allow me to answer and corrected Deepa's question.

'How do you talk to him, dear? I wonder how you do. I just could not even tell him my name. I was getting so nervous.' One thing I liked about Rani, she had no pretensions.

'But you're very beautiful Rani. Very smart. You shouldn't feel that way.'

Although I said this to Rani, I felt that she was right. This man armed with his superlative charm was not at all accessible. It would not have been possible for me either. But for that accident. That extraordinary situation. It made all the difference. I thanked Mukul in silence.

'Why don't you tell us how far you have gone?' Rani was eager.

'Up to the nose. That too from the chin upwards.'

'What do you mean?' Both of them chorused.

'I mean I was trying to sketch his face. From his dimpled chin upwards. I've finished his nostrils so far.' I smiled.

'Oh, you and your brush!' Rani said brashly. Deepa looked at her with pity,

'Dear Rani, there are so many other things to talk about. You are not going to go on a date with this guy.' Deepa's voice was dry.

'I should rather not.' She sounded awfully bitter. Yet, she wished sweet dreams to us and so did we to her.

'I am worried for that girl,' Deepa said while massaging night cream on her face.

'Come on Deepa. She'll get over it.'

'I'll try my best to take her mind off that illusion.' Deepa was as usual motherly.

Next day, I went to the hospital with Deepa and Nandan. A bit early. We went without Rani's knowledge. She was busy with rehearsals for Holi. The boy was alone when we reached there. He was not sleeping. His terracotta body was getting back the tanned texture. Dr Sen was there today. But no other visitor. Deepa and Nandan stood away from the bed. I asked the boy what he liked to eat and he told me that he liked raw mangoes and *pitha*, a special Bengali sweet. Both were not available at the moment. Mangoes were yet to grow and *pitha* would be prepared during winter season with special winter fruits. I promised to bring him some other sweets the next day. I gave him some games, a bagatelle board with balls, some easy jigsaw puzzles which he could work on by himself and forget his pain and boredom for the time being. Dr Sen said that he had come to know something important about the boy. He wanted to talk to me about this in his chamber, and not in front of the boy. Deepa was not interested. She and her boyfriend left the hospital for some dark corner of Shantiniketan; to feel each other better in the darkness.

When I came out of the room with the doctor, I saw Leslie coming. There was a tennis racket in his hand. A white unbuttoned T-shirt. A beckoning bare chest. A pair of tennis shorts and a pair of long lithe legs. Apparently, he had been playing tennis with the Japanese boy, who was also with him with a racket and a ball. They stopped and Takahashi wished us.

'You have come early today?' Leslie Fraser asked me.

'And you've come late.' I retorted spontaneously.

Immediately, I blushed. Deeply. I lowered my eyes. What were we coming to the hospital for? Not to see the boy, but to see each other? Not to comfort the helpless, but to relish each other's company? I quickly went away with Dr Sen to his chamber to know more about the boy. After a few minutes Leslie Fraser also joined us. Alone. His Japanese friend was not with him. He was holding a beautiful geranium, found in plenty in the hospital garden. He held it out towards me and as I was hesitating in front of the doctor, he said with a geranium smile, 'This is from Mukul. He asked me to give it to you.'

I remembered the flower vase in his cabin, on the bedside table with a bunch of bubbly geraniums and thought to myself, I was with him so long! Why didn't he give it to me himself? My eyes might have revealed my question. Dr Sen smiled and commented with a touch of humour in his voice, 'This small child is pretty sensible and smart I would say.' I blushed and avoided the blue bubbles of my amused companion. I wondered if it was really from Mukul.

Dr Sen told us the story of the boy. He was from a poor village background. His father was a carpenter and worked for some contractor. He lost his mother some two years ago. His father remarried. The new mother was not very kind to him. To add to his woe, his father went to work in some foreign country, perhaps some place in the Middle East, to earn more money. His stepmother stopped him attending school and he had to go to help his uncle, his stepmother's brother, who was a construction labourer. His childhood grew along with the height of the concrete buildings. To read, he had the brand marks over the bricks and cement bags; to play he had the mosaic slabs to fit. And to shelter from the savageness of this pseudo-civilised world he did not have a home, not even the stepmother's house where he was an unwelcome stranger. He escaped from the heartless, concrete grips with an older village boy and found employment as a dishwasher-cum-servant-cum-attendant in a tea stall, on the national highway, just a few kilometres away from Shantiniketan. After a few months he escaped from there too. With Nilu, one of his co-workers he reached Shantiniketan to work as a labourer on the new railway track. That was approximately fifteen days before the accident. Nilu stayed with his brother in the outhouse of some rich man, for whom the brother worked. They allowed Mukul to stay with them. However, they never came to see Mukul in the hospital. Mukul could not tell their exact address. But he had told Dr Sen that he would be able to go to Nilu's place, if he was taken to the railway construction site.

'Hope we'll be able to take him there soon.' Dr Sen concluded the story and fixing his eyes on Leslie said, 'I feel you should meet the police officer tomorrow. I'll talk to him too. You may very well leave for Calcutta in a couple of days. Don't think you have to stay any longer.'

For a few moments the words did not sink in. As if I expected that this would go on forever. I would keep on meeting him by the side of the sick bed. Perpetually. Getting healthy and healthier. Enriched with more music in my ears, more beauty in my eyes, more wildness in my heart. And now suddenly, I was impoverished. The dry Ajay River bared its gritty ribs. The rainbow lost its colour. The sea reduced to a bubble, with cold emptiness. Next few minutes only one feeling was hammered in . . . He is going. He is going. He is going.

Dr Sen said, 'Goodnight Lucie,' and I woke up to a bad evening.

'See you tomorrow, Doc.' His words sounded a bit heartening. I would be able to see him tomorrow at least. And tomorrow is a whole new day as they say. I looked up at my god, my dream. I saw both of us with Mukul in between us. I felt better.

When we came out in the open, Leslie Fraser asked me, 'How will you go back?'

I showed him my cycle under a tree.

'I see. But what about me? Takahashi gave me a lift while coming. He had some appointment, so he left early,' he said and I saw the moon in his blue eyes. Moonlight on his blond hair. It was a moonlit night, just two days from today there would be a full moon, that full moon would be a special one, the Dol purnima or Holi purnima. The night of the colour festival or spring festival. I had seen Kanchenjunga draped in moonlight so many times, I had seen the Taj Mahal dreaming under the full moon once. This was no less a spectacle. The sunshine complexion was now a silvery symphony. Light and shade had sharpened his classic features. The colour of the night had spread a gossamer softness. His tall, erect figure was a Michelangelo carved on a time warp, mystifying the ever-expanding moonlit space.

'The night is lovely, isn't it? Ideal for a long walk,' he said with some expectation in his voice.

'I wouldn't prescribe it. You may get moonstruck, you know.'

I tried to make light of the moonlit heaviness. He was amused and his laugh swayed the sound waves. This time I wanted to amuse myself and not him, to get rid of a nagging feeling. He is going: He is going. A leaking tap. I took the bike. The kickstand was pushed up and the wheel rolled.

'Please, take a rickshaw from there.' I pointed at the rickshaw stand across the ground, while I got on to the bicycle, and was all set to say goodnight.

'No, I won't,' a deep steel voice stupefied me. Next moment, a steel hand grasped the handlebar of my bicycle. Never before had I seen his face so close to mine. It used to be high up. Near the cloud cluster. Now after sitting on the saddle of the cycle, I nearly reached his height. He almost whispered, so close that I could feel the air between us quiver, '*Andando*. I mean let us walk. Let me walk you to your hostel.'

The very next moment he bent down and I heard the tyre valve hissing. His naughty childish way of doing things! I had to get down. The cycle with the deflated tyre was parked in the cycle shed of the hospital and we started walking. We walked in silence for some time. The silvery moon had painted the red earth gracefully grey. A pleasant southern breeze was spreading the wild smell of some unknown savage night-flower. Perhaps, a night fly was waking up somewhere and shaking off a droplet of dew from its wings. The road was half-empty. A few rickshaws and cycles were passing at long intervals. We did not talk for quite some time,. but the silence talked volumes to me alone. Finally, I heard his voice as if from the other side of the universe,

'Hey! *Que pasti*? Where are you? In some other world?' he asked and lit a cigarette. I couldn't answer. So he went on again, 'Are you disturbed? Can I help you?'

Without looking at him I could see through his design. Yes. *Maybe, most of the girls had always felt distressfully disturbed in his perfect presence and turned to none other than him to get rid of* the *fatal feeling. Remedy of snake venom is only more of it in a syringe.*

'Thanks. I'm fine.' I forced a smile, knowing very well I was not. I remembered Mom. I gathered the armour against my failing heart. I dreamed.

My medieval knight was back by my side. My Darjeeling antiques. The ancient smell of the bees wax painted on the walls. These days of mine would be stowed as antique pieces, in my memory with the smile of the sea, the smell of the wildness. Would they have any antique value for this man too? I threw a glance at him through the corner of my eyes. His lips were moving. He was asking me something, perhaps.

As I did not reply he enquired, 'Dreaming perhaps?' Not getting any answer from my side he asked again, 'May I know what are you dreaming about?'

'I am not dreaming. I was thinking about the boy,' my words floated very softly in the silvery silence. He didn't talk for some time, and then said,

'Yes, it is so strange. Stepmother, her inhuman behaviour . . . the very stuff of fairy tales. Do they really exist? It is hard to believe.'

'Oh no, Mr Leslie Fraser, it is not. I don't think any trait of human nature, positive or negative, ever gets extinct like the dinosaurs,' I said and felt that *'all of it remains there, maybe, invisibly, like the stars or the darkness, now, hidden under this shining moonlight.'*

'Well, what about women? They have always made it tough for men. Right from the days of Adam.'

'How stupid! You should thank Eve for this life today. Such a beautiful life. But for her it would have been just zippo.'

'Really?' he looked at me with a twinkle in his eyes. I flushed to the root.

But concealing my embarrassment I hurriedly said, 'I meant that the life in Paradise may have been perfect, but I am sure, it must have been monotonous. I . . . I feel that Eve, a woman, had the guts to rebel against the system, and create something new.'

Yes, I always thought that it was curious, courageous and creative Eve who should be considered as the creator of this life and not the dumb and dud first man who, in the beginning, meekly followed the system and then the woman. Her blasphemous, billowing blunder had flooded the blandness with blooming bubbles of love. An eternally stretched, stale and straight-line relationship between one man and one woman has been broken into numerous small, varied, fragments, curved and curious. Millions of shapes, very much the same yet so very different. Eve paved the way for re-, re-, re-creation of love throughout the eternal life; every time new, although basically the very old same. She could feel the infinite potential of it and did not allow it to stagnate between one man and woman in one particular way, however perfect that may be. I thought of the bubbles of love once narrated by Leslie Fraser. I wondered if he was right perhaps. I got lost in my thoughts.

Leslie Fraser's voice floated through the silence and broke into my thoughts, 'I think, you think and dream a bit too much. Why don't you act a little more?'

'What do you mean, Mr Fraser?'

'Oh nothing. Just kidding. But will you call me Leslie and I'd like to call you Lucie.'

'Oh yes, why not Leslie?'

'Lucie, you see our names rhyme, don't they?'

Only the names do, I was about to say, but zipped up my lips. And he unzipped his. From the Garden of Eden he nosedived straight on to the barren red terrain of Shantiniketan.

'I don't think you have good restaurants here, to sit and have a cup of coffee.'

'You will find a couple of good restaurants In the adjoining town.'

'I've been in the town but could not see all the restaurants there. The one that I saw I didn't like it at all.'

'We have beautiful open-air restaurants. Peace and quiet are served along with food.'

'Tell me, how the students go out on a date here? How do you . . .'

I interrupted him promptly, 'What's the problem? I go out on a date almost every day.'

'What!' He stopped abruptly. And gave a sharp look at me. 'You must be kidding!'

'Certainly not. I go out on a date almost every day. With Nature. He is the Mr Rare, you know. Today also I'm out with him and you are playing gooseberry.'

I giggled and expected an echoing laugh penetrating the silence of the evening. My senses were so eager to absorb it. To my surprise, he only smiled sheepishly and slowly turned away his face. I saw his perfect profile, a bit too perfect. I noticed his Adam's apple move up and down as if he swallowed hard and he almost murmured to himself, 'You are just amazing.'

We walked a little longer and I stopped near the gate of our university campus. My hostel was just fifty metres away from the gate. At night the big iron gate remains closed and only a narrow, small four-foot high side gate allows entry and exit. I went inside the campus, and from the other side of the gate wished him.

'Thank you very much, Leslie, I enjoyed the walk. Goodnight.'

In answer he gave me a very strange look. The next moment his supple body leaned forward, bent over the gate. A tight close-up of the classic face, a talon touch on my shoulder, and a sweet darkness where his breath whispered on mine and my lips blended with his. Even teeth melted. Two melting mouths. One liquefied universe.

How I came back to the hostel that night, gathering up every part of my consciousness which was falling apart, after that shockingly unexpected first kiss, I don't know. I just ran away from him. Very fast, without looking back even once, at the boy, who had just gifted me the sweetest souvenir of my life. The first kiss. He added a new experience to my life. In fact, he had added one whole chip where this micro kiss would be stored forever and be processed again and again in macro magnitude. On the headlong flight the whole process was repeated over and over again in my mind. After reaching the hostel I threw myself straight on the bed, I lay still for quite some time and felt the heat of his warm fleshy lips melting on mine. Then, I sank my face in the softness of the foam pillow as deep as I possibly could. I need darkness, a deep darkness, only that can mirror my bare self to me. I need to see myself, I need a meeting with myself more intimate than the organic mating.

Why and how could this happen to me? There was a Joy waiting for me with his tea-flavoured smile, with a design of a home near the Happy Valley Garden. In his last letter also, the warmth was sealed safely inside the envelope. Maybe, the degree of the warmth was always known to me, maybe the quality of the warmth heated me in the same steady way. Maybe, there was never any written or uttered commitment that I would be the definite thing to happen to his Happy Valley Garden plan. Maybe, he himself would find someday some London delight much brighter than his childhood crush. Yet how could I be magnetised by the one, for whom no road would lead towards a home? Who would be going in a day or two. I couldn't blame him alone for tonight's fantastic folly. There had been a strong undercurrent deep in my heart, I couldn't deny it. There might have been seduction in my eyes, in my breath. Initially, I tried to convince myself it would be a common tendency of an artist to love all beauteous things.

Yes. He was beauty personified. He had everything;—a strongman's body, a lover's eyes, a divine dimple on a macho chin, a wavy romantic curve on the thin satin-blade lips, a deep sea-like voice, a dream-like smile. Height and weight, length and width, colour and texture, lines and curves were all so perfectly arranged and balanced that if he were a picture I would never have disturbed even a single dot. He was so breathtakingly handsome that the phrase 'to see him is to love him' might have been meant only for him. It was so difficult not to love him, but it would be even much, much more difficult to love him, HIM, I meant. His beauty would be misleading. One could try to reach the depths.

But how? Take off the outer layer of charm, under it lies another layer of beauty, under it still another, and there is still one more and one more and you are lost in the jungle of charm and beauty, brilliance and radiance. Where is the man with the blue longing and the oceanic passion? Or even something and many thing more. How to know? How to skin off the brilliance of sun once, twice, a hundred times to know the inside soul story. Or would that be the real sun without its layers of brilliance? What do we love in a person; everything about him, something about him or nothing about him? He just happens to make me know myself, enjoy myself, and love myself deeper. Is this called love?

That is why at this moment rather than thinking of his perfect portrait or his agreeable aggression, I can feel every atom of my body. The kiss is percolating through every atom of my existence, energising as well as paralysing them. I am absorbed in myself Yet, I am not very sure it is love, or the beginning of it or the end of an infatuation!

As for him, why did he do this? He definitely did not mean anything. It was just a flirting flicker for him. These whites are quite used to it. The moonlit night wove a web of romance and he was probably caught in it for the moment. Just a passing feeling like a spark of fireworks. He couldn't possibly have taken a fancy for me. He hardly knows anything about me, my roots, my soil, the expanse of my life or the depth of my thoughts. He has also seen many blinding blonde and non-blonde beauties all over the world. Why did he do this then? Why did he want to mercilessly pluck the strings of my heart? Already his majestic charm had caused a quaking agitation in the cells and atoms of every layer of my human form and senses.

Now, his kiss is penetrating my senses, reaching deep down, maybe towards something which is called the soul. I am scared. I don't want it to reach there. He can't be serious about it. We know a kiss is nothing very special for them. Had it been an Indian boy it would have had a different implication. Had it been Joy . . . I could not think any more. He had kissed me on the cheek occasionally. Kissing is not a common Indian activity, at least in public. Indians mostly never kiss anybody in public other than very small children. Or a motherly kiss on the forehead of a child. However during Christmas days in our house when Joy used to come to celebrate with us, a child Joy, he used to kiss me on my child cheek. That's why a kiss by an Indian boy would have meant something definite. But what about a white boy? For them kissing is just like sipping a glass of wine. Sip at sherry, sip at champagne, sip at lips.

We don't know much about the feelings of the white mind. My great grandmother was an English lady. There was hardly anything I knew about her, except that she had eloped with my great grandfather. Then, she had lopped off the romantic brown connection and gone back to white England with a white man, after fifteen years. Two daughters she left behind and one daughter she took with her. Great Grandfather had not married again. But his blunder had been repeated again by my granny, my grandma's sister. With white blood running strong in her veins, Granny had had a ruinous affair with a Portuguese Army officer. Now, she was a spinster with a lonely art studio. *A snail without its shell. A guitar without its strings.* Her soul was now in exile in Siberia, without the white man and yet all covered with white and white. Colourless and cold. That was why, although somewhere inside me a thin white vein had been throbbing all through, my feelings had an inbuilt strong aversion towards this white hallucination. I decided not to meet him again.' One or two more days. Then, he will go. Why go for this fragile pleasure, which will not last and will hurt forever. I am an incorrigible Indian, looking for stability, reaching for a home.

To the boy and his recovering health. Next day. This time I went in the daytime. I wanted to see the patient and nobody else. I wanted to repair the damages to my so believed-to-be impregnable fortress. So many advances I had resisted so far, with a mere smile on my small lips and with a big Joy tucked away somewhere in my consciousness. I would get over this one too. However, I would never forget that first kiss of my life, neither would I try to do so. It meant so much to me. I just wanted to ruminate about it for the rest of my life. I would relive the dream every now and then. Why face that fantasy? I would fan my fantasy within me. I had no idea about how to proceed after what happened yesterday. Where do we go from there? How does one get back to normal life once again? Wasn't it the climax? What could happen after this? Just slide down the slope of reality. A voice nudged me from inside, No. No more of this wild wandering. Don't proceed any further, else this majestic moment will become miserably mortal. Leave it here and let it live forever. He will be leaving Shantiniketan soon. But this magic moment will remain with me forever. Our last meeting. Our first kiss. No dream can be better than this. I do not want my dream to come alive, I want to live my life like a dream.

Mukul, however, asked the realistic question directly with his terracotta simplicity.

'Where is the white Sahib? Won't he come today?' I shrugged my shoulder.

'Why? Don't you stay together?' I blushed at the child's naive question. He had almost always seen us together. He had drawn an easy conclusion.

'No. I stay in the hostel. I am a student. He is a foreigner.'

'You go to school. Great. I also used to like going to school. I had many friends there. I used to get free snacks, too. Mummy used to take me to the school and bring me back. Why did the guy upstairs take her away from me and leave me alone?' I saw a sad shadow shuddering in the liquid eyes. I had no reply for the question.

'Why didn't you wear a bindi? You look so beautiful with a bindi.' His eyes were fixed on me. Two smoky eyes. It was meaningless to explain to him that a bindi does not go with a western outfit. I touched his face and smiled, 'Next time I shall.'

'And put some flowers in your hair. Red Palash.' As I listened to him I felt that I was a doll in his small hand, being decked out by his imagination.

In the evening my imagination spread its wings as I confined myself within the four walls of my studio. Prof. Pierre, our visiting French professor, was very happy to see me working in the evening. He used to take special interest in my work and that of Ganeshan, a boy from Tamil Nadu. We used to get special training from him and could work in the studio whenever we liked. The watchman knew us and would open the door for us. Our professor also used to work long hours.

Although I kept myself busy in painting and in panting during the dance practices for the Holi festival, my heart pined for him. I could not stop thinking of two aquamarine wonders wandering along the hedge of the autumn-brown eyelashes. In search of someone? Would he really look for me? Would he come to my hostel to meet me? I went back to the hostel, very late from the studio. Nobody had called for me. I missed the pleasure I had got used to, the last few days. I missed the company of the sunshine complexion, the rocky structure and the echoing laughter. I consoled myself that I should not get addicted to it or anything. *'Addiction dictates you, unless you dictate yourself,'* Mom used to say. I should get used to my normal life. That kiss would be the last time that I would see him, or touch him. A rosy end.

But a thorn kept pricking me all through. 'Couldn't he drop in once to say goodbye?' With two teardrops, I tried to wash away the bleeding wound and bandaged it with layers of busy schedules. A lot of work with brush, with music, with dance. This was Holi time. Dol in pure Bengali.

The colour festival was just like it had been in the previous years, except for a missing feeling somewhere in the subconscious mind. A desert missing a mirage. The sweet sleep missing a dream.

The festival used to be an open-air extravaganza, unique in its own way. In the early morning, students of all ages, wearing yellow saris or dhotis with red border and red scarves and decked out with red Palash flowers all over, would dance in a unique procession through the lanes and by-lanes of the Ashram. They would shower the audience, on the roadside, with red flowers and red-coloured powder. It was a spectacle! They would dance to the tune of the chorus, sung by a group of students and teachers on the open-air stage. The dance-procession would cover around two kilometres and then gather around the stage. A few more songs and dances by small groups would be performed on the stage then. By ten or ten thirty, the formal festival programme would be over, leaving the students and all others to indulge themselves in playing with colour. Only with colour powder or *abir*. Any liquid colour sprayed in public was strictly prohibited in Shantiniketan, unlike in the other parts of India. I had always been a participant in the dance procession for the last three years. This year also I was very much there, celebrating the festival of colour, spring and youth, only this time the aquamarine blue had spilled over, and added a bluish tinge to the red *abir*, to the yellow spring, to the green youth. A shade of blue fraught with pain.

In the evening there was a dance drama. I did not take part in it. But I was an active organiser behind the curtain. This was also an open-air programme. The stage had to be set properly and the work of setting the stage was given to me and three of my friends.

I could not go to the hospital. There was just no time for me. There was just no time for me to look at myself It was all work and no brooding. Only a pricking feeling of the absence of a foreign element in my existence, consciousness and memory. A bit of grit missing in the shell of a pearl oyster. Every now and then, I had hoped to chance upon him. He might have extended his stay to see the festival, record it in his camera. I wished. But I could not find him anywhere.

The festival of youth got over for me this year, without celebrating my youth; no confetti of touches, no champagne of kiss. But, around eleven at night when I returned to the hostel, with loneliness spilling all over, my childhood called me. Yes, it was Joy. He rang up from London to wish me a happy Holi and we recalled our Darjeeling days of squirt guns and coloured fun for a couple of minutes. We talked for quite some time over the telephone and that was indeed a happy ending to my festival day. I suddenly discovered with Joy, it was not my youth, but my childhood that possessed me, even now. Those budding feelings of the last few days in Darjeeling had been nipped. With him I became a child and forgot the pleasant pangs of youth.

Next day was again to childhood. Early in the morning I went to see the boy in the hospital. It was a holiday in the university. I wore a twilight-red sari and a small dark red bindi in between my eyebrows. I put a few Palash flowers in my hair. I took some abir and lots of sweets with me. Mukul's forehead was covered with a white pale bandage. But his eyes brightened as I entered. He looked at me as if! was the eighth wonder of the world. With the permission of Dr Sen, I marked his two pale cheeks with two dots of colour. For the first time I saw him smile. The dark pod opened up to show the bright peas inside. He was happy, very happy.

'Would you like to put a little colour on me?' I asked and held out my hand with the abir container in it. He shrank. 'No Didi. You are looking so pretty. I'll spoil it all.'

Dr Sen nodded his head approvingly and threw a naughty glance at me. I wished him a happy Holi and put abir on his feet. That is the way you greet your elders during this festival and get their blessings.

We had some sweets, followed by sweeter conversation. Mukul told me how much he liked all the games and books and pictures I had given him. He was enjoying talking today. He said that he had read some stories from the books with the help of the nurse. He also said that his head did not hurt much now. I went to Dr Sen's chamber where I was offered some more sweets. An empty visiting chair by my side shared a vacant feeling with me. I had to work very hard to control myself from asking about our common friend.

Dr Sen told me that the boy was recovering and within another three days, his bandages would be removed. If the stitches heal well, he would be kept under observation for two more days and then he would be discharged.

'And where will he go?' I asked the doctor.

'Maybe to his stepmother, maybe to the friends he was staying with, before the accident. This Fraser boy has promised to give him enough money as compensation.'

My heart leaped wildly as he uttered the name. He did not say anything further about him, however, and continued, 'By the way, Lucie, you may have to go once to the police station as a witness, for the inquiry they are conducting. Just a formality; now that the boy is okay, they will most probably close the case. I have spoken with the man in charge. Don't worry. It will be like the other day, you know.'

I saw a ray of hope that Leslie would come to attend the inquiry proceeding too, although the idea of seeing him in the shadow of prisons, depressed me. 'I thought it was over. Why is it required again?' I asked.

'Well, this is the way the machinery works. It takes time. I registered the case on the day of the incident, as a part of my duty. There was a preliminary interrogation. They are doing their regular duty now. I don't feel, there is much to worry about Fraser. He is home and dry now, I believe.'

Is he home? I wondered. Would he ever be home or want to be home? And would he ever want to be dry, the man with the blue passion? And this child. Where would he find a home now?

III

The Wild One and the Mild One

TIME PASSED SOFTLY along the much-trodden lanes. The kiss was showcased in memory to be visited every now and then. And in spite of all the aversion towards the white enigma, and all philosophical thoughts about keeping the fantasy immortal, the senses started feeling starved, memory started demanding more storage. A will-o'-the-wisp. And my desire overstretched its elongated giraffe-neck. Sometimes, I even thought I would try to get his Calcutta address and contact him. He had not given me any address or contact number on his own. He had given me just one farewell gift, the first kiss of my life. And that's that. The end of the road. The limit of the horizon. The lonely spring wind groaned in the darkness imprisoned in the entangled aerial roots of the enormous ancient banyan tree. I felt lonely. The lonely lost bow of a violin. The music devoid of melody. But Mom's face bobbed on the melancholy horizon; and whispered in my ears, 'You have a sky of freedom, a nature full of colour, and a life full of years ahead of you. Why should you worry at all?' I consoled myself I controlled myself I went to the library.

The world of Picasso, Gogh and Gauguin, Dali and Abanindranath, Cézanne and Lautrec, De Vinci and Michelangelo. The pages of Michelangelo distracted me again. The history of art was not so easy for me to mug up. Neither was I in a mood to brush up my brushes. I hadn't been to the studio since Holi. I took some outdoor assignments. This time I went with my classmate Radha, and the Cambodian student Tan (his actual name was long, but we all used to call him Tan). I was afraid if I went alone I would end up brooding and do nothing.

We went near the railway construction site. The others got busy sketching the landscape, while I asked some of the labourers about the boy Nilu, Mukul's friend. Nilu was not there. Some labourers told me that he had not come for the last one week, perhaps due to temporary illness. My canvas didn't get much attention from my pencil. It was not a sketch, merely a sketchy affair. The others were surprised at my improbable 'improvement'.

'Lucie, what's wrong with you? Aren't you interested anymore in drawing?' Tan asked me. But Radha explained on my behalf that as I had talked to those labourers, I had lost my concentration.

We packed up and went back to our classroom to attend a lecture. After the lecture I was about to go back to the hostel, when I met Ganeshan. He was coming towards me. 'Where were you? Pierre-da is gunning for you.' (in Shantiniketan teachers are not addressed as "sir". *Da* with the first name is used. *Da* means elder brother.)

I rushed to the studio. Ganeshan also came with me. He had already informed me about the professor's annoyance over my absence.' I was prepared to face the music. Although the professor was a gentleman, and not as eccentric and wild as most of the artists are, like any devout art lover he could not tolerate insincerity. So I went to him, head bent, brush dry, and a bit ashamed, perhaps. However, he could not go on long with his lecture on total devotion to work if one wanted to be a good artist. He stopped just after a couple of sentences and I saw the transformation of his scowling expression into a smiling one. Over our shoulders, he looked at the door of the studio and said in an elated voice, 'Bonjour. Come on in s'il vous plait.'

And they walked in. The young Italian lady, the new lecturer in Italian Language, and by her side, the long lost Leslie. I was shaken. He had come back. Had he gone back at all? Could we resume where we had left off that evening? How? I had no idea. I wanted to keep my eyes down but could not. He was in a Bengali outfit, a set of milky white kurta and pyjama. The radiance of white made his golden complexion smile. I could not take my eyes off for a few moments. Inside me started the wild beating of Santhal tribal drums. He broke my trance by saying a 'Hello' and smiling with that killing curve. I saw the thin soft satin blades. I recollected the touch. I ruminated on the taste. I turned as still as our handmade sculptures while the drumbeat grew even wilder. I wished both of them but couldn't hear my own voice. Then, I turned towards the professor and wanted to take leave of him, Well sir, from tomorrow-' But he didn't allow me to finish.

'No tomorrow. Today. You carry on with your work, I shall take them out: By the way, Monsieur and Mademoiselle, these two are my most brilliant students, Lucie and Ganeshan and these are . . .' he went on with the introduction. Madam Maria, the Italian lady warmly shook my cold hand and Leslie told the professor 'I know her', while he was almost staring at me.

'Do you?' the professor asked me, looking a bit surprised.

I said hastily, 'Yes sir, we have met before.' Leslie did not seem to have liked my answer very much and frowned. The Professor got annoyed with himself

'Oh la la! Shame on me. It seems only I have missed your face, every other person seems to have seen or met you. How could I possibly miss such a face!'

'Don't worry Pierre-da. I'm also every bit as blind as you are. I haven't seen him before either,' Ganeshan said and they laughed. His voice mingled with others.

The three went out through the side door to the class area. In Shantiniketan, study is mostly an outdoor affair. Like sports, like farming, like gardening. Tagore believed, study is also as natural as those activities and not something artificial to be injected in the painful penitentiary named school. So, most of the lessons given here are out in the open, very few in the confinement of classrooms. The concrete seats for students and teachers are arrayed under the shady trees or under concrete canopies. A moderately modern touch to the original tradition. The blue slate of the sky, the green scribbling of nature, the fresh lessons in the open air, make the study healthy and refreshing. To feel the world with your senses, and letting it seep into your mind. Our French professor took them to such an outdoor 'classroom'. To sit in the midst of nature, with the beauty of nature.

Ganeshan and I were left behind to do our work. The resounding drumbeat was dying away. I opened my unfinished work and looked at it blankly. I was so stupid. I never knew that there was something in me which could beat like a drum. The sound faded out but left all my senses numb. Mechanically I fixed up my easel, opened the colour box and put colour on the palette. Instead of doing anything on my canvas, I started mixing the colour on the palette, mixing and mixing and almost wrestling with my restless brush.

Was the brush restless or the hand or the veins in the hand, or the blood flowing in them? I could not make out, but I was desperately trying to bring myself back from the brink. This was one I hardly knew: a shaking shameful shadow of myself. I started rebuking myself. So far I had enjoyed this man's charm, my senses had relished his exquisite exterior, just the way I used to absorb a Beethoven or a Bach symphony, or soak in the beauty of a Mona Lisa or of a bright landscape by Van Gogh. It had been fulfilling; it had been refreshing. It had been an impalpable pleasure. It had been a dream. But today it hurt. The hurt was real. Why and how I could not figure out. Only I felt it. A disturbing pain. A dumb bell. The giant bell at the Bell Tower started swinging madly; no sound rang out, only the silence was wrung out from its hollowness. The clapper broke and was lost beyond the reach of time. Ganeshan looked at me. His brush was quite creative by then.

'Anything wrong, Lucie? I don't think you are concentrating. Can I help you?'

A gust of spring wind danced into the room and made my hair and forelocks unruly. I had to push my hair back behind the ear. I smiled at Ganeshan and thanked him for his concern with my eyes, but continued to scratch the palette with the brush. I did not want to spoil the work I had done so far with so much heart. One single wrong stroke and this still life would forever be still and have no life at all. So, I pulled down the blinds around my senses, tautened the strings of my inner violin, closed my eyes to enter the revealing darkness, and took up the brush to start working.

'Holi is over, are you still playing with colours?' a severe pull on my tautened strings and I opened my eyes to see Leslie by my side. He was looking at my face with an amused smile on his tenderly strong lips. It was a killing curve. I gave him a blank look.

'You have a smudge of colour on your cheek.'

He kept his smile alive. My hands were smeared with colour, I noticed. I wanted to wipe the colour off with the other side of my palm and he laughed. 'It's getting worse.' Ganeshan also started laughing. I messed up my face. Leslie took out a milk-white hanky from his pocket and holding my chin up with one hand, started wiping off the colour on my cheeks. However, the colour which rushed to my face was beyond any cleansing. As I protested mildly he said, 'Shhh . . .' When I made a sign towards Ganeshan's presence, I heard his soft whisper, 'Doesn't matter.' Deep inside me, the present, the past, the future, all got smudged.

From me he shifted his attention to my unfinished picture. Then he looked around the room: 'Can I see some of your paintings?'

'Not now, please. I have to finish the work,' I pleaded and understood that my wit had deserted me for the time being. Ganeshan came forward to my rescue and said,

'Well friend, it is better that you don't disturb her. Today is surely not one of her days. But you are our honourable guest. I shall show you some of our good works. If you want, I'll take you to our exhibition hall. When there are no exhibitions on for the public, we keep all the best works of our students there. Paintings and sculptures.' He said, with his friendly eyes twinkling.

Leslie thought for a minute. Then, he looked at me and said, 'I'd like to go around with him. Saw a few interesting pieces of sculpture while coming here. If Maria asks, tell her I may be late; she may go back if she likes.'

'What if she doesn't? Should I then send her to you?' I was getting better and bitter too.

'Yea, of course. You may bring her if the professor lets you.' Ganeshan said, 'Let me see if the hall is open or I shall have to get the key. I'll be back in a minute.' He left the room.

Leslie's flexible figure came quite near to me: 'I want to talk to you. Badly. Do you have any idea how much I missed you? Where have you been keeping yourself?'

The confused unsettled red dust was blown away by a strong blue wind. I just managed to whisper, 'Should have looked for me within yourself. Shouldn't you?'

He was going to answer me when another gust of wind rushed in. It blew away the cover of one of the pictures of mine. Yet to be finished. Almost three-fourth completed. A portrait. Mukul's portrait. As I had seen him before the accident. frizzy hair, dreamy eyes, terracotta texture. Leslie's eyes fell on it.

'How could you paint his picture and not mine?'

'You are too perfect,' I came out with an imperfect answer.

'Bad excuse.' He snatched away the brush from me.

Before I could stop him he drew long straight yellow lines over the frizzy hair. Then, he straightened the nose with a red line. Started lightening the complexion by smearing white colour. My labour was spoilt. Yet, he had me in stitches. He laughed too as he could not change the black eyeballs into light blue and dabbed two solid colour blobs inside the eyes. How easily he could spoil a thing and how sweetly too, I wondered. Ganeshan came in jingling a key and took Leslie away. Leslie looked back once and made a sign which indicated that I should wait for him there till he came back.

As expected, Madam Maria came in within a few minutes, looking for Leslie and I had to send her to the hall. Then the professor got busy with my painting, instructing me on all the little details as I had finally started painting under his close supervision. Today, I wanted this close guidance. With his helpful instructions, I soon got into my stride. All outside distractions were blocked off; the doors of hearing were locked. The windows of smelling safely shut. Only a flame lit up my eyes and the picture gleamed with a glorious glow. The lines sang in my ears, the colours smelt. I went on with the creation in my habitually crazy normal way.

How long I had worked I could not say. I got a light pat on my shoulder and descended from the world of lines and colours. The Professor was appreciating me. I saw satisfaction in his eyes.

'Well done. But now you should rest. The finishing touch will be done tomorrow. Let's go now. They've been waiting for quite some time now.'

I looked around me and saw Leslie and Madam Maria standing in the corner. Ganeshan was packing up. He looked at me and grinned, 'You better wash yourself first. You're all coloured.'

I looked at my hands, arms, my clothes; colour was everywhere. I was not wearing my pinafore, as I had not been ready for a real painting session. After washing off the colour from my body and face, I stepped out with the others in the twilight tapestry of nature. I looked at my watch and understood that for about two hours I had worked madly, shutting off my senses from the world. Ganeshan told me he had showed the guests around the entire Kalabhavan, the Fine Arts department. He had shown them the paintings of the students. The works of some of the great artists of Shantiniketan. The musical murals. The soft carvings on hard stones. The rich relief work on the earthen walls of humble huts. The eucalyptus-tall, life-oozing big sculptures of Ramkinkar Bez. Kept outdoors. Growing everyday with nature.

Madam Maria invited us to her official quarters. It was nearby. Ganeshan requested to be excused and turned left towards his hostel. He, was a strict vegetarian Brahmin from Madras or Chennai, as they call it now. He would never go to a foreigner's party. I was feeling exhausted so I too excused myself I said bye to all of them, and turned towards my way to the hostel. Leslie called out to me from behind, Wait a minute. Wait a minute. Have you seen the boy? Mukul? How is he?'

'Fine. Will be discharged soon.' I stopped, turned and could not help asking, 'You're supposed to be in Calcutta?'

'I never left Shantiniketan.' His naughty smile flashed. Then he answered the question written in my eyes, 'Well, that was the schedule. But I didn't follow and just stayed here.'

'Police . . . ?'

'I did not ask the police officer. Did not feel like going. Just like that.'

'Your professor?'

'She got upset. So, she came here,' he laughed as if enjoying his own achievement in disturbing his professor. Then changing his tone to a normal one, he said, 'That's why I could not find the time to go to the hospital. Can we go to see him now?'

Before I could say anything, he had told them that we would be going to the hospital to see the boy. Madam Maria did not seem happy. She objected, 'Why not go to the hospital tomorrow? I intended to open a bottle of champagne today.'

'Any special occasion?' the professor asked.

'Of course. Finally I have made some good friends, after having been here for almost three weeks. Thanks to that Holi festival, we all could get acquainted. Doesn't it call for some celebration?'

Her beautiful square face lit up with happiness. Her sandy hair had, as if, sucked the twilight from the sky. I got the drift and slowly started moving, in order to remove the odd person out there. But I could hear Leslie's voice quite clearly behind me, 'Some other time. Today I must go. Okay, adios.' I heard some quick footsteps coming up behind me.

'Hey, Lucie, why didn't you wait for me?' He was a bit demanding.

'Well, champagne is not my cup of tea. You know.' He laughed at my words.

'But we shall go to the hospital,' he said, as we walked side by side.

'I've already seen the boy this morning. Tomorrow they will remove his bandage,' I informed him.

'Okay. Let's go for a walk. For a cup of coffee. To that open-air bistro.'

'I'm sorry. I can't go. I am terribly tired.'

In my mind I was clearly visualising the oddness of my dishevelled presence in the crushed, colour-stained clothes, by the side of this too perfect handsome charisma in the crisply ironed milky white Indian outfit.

'That's why you need a cup of coffee. Very strong. The way you worked! It was amazing. Do you always work like that?'

'Sometimes, when I am possessed by some craziness.'

The aquamarine ray sailed through the fading waves of twilight, as he said, 'I don't want you to be possessed by anybody or anything else. I was really hurt when you didn't look at me even once, after we came back from the hall. We waited for nearly fifteen minutes. Then, the professor asked us to go and see other things. That boy showed us the whole university, I believe. We also had a cup of coffee at your open-air students' canteen to kill some time. This has happened for the first time in my life. A girl neglected my presence for fifteen full minutes! Well, that tears it!'

'Don't take her for a girl, it was a blind brush, so, brush aside your hurt feelings.' I smiled, 'I didn't mean to give you the brush off.'

We were walking very slowly. The twilight had dissolved into light darkness. The moon was yet to spread its silvery web. We were passing by the side of a bamboo clump. The green foliage had turned coppery yellow. Hundreds of sparrows were chirping while settling in for their night's rest. Tall, slim and arching bamboo stems and their cute conic leaves were shaking and quivering a bit under their frivolous hopping and flying around. A nice backdrop and a nice background music were provided for us. We both stopped and looked at it.

'Here they take shelter at night to rest their tingling wings.' I pointed out at the bamboo clump shrouded in green darkness.

'Come on, let's move,' he sounded a bit impatient. 'Wouldn't you like to sit here?' I wanted to be in that picturesque spot.

'You like it here?' he asked in surprise.

'The moon will come out soon behind this bamboo clump. A Japanese picture. A silver circle and a few dark lines, curves and spots. Would you like to see?'

'I would. Come on, let's find a place to sit.' He held my hand, and gave me a little pull. A palm against a palm, fingers twined around fingers, we advanced. And the bottled blood sloshed around. The red stony earth relished the grassy goose flesh.

We chose one circular seat under a Peepul tree. One of my favourite spots. I had sat here often. With friends, with myself, my thoughts, my dreams. Today, I sat there with my blue blunder. We were not alone. In the evenings the concrete seats of the outdoor 'classrooms' would be mostly occupied by dating couples, friendly groups, even resident families, who wanted to enjoy nature's magnificence. It was no exception today. A group was sitting a few yards away from us. Some on the seats, some on the red rocky ground. Other smaller groups and couples were also scattered here and there. Although one could hardly recognise the persons, but their figures and activities were dimly discernible. Darker solid images against diluted darkness. Moving pictures in light and shade with faint sounds. Moonlit nights were usually a time out for people here. Although the main roads remained almost empty, but the Ashram grounds would be teeming with talk and laughter, humming and songs and some vibrating silence between a few twosomes. A melodious voice was singing a hymn to nature, written and composed by Tagore. And our two hands were feeling the wonder of nature. The primitive, the prospective, the ageless, ultimate wonder. Five fingers against five fingers and an infinite series of feelings. One mirror in front of another mirror. Infinite number of reflections.

When he finally freed the grasp in order to light a cigarette I felt myself shaking. Not like a trembling tree, not like a rippling river. Like the tiny flame of his cigarette lighter.

'Lucie, why didn't you meet me all these days? I was getting mad.'

I hung my head and remained silent. I could not open my lips as they were reliving the moment. The moment when my lips received the first male touch. I could not dare to look at him. The white flowers opened their eyes in the darkness. The blue flies spread their dream wings. A green smell of the yellow bamboos enlivened the evening. I could not say anything.

So, he said again, 'Well, there was nothing to feel so bad about that evening. It was just natural. I am sure you know that you have the cutest lips in the world I have ever seen. I couldn't resist their charm.' So, that was the only reason! A dry leaf fell silently on my memory lane. I still couldn't say anything. He said in a serious tone next time,

'Believe me., the first time I saw you I could not take my eyes off your lips, so small, so cute, just like a dollop of strawberry jam. They are unique. And when you talk they look so charming . . .' I was getting an uneasy tingle through my spine and the jam analogy jammed my imagination. I heaved a sigh for a dreamless mind and interrupted him.

'Never mind. Now, may I say something?' I tried to change the channel.

'Yes, go ahead.' He was curious.

I did not want to add a drop to the ocean, I also knew that he was quite self-conscious, yet, I could not help saying,

'You are carrying this Indian kurta pajama much better than most of the Indians.'

'For that matter, I look best in any outfit, Eastern or Western. Not only women but even men of those countries have complimented me on that.'

'Is this the first time you are wearing an Indian outfit? How did you get it?'

'Leena brought it for me from Calcutta. Oh, she is the daughter of my professor, Meera, I told you about. I wore another pair on the day of Holi. That was the first time.'

I felt my darling darkness adulterated and my mind fractured.

'Where are they now? Why aren't you with them?'

'Because I want to be with you.' Even the hollow bamboo stems filled with thrill, as he said this. And he continued, 'I mean it.'

'But you never looked for me.'

'Says who?'

'You didn't come to our hostel . . .'

'Well, that's because it is a girls' hostel. Too many girls.' He smiled mischievously, 'Who wants to be the target of so many ogling eyes?'

'I am not going to buy it. Ogling eyes are far too common for you. We met just by chance today, and you are . . . .'

'By chance! My ass!' This time he interrupted me, 'Excuse my French. Do you think I went to your studio to see some blasted lifeless art objects? I'm not an arty-crafty kind of guy. I tried yesterday too. The studio was locked. When it opened, two other students went in. I did not know them. I waited for some time, then some enthusiastic painter asked me to be a model and I flew the coop. Today, I tried my luck again. Mark told me this is the best place to meet you in quiet. He was right. Finally, I could see you.'

'Didn't you see me at the Holi function?'

'Yeah, I did. You were dancing in the yellow red sari and those red flowers around your neck, wrists, head, and, all over. I was just by the side of the fence, you danced past me, I couldn't call you. In fact, I wanted to. I am capable of doing many wild things. But that day somehow, I restrained myself. Not that I'll always do so.'

He dropped the cigarette stub, came dangerously close, and put his strong arm around me. And just then, over his square, firm shoulder I looked far and my eyes sparkled.

'Look, who is there!' A loud whisper came out from my mouth. He got startled and looked back. Both of us saw it come out. The nearly round full moon with the doodles of bamboo stems and leaves on its face. *Scribbles of reality against the perfection of dreams.* Neil Armstrong had indeed hopped on it in order to take away all the hype heaped on it for centuries by poets and writers and lovers, yet, it would be still the only glorious spot of hope in the bleakness of the night.

The arm around me had loosened, and I stood up. 'Sometimes, you act wilder than I,' he mumbled. He stood up too and started walking with me towards my hostel. The moon was moving with us like the cursor along with the words on the computer monitor. He asked, 'When shall I see you again?'

'Tomorrow. In front of the hospital. Where we first met.'

'I met you before that, when you were coming along the lane, at the spot of the accident. It was me who sent the rickshaw and followed you to the hospital. I took the main road while you were going along the lanes and alleys.'

We were now passing through the mango grove. The smell of the mature mango blossoms was all over. The compound wall of my hostel was now clearly visible. I stopped, picked up a fallen twig with green granular mango buds. I put it in my hair. In Shantiniketan, we were fond of following our own unusual fashions. Putting twigs, even dry ones, in our hair, decorating the forehead with a small round petal instead of a traditional bindi, or adorning the watch strap with a small flower. He was looking at the moon through the criss-cross of the mango branches.

'So, tomorrow at the hospital. Hope, I won't look as awful as I did on the first day.'

'Who says you looked awful?' he came close. Automatically I moved back a little, to feel a solid tree trunk behind me. He came closer and no, didn't touch me but stretched his arm to lean against the trunk.

He went on, 'I'd say you looked very refreshing. Your face was wet, and tiny water drops stood on the curls on your forehead with the sun on them. It was something like, like . . . I'd say, a natural tiara . . . I wanted to touch them in fact.'

And he touched them now, fingered them rather with all fondness, twisted a longer one around his first finger. No wild waves and no white horses, I dived in the calm, caressing depth of the aquamarine blue.

The white man gifted me a white night. Feelings and emotions and thoughts went throbbing through every vein. And they were not white, they reflected every possible shade of the colour spectrum, I would say. I recalled his touch, his walking hand in hand with Madam Maria, his gazing eyes, his fair guest Leena's gift, his deep-sea voice, girls' ogling eyes', one pair of them might be mine too. The motorbike, a pool of blood, a covered helmet, the mesmerising charm, the brown hedge of eyelashes, a protruding Adam's apple, white bandages and stained cotton wool, two long white downy legs with red-soil-coloured knees, a dimple on the chin, a killing curve on the lips, a white kurta, a long strong neck, a stained hanky, my stained hand on his white hand, a misty moon. All were mingled and juxtaposed with one another. One was focused and the others went out of focus, one by one. A tangled imagery, a confused consciousness. I did not understand what was happening to me. I couldn't name it.

I met him the next day in the hospital. He was waiting for me near the porch. We had fixed the time last night, before departing. It was a bright afternoon. Our eyes greeted each other so passionately that the 'Hi' sounded like a real low. Our hands by this time had got so harmoniously tuned to each other that they hugged and the fingers started crooning softly to one another. We went into Mukul's cabin. I got a shock. The terracotta body was sitting on the white bed, with deer eyes wide open. The heavy bandage around his head had been removed. And there was not a wisp of that spectacular frizzy fair. It was all cleanly shaven. A strip of a light bandage had been tied around his head. A colourless bandanna. There was awe in my eyes. Leslie noticed it and asked with concern, 'Something wrong? Are you okay, darling?'

I pointed at his head, 'Look there Leslie, he has lost all his beautiful hair. It's a cruel sight.' My voice choked. The nurse told us that it had been necessary for the operation.

In fact, the hair had been shaved off long ago but a heavy bandage had hidden the hairless head. Leslie comforted me with his arm around my shoulder, 'Don't worry, dear. The hair will grow again. What's so upsetting about it?'

How could I make him understand that his appearance had lost its character? Hair is the dream that gives the real skull a spectacular life. How could I bear such a sight? Maybe temporarily, but it was the handicapped appearance of a terracotta childhood. Mukul, of course, didn't look disturbed. Today he talked and laughed freely.

'Don't worry Didi. My hair grows very fast. Once my stepmother was angry with me and got all my hair shaven off I got them back soon, she never punished me the same way again.' He laughed. It was nice to see him lively as a child should be.

Mukul accepted with silent thanks, all the chocolates and games we had brought for him.

'I like to play the games. It is so boring here otherwise. When can I get out of this boring hospital?'

Dr Sen told him that he would be discharged after two days. But he would have to come back after a few days, for a check-up.

'Where will you go?' I asked Mukul.

'I'll go to Nilu. Did he come to meet me? Will you tell him to come and take me?'

I did not tell him that I could not meet Nilu as he had not been coming to the worksite for last few days. I just assured him, 'Don't worry. We shall take you to his place. You just show us the way.'

Dr Sen asked him, 'Don't you like to go back home? To your own people?'

I saw fear creeping up into his eyes. He protested strongly, 'No, no, never. Don't send me there. They will beat me to a pulp. Please, don't.'

He was tearful. The doctor and I comforted him and told him that we would do as he wished.

As we came out of the hospital, a foreigner waved at Leslie. I had seen her before but was not acquainted with her. I always wanted to keep my circle small and limited, as much as a cosy corner could accommodate. It seemed she was waiting for Leslie. Leslie quickened his steps and I slowed mine. I could only catch some words 'Hi Susie', 'why now', 'can't wait'. I went towards the cycle shed and unchained my cycle, when Leslie came near me and said,

'Listen, I've got to see Prof Bose immediately. He's sent a message for me. Crazy guy. Doesn't know anything but books and theories.'

'Go ahead. And don't talk about elders like that.'

'Hasta luego.' He sat on his motorbike and the girl sat behind holding his waist. They were gone along with a gust of the hot midday wind. I was left behind with a small shadow of mine. The shadow, a body complements; the dream, reality supplements. A shadow is not unreal. Nor is a dream. Only a ghost does not have a shadow, as its body is not real. I don't want a ghost reality. I adored my shadow. In fact, right at that moment I wanted it to be long and long enough to reach the study centre of Prof Bose.

'Lucie. Of all people! What are you doing here? Are you okay?'
Turning round, my dream discovered a reality named Biman.
'I'm fine. Came to see a patient.'
'Me too,' he grinned widely.

Biman was a research scholar working under Prof Bose. A serious looking bespectacled scholar. I had met him at one of our painting exhibitions. He had showered me with praises on my creation, which had quite overwhelmed me. I had got the wrong message and gifted him that picture later. He had got the wrong message too. He had gifted me a letter. Asking for a quiet meeting in a quiet place. Deepa had intervened effectively. She had gone with me to make the quiet place not so quiet, and in her unique way had talked about my engagement with a super boy in London. Biman had never again sent me any letter, but had remained a good friend. Deepa used to tease me that he had not given up all hope. Rani had advised me to go for him as she was a bit doubtful about the loyalty of my childhood Joy-friend. Toy-mate.

'Once they go to some Western country they lose their virginity, they lose their fidelity. The women there, dangerous species, you know.' She had always been so uncomplicatedly clear about her views of life. 'They can sleep with anybody.' She had said.

Rather they can slip into any body, I had thought.

Rani had further advised, 'Biman is a good scholar. His father is our university professor. You will be happy if you marry him.' Happy? Maybe the way you feel about a car race in a video game, not feeling it the Schumacher way. An impoverished replica. A dream is not a replica. It is a real revelation, I thought but never said anything. Because of my small mouth, because of my big dreams.

'I should not disturb you. You seem to be lost in your creative thoughts.' Biman was too civil to be persuasive. But I pursued my new-found feelings.

'Come on Biman da, don't you tease me. How is your research going on?'

'Just going on . . .' he would be always so humble. 'I am not satisfied with the way it is going on, however, Prof Bose thinks it is great.'

'Are you going to his study centre? I've not seen it so far.'

'Do you want to see it now?'

I nodded with a smile and noticed the change. An immediate facelift. A snappy smile.

'Come on, I'll show you.' His scholarly eyes scaled a happy height and shone behind the glasses.

Both of us rolled on our bicycles and soon entered right into the big and sophisticated study centre of the famous Prof Bose. I had seen Prof Bose, listened to his lectures many a time, but had never been in this centre. It was really wonderful. Books were stacked neatly in numerous cupboards. All neatly bound with golden letters glittering on the spines. Well-garnished mental food to make people knowledge hungry just by seeing the face of it. Yes, the professor might be an old man, he might be dealing with the dead and old, but old wine was definitely served in a very modern bottle. Through the glass I could see the computer room too. Five monitors. Two people were working.

'I requested you to come and see it so many times, you couldn't make time!' Biman said. There was a touch of whining in his voice.

'Well. Today I like to see the place, can I?'

'Yes, indeed. Be my guest.' He cleaned his specs nervously with his hanky. Then he took me to all the places, showed me the manuscript section. Old handwritten manuscripts were neatly wrapped in red velvet-like cloth and no one was allowed to touch them without special permission. Microfilms of the manuscripts were used by the students in general. He was working on some microfilm of a very old manuscript. But he knew my interest. So, he brought another one from the clerk and showed me some beautiful old miniatures. Time could not blunt their subtlety. I got engrossed in them. Next, he took me to the computer room. Two students were already working. Biman started explaining things. He opened his file with a secret password and showed me his thesis. He had written quite a few pages. Almost a hundred. I appreciated it and asked him to allow me to do some nonsense sketches with the paintbrush.

'Let me show you. I am a dab hand at operating the computer,' somebody said from behind. The next moment the handsome body was at hand. He straightway quitted Biman's file and his deft fingers flitted about from key to key. The monitor blinked at us with two names emblazoned in a very large font in capital letters: LESLIE AND LUCIE

He wrote some commands and the whole monitor flashed rows of the names:.

LESLIE AND LUCIE
LESLIE AND LUCIE
LESLIE AND LUCIE
LESLIE AND LUCIE
LESLIE AND LUCIE

The names then rolled on to each other and after mingling for a few seconds, rolled back to their previous position. It continued. He asked me to tap on the 'page down'. I tapped. On and on. The two names rocked and rolled, on and on. They seemed to have occupied the whole memory of the computer. We looked at each other to see one's name emblazoned in the other's eyes. A computer could not possibly comprehend the chemistry of these two names, but the human mind could. I could not find Biman anywhere in the room, when I turned round. The shallow saffron rivulet, lost in the expanse of the shimmering reverberating red earth. Straining my eyes, I caught a glimpse of him in the adjacent cabin through the translucent glass. A lonely, vibrating string on the Ektara, the one-stringed instrument of the Bengali nomadic and spiritual folksingers. But I could hardly empathise with him.

A clear collage emerged on an infinite canvas. My arm, Leslie's hand. My fingers, his nails. My eyes, his eyelashes. My chin, his dimple. His lips, my smile. His hair, my fragrance. His light, my transparency. Together they made sense. How did that one whole ever get severed? And why?

I was unable to talk for quite some time. Leslie was explaining something about the mechanism of the animated effects, which I could hardly follow. So, when that Susie girl came and they again went inside Prof. Bose's cabin, I came out of the building, carrying a stranger's body. Life's reality dreamt my dream. The strange collage escalated higher and higher, till an earthly call messed it up. I was in my hostel and Rani brought the message about a call from London.

Obviously it was Joy. He informed me that his father had had a heart attack and he would be coming to India.

'When did that happen, Joyee?'

'This morning. He is in ICU now. Mummy needs me.'

'Why all of a sudden . . . ?'

'Not quite. You know Polly and her rotten way of doing things. She did something terrible. Daddy could not bear it.'

'Drugs or boy?'

'Boy. But can't explain everything over the phone. Can you make it to Calcutta? I'll stop over there for a few hours for the linking flight. Day after tomorrow.'

'I'll ask Mom.'

'You are still a good girl. Typical Indian. Okay. I'll give you a . . .' His unusually serious voice broke off as the call got disconnected. It happened many a time, especially with long distance calls. He did not ring back again. Maybe because the news he wanted to give had already been given.

The disturbing news, the collapsing collage. And a nostalgic Darjeeling panorama. I lay down motionless on my back. Naresh Uncle, his jingling jokes, his Kanchenjunga-white affection. His two broad shoulders. Joy and I perched on them. His one broader heart at the moment, being treated in the hospital. Hospital. One terracotta body. He would be discharged from the hospital day after tomorrow. 'Who will help him if I am gone?' I could always request Dr Sen to keep him for one more day. I would return the same day by late evening. To look at the glass-bead eyes, to be blinded by my blond blunder.

At the moment, a happy valley loomed large. The pine needles pricked, the rhododendrons summoned. I was dragged out of inertia. A call to the local railway booking office at Shantiniketan, confirmed that no ticket was available to Calcutta, for the next four days. But they suggested that it should be available at the main booking office at Bolpur railway station. I took a daring step. I decided to go to Bolpur and get the ticket booked for the next day. A call to Goa from a nearby PCO booth, did not connect as the lines seemed to be faulty. That's why Joy's call had got disconnected. I believed that Mom would permit me. I had to ask my local guardian here to talk to the hostel superintendent. The ticket should be booked first. I took another daring step. I took a cycle rickshaw and started for Bolpur. Taking permission of the veiled voice, would mean wastage of time. I preferred a rickshaw, as under its low hood I would be less recognizable. Even the curtain, used for rains, was pulled down to hide me completely.

Yet, I could not remain hidden. After getting my tickets booked for the to and fro journey, when I came out of the booking office, a pat on my shoulder shocked me and shook me. It was him. That dangerous droop at one corner of the lips and that killing curve at the other.

'What are you doing here?' he asked me, staring at the ticket in my hand. I was yet to put it inside my purse.

'Shouldn't I ask you the same?'

'Oh sure, sure. I'm here to see them off, Meera and Leena. They are going back to Calcutta today.'

'And you?' my voice shook a bit, perhaps. The collage was looming large. My senses were collapsing.

'I would have but for that small accident. They have not yet given me permission to go. My work has also suffered. I haven't been able to complete my assignment yet. So . . .'

Swallowing a hard lump I said, 'Well, then, see you later.'

'What do you mean by see you later? Come with me.' He held up his aggressive chin, gracefully. 'I want you to meet them.' The afternoon sun left a haughty blonde shade on his aquamarine depth, before hiding in his abundant hair. The Darjeeling ice melted. My eyes got drunk. *Why didn't I get see-sickness sailing through this ocean of charm and beauty!* The conscious mind said feebly, 'Oh Leslie, some other time . . .'

'Ahora mismo.'

He did not allow me to talk any more, grabbed my hand and pulled me along with him. We reached the platform. The train had not yet arrived. A small station with two narrow platforms, a few narrow benches, and a row of food and tea stalls. Tolerably crowded with people, swarming with flies and adorned by some withering plants. While walking he asked me,

'Why didn't you tell me before leaving Prof. Bose's place? And why are you here?'

'To get a ticket booked.'

'Are you going somewhere?'

I had to try hard before coming out with a white lie, 'No. It is for a friend. She couldn't come. She's not . . .'

'Don't tell me if you don't want to. I can't stand a lie.' His eyes invaded mine.

'Listen . . .'

'Never mind.' He waved his hand deprecatingly. My heart sank. How to tell him about Joy? And why? 'Why am I feeling so awkward about telling him about Joy? It is strange. Never before have I felt the same way. Ganeshan knows about him. So do some other boys. He has never been a secret. What is stopping me now from declaring openly his existence in my life?' I pondered and decided to open my small mouth.

'Hi!' Leslie waved at somebody just then. The words remained inside my corked mind. We went where they were standing: mother and daughter. Two graceful refined sophisticates. We were introduced. The moon met the remote-controlled satellites. They talked about their plans to visit some major tourist spots of India. I remained mostly silent, looking at the never-ending rows of wires hanging endlessly all along. over the long, long railway track and tried not to listen to their conversation as I heard Leena call him 'darling' a couple of times. The train arrived soon. It would stop here for two minutes only. They got into the air-conditioned coach. The coach was almost empty. Only one couple was sitting and a renowned singer of international fame, got into the same compartment. We said goodbye. I saw Leena put her arms around his neck and kiss him softly on the killing curves. I saw her matte lipstick on his male lips. I got my signal and the train got its. With heavily clanking wheels and hinges, the train started moving along the track.

As the train started, Leslie started moving slowly with the train. I did not. Leena was standing at the door and waving her hand. Her coach went past me. Another and another, when I saw a small child running with the train to catch up with it. His hands were trying to reach for the train and from the door of a second-class coach passing in front of me, a village woman was stretching her hand as far as possible, to reach for the boy and crying. But the train was gaining speed and the distance between the two hands of the mother and the son was increasing. The boy was going dangerously near the train. I could not but shout 'Stop him, please stop him!' and started running to hold him back. Maybe more for my sake and less for his. I did not want to see another accident with blood and tears, life and death all tangled with each other. Now, Leslie ran faster. He rushed past me and jumped into the speeding train. Dangerously. Yet home and dry. By that time I and a couple of other persons had got hold of the boy and stopped him. We saw the train slowing down and soon it stopped. Leslie had pulled the chain. The son was handed over to the mother. I had to explain the whole thing to the guard who had come down to examine the situation. In an abusive language, he scolded the poor village woman. Grumbled a lot and then spattered the *paan* spit on the platform and went to his own place with the dull green flag furled, like his anger.

Leena had come down in the meantime and Meera was watching from the door. I was afraid there would be another farewell formality. Her lipstick would be faded further. Well, this time it was only pressing the flesh with both mother and daughter. And a little fluttering of the painted eyes, 'Finish your work as soon as you can. We'll be waiting for you.' Leena's words were almost lost in the sound of the train.

'Why did you jump into the running train? It was so risky,' I asked him while walking back to the motorbike stand.

'You were worried for me? *Por que*? This was no big deal. I have done many more dangerous things. I can afford to. Look at me. I am so strong and athletic, am I not?'

I stared at him. I wanted to touch each column of the strong solid construction, each· leaf of the energetic exuberance. Leena's lip-gloss on his lip held me back. I didn't answer.

So he said, 'To be frank, when you shouted and started running for the boy I lost my head. Why do you get so concerned for others? Why do you want to protect everybody from getting hurt?'

'Because I don't want to get hurt myself,' I replied. Or to hurt my dreams, I said to myself.

Leslie did not allow me to take a rickshaw.

'We are going back together.' The mesmerising masculine master in him commanded. The deep-sea voice echoed deep inside me. He took out his motorbike and sat on the seat.

'Hold me tight. I drive the thing flat out you know.' A naughty smile lit his face. I was hesitant and he got impatient, 'Are you scared?'

'Of what?' my eyes asked.

'There may be another accident?'

'The worst accident has already taken place for me. I met you.'

'You regret! Do you?' The way he said it, he actually meant 'How could you possibly!' Next he honked impatiently. 'Now come on, what's the matter with you?' The matter was serious but I didn't expect him to realise it. Yet I said, 'You see, Leslie, if I go with you like that, people will talk. This is not your California or Tasmania.'

'To hell with the wagging tongues. Will you sit?'

Just like the speed of his wheels, just like the ripples of his rocky arms, just like the effect of his liquor-charm, his insistence was sweeping, strong and overwhelming. I had to give in. I sat behind him carefully, grasped his strong shoulders, and kept my body away from touching his. Lest my sloshing senses should uncork themselves. Yet, on the, bumpy rough roads, with every jerk I could feel my frail frame brushing against his rock-hard back. And a fountain of feelings would gush out. His silky flyaway hair, blown by the wind (today he was not in a helmet) was caressing my face like a soft passion. We remained mostly silent as his motorbike breezed along. I doubted if it would be a safe landing at Shantiniketan. I was a bit lost in thoughts, with the collage blooming and drooping inside me. All of a sudden, I noticed Leslie was going by some other road. I thought maybe, he had chosen this road so that he could drive his motorbike faster as this road was less crowded, most of the time. But he took a right turn and before I could comprehend or protest, he had stopped by a bungalow.

He got down from the motorcycle while I did not. Sitting on the pillion, I asked him, 'Where on earth have you brought me?'

'This is the place where I stay. The cottage of Ganguly.

Come on, get down.'

'I won't. This was not in our plan.'

'I never go by any plan. I just hate to. I felt like bringing you here and that's that . . .' he shrugged his masculine shoulders.

Going alone to a man's house where he stayed by himself! Had I ever done it before? No. Indian moral standards do not approve of it. So although the man was housed inside me to occupy every inch of myself, I did not dare to physically enter into his house. I got off his bike and walked towards the main road to get a rickshaw and go back to the hostel. The evening shadow was setting in. The road lights were yet to come on. The sky was covered with the flapping wings of the birds, flying back to their night shelter. My wings had started hurting me. A little rest. A shell-like shelter. A green darkness. A mauve dream. I needed very urgently. Suddenly, why I can't I say, I got scared of the collage. I tried to escape. So, I said 'Goodbye' and started walking. It was a narrow alley. A row of big bungalows and posh cottages with huge surrounding gardens. These belonged mostly to the retired military officers or bureaucrats who had chosen to settle in the midst of peaceful nature. Some of these cottages belonged to the film artists who would occasionally come and stay there during their rare leisure time. There was hardly anybody seen around.

I speeded up. But within seconds I was hit by a tornado. It literally swept me off my feet. My senses shut off and opened a few seconds later, only to discover myself in his arms. He was carrying me towards the locked door of a small cottage house. He put me down on my feet. The door was unlocked and a light was switched on. In front of this small cottage, stood the main bungalow where the owners of this house, the Gangulys, lived. But they were now out of station for a couple of days, and the caretaker and the cook stayed in the outhouse. Leslie told me. There was a lovely verandah with two rocking chairs on it. I preferred to sit there. I was still trembling with the depth of feeling that the strong grasp of his arms and the rocky touch of his terrain had generated in me. The dream body was so close and that I had actually touched it all over, I couldn't believe. The collage was shaping up. Growing. Filling the whole universe. I closed my eyes and remembered Mom. My red-earth reality.

His voice came floating in.

'Why don't you want to go inside? Are you scared of me?' He was smiling.

I couldn't say anything. I was not myself I sat down on the chair, sweating. He came closer to me, 'Hey, Lucie, are you okay? Well, I didn't mean to scare you. You were getting far too obstinate. I had to use a bit of force, but believe me I don't mean any harm to you. I just can't.'

His aquamarine charm was casting its catastrophic spell on me. He wiped the sweat on my forehead with his pink palm. Then, he bent over to reach my lips. I covered his lips with my hand and gave a light push away from me. I could still see that matte stain on his lips and I didn't want to get stained. He moved away from me, went inside and brought a glass of water for me. I didn't know how he could understand that I was feeling terribly thirsty. Eagerly, I took the glass from his hand. But before I took a sip, a sixth sense disturbed me. I held it in my hand looking at my reflection in the water. He started laughing, his usual, resounding laughter. His erect body was shaking and bending. I could not even smile. He soon controlled his laughter. The dimple on the chin came back to its original shape and he asked me, 'What do you suspect? It's drugged? Colourless liquor? Poison? Look.' He drank the water himself. Suddenly he looked grave. Very grave. Like the face of midnight. His deep dimple got deeper. How he could see through my doubts I don't know. I had never before seen him like this. He looked towards a moving dot of light across the sky, an aeroplane, perhaps.

He said gravely, 'Come on let's go.' He was serious. And I became serene. I looked straight at him and said, 'Yes, but first let me have some water.'

He was surprised. In the half-dark verandah I could not see the details of his Michelangelo face. But his eyes sparkled. Conspicuously.

After giving me water, he sat by me. He seemed restless. He was rocking in the chair quite impatiently. Rock, rock, rock . . . I was sitting almost still. The silence between us was swinging helplessly. I wanted to start a conversation, 'Why don't you sing a song?' I pointed at the guitar box kept inside his room.

'I can't. It is broken.'

'Broken!' I could see through the box a mangled body of a guitar, 'Broken or you broke it?'

'How did you . . . ?' he looked sharply at me, 'The frigging thing could not be tuned!'

A semi-melodic silence followed.

Then, he started, 'Why don't you teach me Bengali? I want to learn Bengali well. Sometimes, it gets difficult with some of the country folks. I get their dialogue recorded for Meera to work on later, but it makes better sense if I understand them.'

'I'm no expert in teaching Bengali. There is a senior girl in the Bengali department, a research scholar. She teaches most of the foreigners,' I said without hesitation as there was hardly any threat from that insipid, bespectacled girl. She had a brilliant brain, but not a radiant appearance or a vibrant heart. Leslie showed no interest. So, we both fell silent again. A grape-soft silence. Leslie illuminated it by lighting a cigarette.

'Why didn't they stay longer?' I asked him.

'She has got some work in Calcutta. Some professor from Delhi is coming. We don't have much time left. Say a couple of weeks. Leena has to get a visa before that.'

'May I ask who she was staying with in India?'

'With her father. Meera's divorced husband. I told you about her divorce. Didn't I?'

As I nodded he spoke further, 'He wouldn't have allowed her to go, had he been alive. That martinet. Kicked the bucket a couple of months back. Leena is now free. He would always accompany Leena, whenever she went to the States to spend her vacations with Meera. They would stay separately and Leena would come to meet Meera, as and when he wished.'

'That is quite natural for an Indian. We hate divorce.'

'And do not hate a life of pretensions, when there is no love left between two persons?'

'Love should be lifelong, if it is love at all for us. Time is the touchstone of the purity of love.'

'Very funny.' He smiled. Rocking had stopped already.

He took a long puff and almost sneered, 'Very strange. You go by the length of it. Depth does not matter? A few moments' pleasure can be very deep, or should I say profound? You cherish. it your whole life. Life means those few invaluable moments. Not everyday drudgery. Drudgery lasts very long. True love lives intensely and dies like a gallant hero.'

So this is what he thinks about love and life! The intense love and its instantaneous death. With every girl a moment of depth and with the next one, a deeper quest. He can afford to, as there will never be any dearth of women in his life.

My collage started falling to pieces. The colours bled. The happy palpitation got paralysed.

'Go on tossing off a few true-love moments everyday, with every girl you meet and brag about it.' I wanted to shout angrily but my small mouth remained shut. Nevertheless, my eyes might have been talking. He tossed the cigarette stub down and smiled.

'Don't you flash your eyes like that? Those beautiful dark grapes will burst.'

My lips were a dollop of jam. Now my eyes were dark grapes. Can't his dream-coloured eyes see anything beyond food items, or is it that my appearance arouses hunger? I reflected sadly. At the same time, I felt my usual boldness tightening around my sagging self It was a weird feeling. A child kicking wildly to come out of the womb and crying frenziedly when he is out of it. Never before had I felt this red-earth warmth and that deep blue coolness at the same time. The railway track swung open in front of me along with a blurred face. Day after tomorrow, I would be meeting Joy. Should I think anything else?

'What's wrong? Cat got your tongue?' Leslie's impatient voice rang out. I blinked fast to see clearly around myself. Leslie was not sitting on the chair anymore. He was standing close to me, with a naughty smile lighting his face. The moths in my eyes could not help fluttering helplessly.

'Why don't you talk? Lost in dreams about some long lasting love?'

I tilted my head and gave him a sidelong glance, a bit like a famous Bengali heroine. Next moment, I bit my lip remorsefully. *Am I flirting? Trying to lure this Casanova? Shame on me! I chided myself.* Never before had I behaved so strangely. With undulating uneasiness locked inside, I tried to look easy.

'Dreams won't take you anywhere.' Leslie said, 'Savitri (Savtree, he pronounced) did not dream when she outsmarted the god of death.'

'You have read the story!'

He shook his golden head in the most fascinating fashion.

'Susie told me. I was quite curious when you were talking about it. So, I asked Susie. She knows a lot about Indian mythology. She is working on Bengali women. Some anthropological study.' I recalled the gold-haired tall girl who was moving with Leslie in the morning with two melodious eyes. Leslie went on, 'I heard the story of Behula, who just like Savtree brought her dead husband back to life. I heard about Lacseera (original Bengali Lakshaheera). The most shocking story I've ever heard. The wife carries the decrepit husband, suffering from syphilis to the brothel, to a rich prostitute, just to fulfil his desire or should I say lust! And this you say is real love! My ass.'

'Leslie. Please, give it a break.'

And he broke the beautiful Bordeaux glass in which he had given me water. He just casually took the glass kept on a small stool, held it high and dropped it on the hard dry ground by the side of the verandah. Deliberately.

'Would you say it was less beautiful than an iron chest because it broke?'

I stood bewildered. A wilderness of wild savage beliefs. Smashed to smithereens? Perhaps not. My dream-lined durable reality survived.

'Don't you look so lost. I love breaking glasses. They sound so musical. When I was a baby, merely one and a half year old, I had a passion for breaking glasses. It continued for quite some time. Months, maybe years. I have no memory, my uncle told me. Imagine how many costly champagne flutes, Alsace glasses, decanters I must have broken. Must have got a thorough' spanking too.' He laughed, 'My folks used to hide them from me.'

'Not because they wanted to save the glasses. But to save you from being hurt. A piece of a smashed glass could easily hurt a baby.'

He stopped blinking and reflected for a few seconds, as if this had never occurred to him at all. He repressed a smile, went inside and brought his camera.

'Let me take some snaps of yours. I don't have any.'

'I think, in the jungle, your camcorder recorded my movements.'

'Well in just a couple of frames. And not focused on you. I want your snap. You should not smile. I want to capture that pout of your lips.' He looked through the viewfinder. And did not find any view as I turned my back towards him. 'Hey, look here. What're you doing?'

'A photo is a long-lasting thing. Why try to make a transitory moment everlasting? It would be against your belief,' I said as I went near him and took the camera away. 'My god. You are a headstrong girl, aren't you? Never ready to accept a logical concept.'

I did not answer but very calmly handed over the camera to him. He was still disturbed.

'Sitting here in a damn lazy environment you can dream and fantasise about your everlasting things. A load of bullshit. But when you come to the States with me, you will feel the truth, the reality . . .'

It was an earthquake-shock. Even he stopped abruptly. My breathing stopped. The stridulation of the crickets stopped, or did not reach my ears anymore. We looked at each other like strangers look. Even he didn't say it consciously, it was clear. He was agitated and something had slipped through his tongue, through the chink of his subconscious; maybe, something which even his conscious self was neither aware of nor wanted. To stop our embarrassment, his telephone rang. He went and picked up the receiver. I could hear his voice clearly.

'You are coming now?' Pause.

'Well, I had some work, Maria . . .' Pause. 'Can't we make it tomorrow?'

I got up, went near him, and almost whispered, 'I'm going.' But he held my hand with his free one and didn't allow me to go until after his conversation was over. He hung up and shrugged his shoulder, 'Maria is coming.'

'Well, you have made a number of friends here. Mostly women.'

'Friend or no friend, women never let me alone.' Some strange helplessness blunted his supercilious tone. 'They follow me everywhere, women and troubles. Everywhere, wherever I go. Troubles and women. All kinds and in all varieties.'

'You do want them to hunt you and haunt you.'

'Yes indeed. I did want to get mixed up with an accident here or nearly being jailed in Delhi.'

'What happened in Delhi?'

'It was a brawl at the hotel. Some boys made ugly remarks about Meera and me. Leena was not with us that day. Meera is my teacher and we share a beautiful friendship. She is a very mature lady. But they were corked up and you know. I could not control myself, there was a brawl, a couple of punches and we had to go to cop shop and I was almost jailed, but for some lawyer friend of Meera.'

'I'm getting late. I must go now.'

'Why should you go? Let her come. We'll share a drink. All of us.'

'I don't drink.'

'Beer would do no harm.'

'Please. I have to return to the hostel.' And to face the music, in case my secret trip to Bolpur was already known.

He thought for some time with his head down and his hands in the pocket of his jeans. Then he came very close to me, 'Let's have a goodnight kiss.' The aquamarine was deeper, the satin blades were dangerously curved. A leaping expectation for my lips. But a P*alash* feeling possessed me.

I retreated and said, 'Today, I shall kiss you. Okay?'

I went near him. Reached for his lips. I saw him closing his eyes. Brown eyelashes were quivering like the delicate antennae of a moth. With a sweeping swiftness, I dipped a kiss in the depth of his dashing dimpled chin. And escaped. Out in the garden. He came behind, surprised and amused and a bit disappointed.

'Hey, this is not fair, come back,' he shouted.

'It is. I did the way I like it most.' I giggled and went out of the garden gate. It was decided that we would meet at the hospital, the next morning. He wished me goodnight for a change.

'I should wish you a good evening with a ravishing Italian beauty,' I said with a small smile on my lips and a wisp of smoke in my heart. Or, was it smouldering jealousy?

In the hostel, Deepa started grilling me. She informed me that although the superintendent did not know about my trip, but some students had seen us together at different places. Some on the motorbike behind him, some at the station and things were obviously exaggerated, like I had been glued to him on the motorbike or we had been walking arm in arm at the station. Deepa didn't believe them all with her excellent logical sense.

But she asked me point-blank, 'Have you got something going on with Lesile? Are you really serious about this out-of-the-world, out-of-our-culture boy? Are you going to dump your London boyfriend?' It was typical of Deepa to come out with a series of queries.

'He is not a London lad. He has gone to London just for studies,' I said, 'and there is nothing happening between Leslie and me. We're friends.'

'What were. you doing at the station then? Why did you come back so late?'

'We saw off his professor and spent some time together.' 'It is dangerous. To spend so much time with such a flame and not get burnt! I don't believe it. It's just not possible. Just go and see in the International Student's Hostel. We heard there is a tremendous competition among the girl students. Almost everybody is trying to. make a move on him. And I believe he is flirting with some of them too.'

'I am least bothered,' I said with gloom lining my face. 'Something is definitely going on between you two. I am sure. One can't but fall for him after being so close to him for so many days.'

My small mouth opened wide on this rare occasion. 'Well, even if I accept your logic, will you tell me why he would fall for me? With girls following him at every step, why should he have any special feeling for me? Why? I don't have anything so special about me. No great looks, no great background, no great wealth. Why then?'

Although I was talking to Deepa, all these questions I was actually asking myself. Each word was a piercing nail. N ails and nails in the coffin of my fateful affair. Deepa thought for a moment, seriously, then said, 'You may be right, Lucie. Absolutely right. This boy has to spend his few days here, and so has made friends with you. They need it, these foreigners. They have to have some woman companion around them. Look at all our Western friends. Yes, now this boy had that accident and so you were his natural choice to come out of the mess. In the process, he's having a good time too. Wise up, my dear, wise up.'

The last nail in the coffin. It was difficult, very, very difficult to hold back tears. Yet, I did. Deepa was a coolheaded reasonable girl. She might be insensitive but her judgement of things was pretty reliable. Faintly I almost expected her to tell me like my granny: *'Love starts blindly and ends blindly.'* Or she would probably give some comprehensive logic, *'The most ordinary flower in the garden can very well attract the most colourful butterfly.'* But she did not and her explanation of the things was quite acceptable. We both remained silent for some time.

Then, like a mother she held my hands affectionately and advised, 'Lucie, don't get seriously involved with this boy. I know it is very difficult to spend hours with him and not to fall for him. So, I would say you stop seeing him. You don't need to see him again, do you?'

'No,' I had to agree. There was no logical need. Nothing. Only an enormous empire collapsed inside me, and I saw myself among ruins and ruins. As vast as the Harappa and Mohenjo-Daro.

Deepa continued, 'It would be better for you, dear. And I feel you should not be bothered; after all you do have your steady affair going on with your childhood friend at London.'

Yes, I forgot about Joy and my meeting with him. I tried to draw his face in real colour. I could not. Deepa was saying something I could not hear. Presently, she held up my chin and added, 'Here also there are so many boys who wanted to be in the line. Some of them still do.'

She laughed in order to make light of the heavy weather around. And I thought of the queue behind me. The length of the queue, or the numbers did not prove my worth anyway. Even one single man in the queue could have given me all. But who was that single man? I avoided the thought and said goodnight to Deepa. Both of us switched off our bedside lamps.

I looked through the window. Moonlight was fading and some stars were twinkling. I felt homesick, without any home anywhere. I missed Mom. Terribly. I recalled her face reciting, 'Twinkle twinkle little star, how I wonder what you are.' I could not understand why people wondered about the stars. Do we know what life is, although we are living every moment of it? We are brought here without our permission, in this mess called life. I was feeling confused, I was feeling wretched. I tried to think about Joy and my meeting with him. He would be waiting for me at the railway station. The station, the running train. He jumped up into the running train. Oh no, he was not Joy. Joy would be at the airport. I heard the big clock, in our hostel lounge strike eleven. Deepa was fast asleep. I wanted to talk to somebody, to listen to somebody, badly, to help me keep away the avalanche of memories, of the dark dimple, aquamarine blue, olive green kisses.

I got up and went to the small room, adjacent to the lounge. I had to make two calls. One to London, one to Goa. I got the London call immediately, but didn't get Joy. His answering machine asked me to leave my message. My purpose of talking and passing some time and not thinking of anything else did not work. Answering machine! Not an assuring one. Yet, I said, 'Joyee, I look forward to seeing you.'

Next, I talked to Mom. Mom was at first very worried. 'Something wrong Lucie? So late at night?' she asked anxiously.

'I am okay, Mom. Joy is coming to India. Uncle had a heart attack.'

'My God. But we have not been informed.'

'They must be too busy and worried, Mom. Joy wants me to meet him at Calcutta.'

'Of course, you must go. In fact, I'll ring them up tomorrow early morning. I'll talk to your superintendent too.'

'Mom, there is something more.'

'Well, what is it?' Mom sensed trouble from the pause that ensued.

'Lucie. What's it? You seem troubled. Everything okay? That small village boy, is he all right now?'

'He is. He will be discharged, day after tomorrow.'

'Then? Any problem with the police?'

'No.'

'Has Joy told you something?'

'Oh no.'

'Is it some boy there, in Shantiniketan?'

'Mom, can't you come to Calcutta too?'

'You are upset, aren't you? Speak out dear. Tell me everything.'

'Mom, is it wise to get involved with somebody who is breathtakingly handsome and who has numerous girlfriends?' A nineteen-year-old innocence asked a mature wisdom.

'My God, Lucie, baby. You are not seriously involved with anybody, are you?'

'I don't know. Please, answer my question.' Tears rolled down my cheeks. Some rare experience for my eyes, my cheeks, my memory. I never saw my Mom cry in her worst time. Neither had she taught me to do so. Tears were almost strangers to my eyes and I wanted them to be so, always.

'Tell me about the boy. Who is he?'

'A foreigner, from America.'

'A white man?'

'Yeah.'

'Oh no. Not again. Grandpa suffered. Aunt has been suffering. You must not.'

She paused for a few moments and abruptly said, 'Go to Calcutta, meet Joy. Go to Darjeeling with him.'

'My exam is just around the corner.'

'I know. But I don't see it would make any difference. Rather it would help. The tour will help you to forget this boy.'

I remained silent as I was figuring out the chances of burying the white passion under the white snowline of Kanchenjunga. Mom interpreted the silence wisely.

'Do you really want to go for him? Are you deeply involved with him? You know what I mean.'

'Oh no, Mom. No.'

'Well then. Don't get physically involved. Remember, it is always difficult to be sure about a white person. He can leave you any day anytime.'

'Yes, I know I'm not white.'

'It is not because you are brown. It is because he would leave even a white girl just like that. It is the way they are. And you already know he is a womaniser. You should be strong,' Mom spoke after a pause of a few seconds.

'Lucie, dear, don't you dream. Cinderella is a dream. Think about Diana. You know about her. In reality. Don't you? Do you want to end up like that?' Still she did not get any answer. So, she said with finality in her tone,

'If you must have him, don't make yourself too available. Keep a distance. Distance always lures. Don't be too close. I would have loved to come to Calcutta, but I want you to meet Joy alone. I think that will help a lot. After meeting him, you will understand yourself better. I always thought you two would make a nice couple.'

Our burning shop singed my memory. The Happy Valley Villa and Joy and I. A burning smell filled my senses. Mom said,

'Don't worry Lucie. Go to Calcutta and Darjeeling. See how you feel when you come back. You will definitely get over this temporary infatuation. I'm always there for you. Go to bed dear and sleep well. I'll talk to you tomorrow.'

I went back to bed and pondered over Mom's words. Mom never dreams. But I had my own idea of life. I tried to get some strength out of it. *Dreams are dreams and fact is fact. Both are reality. Dreams are real. They form an inseparable part of our consciousness. As sleep is an activity, a dream is a reality. But don't mix up dreams with life. Don't expect the dream to come to life, nor life to dissolve into dream. Keep them apart. That is the safest way to avoid trouble and enjoy both of them. I always believed it as a theory, only now did I realise the meaning of each word. Yes, my dream with Leslie will be out of my life. I must not mix it up with my life. It was a dream, it will always remain a dream. And my life will continue as my life.*

I repeated it again and again, although every moment I felt that dreams and life were overlapping each other. The sea and the sea beach. Now it was the beach, now the dance of the sea waves. Now the sea was rippling and now the beach lay bare. I also remembered my granny's face. Pale white. She got her love life entangled with a white livewire. Love did not remain alive for her. The wire tied her down to an empty nothingness.

But do I love this boy? What is love? Do I actually know it? If I don't love why does it hurt so much? Will it hurt this much, if Joy loves some other girl? I can't think at the moment. I should only follow Mom's words. This was a dream and I enjoyed it thoroughly. Now, the dream is trying to find shelter in reality. Why? Is it always necessary for a dream to seek its shelter in reality? Or for reality to seek refuge in dreams?

Early in the morning next day, I went to my local guardian's house. Mom had already talked to them. I got a consent letter from them about leaving the station. Next, I went to the hospital. Mukul was waiting for me impatiently.

'Didi, I don't like it here anymore. It is boring.'

'I'll talk to doctor uncle about your discharge today itself.' This was because I wanted to take him 'home' myself and my trip to Darjeeling would mean I would not be able to take him to his place. I would never allow that to happen. I must see him happily back to his normal life again, I promised myself

'Didi. Bring your head near me. I'll put this flower in your hair,' he said, taking out a sprig of Palash from the vase. 'Why don't you always put flowers in your hair? You look gorgeous.' He put the flower in my hair.

'I think you can sing, Didi, like they sing in the films. Your voice is so sweet.'

'I can't sing Mukul, I paint. I'll paint a portrait of yours when your hair grows back to normal. Now, I'll take your leave.'

'Will you go so soon? Why do you look sad today? Did your mummy scold you?'

His innocent insight had wisely discovered my distress so easily.

'My mummy stays far away from me. She didn't talk for long. So . . .' I had to make this up. At this, he burst into tears. Over my shoulder. In between sobs, he groaned, 'And my mummy has gone so far away from me. I can't talk to her, ever.'

The nurse and I had put a lot of effort to comfort him.

But I could not get him discharged that day. Dr Sen was out of station and was expected to be back in the afternoon. The doctor in charge did not agree to discharge Mukul without Dr Sen's permission as he had specifically asked him not to take any decision about Mukul without his permission. I decided to contact him in the afternoon. However, a doubt kept on niggling me. What if he does not come in the afternoon? How can I go to Calcutta or Darjeeling in that case?

My short meeting with the hostel superintendent sparked off an unexpected effect. Deepa and Rani came to know about my programme and they were very excited.

'It's real good news. He is coming at the right time.' Deepa gave her expert comment, 'Go and have a nice time. By the time you come back your white Casanova would have gone. The timing is really great.'

I looked up at the time. It was close to my meeting time with Leslie. I hated to stand him up and went out of the room on some pretext to call him. I wanted to be excused. There was no reply. I went back and told my friends about the problem, concerning Mukul.

'Maybe, I should come back from Calcutta. One day won't matter. But to go to Darjeeling . . .'

'This is idiotic dear,' Rani said. 'You can't cancel your Darjeeling programme for this god damned village boy.'

She could hardly understand how much that boy meant to me. I did not expect her to realise it either. Deepa sounded wiser, as usual.

'I shall personally talk to Dr Sen and see to everything. Don't you postpone your Darjeeling tour. Come back just before the exam.'

'Right. You must not be trapped by these Western boys. They are only after your body. They don't have any chastity about them. They don't mind sleeping with any girl they meet. Even the girls don't mind,' Rani said. These were the detergent words used by Deepa to brainwash her, so that she could abstain from following the hallucination of a white lure.

'Their culture is different, dear. They don't care about the body,' Deepa commented.

I recollected an excerpt from my grandpa's diary.

And we care so much, although our scriptures have stated that a body is nothing but an outer outfit of the soul, which is changed again and again. We lose all our energy in keeping that outer clothing stainless. Women in particular. There is no redress for their stained dress. No remedy. Even the immortal imperishable eternal soul cannot improve it. As if, in the world of illusion, the so-called sin of women is the only real thing!

I heard Deepa say, 'Premarital sex is not wrong if you marry the same person. After all, if you have a long affair before marriage, how can you avoid sex?'

She voiced the common belief of the modern generation in India. She was talking from experience. She looked at me as though for approval and got it.

'I don't love loveless lovemaking,' I announced.

Rani got disturbed, 'My gosh Deepa, you said the other day that it was wrong, to have sex without marriage.'

Deepa had to be careful now.

'I meant that the Western people indulge in sex and only in sex and do not marry after sex. That irresponsible and sinful relationship does not suit us. Okay?'

What about making loveless love with your stranger spouse, after an arranged marriage? I was about to ask but held it back and without stretching the conversation any further, I rushed to the studio. I had to finish the incomplete work of mine before my trip.

After a tiring session at the studio I came back late in the afternoon. Then in my room, I tried to concentrate on my studies, when our lady attendant came and told me that there was a male visitor for me, in the lounge. Women visitors could come to the rooms directly while male visitors had their boundary limited up to the lounge. They had to send a message to the girl inside and wait for her in the lounge. I thought some of my classmates had called on me to give me some books. In fact, I had sent for some of them to do so. I wrapped the dressing gown around the maxi and went to the lounge, only to discover a crowd of girls and a blond head blazing above them. It seemed all of them were acquainted with him as they were all talking in familiar tones. As I entered the room, Leslie stood up. I again cursed myself for my dishevelled appearance. Neither had I combed my hair after shampooing nor had I controlled them with any bobby pin or hair band. It was all a wavy mass. I didn't have kohl around my eyes. No bindi on my forehead. I was just myself. Nobody showed any sign of leaving the lounge.

'Good afternoon,' I said and he just nodded half-heartedly. Without looking at him directly, I said in a low voice, 'Sorry, I couldn't make it in the morning because I had some urgent work. I called at your place, but nobody picked up the phone.'

'The doctor wants to see you,' he said without paying much attention to what I said.

'Good news, so he has come back. Did he agree to discharge Mukul today?'

'I don't know. Isn't he supposed to be discharged tomorrow?'

'He was. But due to some urgent-' I could not complete my sentence.

Deepa came running and said, 'Quick, Lucie, call from London.'

'Must be Joy!' I said spontaneously and ran so the call did not get disconnected, which happened many a time in case of an ISD call. In a hurry, I forgot to ask Leslie to wait.

'Hello. Joyee.'

'Hey Lucie? Got your message yesterday,' a very feeble voice reached my ear.

'Joyee. Please speak up, I can't hear you.'

In reply a muffled wave of sound baffled me. 'Joy, speak up, louder, I can't hear you.'

He said something and I could decode only Lucie and Calcutta these two words. It seemed he could hear me. 'When will your flight reach Calcutta?'

This time some mechanical noise maddened my ear. Apparently, it was a one-way communication. He could hear me, but I could not. Disgusted, I hung up the phone. He would call again. He did. Within a few seconds.

'Hello. Hello.' This time it was total silence on the other side. After saying hello for two three times I had to put back the receiver. I waited for some more time to hear a ring. A ring came and stopped before I could pick up the receiver. A snapped line, a snapped mood. I went to my room to change.

When I went back into the lounge I saw Leslie talking with Deepa and the others. Rather, listening to them. I saw Rani sitting by his side and staring at him. Her sunflower eyes were soaked in the midday brilliance. Her mind might have been worldly wise, but her eyes were unwisely wide. As I approached Leslie, she came near me and whispered, 'Are you going out with him again? I heard you'd promised Deepa yesterday not to see him again.'

'I'm going to see Doctor Uncle. He's called me.'

'May I come with you?'

'You can't stand the hospital smell. Nor the Western spell. Can you?'

'I thought together we can help each other.' The honest sunflower eyes touched me deeply.

'We're getting late I'm afraid.' Leslie came near and looked into my eyes with impatience. The sunflower drooped even in the presence of the bright sun. Perhaps, my shadow fell in between. Rani almost ran away from the room.

We walked in silence and not side by side. He was walking with long strides. I walked slowly and deliberately fell behind him. Near the gate, along the boundary wall of the hostel premises we had the cycle shed. I went to take my cycle out. He stopped and looked back.

'Why the cycle? I have my mo'bike there, near the Bell Tower.'

'I shall go behind you to the hospital. You proceed on your motorcycle.' Then without his asking I explained, 'You see, yesterday everybody was talking about us. Please excuse me.'

He thought for a moment. Then said, 'Would you mind walking with me?'

'Walking? But the hospital is pretty far. It is hot out there.'

'We are not going to the hospital.'

'What do you mean?'

I looked directly into his eyes for the first time today. A red, angry tinge was mixed with the aquamarine romance. I had never seen it before. The blue crystal cracked with a red-hot impatience, 'If we can get out of here, I would like to say something.'

He looked at the gateman who was gaping at us, or to be precise, at him. With him around, I could hardly attract anybody's attention. However, leaving the cycle at the stand, I went out of the hostel premises with him. He took the first turn left, to get out of sight of the hostel curiosities. I followed him. I was waiting for his outburst about not keeping the appointment any moment and was groping in my mind for some white lie. However, I got terribly shocked when he asked me in a granite voice, 'Who is Joy?'

I looked up at him. He was looking straight ahead of him. The perfect lines of his face got a bit stretched and hardened. The cutlass curve on the satin pink blades was missing. I was not at all prepared for the question.

'My friend,' I answered.

'Only friend? You've never told me you're engaged.'

'Engaged!' I was shocked again. 'Who told . . .' And I understood that it could only be the work of my well-wisher, Miss Deepa.

'The way you rushed out of the room I was worried. Then, your friend told me that was because it was a call from your fiancé. Why are you telling me a lie?'

'It is not a lie. I am not formally engaged to him. No.'

'Informally then, I suppose. And you are going to Calcutta to meet him tomorrow?'

'How does it matter? Why are you asking me this?'

'This is not the answer to my question.'

'Yes. His father is sick. But will you please tell me why did you come to the hostel?'

'I came to your hostel . . .' he broke in between. 'Well, it doesn't matter, now that I can guess why you didn't come to the hospital this morning. But there is one serious reason. We have to go to the police station now. Doctor Sen asked me to inform you.'

Both of us walked in silence. Like two strangers. As if those last few days never existed and all the green grandeur had never grown. It was only barren branches. 'Dreams are dreams and life is life.' So far we had been sailing in dreams and now we were limping through life. Both were real, yet so different. We were nearing the Bell Tower, when I said to bring back some friendliness, 'Why do you want to go to the police station on the motorcycle? If you barrel to the police station that would be damaging for you.'

He did not respond. I stopped by the side of the bamboo clump. Today it was a bit early but the clump was full of lively chirping and hopping sparrows. Nothing changed here. Dreams and life were all rolled into one.

I saw the motorcycle. He was walking towards it. I almost ran to catch up with him.

'Leslie, let us go by rickshaw.'

'You mean if we sit side by side in a rickshaw your people won't talk?' I could not look into his eyes. Bitterly he said, 'I just don't understand why your people think and talk so much about others. A nosy bunch of idlers.'

I don't understand either. Which way the red dust blows and why? Aloud I said, 'Your rash driving should not be exposed to the police.'

'I hate rickshaws. They give terrible jerks and take so much time!'

'In that case why don't you sit on the pillion?'

'Who will drive?' He stopped and looked at my smiling face. 'You don't mean . . . you . . .'

'Yes, I can drive very well, very safe. Please, come on.' During my days in Goa I had learnt it. There, it would be a very common sight to see girls riding two wheelers. Leslie gave me the key. He kick-started the motorbike. I took the driver's seat and he sat behind me. But he did not require the support of my shoulders. Was I relieved or disappointed? I didn't ask my mind.

'Is Mr Fraser nervous? Sort of police-phobia?' I asked him on the way as he was very quiet, quite unlike himself

'Nervous! No way. I have been in a jail for a few hours.'

'What?' I was not prepared for this.

'Yes. In the Middle East. I forgot my papers at home and got into trouble when I drove a little fast. This is nothing new for me.'

'Why don't you saddle your wildness? It may really harm you one day,' I muttered more to myself.

In the police station they were waiting. Dr Sen, Mukul and Mr Ganguly. I asked Dr Sen about Mukul's discharge today and he showed me the paper. It was ready. His discharge certificate. Mukul's bright eyes discharged electric vivacity. 'I'm free at last.'

'He is discharged today.' Dr Sen said, 'The case will also be finally settled today. I already talked to the officer in charge here. He agreed. Everything is going to be okay. You need not worry any more. No more daily rounds to the hospital for you. Mr Fraser too will be free to go back to Calcutta and carry on with his work schedule. Mukul will go back to his own life. All the problems will be over today.'

Yes, Dr Sen was right. Everything would be over today. The accident and the boy had strung us together. Now, Mukul would go back to his own world. And Leslie and me, to ours. There would be no occasion, no excuse to meet each other. This shelter-less terracotta boy had provided a shelter to a soft white dream. A milky pearl in a red oyster shell. It would be lost somewhere in the red hilly waves of this rustic rapture.

Tomorrow, I shall go away. When I come back, he will not be here. The white man, his white words, his white surf feelings will belong to another world as they did earlier. The white smoke is encompassing me. But smoke never stays. The wisp of white smoke will slowly disperse into thin air.

I reflected and the arid red earth of Shantiniketan cracked in silence.

After the necessary formalities at the police station we went to the hospital in Dr Sen's car. Mr Ganguly left on the motorbike. The nurse and I packed Mukul's things. He had maintained all the games and books nicely. Nothing damaged, nothing torn. Only the new books lost their new smell and the games lost their shine. We packed all those and his clothes neatly. Leslie and Dr Sen stood outside in the corridor. I stole a glance at him. My eyes met his. I did not see the soft blue light of love or liking or flirting. It was hard blue sapphire. Uncut. Dull. Mukul held my hand and drew my attention.

'I'll come to meet you everyday. You will show me your place, won't you?'

'Yes, Mukul. I will.'

'Will you come and meet me often, after I leave the hospital? Today you will see my place, won't you?'

'Yeah, definitely.'

'Promise?'

'Promise.'

In my mind I also promised, I'll take you to some school. I'll find out some good job for you. There should not be any more bleeding on the rough edge of life.

Leslie went past me. He went near Mukul, bent down and extended his big white hand. A warm handshake. Mukul's eyes were sparkling. Leslie smiled and gave him a fat envelope. Mukul took out a wad of notes from inside the envelope. The new untouched bank notes looked like strangers to him. He smelt them. I too liked the smell of new notes very much.

'So many. Why should I take your money?' he asked. A naive question, like a glass of pure natural water.

'My gift for you,' Leslie tried to explain in Bengali.

'He is too young for money, Leslie.' Dr Sen echoed my feelings.

'He'll need them doctor.' Leslie tried to justify his action.

'Yes, provided he can keep them with him,' I could not help saying.

'Lucie is correct. People will rob him. He has no home of his own. Think of that.'

Dr Sen elaborated. Mukul gave the wad back to Leslie, 'I don't know what to do with it. You take it back.'

Dr Sen and I had to persuade him with a lot explaining that he would need the money for further treatment and good food. At last, he accepted but handed it over to me.

'You keep it, Didi. For me. You know better what I'll require.' I had to take it. 'I have to buy one bicycle for poor Nilu. He goes to work on foot. He does not have shoes. He gets blisters walking on the hot road. I can't ride a cycle. But I'll sit behind him. Can I buy one with this money?'

'Yes, I'll get him a bicycle. But for now, at least for the next two months, you must not work, you have to rest,' I almost commanded.

'No work? I'll get bored sitting in that outhouse.'

Well. I shall give you books and some other interesting work.'

'What's that?'

'Tell you later. Now let's go. We are getting late.'

Dr Sen was going to call the driver, when Leslie requested him to give him the car key. Dr Sen was a bit hesitant. Leslie smiled and said, 'Don't you worry. You'll get it back intact.'

So the two of us started for an unknown destination with a small wonder sitting between us. He told us to take him to the railway construction site. From there, he knew the way towards his residence. On the way, I showed him my hostel. Its walled boundary. The second storey of the hostel was visible from the main road. I asked him to come again to meet me whenever he got time. He gazed at it. Turned round to see it for a long time. He was memorising the location. I knew the way to the railway track. Directed by me, Leslie took us there. He was driving cautiously today. When we reached the site, Mukul looked happy and excited.

'Look Didi, the track is longer now. But all the other things are just the same as they were, when I last saw them,' he wondered. As if he expected some conspicuous changes in the big world, keeping pace with the ups and downs of his small life. From this point onwards he started directing. I looked at him. A homeless helpless lonely heart. Yet, he had brought the two most remote corners of the earth, under one beautiful shelter of a unique relationship. Yes, it was he who had painted a crimson canvas with his own blood and drawn us together. In my mind, I thanked this terracotta innocence and his pleasant presence in my life. Temporary but tremendous.

We dropped Mukul at the gate of a big bungalow, away from the main town. A big heavy iron gate was opened by a gatekeeper. Mukul greeted him. Leslie was standing near the car. I went with Mukul up to the gate. Mukul made a sign to bring my ear near his mouth. As I stooped, he said in a very low voice, 'Sahib looks angry today. Did he have a fight with you?'

'Oh no.' It did not sound credible to him.

'Give him back his money. I saved a hundred bucks before the accident. If I need a little more at times you will give me, won't you?'

'Of course Mukul, I will. But his gift is also yours.'

He went inside the gate and waved his hand towards us. 'Please, come to meet me here sometime.'

'Take care of yourself Mukul,' I almost shouted at the disappearing figure seen through the iron bars. We noted the address in our memory. One responsibility, one hospital connection was over. But I did not feel healthy nor happy. Right now, I had a sort of empty feeling.

That's it. The end of a trip. The breaking of a chandelier. My peacock blue chandelier. A sickness is over. Another is spreading. All over me. Tomorrow I shall go away. To Calcutta? To Darjeeling? To a no-feeling land? And back to where? The red-eyed barrenness.

IV

The Colour Called Love

WITH AN EMPTY HEART I started the return journey. I looked out of the window of the car to see that we had left the asphalted road and taken a dirt road across the vast rugged field. A very rough journey started. I heard Leslie mumble, 'What a kidney buster!' The main town was rolling away into the distance . . . I did not ask any questions. *'Let it be a de tour. This is, in all probability, the last few minutes together. The last few crystal drops dangling from the broken chandelier. After this, our sky will be divided. My hostel room with the mammoth murals of memories. Leslie will go back. Where? To the tennis court? To court the Italian beauty? To have love games with the other girls?'* I didn't dare to dream about the nightmare.

Leslie said in a midnight voice, 'We've lost our way. Do you have any idea where we are?'

No, I did not have, in the least. I only knew that I was by his side, like the pause following a word. I shook my head in silence.

'Don't know much about your town, I can see.' He was smiling. I felt he was enjoying himself 'Didn't we go by this way?'

Again I shook my head. Definitely, we had not taken this path, while going to Mukul's place. I looked about for somebody to help us find our way out. This area was a small tribal settlement. A few thatched houses and shacks under the sparse shade of the skeleton trees. Barren ground and bare trees. Greenery was as scarce as our words. Only thistles and weeds adorned the red earth. The goodbye ray of the setting sun had added one more shade to its original red. We advanced in the smoky red dust. I had never been here before. No other vehicle could be seen anywhere. A few Santhal men were walking along the dirt tracks. Mini dhotis and gamchhas around their waists. Topless. In top class shape. Warm black chests as if moulded in an ice cube tray.

'Let me ask them,' I ventured. But he shook his golden head and drove on.

'Nothing to worry. I'm looking for the main road. Once we get to it . . . rest is easy.'

He was correct. There were only a couple of main roads in the town and even if we reached anyone of them, finding the way from there would be no problem at all. But at the moment, we were moving along a dirt road with vast barren rocky ground stretching to the horizon all around us. And we were lost. Strangely enough, I was not worried at all.

Doesn't my world always get lost when I find myself in his eyes? Isn't it better to get lost together today than to lose each other tomorrow? Let this cut-glass moment hold us together before the timeless hand of time breaks it into pieces. The two wings of a butterfly blended into one on a flower-moment.

My dream broke as I heard him exclaim, 'Wow. What a sight!'

We were going past a group of Santhal women. They were dressed in slinky outfits. Red flowers placed in their neat buns. White smiles stashed in their eyes. Tribal passions hummed on their lips. They clasped each other's willow waists and swayed their slim hips while sweeping across the field. t always admired their incredible vital statistics and natural vivacity. Even after a whole day's work, in some farm or at some construction site, they would be in dashing form, with their spirits running high. No wonder, Leslie got turned on by their beauty. Beauty of form. Shape. Life.

Our car stopped with a screech suddenly. Leslie got down and made a sign to me to come out. I came out, looked in front of me and my eyes snapped open. Wide. Very wide. It was a spectacle. A small shallow lake. With plenty of bamboo clumps on its three sides. On the far side of the lake the countryside was full of red rocks and hillocks faded into the red splendour of the setting sun. A flat natural canvas, where emptiness and earthiness all blended into one and the dividing horizon was missing conspicuously. The dying sunlight had coloured the life of the lake. It was swarming with lively migrant birds, ruffling up their feathers, shaking their webbed feet and cheering up the vanishing glory. Their black bodies, with yellow rings, concealed the water of the lake completely. It had become a lake of floating chirping birds. We walked a few steps forward but didn't go too close. They might get scared.

'How do you like it?' Leslie's voice echoed after a long time. 'You can make a good landscape out of that, I presume.'

A feeble nod from me answered his question. His camcorder recorded the beauty of the place. Human hands cannot paint that fast.

'Have you been here before?'

I shook my head slowly. I had, never before, set my eyes on a spectacle like this. So Leslie's 'wow' was not meant for those willow-bodied beauties but for this spectacle! It had burst upon his view from a distance, while I was lost in my dreams.

'After some time the sun will go down and the flight of these birds will cover the sky, you will see,' he told me.

I could imagine it. They would leave the water alone, cold and lifeless. Leslie stood leaning against a tall Tal palm, as erect as his body.

'May I ask you a question Lucie?' he suddenly asked, 'Do you love that boy, Joy?' The open space, in the shape of an inverted bowl, closed in around us.

'To be frank, Leslie. I still don't know what love is.'

I could not speak further. My small mouth acted as a cork for my frothing feelings, as usual. But he was obstinate. 'I can't believe that. Be honest, will you?'

A rugged barrenness spread over my consciousness. I could not think. I spoke very softly, almost to myself,

'Well, I doubt I am in love with so many. Sylvester Stallone, Pete Sampras, Rahul Dravid, . . . even dead men like Van Gogh or our Bengali poet Sukanta Bhattacharya.'

He started laughing. His resounding laughter.

'There is nothing so amusing about it. I get obsessed by them, I th . . . th . . . think about them . . .' I was trying to get back to my normal self

'Enough. Enough,' he interrupted me. 'This is not love. This is a teenager's infatuation. But you are not so immature. I won't buy it.'

'What's love then? Can you tell me?' I didn't know where our conversation was leading to.

'Tell me, how do you feel about this boy in London?'

I noticed a restlessness among the yellow and black wings on the lake. In the fading light, the birds with ruffled feathers were looking like liquid ripples. Strangely enough, I imagined snow on their wings. Snow of Siberia. And I remembered the snow of Darjeeling, Sandakfu and Joy. Yes, I had to tell him about Joy, Leslie was waiting. All ears.

'We grew up together. We used to know what the other was thinking about or going to do.'

'Why used to?'

'Because we were separated. Around four years ago.'

'Till then you were dating regularly?'

'We were too young to date!'

'How?'

'He was a smart kid of seventeen.' A long shadow of white Kanchenjunga fell on the red earth. 'I was fourteen and a half.'

'You have never met since?'

'Only once. He came to Shantiniketan.'

'Can't you sometimes speak a little longer and let me know about him and how you communicate nowadays? Always a sketchy answer.'

I smiled faintly at his outburst, lowered my eyes but did not speak.

'Must be writing and talking regularly, I presume. All these four years?'

My big nod drew his little attention. So, I opened my mouth.

'Why are you asking me all this? I have never asked you about all the girls galore you have. Have I?'

Leslie picked a long reed from the nearby clump, started splitting it lengthwise and said,

'But Lucie, I am afraid, if we use a balance, this one man of yours, would outweigh all these girls of mine put together. What do you say?'

I picked a small wild flower from the thorny weeds. Tiny multicoloured petals, almost like granules, bunched in the form of a flower, a proof of the most delicate handiwork of nature. And love is even more delicate, and may be even more delicately wild.

I looked up at Leslie and answered, 'I would say, don't weigh them in the first place. Leave all of them alone in their own places. Leave Joy alone, leave Leena alone.'

'Leena. Oh, I have seen her only after coming to India, to be more precise, to Calcutta. It was just about two months ago.'

'And you have seen me after coming to Shantiniketan. Say, just two weeks ago.'

'Have I? Oh yes. It is strange, it seems as if I've always known you.' And just then we heard the fluttering of wings above our heads.

'See, our cranes are flying.' He pointed at the flying birds. With the setting sun on their wings they were flying away. The space was shaken by the restless fluttering of their wings: A couple of feathers were shed around us, like dreams from heaven. Their wild chirping enriched the air. I felt a splitting agony inside. And my small mouth opened wide, for a change.

'They are not our birds, Leslie. They will go back to Siberia or any other foreign land where they have come from. They will shake off the last drop of this red-soiled water and flyaway, all dry, all clean.'

Deep inside, an aching organ shook off a drop of tear.

Leslie came close and put his arms around me. 'Lucie-,' very softly he called me, bending his body and bringing his face very near to mine. A marvellous pain started dripping. The vacuum inside me was blossoming. 'Yes Lessy,' I replied with my eyes down to the red rocky earth.

'Did you call me Lessy?'

'Yes. I think that rhymes better with my name. Remember, what you said once about our rhyming names?'

'Yes, I do.'

'Would you allow me to call you Lessy? Well, I know there is nothing less about you, you have everything in excess, everything. And much more in excess, but only for rhyme's sake, can I call you Lessy?'

My small mouth had really grown big! The arms around pulled me closer. He started twisting my soft curly forelock round his strong fingers.

'You know something? There is everything less about Lessy if Lucie is not around him. And that is love, I believe.'

Every pore in the body of the air around, swelled with these words like coloured balloons. A riot of flying, sweeping, bursting colours. The world spread its iridescent blue peacock fan in the sky. There was no suddenness in this kiss, it was impatiently awaited by the lips, repeatedly created in the dream, and invariably expected in reality. Yet, when it was recreated impatiently in reality, the wild expectation got reduced to dreary, flimsy, depthless cut-outs. In his iron arms, pressed severely against the rocky contour of his body, I perished in mesmerising pleasure.

The lips were liberated and the long embrace was unlocked, as a giggling sound brought us back to rugged reality. A group of Santhal women were looking at us and laughing in amusement, with the setting sun brightening their pitch-dark eyes. The red and white flowers in their hair were rippling in ecstasy. The yellow wee buds on their noses were whorls of passion. The brown flames of their frames were fermented desire. They swayed past us as we slowly moved, got into our car and started.

We did not talk. Leslie was humming. For a few minutes my world turned into a cloisonné vase. With an ikebana of words and touches and kisses. All transitory. All ephemeral. All dreamy. My vase broke with a sharp jerk. From a lower level of the dirt road our car had jumped on to the main asphalted road. We had found our way. From dreams towards dreams?

I could not find any words when Mom rang up in the evening and asked me to go to Calcutta the next day. A cool breath of the indifferent Kanchenjunga on my neck. A prehistoric vision of yesterday. Joy, Mom, Naresh Uncle, hospital. A sliver of a teardrop. Joy had left a message with Deepa about his flight time. It would reach Calcutta around eleven and he would catch the flight to Siliguri after about three hours.

Why should I go to Calcutta? Or to Darjeeling? I am in love and I'll celebrate. A firefly flickered in the fragrance of the mango grove. *Yes I am celebrating my love. But for how long? The mango blossoms will soon droop. The red shimul grandeur will burst into ethereal white puffs. The red-hot summer wind will blow in a shimmering vast vacuum. And then?*

But I have always been a disciplined daughter with a lot of unruly dreams stashed inside. What should I tell Mom? How shall I explain to Joy? Yet, why should I sacrifice my chandelier moments? Somebody answered from inside,

'For some diamond ones.'

Leslie's voice echoed, 'Isn't a diamond dead? Dead and dull? Isn't that which we may lose more valuable that which has a life ebbing away every moment?'

My loyal friends, Deepa and Rani, woke me up in the morning to catch my train. It was pretty early. I requested Deepa to tell Leslie about my going to Calcutta.

'I'll come back in the evening. Tell him.'

'Not going to Darjeeling?'

I shook my head violently and left for my journey. From Shantiniketan to the station. To Calcutta railway station. And then to the airport.

Long Howrah Bridge. The turbid Ganga. Trillion waves. Trillion heads. Calcutta is a city of crowds indeed. Over-overloaded buses. Tired traffic lights. Broken cellophane sky and broken celluloid roads. Under them runs the Metro, India's only underground rail. Sleek and ultramodern. On the ground, rickshaws are pulled by men. Carts are pulled by men. Primitive, ultra-obsolete. It hurts Calcutta to give up its old but she grows with the new at the same time. A grey-haired city.

Dumdum airport is far away from downtown. Traffic was at its peak during this time of the morning. The Metro did not run up to the airport. So, I went to the airport by taxi. It took nearly two hours and instead of my welcoming Joy, he came and greeted me as I got down from the taxi.

'I thought you could not make it.' He smiled.

'I was caught in a traffic jam.'

'I know,' he said. He was sweating profusely. My hand automatically advanced to wipe his wet forehead, and automatically stopped, like in our adolescent days. But now I was no more an adolescent girl and my hanky, after an initial hesitation, touched his forehead. However, he smiled shyly and took the hanky himself and wiped his face.

'All my hankies are soaked. You have to supply some more.' He smiled.

'Let's go to some good restaurant.' I suggested.

'Yeah. It is now lunchtime here. Let's have something.' And we went to the cool and cosy restaurant of the Airport Hotel.

He told me all about the unhappy episode of Polly with a Kashmiri boy. Boys from Kashmir are generally awfully charming. She got involved with one such Muslim boy, a dealer in woollen clothes. With him she ran away from home. Went to Nepal. The boy abandoned her after two days and Polly contacted her family to take her back. Naresh Uncle got a heart attack. Ramesh Uncle went to Nepal and brought her back. Fifteen-year-old Polly. Almost four years younger than I. I remembered her when she was just three or four. In a jumpsuit. *From peek-a-boo to pick a boy.* The transformation was phenomenal.

Joy was sitting next to me. I noticed no spectacular changes in him. London's sophisticated touch and cool air had not given him a new shape. He was the very same old Joy. Obedient and dutiful to parents, concerned about his family, caring and loving.

'You have changed a lot.' He fixed his eyes on me. Yes, I had changed. Touched by a man. Felt reality through dreams. I always told Joy all the big events of my life. But the biggest one remained concealed inside me. I tried hard to tell him about Leslie, as a friend at least, but my small mouth did not allow. Or maybe a huge guilt feeling?

What if I tell him about Leslie and he severs our age-old friendship? I can't imagine such a phase in my life, when I don't contact him and don't get his signal back. For every happiness, for every sorrow, for every success, for every failure. Why can't I tell him about my love? Love is not happiness, love is not sorrow, love is not success, neither failure. Love is a feeling named love. When we are in love, we feel just love. Just like when we skate, we just skate. We don't walk, we don't run, we don't fly, or maybe we do it all. Just as we dream. We don't see, we don't hear, we don't think, or perhaps we do all. We dream. I am in love. I am in dreams.

'Earlier, you used to talk less. Now, you've grown dumb. What's the matter with you?'

I blushed and Joy interpreted it wrongly. His hand held my hand on the table. Soft oily sweating palm. It was as if my one hand was touching the other one. So very familiar. Even after so many days. No goose flesh, no rush of blood. Fortifying comfort. Till the other day I was content with it. My ultimate shelter. Today, I am shelter-less in love.

'Lucie, look up. You have never felt shy with me!' His hand pressed mine.

Never did I feel shy with him, neither now. I was avoiding his eyes to avoid feeling embarrassed. Or guilty. His fingers lifted up my chin and I had to look into his tea-coloured eyes. A dream nestled in them. A Happy

Valley dream. A hard lump choked my throat. On the pretext of going to the toilet, I left the table.

My eyes were burning and my insides too. I splashed water on my face. My reflection on the mirror mocked at me. For the first time in my life, I despised myself and hated my face in the mirror. But the very next moment my eyes got glued to the mirror in shocked amazement. The bubbling blue, the burning gold, and the most unearthly curve of all. An uncontrolled scream. Followed by swooning consciousness. An extra-large hand on an extra small mouth and two struggling bodies pushed each other out of the ladies toilet. The girl tried to shove the alien boy out, and the boy tried to drag her out with him. Fortunately, for us there was no other woman in the toilet at that time.

We rushed to a nearby corner. Joy could not be seen from here.

'What are you doing here?' The perplexed words came out of my mouth.

'Looking for you. Why didn't you tell me you were coming here?'

'I told you I'd be coming to Calcutta today.'

'But how, when, for how long . . .' Already most of the eyes were watching this out-of-the-world beauty and perfection. Now, his impatient voice raised a few eyebrows around us. One waiter came forward and tried to help me.

'Yes madam. Any problem?' I shook my head feebly.

'Goddamn nosy Indians,' Leslie muttered angrily. I saw anger in the waiter's eyes. He could not follow his accent but felt abused. I sensed trouble.

'Sorry. I am so sorry, brother,' I said to pacify the waiter and dragged Leslie away.

'I beg of you Lessy. Don't make a scene.'

'Come with me then.'

'Just a few more minutes. He is flying to Darjeeling.'

'Let me go with you and meet him.'

'No. Oh no.' A purple appeal sprang up from deep inside me. 'No Lessy, please don't do this to him. His father is in the hospital, seriously ill. Please.'

I was extremely apprehensive that Joy would know it all the moment he saw Leslie by my side. Uncle was seriously ill. Polly was upset and derailed. He would not be able to take it. The vulnerable tea bud.

Leslie looked deeply in my eyes. For a moment the passionate aquamarine grew compassionately still.

'Very well. I'll be waiting for you in room number 313.' Before I could tell him about my return journey at six, he flashed past me, whistling impatiently. I hurried back to Joy only to discover he had also left the table and was looking for me.

'Where were you, Lucie? You took so long. I got worried. I have to catch the Siliguri flight now. It's time.'

I just hung my head and expanded my small lips as far as possible in a vain attempt to smile. My inside was shaking like a revved-up plane. Maybe, out on the runway at that time no flight was taking off, but my ears got deafened by the roar of a flying plane as I saw Leslie sitting at a table at a distance smoking peacefully. Joy's back was towards him. My pale face, my shaking existence again gave a wrong signal to Joy.

This time he put his arm around me and said, 'I know how you feel. Don't want me to go. But I've got to, you know.' He helped me walk with him. Or rather totter with him. 'Can't you come with me to Darjeeling now? Should we try for a ticket?' he asked me. 'Mummy will feel better if you come with me.'

'My exam, Joyee . . .' I faltered.

'Oh yeah, you told me. Bad timing. Come when I go back, won't you?'

I nodded in silence. We went to the airport. Before going into the security zone, Joy suddenly hugged me. For the next few seconds I could not feel my thumping heart as much as I could feel his. He tore himself away from me and a cold-tea face looked at me through the barrier glass of the security zone.

For quite some time, I could not move at all. Even after Joy went out of sight. Out of sight, yet not out of mind. Rather, I was out of my mind. An utter confusion. The bustling airport, the honking busy traffic, nothing was disturbing me. I was much more disturbed by the inner turmoil. I would have stood there forever had not a trolley hit me on the back. The man behind the trolley appeared to be a Japanese or a Korean. He apologised with a slight bow, and I came back to this world. But at the moment, my world would be room number 313 in the Airport Hotel. A few minutes' walk from the airport.

Although I was so used to hotels and hotel rooms, it was a very new experience for me to go into a hotel room, alone. The door was ajar. I knocked and did not get any response from inside. So, I entered slowly. A beautifully decorated room but the best piece was missing. I looked around me, when all of a sudden, a tornado hit me on the back, spun me, swept me off my feet and flung me on to the bed. A silky soft touch under me and over me the splashing blue waves of the sea down under. He crushed me against the soft bed and started kissing not only my pout but every inch of me. I could do nothing but close my eyes, my darling darkness. Wild darkness. *In the dark, darling, I feel the light in you* and there was a blazing light of fire all around, torching my senses. Yet, deep down I heard the murmur of the distant sea. Mom's voice. Not too close. Not too close. Too close, opened up two wilted petal-like eyes of my granny. When Leslie was trying to unhook my bra my sea-deep mind murmured, 'No Lessy, no Lessy. Please.' I kept struggling with him and much more fiercely with my own ignited self 'I'm not ready for it. Please.'

But every bit of me was ready for it. Ready to mix with every bit of him. To know the unknown, to explore the ultimate. His voice dived deep into my heart, 'Oh Lucie. Be game. Dive in. Dive in.'

I could not see his perfect face, perfect form. It was too close to be seen. I saw the face of Mom. I smelt the burning shop. Mom burnt her house in order to save her home. Her eyes pleaded with me to burn down my desire in order to save my love. Again I struggled with Leslie, with myself Resisting him physically, was impossible for me. So I used my weapon, my strength. My words. As soon as my lips got free for a few seconds, I squeezed the difficult words out of my small mouth, 'Oh Lessy. I'm all yours. Why do you have to use force on me? Why?'

The storm subdued. The riding white horses got flattened on the sea surface. Leslie sat up. A shadow of dissatisfaction darkened his aquamarine. He left the bed, picked up his shirt and put it on. I buttoned my shirt and went near him, rested my head on his back and sobbed, as I could not hold back my tears any more.

'I am sorry. But I love you, Lessy. I love you. Don't spoil it, please.'

He listened in silence and then started laughing in bewildered amusement. If his laughter could be translated into words it would mean, 'What a jerk! Making love is spoiling love or making it!'

'I am an Indian. A common Indian girl,' I spoke through tears. He turned. Wiped off my tears and smiled with the familiar curve.

'Forget it. Let's go out and see the city.'

His words stopped my tears. A cold wave ran down my spine. It was already half past four. Through the window, one could see the dying light of the sun. Darkness was rolling in. In this part of the world, sunset is pretty early.

'Oh God. I've got to rush. Right now.' I started towards the door.

'What is it?'

'My train. I've got to catch the train at six. Back to Shantiniketan.'

In my mind, I was horrified at the extreme difficulty of reaching the station before six, due to the heavy traffic jam during this time of the day. Then I held his hand and gave him a light tug, 'Aren't you coming back by this train? Please, let us go back together.'

As if I was very sure he came here only to follow me and would again go back, following me. To the red serene earth. His only destination. And the two of us with a green destiny. My darling darkness spread its rainbow wings. I closed my eyes to see its phenomenal flight.

'I've finished my work in Shantiniketan.' His cool, cool words halted the feral flight. My heart suddenly nosedived into a bottomless abyss. I had forgotten the simple fact that his stay in Shantiniketan was not meant to be forever. The red earth of Shantiniketan was not my heart. In fact, his days in India were numbered. All of a sudden, the whole world with the living and the dead, with noise and silence, with emotion and inertia took off like an aeroplane and flew away, far and farther away from me. A cold flattened out runway. A runaway loneliness.

'Are you okay?' His words and arm around me shook the inertia out of me. I felt paralysed inside, yet my human body responded. My arms held him close. Very tightly. As though, by pressing hard they could keep him forever in their possession. I kissed his deep dimple and a deep agony erupted, 'Goodbye Lessy.'

As I tried to wrench myself away, his two strong arms restrained me.

'You are not going anywhere.' His cool tone was puzzling. His aquamarine waves splashed, as though he took pity on my confused soul.

He twisted my forelocks round his fingers and smiled, 'We shall go back tomorrow.'

'B . . . but you said your work was over?'

'Yeah. I have to get some more work from my professor. I'll persuade her to keep me, for a few more days, in Shantiniketan.'

'What if she does not agree?' I expressed my doubt. My heart was still limp.

'Don't you worry about that. I'll see if I can swing it so she does agree.'

'I've got to go back today. By any means. I have not taken permission to stay out overnight.'

'But you cannot catch the six o'clock train. It is too late for that.'

'I shall take the next one, at seven thirty.'

'No, no. You will reach after ten. At ten, the town is almost empty and asleep. You mustn't go by that. I won't let you.' His eyes rippled, 'Stay tonight.'

The words strummed on my every nerve, 'Stay tonight. Stay tonight.' For quite some time I could not hear the roar of the aeroplanes, which were flying every now and then over the hotel. Then I heard his voice.

'Scared of me?' An unusual softness was added to his voice, 'I won't do anything against your wish. You can count on me for that. You can.' He put an assuring arm around me and started playing with my forelocks. A relaxed easiness.

We sat on the sofa and he ordered drinks, hard and soft. We started exploring each other's world, talking about our childhood, our hopes and disappointments with intermittent interludes of interlocked arms and lips.

'Your body is so soft. I've never experienced such softness,' he said. 'Or maybe I did.' I was all ears. 'In my childhood I had been to a big party with my parents on some occasion, I can't remember exactly what. There was a ten-tiered huge cake. I was mischievous. So were a couple of my friends. We fell on that cake. We sank in that very soft spongy stuff Your body brings back that feeling.'

He sunk in my softness to get that feeling back.

'Should you always compare me with something edible?' I remembered he compared my lips with a dollop of strawberry jam. My eyes with black grapes. I hadn't liked those either. And now my soft body with a spongy ten-tiered cake!

'What's wrong in that? I can't make up things. I say just what I feel.' He kissed my forelocks.

'And you feel I am just a thing to be eaten! Insulting.'

'Why? Why do you always want to be compared with the moon and the sun and the clouds?

Why not some real earthly thing?'

I had no objection to real things. 'But why eats? They get over as soon as you eat 'em up,' I argued.

'You are just you.' He sealed any more argument with a burning kiss.

He was getting wilder and sensing an imminent surrender on my part, I warned him, 'Lessy, you promised . . . if I don't wish to . . . Didn't you?'

'Why do you people feel so inhibited when it comes to sex? Don't you love me? After all, what is love if you don't make love?'

A deep flush crept up my neck. My eyes drooped and I hung down my head in a pleasant embarrassment. Never before had I discussed sex with a boy, face to face. My silence agitated him.

'After all, love is sex. Yes, it is. You may add a lot of rubbish romantic nonsense to it. But that is not real. No way.' He shook his golden head impatiently. A patient silence followed as he sat up and looked at me with expectation and I gazed at the human perfection with my imperfect impulses. The cold bottles gathered hundreds of droplets and stared at us as if through the compound eyes of a honeybee.

Soon I felt a bit stronger. 'Come, Lessy, I'll show you something.' Holding his hand tightly, I took a bewildered Leslie to the balcony.

'Look, Lessy.' I pointed at the moon to pinpoint the difference between love and sex, *'Look! Moonlight is nothing but sunlight. But is it the same?'*

I had to spend the night in the company of the lonely moon in the sky and lovely moonlight. Leslie had to go to his professor Meera as she had called him suddenly. Leslie informed me over phone, at around eleven at night, that he would not come back that night as a party was going on there.

He was not there in the room. However, Leslie's presence inside me filled my existence, my senses completely. A spectacular spillage. It was all so new for me. I remembered his every touch, his every kiss, his every loving word. They were so very unique. The newly born world in the newborn vision of the newly acquired eyes of one blind by birth. The thrill of exploring each other's world. Even exploring oneself extensively. Never before did I know that my lips could be so delicious. My shoulder could be the resting pad of some wild passion. My long black hair could weave the patterns of a white desire. And I, with a few vital statistics and a lot of non-vital details could be the shelter for a wild wandering wonder.

A wonder indeed. Leslie did not turn up till late afternoon the next day. He did not call me either. My eyes ached and my heart throbbed in pain, but my mind comforted me. He never loved you. Never wanted you. He wanted your body. So, it is better this way. Much better. *Love cannot do without the body. But the body is not the embodiment of love.* My old, inhibited, Indian mind tried to console me. But could it possibly? The hands of the watch turned into stings and attacked me. I was placed unarmed in the apiary of time. With agony filling up my veins and tears rushing to my eyes, I left the hotel without enough money in my pocket. Leslie, had made an advance payment for the stay. But the cost of food was high and I was not carrying much cash with me. However, the train fare could be managed.

The train reached Shantiniketan quite late. Incidentally, among the passengers, I found an acquaintance from Shantiniketan. A senior student in the English department. We shared a scooter rickshaw. The hostel was almost dark. It was almost eleven thirty. Due to early morning prayers and classes the students used to go to bed early. With my key I slowly opened my room and crept into it. Deepa was fast asleep and quite unaware of my presence. Although I was no longer in the train, yet the train of events of the last few days kept flying past my mind like the lonely lean poles by the railway track. The toy train of Darjeeling. The dancing speed. The train grew, the speed grew, the sound grew, and my mind derailed. My darling darkness blinded. It could not dream. For the first time in my life.

A few white lies to my friends and the superintendent saved the situation the next day. But the black truth hovered around the horizon. No hews from Leslie. The deep anguish of missing something, missing everything tormented me. Missing Leslie, missing our moments together was painful. But the agony of missing my dreams, the perfect shelter of this imperfect life was unbearable. I could not reach my god. In order to relive the dream, I went to the place, where we had first met. The accident. The crimson blood. Mukul's face floated up in my memory. I went to see him. The bungalow gate was opened by a middle-aged lady, who was taking a stroll around the garden. To my utter surprise, she informed me that she did not know anybody by the name Mukul and no small boy stayed at their outhouse. Did I lose everything? All of a sudden? Just the way I had got everything so unexpectedly?

You are gone and you are gone and the red earth bleeds;
A small life, too many big dreams are all but dead indeed.

No. No. My heart clutched at the oozing strength and shook off the inertia. A dim light, dream-light flashed in my mind. Two aquamarine waves. A crest of frizzy hair. I decided to go to the hospital and find about Mukul. He was supposed to come for a check-up. What if he did not come? I did not think about it. I dreamed. Leslie's address or telephone number in Calcutta was not known to me. I dreamed to get it from Mr Ganguly, Prof Bose, Mark. The studio sheltered me. The brushes and colours. Till all the colour of nature got lost in the grey barrenness of the waning moonlight, I worked. I reached my god.

When the two hands of the big clock of the Bell Tower met at midnight, I came back to the hostel. They always met, at every hour. After every one hour and five minutes. I felt empty like a handless watch. A very conspicuous existence of a dial. Large. But meaningless without those two delicate hands.

Two handwritten messages were kept on my table. Deepa had left them for me. Both Mom and Joy had called. Mom had asked me to call back. Joy's message had good news. Naresh Uncle was recovering. So, Joy would curtail his stay here and go back to London next week. Next week. My exam would start next week. The final semester. I had fared pretty well in all the previous ones. There was no Leslie then, no Mukul. No colour called love. No brush named passion. No moment when I was not enough for myself

I found a bit of my lost self in the hospital, next day. As I went into Dr Sen's chamber I saw Mukul. Everything was not lost. Mukul was still there. The harbinger of our love, if I could put it in an old-fashioned way. He was standing with a nurse, who was attending to his wound. When I had a good look at him the light in my eyes dimmed. The terracotta face was terribly pale. Neither his lips nor his eyes greeted me with sunny warmth. Dr Sen was busy talking over the phone. As soon as the nurse finished her job, I brought Mukul out of the room. His bandage was removed now completely and I could see the scary scar on his head. Still fleshy red, still a little swollen. I squatted by his side to bring my face near to his.

'What's wrong, dear?' I asked him. He could not say anything, rested his head on my shoulder, and started sobbing. I held him tight, stroked all over his dirty shirt. Once, I got soaked in his blood. Today, it was only dirt.

'Please, my dear. Be quiet. Tell me what's wrong.' Looking at him, I felt, my love, my love for Lessy was hurt and sore. Crying and dissolving. I held him still tighter. Let me save my love for Leslie. Let me nurse and revive it. My heart mused. After a few minutes, he rubbed his eyes and looked into my eyes. A damp look. 'Didi, I have no place to stay.'

'What about that bungalow? I went to meet you there.'

'They are gone. Nilu and his brother. They stole something from the house and escaped. I'm not sure they have done it but they think so. The masters. They think that I am a thief too. I am not a thief, Didi. Mummy asked me never to touch others' things. Your fingers get crooked, sore.'

'Where were you all these days?'

'The gardener was so kind. He allowed me to stay with his family for two days. Then the master came to know and asked me to get out.' Tears rolled down his cheeks. I wiped them with my palm. I saw Dr Sen rush past us with a couple of doctors and nurses. Most probably some serious case had to be attended. Or there was some VIP.

'Now where shall I go Didi? Since yesterday I have been on the road,' Mukul asked. He also informed me, 'I tried to come to you, but couldn't find the place.' Yes, of course. He was only ten years old.

'Have you eaten anything?' From his appearance I could feel his hunger and thirst. I took Mukul to some nearby food joint. He was starved and gobbled up two plates of rice and fish curry. I had a cup of coffee. He wanted ice cream as dessert. He had already got used to the taste of imported extravagance.

My next destination was the bungalow of Mr Ganguly. From the outer side of the fence I saw a big padlock on the door of the cottage where Leslie used to stay. An old man, most probably senior Mr Ganguly, came out of the house. He came near the fence and looked at me with questions in his eyes. Mukul was a few metres behind me.

'Are you looking for someone?' he asked in a dry old voice.

Although I came here to take Leslie's Calcutta address and phone number, I could not utter a single word. I felt embarrassed, awkward. My small mouth remained shut.

'Yes, please tell me. How can I help you?'

Shaking my head meaninglessly, I turned around and walked very fast to get out of his sight as early as possible. Mukul ran with me. I should have said that I had lost my way, but I could not lie impromptu.

My awkward feeling took me straight to the hostel. I remembered I had to study for my exam. Mukul came with me. During the day, it might not be difficult for him to move around the boundary of the hostel. I even requested our gateman to allow the boy to rest in his shed. I asked Mukul to be there at sunset and I would arrange something for him. In my mind, however, I was not at all sure where to take him. Next, I tried to concentrate on my books and two glass-bead eyes, reflecting the whole hollow homeless world, popped up from the pages of the book.

I missed Leslie even more than ever. I needed him badly.

'To solve the problem together. Everything about this boy, we have done together and now he should be by my side to find the final solution. Why doesn't he appear in front of me this moment, save our love and save this poor child?' I thought, and was dead shocked the very next moment to see him coming in through the door. He came in sharply and closed the door behind him. Before I could rub my eyes to confirm the correctness of my vision, they closed and plunged into darling darkness. Spongy mouths, liquid teeth. A few fountain moments.'

It was happiness all over to see him once again, it was madness all over to touch him once more, but it was still more. It was love. Love does not know happiness or unhappiness. When united, or when separated what you feel is love. My feeling of love got mingled with a sense of benumbing fear.

'Are you crazy? How did you come here? How?'

'Simple. Bribed the man out there. He told me your room number. Nobody was around. So, I took a chance.' He smiled with the same killing curve. 'But you are shaking. Why fear so much!' the very same cool, deep-sea voice.

'What if somebody has seen you?'

'Who cares?' he shrugged his shoulders.

Nothing would happen to him, I knew. He was not a student of this university. But I would be expelled. All this I could not explain to him. Opening the door, I almost flew out of it. Two girls were going along the passage.

'Anything wrong, Lucie?' one of them asked. I shook my head nervously.

'Before you start painting your picture, colour your face dear. You look so awfully pale.' The other taunted me. 'Too much of white company, I believe.' Next, she whispered into my ears, 'People say he has left. Has he? Who else will know better than you?' They laughed loudly at their own joke and walked away gingerly.

I ran to the lounge. One girl was sitting on the sofa. She was reading some magazine with great concentration. I sat in front of her and with a thumping heart opened a newspaper in front of me. From here I could see the passage to my room. The girl was sitting with her back to it. Girls were coming and going. Deepa came in. Instantly, I took her away in the open.

'There is a problem.' I swallowed hard.

'What's the matter?' Deepa's roving eyes caught me unawares. 'Are you okay?'

I was trying to explain the situation, when Mukul came running.

'What is he doing here?' Deepa looked puzzled. 'He was discharged from the hospital the other day. Wasn't he?' 'Yeah, but not from the complications of life, Deepa,' I said.

She nodded her head seriously, 'I see. This boy has created some problem for you?'

'Let's go out and talk.' We came out of the hostel premises and I briefed Deepa about Mukul.

'I cannot let him roam around on the streets, homeless,' I concluded.

'What will you do? What can you do? Why doesn't he go back home? We can take him there.'

'I don't have any home,' Mukul spoke out very boldly. He was right, perhaps. After publishing and broadcasting the ad when nobody came to see him even once, he could not call his birthplace a home. Not even a shelter. It could be, at the most, a museum carrying his mother's memory. Who lives in a museum other than a few dead mummies?

Soon I saw Leslie coming out of the hostel premise with three girls. He walked towards the Bell Tower, away from us. I heaved a sigh of relief He had managed to escape without anybody's knowledge. Deepa went back to the hostel and I did not follow Leslie. At heart, I was content and filled with spring tide. But at hand, I had a difficult problem to solve. A place for Mukul. A shelter. Even if temporary. We went to the hospital. Dr Sen was free this time. He greeted us. I told him about the problem. Dr Sen looked serious. He turned towards Mukul and said, 'You should go back home, child.'

'I'll go to Papa. I won't live with my stepmother. Don't send me there.'

Beads of tears blurred his eyes. I held him close to me. Slowly I talked, with some awkward pauses in between.

'I have one request Doctor Uncle. It may be asking for too much. Can't you keep him in your hospital for a couple of days? As a patient?'

Dr Sen started scribbling on the writing pad in front of him. He looked thoughtful. I widened my small mouth and said, 'I'll definitely make some arrangement for him in a day or two.'

'I understand your feeling. Let me see.'

'Keep him in the general ward. Single-bed cabin is not required now.'

'Wait a minute dear. I'll have to check the occupancy position. If it is not very crowded I shall arrange it.' He then called some official and started checking the record. I waited with my fingers crossed. Mukul stood leaning against my chair.

'Yes. I think it may be possible,' he said while going through the records.

Mukul was taken to a general ward. Ten beds. Six were occupied. Number seven would be his address for the next couple of days. A new address to be found later. A shelter. For Mukul. For my love?

I went to the house of my local guardian early morning next day. A request for keeping Mukul at their place for a few days was not directly turned down. They informed me they did not require a full-time servant. The children were grown-up, going to college and both husband and wife worked in the local state government offices. They also suggested that they could find a job for him in the nearby stone quarry, where labour was required in large numbers. The workplace had a slum built nearby.

He could stay there. A very stone-solid solution to this delicate human problem.

'Well, I'll let you know.' I could all but mutter.

'It will be done. I can assure you. I know them pretty well. You may bring him in a day or two. Everything will be arranged.' The wise man promised. I visualised the childhood crushed under stones, and my love sheltered in a black airless pit. A suffocated, depleted world with dreamless incomplete reality.

Leslie's telephone call brought back my dreams to some extent. He had been sent here for a few more days, mostly to work in the nearby villages. Among the *sadhus, tantriks and bauls.* All those occultists. Found in plenty in the nearby villages of Shantiniketan. The barren red earth bred them in abundance. Leslie would be filming their interviews and record their ways of life in his camera. He would be away most of the time, I would be studying most of the time. A few rare green moments on the red earth.

That evening, in one such moment, I told him about Mukul. In brief. His problem and the way I solved it.

'You are brilliant, Lucie. I'd not have found out such a fantastic solution so quickly.'

'Can't say fantastic. It is just temporary,' I said looking at the flying street lights through the car window. Today Leslie had come in Mr Ganguly's fiat. We were moving around aimlessly in that.

'And nothing temporary can be fantastic, eh?' he sounded a bit ironical.

We remained silent for some time with a silent presence of a third person in between us. Then Leslie said, 'Let us go to his place once. I can offer them enough money and it can work. What do you say?'

Suddenly I smelt money, the smell of new bank notes, and my very dear mesmerising male-musk was overshadowed.

'Money can change minds. Temporarily,' I replied.

'We may try. But Lucie why are we talking only about Mukul? Why not talk something about us? We met after a long time. Like to go to a restaurant?'

'Oh no Lessy, please excuse me today. I've got to go and study.'

'What do you mean? The whole day you remained invisible and now . . .'

'Now, I am untouchable. Touch me not.' But he touched. He pulled over, rolled up the car window and holding me tight against him he fondled my lips with his. It did not last as long as it used to. He started the car soon.

'It was so different, Lucie.' He seemed to be quite dissatisfied. I felt hollow like the bamboo stem.

'I think you are losing your temporary interest in me,' I uttered bitterly.

'Oh dear.' He put his left arm around me. A warm arm. Armed with love and security. 'It seems you are far too disturbed by that boy.'

'Will you tell me what was the difference? I didn't feel any.'

'You are crazy.'

'Yes, I am. Please.'

'Something was amiss. You can feel it. Difficult to explain.' He was trying hard. 'Your body is always so soft. Today it was a bit stiff. It seemed you resisted me.'

'Absurd. I want you more than you want me.'

This argument was not going to end soon, I knew. I bade him goodnight and departed for the land of art and artists. So far life had been like this red rugged plain of Shantiniketan. Plainly created, with a few trees and bushes scattered here and there. A few flowery' touch. That easy landscape of my life had completely changed overnight. So many incidents, so many experiences, so many feelings, all squeezed into a small period of time. *A poem of Tagore written on a grain of rice. Or a more modern version of that, a microchip.*

Dr Sen called us to his chamber the day after next. In the meantime, Mom advised me to cut off my white connection. Joy was disappointed to learn about my inability to come to Calcutta due to my exams. And I could not find any way to settle Mukul, the way I wanted to plant a seedling. So our three heads met together. Dark, grey and sunny. In the doctor's chamber. Leslie said that somebody should go to Mukul's home at once. To get an idea about his family. To decide on the course of any future action. Surprisingly, Dr Sen was also thinking on the same lines.

He had already collected a lot of information about his village and his home. He wanted to send one of his officials, Mr Kundu, who hailed from a small town very close to Mukul's village. I wanted to see it myself. In this matter, I just could not depend on anybody.

'What about your exam?' Leslie wanted to dissuade me. 'I still have two days. Tomorrow we can go,' I said.

After a lot of discussion, it was decided I would go with the official. It was decided to keep Leslie out of it as his presence would perhaps create unnecessary curiosity and the real purpose would be lost. Leslie was not very happy to be left out. But accepted it with a resigned smile. Mukul was not informed about it.

We reached the village around ten in the morning. It was a typical village on the border of Bengal and Bihar. Rugged terrain, fields of corn, pieces of farmland with stubborn stubble and a few struggling shacks with broken windows, leaking tiles and a few thatched Third World cottages. A dream of California and Australia is much nearer to me than this place, a few kilometres away. It had been so always, even before Leslie's presence in my life. Are dreams closer than reality? And why only me? Deepa, Nandan, Dr Sen. Who among them is closer to this village, dressed in natural tatters and shattered with poverty? Even Mukul!. Was it only his apathy towards his cruel mother or was it that he had developed a distance from his native place after getting a taste of the city's varieties? Apart from the cruelty of a stepmother, what novelty could this place offer to him? Rusty dust and roasting heat, drying-up wells and the wrinkled face of the mother earth? I noticed : Time is almost static here. Change is a stranger. Few things are short-lived, including Pandora's hope. The reality behind our dream civilisation. It is like the skeleton inside our body. We know it is there, and we try to forget it. Yet, it lasts much longer than our dream body and short-lived youthful appearance.

Yes, now I realise Leslie's view of life. Anything temporary, anything short-lived is not worthless. Transitory life is so much dearer than the perpetual nothingness before and after that.

We reached Mukul's house after asking a few people. A roof of tiles. A body of bricks. In a better condition than most of the others. His father must be earning well in the Middle East, I thought. The door was open. A few chickens were pecking at some grain. My companion called out, 'Anybody home?'

A woman came out. She was holding a child, half-sitting on the curve of her waist on the left side. A running nose. A miserable thatch on his head. A few dried-up tear tracks on the cheeks. Her body was a bit bent on the right side to keep the balance. She was young. In her late twenties, perhaps.

'My brother has gone to work. No male member in the house. You come afterwards,' she informed even without our asking anything.

'We have come to talk to you,' I said.

'I don't know anything about voting cards or counting of male and female members. Only my brother knows,' she said. Another woman, almost her age, came out with two turmeric-yellow hands and a vermilion-red parting in her coal-black hair. Her eyes were moons in the afternoon sky. A life trapped in the rut. Her brother's wife. I guessed,

'We want to talk about Mukul.'

The first woman was almost startled. Then, changed her expression of shocked bewilderment into innocent ignorance. She was an actress.

'Which Mukul? We have four Mukuls in our village. Which one do you want to meet, Bagdi, Nayek or . . .'

'I'm talking about your son Mukul.'

'I have only one son. Keshta. See.' She showed the boy she was holding.

'Don't you have any stepson named Mukul?' I doubted if had come to the house we had been looking for. She remained silent for a few minutes. The other lady went inside, as silently as she had come out, a few minutes ago. Mr Kundu repeated the question.

'Fucking wretch. Evil spirit. Why are you asking about him?' The language, the expression belonged as if to a different plane or a different planet. I was not at all used to hearing such filthy dialogues. Mr Kundu took charge of the situation, 'Do you know he is sick and lying in a hospital?'

'Deserves it. Stole our money and ran away from home. That son of a bitch. God has taught him a good lesson. Now, when he comes back he will be cut to shape.'

'Won't you go to see him?' my companion asked. I didn't like to speak to her.

'I give a damn for his sickness. He'll come back on his own. Who'll keep such a rotten egg?'

My companion asked her where her brother would be available and got an idea about the construction site.

It was away from the village, in the town where the official lived. We found out the man. In his thirties. Short and stocky. A few parallel wrinkles on his forehead. The face was as stiff and baked as a brick. He, with the others, was mixing cement and stone in a crusher. The sound was deafening. Mr Kundu took him away, offered him a cigarette at my instance. White puffs of smoke covered his brick face. We asked him if he could come with us to bring Mukul home from the hospital. He didn't even ask why Mukul had been at the hospital.

'That rotten brat. Left home without a word. Months ago. Now he is in trouble, wants to come back. Eh?'

'He is just a child!' I couldn't help saying.

'Child! At his age I used to earn half the income of my family. Child! He doesn't want to work. I used to bring him here and half the day he used to spend, peeping into that food joint to watch TV. And very obstinate. Even if you beat him, thrash him to a pulp, he would go on his own frigging way.' He took two long puffs and threw the stub away. 'Send him back here. But nail it into his head that he must be a good boy and obey us, if he has to stay here with us. He can't have his own rotten way,' he announced after a brief pause.

'Must he work with you here? He is too tender for that,' I said.

His charcoal-eyes smouldered in anger.

'We have our own standards, Memsahib. We are poor. If he stays with us he has to work for his food.' The rude words spouted from his wide mouth.

'Doesn't his father send money for him?' I asked.

'Who the hell are you to question me? I can do anything with our money, with our child. Mind your own business. We may be poor, but we are not your slaves.'

He started walking back to the crusher. Mr Kundu walked fast and caught up with him. As I made a sign to. him, he showed our trump card to that man, 'Listen, what if we pay for the boy's food and school?'

The brown hairy legs with cracks and scars stopped immediately. He turned around with. charcoal on fire. Looking for more fuel.

'Money. You will give money for him. How much?'

'Say five hundred a month.' The bad-tempered brick face got plastered and painted with 'distemper' decency. He grinned showing his jaundice-coloured teeth and shaking his flabby lips.

'If he works here regularly, he would get not less than seven hundred a month. Can't settle for anything less than that.'

'All right.'

'Must pay in advance.'

'Yes.'

'Done. You send the boy here. We shall take care of him.' His tone changed suddenly. 'After all he belongs to us. All motherless children are a bit difficult. We'll handle it with care. Don't worry.' He shook one earthworm off his leg. Trampled upon it again and again, upon the writhing body, till it was crushed completely. My flesh crept and I retched.

We came back from the village before lunchtime. Went straight to the hospital. Dr Sen listened to the factual description given by Mr Kundu. I did not feel like talking. Dr Sen asked me, 'Then we should send Mukul there? What do you say, Lucie?'

'He will not be happy.'

'He will be safe. He doesn't have to drift around.'

I had a serious doubt how safe he would be there.

Dr Sen said to Mr Kundu, 'You better take him this evening only. He is getting bored in the hospital. This morning he went to the local market to purchase chocolates and a ball. And he has been bouncing the ball in the garden, ever since.'

A pricking sliver in my mind. Silent haemorrhage. I met Mukul. He was playing with the ball in the lawn. He flashed a smile and came running to me. I kissed his hands. Bent down and hugged him. No ceremonious farewell to innocent childhood. Mukul was, however not an epitome of childhood for me, he was the symbol of love. My first love. I could not talk to him today. I could not even look at him directly. I escaped his glass-bead eyes, reflecting my cowardly helplessness. In the porch, I saw Leslie talking with Dr Sen. He seemed satisfied that Mukul would be going home. Would it be his home? We purchased a few things for him and gave the stuffed bag to the doctor.

A late lunch with Leslie in a less crowded restaurant was insipid. At least for me. Leslie tried to convince me that this was the only way Mukul could be settled.

'After all, he belongs to those people, that family.'

'No, he does not. But he will, if he is left with them.' I thought to myself and said, 'Nobody cares for him there.'

'Now that they are getting money, they will. These suckabuck schleppers!' He spoke with disdain.

'Monetary influence is momentary.' In my mind, I thought. How long could we continue this shielding act with money against those 'suckabuck schleppers'! I would go, Leslie would go, and if they ill-treated him we wouldn't even know.

'Maybe, his father will come back soon and things will change.' He tried to comfort me with reason. I remained silent. I nibbled at the sandwich and thought about the cactus language of his stepmother and the rude manners of his uncle. The whole world turned tasteless in my mouth. I saw that crushed lump of the earthworm on my plate and could not eat anything. For the time being, I accepted the decision as a temporary one and decided that after my theory exam I would find some other alternative.

After lunch, I went back to my hostel to study. No doubt, I could not concentrate properly. For the first time, life meant so much more than a few black and white words printed in the books. Deepa was also studying at her table. By now our friends had come to know about his return and had accepted that we were closer. How close they didn't know exactly and each guessed in his or her own way. Deepa looked at me and commented philosophically,

'You are learning more from life now than from these books, I believe.'

I did not reply. So she added on, 'There's nothing wrong. I have gone through this stage already. Only the time is not proper. It is exam time. One needs a little less disturbance.' She stopped again and waited for a reply. I didn't wish to open my mouth.

She now sounded a bit ironic, 'Besides, with such a Casanova foreigner, feelings of uncertainty and insecurity are also quite a bother, aren't they?' now she asked directly so that I would be forced to answer something. I told her my true feelings.

'It's got nothing to do with Leslie. It is Mukul.'

'Mukul! Yes, I forgot to ask you what happened to him. Got so busy with exams and study and what not.'

'He doesn't have a shelter. We've been forced to send him to his stepmother.'

We then discussed the situation for some time. Rani came and joined us. She was feeling great nowadays. Her parents had come to visit her. They had brought the great news that her marriage had been settled. The boy was an engineer in one of the multinational companies in Dhaka. All set to go to a 'foreign country' soon. The wedding would take place before that. After Rani's exam. Both Rani and Deepa felt the correct thing had been done about Mukul. What else could be the alternative, they asked me. I could not answer. But my mind was dreaming. A shelter for a green innocence with two loving hearts together. This was my way to survive. With the shield of a dream. Perhaps, it is true for almost all. Our soul, covered with scratch-prone reality, would be bared and wounded every moment if it is not protected by the lining of dreams. Dreams and hope.

Leslie came to my hostel in the evening. He was worried about me. We walked down towards the railway track, hand in hand. Now that everybody knew about us, I felt free about moving around with him. I had also realised Leslie's angle of thinking about short-lived and long-lived feeling and relationship. I didn't think much about the future. My exam, including the practical assignment, would be over in a few days' time. Leslie's stay at Shantiniketan was to be even shorter. Exactly how long he could not say. The perfect Leslie way. I did not want to think of what would happen after this time was over. My present was filled with too much pleasure and pain to think anything about the future. I was only aware that I was very happy to get into the web of a universal feeling called love. And love is a timeless thing, with no past, no present and no future.

On the way we didn't speak much. Near the track, we sat on a hard rock. The two parallel lines. Never meeting each other. Like life and dreams running, side by side. They should never meet. The reality rail would be derailed. A new track, by the side of the old one, was under, preparation. The labourers were going away as darkness was closing in. Leslie held my hand and smiled, as the last one of them left with his small basket on his head.

'I never imagined I'd have such unique dates.'

'Why? Did you always have it on the sea?'

'I wish I had! No such luck for that matter.' He shrugged his shoulders.

'You mean they were all city lights?'

Henodded smilingly and started twisting my forelocks round his fingers. His favourite activity.

'Must have dazzled you enough. Why with a firefly then . . . ?'

'Because it has fire. It is natural. I've always been crazy for natural things.'

'You were in the forests . . .'

'Hey, natural does not mean savage.'

'Yes. You are right. Mukul is natural and we have handed him over to some savages.'

Leslie took out a pack of cigarettes and lit one. 'I see. You are still thinking about the boy?'

'I just can't help it.'

Darkness was setting in. The area was almost empty. One goods train passed along the track. Very long train. Deafening metallic sound. Sound of speed. Sound of monotonous speed. But when it faded into the distance, a refrain of a nostalgic piece of music sounded and resounded all over. Leslie gave me a loose hug.

'Can't you think about us and only us, when we are together?'

I wanted to say that could we have been together but for that boy? Could we have known each other but for the boy? I managed to say, 'Lessy, we owe our love to him, don't we?'

'Don't be so sentimental, Lucie.' A very cold tone came out from within his very warm body, throbbing against mine. He kissed my lips softly, a comforting gesture. Yet, I didn't get any comfort.

He rested his head on my shoulder and said, 'Let us go to my cottage today. I've had enough of moonlight. Let me enjoy some sunlight, Will you? You will then forget all these small trivial things. You will have the best dream of your life. You could never have dreamt such a dream ever.' He kissed my neck with sunny warmth. I did not melt though.

'Lessy. Please, not now. Please think seriously about Mukul.'

'Lucie, you always think about the boy, nowadays. I feel neglected.'

Really, he could not be neglected. How could he be? I imagined some huge balance. On one side, six feet two inches tall, strong and striking youth with Grecian perfection, aquamarine charm, and mesmerising persuasion. On the other side, the terracotta imperfection, with a small flat nose, fragile glass-bead eyes, with helplessness and deprivation. How could the second outweigh the first one?

At night of course, that small stature outgrew its size. I dreamt that Mukul, about the size of a small housefly, was in front of the New Empire State Building. Then, he started growing and grew taller and even taller, and the sky-kissing human insolence got hidden behind the colossal human helplessness. I could not sleep properly, neither could I study properly. My memorable moments with Leslie lost their magic touch. *A sitar with two strings. The missing third causing a mess of the music. We were a bit out of tune.* I didn't like it. I never wanted to have it this way. But things were out of my control. The next time, when we met in the study of our library, we related to each other like the front and back covers of a book. An ocean of words in between, but distinctly distant.

V

The Homeless

AN UNEXPECTED and unusual call from Leslie disturbed my preparation for the exam.

'Tomorrow is your exam. I think you should concentrate. Already, you've had enough disturbances. Don't want to disturb you further. See you tomorrow.'

I didn't like the tone in his voice. I've sent Mukul to some hell. And where am I sending my love? I thought. After a short struggle with the books and notes, I went out on my bicycle to Leslie's place. I was not sure he would be there. Yet, I tried my luck. This was the first time I was going to his place on my own, all alone. If he was there it would be a surprise for him. Would he like it? How much? Would we find our lost tune? What if he took me in this time? Mom said, *'Men lose interest if they know too much about a woman.'* With all kinds of doubts and fears gnawing at my mind, I opened the fence gate and entered with my cycle to see a crowded verandah. Leslie and Madam· Maria were sitting on the rocking chairs. She was reading out something. Her eyes were on the pages of the book. Leslie was sitting facing her and his broad back was towards me. I hesitated for a few seconds. I was even considering going back in silence. It was already half dark. The verandah was about fifty metres away. The premise was not well lit:

The light of the verandah was not very bright and complemented my' mood: I could sneak out. Because I knew today was not the day to restore the lost tune. But before I could make up my mind, Leslie turned round. As if he felt some presence, sensed my smell.

'Who's there?' his vibrating voice gave me the usual goose bumps. Next, he came down quickly near me. 'Lucie! How come . . . ?'

'Am I disturbing you?' I whispered.

'Don't be silly. I just can't imagine . . .' I couldn't see the lines of his face in the darkness but his voice sounded happy and excited. 'Come on in.'

'I don't think you have a third rocking chair. How would you accommodate me?' I asked in a low voice and he replied softly, 'Very easy. On my knees.' We held each other's hand and went to the verandah. Maria was inquisitive and when she saw me I could definitely say, she felt annoyed. The square face turned rectangular. I saw a bottle of drinks and two glasses on the table. They were drinking.

'Oh hello! How're you?' she said with a forced smile on her lips.

'Fine, thank you, madam. Good evening.'

Leslie, in the meantime, brought one stool from the room and sat on that. I sat on the chair.

'Bring one more glass, Leslie.' Maria was courteous.

'Oh, no thanks. I won't drink.'

'You don't, I believe, do you?'

'Occasionally. In Goa at parties, during Christmas or the New Year.'

'Are you a Christian?'

'My mother is.'

'And your father is not?'

Leslie, perhaps, understood my uneasiness and asked, 'Do you want some coffee? The kettle is on.'

'Oh, thanks.'

'Why don't you go inside and help yourself?' Leslie said with a twinkle in his eye and helped me out of the uneasy situation. When I came back with the coffee after a deliberate delay, I saw both their heads were almost touching each other on something, over the table.

I took my seat. Madam Maria looked up.

'I am getting some lessons of English from Leslie, you see. My English is not good. Just okay. Here I find difficulty to talk to people. To explain things, you see. I also want to work in America. So, I must know good English, you see. Leslie is very kind to give me some time and teach me English.'

Leslie never told me this. I felt hurt. The coffee tasted bitingly bitter.

'I am sorry. I didn't mean to disturb you in the middle of a lesson. I had no idea.' I got up from the chair and turned to go back, when Leslie called out, Wait, wait.' Then he came near me and said, 'Our lesson will be over in another twenty minutes or so. Why don't you go inside and watch TV? Then, we shall go out for dinner.'

In white custom it was quite all right. But to Indian tradition, it sounded quite rude to invite only one to dinner in the presence of another. So, I had to say in spite of the possibility of the crowding presence of a third one.

'Will you come with us, madam?'

'Thank you. It is a pleasure. I just get bored here. Classes and library. And nothing more special, you see. Sometimes, a visit to Professor Pierre's studio. That's all. The movies they show and the dramas they stage are mostly in Bengali. No Internet connection available. Really very dull. I escaped twice to Calcutta. There I meet many Italian people, you see.

'You can go hiking on weekends. Nature is beautiful in this area,' Leslie suggested. She did not like the idea much though.

'Dear Leslie, I'm no great nature lover like you. I like to socialise, you see. Mixing with people, discussion, things like that.' As she was not very fluent with English, she supplemented her talk with a lot of expressions on her pretty square face. Eyebrows danced, eyes fluttered, lips pouted.

A dinner, with three at the table. I never liked the idea. Yet, I did not want to go back to the hostel either. I would not be able to concentrate on the books, I was sure. So, I went inside Leslie's bachelor's den and started viewing TV and reviewing the watch every minute. Leslie kept coming in every now and then for taking pen, notebook, water, paper, and for taking a little care of me, with gentle caresses. Every time I got a wine-smelling, love-smelling delicious kiss. In that room and later at the dinner· table, sitting with him and Madam Maria, for the first time I wondered how the mere presence of a third person could actually enliven a stagnating friendship, stimulate a staling relationship, and straighten up a sagging love saga. At the restaurant, with legs playing footsie under the table and eyes plunging into each other's depth, we felt happy again, after quite some time. Leslie gave the good news that evening. He would be celebrating his twenty-fourth birthday, the next Monday. Luckily, it would be the last day of my theory papers. Madam Maria wanted a big party and Leslie promised it.'

After a couple of days, when one more exam was over, I was not feeling very satisfied. As expected or feared, I did not fare well. Slowly, I walked towards my hostel and did not accompany the others who were going to the dining hall for lunch. I did not feel hungry. What would happen after exams? After Leslie's exit? I tried to visualise the life ahead of me, when I saw a still life in front of me. Under the mango tree of our hostel premises, with broken glassy pieces of sunshine on the body and an unbroken solid shadow on the face. A life without life. Mukul saw me and came running. He hugged me tightly, started rubbing his lightless face on my chest and an uncontrollable sob oozed out from his young, innocent soul. I stroked his spiky hair. I did not talk for a couple of minutes and only felt the warmth of his tears on my motherly bosom. The gatekeeper under the shed, was staring at us. Although Mukul's tears were filtering through my senses, deep. down into my heart, strangely enough I was feeling relieved to see him again. Out of that hellhole, into my arms. I got rid of that pricking guilt of sending him back to his unfeeling family. I allowed the first burst of pent-up pain to slowly subside. Then, I called him in a low voice, 'Mukul, you are a good boy. Don't cry anymore, dear.'

He loosened the hug. Looked up at me. His eyes were washed clean. A wet whiteness. And a little above that, the reddish brown scab, carrying the tale of a colourful love.

'What's the matter Mukul?'

'Don't send me there, Didi. They kept me locked in a room, did not give me any food.'.

'All these days?' he nodded. 'Come with me.' I took him to my room. As he was a small boy of only ten, a few minutes inside wouldn't matter. I called our room attendant and requested her to bring my lunch to my room today as I was not feeling well enough to go to the dining hall. I paid her a little tip for the extra work.

Mukul described slowly the story of the last few days. They abused, they scolded. They told him, 'Do you really think they'll be paying for you every month? We don't live in a fool's paradise. They have paid once and never will they come again.' They inflicted their delayed punishment on him for his leaving home, by locking him in a room without food and water. His uncle's wife gave him water and a handful of rice and *dal* on the quiet. Mukul informed her, that she was very gentle by nature. That's why she, too, was regularly tortured by them. I remembered the blank face with a big red bindi on the forehead and a just-don't-know-what-to-do look in her watery eyes. She came, she saw us and went back very silently. A typical Indian village woman. A gentle, tolerant, fruitful tree. Inured to suffering.

Mukul washed and cleaned up. I gave him one of my T-shirts. It was quite loose on him. He wore one of my shorts too, which looked oversized on him. He was ravenous and when food came he gobbled it all up in a couple of minutes. Then, he flaked out on my bed. I had a few biscuits and fruits. I looked at the huddled small body, surrendered to a peaceful rest. The kind he had got used to, in the hospital for nearly twenty days and which he had not got for the last couple of days. A checkmated childhood. How could I save him? I opened my book for my last theory exam, day after tomorrow. I could concentrate immediately. After three hours or so, Deepa's voice brought me back to the earth from the world of Futurism, Cubism and Dadaism.

'Hey Lucie, why on earth is this boy here?'

'Shhh . . . don't shout, please. Let him rest.'

'Nitwit, are you going to keep him here? You will invite trouble for yourself and me too.'

'I'm not going to keep him here. I shall take him away as soon as he gets up.'

'Why is he here? He was sent back to his family!'

'They tortured him badly.'

'But what'll happen to him now? Where will he stay?'

'Certainly not here, dear. Your days in the university may be over soon. You may not continue with the advanced diploma, but I have to be here for my post-graduation, for even research work. I don't want to be in trouble.'

'Don't worry. Just bear with his presence for one more hour.'

Deepa did not seem to be very sure about Mukul. Neither was I. But I had some idea in my mind. I am not the kind to give up easily. In the evening when Mukul got up, I changed and both of us went out.

Just near the gate, I met Leslie. He had come back from his village trip. From his ruffled hair and dusty sneakers it seemed he had just returned. His face looked a bit tanned and when he looked at Mukul, he was stunned. He could not talk for a while. Neither did I. I just gazed at his face which looked so fascinating in his bewilderment. Never before had I seen such an expression on his face.

'Namaskar, Sahib.' Mukul was normal. 'I'm back.' He was grinning.

'What's going on here, Lucie? Will you please tell me?' Leslie asked in an annoyed voice.

'Yes dear, are you coming directly from the village?'

'Yea, I thought I'd pick you up on the way to my place.' I looked at his motorbike under the tree, a few yards away from us. We walked towards it.

'You must be very exhausted and hungry, Lessy. Please, go to your place. I have to go to Dr Sen.'

'Dr Sen. Are you going to request him to admit this boy to his hospital again?'

'No. This time I'll request him to keep him at his home for a few days. As a domestic help. He can do household chores.'

'You are a master of the quick fix. Why has he come back?'

'Long story. I'll tell you later. You need some rest first.' 'Rest! I don't need any rest. I'd rather take him to his village at once. Tell me the address. Whatever might have happened there, it is his home after all. How long are you going to shelter this runaway child? He should get adjusted to reality. He would have perhaps. It is only because you are indulging . . .'

He did not finish the sentence, or could not as he looked into my eyes. Those eyes, perhaps, reminded him that he had been a runaway child himself and was a runaway adult even now. Was he not moving from place to place, person to person, job to job as he was not at peace with himself, as there was no home for him to go back to and relax with his own self? He had been tormented by some abstract liquid dreams, and Mukul, by concrete solid reality. Both were running. For a shelter? Where?

'Where is Dr Sen now? At Home? Or still in the hospital?'

'I'll call at his residence and make sure.'

'Sit behind me. Both of you. You and your man Friday.' He kicked the starter. I thought he would betaking us to our destination, so got ready to go with him. Initially, Mukul was not ready to ride on the motorbike. But I promised his safety. He sat in between Leslie and me and held him tightly. To my utter surprise, Leslie did not take the road to the hospital. His bike flew towards Purvapally. To his cottage. Mukul closed his eyes and giggled and screamed all along, as if he was sitting on a roller coaster. We reached safely and before I could say anything, Leslie declared, 'Don't ask me why I've brought you here. I'm not going to answer. Just get into the kitchen and get me something to eat. I'm going to take a shower.'

The usual, Leslie way of doing things!

I switched on the coffee maker and started preparing some toast and omelette for him. Mukul helped me with his small hands and mature handling of the kitchen work. He washed and cut onions and vegetables very fast. And very happily. With a smile on his face and a light in his eyes. He laid the table also quite nicely. When Leslie came out, we were waiting for him at his small dining table with snacks all laid out. After a thorough bath, his complexion was shining like snow under the sun and blinded my senses. His cheeks were rosier than roses, and a male bluish shade along the jaws did shake me to the roots.

'Do you want anything else Sahib?' Mukul asked.

'I do,' he said looking at me and smiling meaningfully.

'Why don't. you go and bring some flowers from the garden? She has no flower in her hair, you see,' he said to Mukul in broken Bengali.

'Will they allow me to pick? I saw so many beautiful flowers in the garden.'

'Don't pick too many and if somebody tells you anything, tell him you are my guest. Okay?'

Mukul ran out of the room and I ran into Leslie's arms. The next few seconds nothing existed for me,—the world, the worries, the wanderings. I changed into a dream, the world would have liked to cherish.

Mukul came back with a bunch of flowers and a few leaves. One flower he wanted to put in my hair. Leslie took it from him, he was still holding me in his arms, a little loosely.

'Give it to me,' Mukul shouted, stretching his arm. The flower was out of his reach. He pleaded, 'Give it to me Sahib, that's for Didi.'

'I know.' Leslie put it in my hair, just behind the right ear, and held my chin up for a better view. His eyes showered honey. I glanced at Mukul. His heavy eyelids looked much heavier. I took one flower from the bunch and went near him, so that he could put this one in my hair.

He shook his head, 'You look great with that one. This is for decorating the table.' His words were moist.'

He then moved quickly to the shelf and got hold of a cocktail glass, very beautiful, very fragile, and arranged the rest of the flowers in it. He kept it in the middle of the table, and looked at me with the expectation of getting appropriate appreciation. I kissed his artistic hand and Leslie caressed his bristly head. I gave him a glass of milk, a few pieces of fruitcake and biscuits.

'This boy has a taste for art. His mother must have been artistic,' I said to Leslie and poured a cup of coffee. Mukul sat on the floor cross-legged and started munching biscuits noisily. I put my index finger on my lips and he corrected his action.

'Why don't you ask him to go to the verandah?' Leslie said in an impatient tone. I wondered why, as Mukul had already stopped eating noisily. Yet, I thought Leslie might want some privacy. As I turned to talk to Mukul, I saw his eyes, his glass bead eyes had turned into a mirror, reflecting me as the most. wonderful sight on the earth. At that moment, it was as if the whole of him had got condensed in those two eyes. I could not tell him to go away.

'How do you like the grub?' I asked him and he blinked, resumed eating.

'Do you like to sit on a chair? There are rocking chairs in the verandah. It's fun to sit there,' I suggested.

'I'd rather sit on the floor. It's fine here.' He shook his stubborn head.

So, I started telling Leslie, in brief: the problems in Mukul's stepmother's house. Leslie asked many questions to get a clear picture.

'I mustn't be too late, Lessy. He'll be in trouble.' I finished my neat narration and got up.

'Wait, please, wait a minute, will you?' he was taking the last bite of the cake. Next he put a few sugar cubes in his coffee cup and poured some black coffee.

As he took the first sip, we heard the beeps of the table-clock. It was seven. It would be too late if we did not start straight away.

'Come on Mukul, we mustn't be late.'

Mukul got up, shook off the bits of biscuits and cakes from his body and clothes and went out humming a Bengali folksong:

Life is so short, oh dear, why is life so short? The world is so big, oh dear, we drift apart.

I hurriedly followed him. There was a sharp tug at my *anchal.* I was about to fall. Leslie came up and held me in his shielding arms.

'Where are you going? Why disturb the doctor, time and again? He has helped us a lot. We shouldn't take advantage of his goodness.' He fingered my forelocks gingerly. He narrowed his eyes as if examining me like a piece of art and finally opened his mouth to speak. 'Let him stay with me, here, for a couple of days, till we find out something better. He can sleep in the storeroom. There are practically no stores.'

'Are you serious?' I could not believe my ears.

'Yes I am.' A shooting smile annihilating all hurriedness.

A pleasure-paralysed moment. Then, with two wings in my heart and a lump in my throat, I threw my arms around his neck, stood high on my tiptoes and kissed his smile.

'Thank you very much, Lessy. You are marvellous.' My eyes and voice got a little damp as I was more than overwhelmed by this, the easiest and the best solution ·of my problem. In my deepest consciousness, I always wanted it, but it had never surfaced as it seemed to be too impossible.

'Oh dear! What a spontaneous reaction. You sure love that boy more than me,' Leslie said.

'This is the first time I kissed a man.'

'Strange. What about your childhood sweetheart?'

'It was a child I kissed then, not a man.'

Mukul's first reaction was not ecstatic. He thought for a while. Then asked me, 'Can't you take me with you?'

'No Mukul, that's a girls' hostel. Boys are not allowed there,' I explained. He nodded as if he appreciated the fact. 'Be here and help the Sahib with his daily chores, will you?'

'I'll do all his work as you say. I'll wash his clothes, iron them, clean the dishes and scrub the floor.'

'Not so much of hard work dear, just a little help when he works.'

'No problem. I can do all. I can massage very well too. With coconut oil and a tiny chunk of camphor in it. It would be so soothing. And the smell would be so beautiful. My mother used to massage me with it. The scented oil.'

His eyes reflected an aromatic memory of his mother. I saw the whites of his eyes dilate. My senses got filled and sedated by the scent of camphor. I thought of his mother whose camphor existence had evaporated, only the smell still lingered in the memory. He wiped his eyes and caught hold of my hand.

'Why don't you stay with us too? It would be fun.' His eyes had started dreaming. Who could say that just less than twenty-four hours ago, he was in the clutches of merciless cruelty?

'You love this boy. You should accept his proposal,' Leslie quipped. 'And how are you so sure that I won't be cruel with him? Better be here to make sure.'

I had to convince Mukul with both facts and fibs before I could finally leave the place. Mukul went out and brought a rickshaw for me. I came back to the hostel with a chandelier in my heart.

After two days, my theory papers were all over. It was party time. A very big day. Leslie's birthday. In my mind I thanked his parents for creating such an exquisite piece of perfect manly grace. I thanked Mukul for bringing him into my life. I had my exam till one o'clock. After that we had to go to our respective professors to fix the schedule for practical exams. We had some liberty and choice in selecting days and topics. Everything was over by four. I could not help arrange the party. There would be, of course no dearth of friends and girls for that matter I knew. The loss would be mine. The party was to be held in a hotel, in the adjacent town. A big hall with red carpets and blue chandeliers. Flowery decorations. Deepa, Nandan, the Austrian girl, all were invited. Rani missed the big occasion as she was out of station with a team of singers and dancers for a national cultural meet.

I was getting dressed in my usual glad rags, a gorgeous sari with gold work and a sequinned choli, but Deepa suggested that in a foreigner's birthday party, we should wear western dresses. I did not have any formal western dress with me here. We were used to casual clothes for everyday wear and beautiful silk saris or *salwar-kurtas* for formal occasions. I had a couple of evening lame dresses for parties lying with Mom at Goa. There, at parties, formal western dresses were commonly worn by most of the people. But in Shantiniketan, even in a foreigner's party so far, we had been wearing our national dress. This time, Deepa thought western style clothes would be more appropriate.

'This is a special occasion. Earlier we attended the parties only as guests. This time it is your boyfriend's birthday party. We must try and impress him,' Deepa argued.

'By wearing a Western dress? Ridiculous.'

'By showing our interest in his culture and customs,' Deepa concluded. Next, she borrowed two beautiful evening dresses from some Nepalese girls. One of our hostel mates, who was deft in make-up techniques was called in by Deepa, the dynamic damsel. I hardly used make-up, only a touch of kohl in my eyes, and sometimes a bindi in between my eyebrows. Today, our make-up girl did something to my face and I could hardly recognise myself in the mirror. Deepa seemed very pleased, though.

'You are looking just marvellous, Lucie. Leslie will not be able to take his eyes off you.'

'Will he recognise me in the first place?' I expressed my astonishment.

Deepa was looking great, no doubt. But it was a strange feeling as if we were going to stage a drama, all decked out. Nandan came formally dressed. He had arranged for a jeep to take us to the hotel. He appreciated our make-up very much. I wanted to give him some time alone with Deepa, so I left them alone in the visiting room. Back in my room alone, I felt like rubbing off the make-up, but fearing it might make it worse I let it be as it was. The party was supposed to start at seven. But we were quite late.

'Boys should learn to wait. They sometimes take us for granted,' Deepa said in her self-assured way.

Finally, we reached the venue at half past seven. Leslie was right in front of the hotel with Mark, Takahashi and Madam Maria. He was in an exclusive designer Indian kurta and salwar. The western dress seemed wasted on me. Leslie and Mark came up near our jeep. Today, he was without his constant companion, the camcorder. We wished the birthday boy a very happy birthday. He was looking terrific as usual, but I avoided looking into his eyes as I was not very happy with my artificial, made-up appearance.

'You look simply gorgeous today, Desdemona. Out to kill?' Mark's words and his appreciative eyes made me blush. He continued, 'Well, first dance I want to dance with you.'

'I dance better than you Mark.' Nandan was prompt, although he did not know much about dancing. We started walking towards the hall.

'Will there be dancing?' Deepa asked.

'Yea, of course. An American's birthday bash. Without a dance it is incomplete.' Mark smiled. Then, he winked at Leslie and said, 'All the girls should get a chance to be in the arms of our handsome hero and feel satisfied.'

'Can Lucie dance?' Leslie asked Mark, with doubt in his eyes, 'I mean, the Western . . .'

'You bet.' Mark knew me quite well. 'In the drama, Pride and Prejudice, she danced so perfectly.'

'As Elizabeth?' Leslie asked.

'No. She was too young for that role. I think at that time she was only sweet sixteen. She was Lydia. Unfortunately, I was not Wickham.'

We reached the hall. Nicely decorated. Mukul came running but stopped suddenly.

'You look like a film heroine, Didi. I've never seen you like this.'

I caressed him, 'Just once in a while. It's party time. Isn't it?'

He too was wearing a smart outfit. Leslie and I had purchased it for him yesterday especially for this occasion along with some other daily casual wear. Mukul took me to Dr Sen. He was talking with Leslie's landlord, Mr Ganguly and his wife. We were introduced. Fortunately, the old man did not recognise me as the girl who had lost her way and peeped into his house. Mr Ganguly's son, Prateek and his wife Reena were also present. There were our French professor, Mark's girlfriend Miranda and a few other foreign students. Some Indian students working with Dr Bose and assisting Leslie in his work. Dr Bose, however was not present. He did not like parties. A typical old Indian scholar. The party was already on. Drinks were being served. Soft drinks for most of the Indians. A lively background music filled the air. I observed that Madam Maria was clinging to Leslie all the time. Mukul took me to a corner table where gift packets were heaped. I was carrying a packet with me and asked Mukul to give it to his sahib.

'It is a gift from you to your sahib. Okay?'

'What's there in it?' he asked.

'A table lamp. In the shape of a hut. A home.' It was made of lovely seashells. With the memory of sea, with the smell of sea. With the heart of a home.

My big gift pack was carried in by Vikash after some time. It was a Spanish guitar. Vikash, a student of the music department had brought it from Calcutta, on my request. The first day at Leslie's cottage, when I learnt of his broken guitar, I had wanted to present him one as a farewell gift. His birthday preceded the farewell, and I did not want to miss this opportunity. For Leslie it was a big surprise. As usual, he did not say thanks in words, but the aquamarine waves overwhelmed me.

'So, you want me to sing!'

When words dream they make a song. Lyrics are not everyday dialogues. Aren't they real? I wanted Leslie to share the dreams of words. Dreams of sounds. Dreams of love. When sex dreams, it is love. Isn't love as real as sex is?

'Please, sing a song for us now,' I requested. No party or function is complete in Shantiniketan if there is no song sung. Specially, songs of Tagore. Mark had already sung a song of Tagore. Now, it was Leslie's turn.

He started plucking the strings of his new guitar. Every nerve of my body vibrated. *After* a little adjustment here and there on the tuning pegs, he sang a song. A love song with a lovely flowing rhythm.

I just can't breathe without you,
I just can't grow without you . . . . baby . . .

If endless space had a voice it would have been this. Everybody enjoyed it thoroughly. So far, only the eyes were privileged; now the ears too. I noticed a wave of thrill sweep over the girls. They came rushing to Leslie, showering him with praise and appreciation. The bottle of champagne was uncorked and the dancing started. Mark was my first partner. Leslie was with Madam Maria. Deepa and Nandan, Mr and Mrs Ganguly, junior and senior, and other pairs were on the floor. Dr Sen was sitting with Mukul and Takahashi did not join. They were holding on to their drinks.

Mark brought his face near me and said, 'Are you in love with that lady-killer, Lucie? You are too intelligent a girl to make such a mistake, yet I'd like to warn you dear, killing ladies is his hobby as well as passion.'

'You know something? The arm of love is longer and stronger than that of the law. When a killer is finally caught in love-net, he becomes a lifer.' I always enjoyed outwitting people with a short but smart answer. I was small mouthed indeed, but not a mush mouth. Mark laughed at the top of his voice at my answer. Leslie looked at us from a distance with Madam Maria in his arms. He was curious. His agile figure was swaying elegantly to the tune of the music. As if the music had a body of its own.

'You think you'll make him a lifer?' Mark asked me directly, with a sarcastic smile.

'I didn't say that. Somebody will, someday,' I replied, without a shred of doubt.

Mark was eager to tell me about Leslie and his liberal liaison with the girls, but I said, 'Not interested, Mark. Tell me about you. You and Miranda. She is so beautiful.' 'Beautiful. Yes. But not as sharp as you are. A bit dumb, I'd say.'

'She is in love with you, Mark. And love blunts one's wit, you must admit.'

He nodded, not very enthusiastically, 'Maybe.' And spun me in a sudden whirl. Somehow I kept the balance, threw an annoyed glance at his chuckling face. We had fun, just like we had had when we had done *Othello* and some Tagore's drama together. In Shantiniketan, all through the year dramas and dance dramas were staged, musical nights were arranged. It was always full of cultural activities. I had taken part in many dramas, some of them with Mark. He had a fantastic memory. During our rehearsals, he used to prompt my dialogues many a time.

The music stopped and we stopped to take a break. Nandan came to me and asked me to join their group. A group of foreign girls and a few Indians were clustering around Leslie. I looked

At the corner where Dr Sen was sitting.

'Nandan, will you please excuse me? Doctor Uncle is sitting alone. I should give him company.'

I went near him and said, 'Why are you sitting alone? Come and dance with us.'

'I can't dance at all, dear Lucie. You go. Enjoy yourself. I enjoy watching you.' He sipped the glass of soft drinks. Mukul came running to me from somewhere. He caught hold of my hand and said, 'I'd love to dance with you, Didi. Please.'

With his words, the music started. For the second dance. The couples took positions on the floor. Mark with Miranda, Nandan with the Austrian girl, Deepa with Takahashi, the French professor with Madam Maria . . . I could not see Leslie. I started with my tiny partner. I was teaching him more rather than dancing. He was only interested in spinning together, spinning and spinning and twirling across the floor and in the process, sometimes bumping into others. A bubbly giggle would follow. He stepped on my feet twice. I remembered Joy. I remembered my childhood. Joy could not dance and used to step on my feet, deliberately. I used to push him and he used to clasp my waist tightly, making both of us fall with a thump. With Mukul in my arms, I felt myself in my chirpy childhood. Small hands, small feet, small hopes. I closed my eyes to feel the retrogression of time while still whirling wildly with my partner. I bumped against somebody. My eyes opened. I met my youth. Leslie was standing in front of me. I looked around. I was no more in the hall. It was the corridor outside the hall. The naughty boy had whirled me out of the hall. He was panting, after a lot of dancing and spinning. He was laughing. Holding his head with both hands, he flopped down on the floor. One hand was on his scar. No pain, no suffering. A life, throbbing with vigour and colour. And a pair of throbbing lips wiped off half the colour from my lips.

Leslie took me into the hall, dancing. Mukul came tottering behind us. He had had his quota of dancing. He sat by the side of Dr Sen. We flowed over the carpet.

'Have you taken your parents' blessings today?' I started the talking.

'No, I don't need it.' He was staring at me and did not seem to be interested in talking.

'Then you must ring up right now. Let's go to the hotel lobby.' I slowed down my steps.

He smiled and said, 'I was kidding. They rang me up. Wished me happy birthday. We talked for some time.'

The regular rhythm was restored and a pull brought me closer to him.

'Don't hold me so close please, one may notice.'

'How does it matter?' he wouldn't listen. 'You dance well. I'll train you to do better. How did you learn it?' 'Mom. I mean my mother taught me. In Goa, the Christians dance on special occasions.

'Why are you wearing so much make-up today?'

'They forced me. Am I looking terrible? Should I go and wash my face?'

'Oh no. But you look better the natural way.'

'May I ask you something? Who gave you this Indian outfit? Leena?'

'Feeling jealous?' he enjoyed my blush and said, 'No, darling. This one I purchased myself with Atanu, a student of Dr Bose. There he is sitting. Can't dance. Most of the Indian boys don't dance I see.'

'I thought it'd be a Western affair. I should have been in a sari.'

'Doesn't matter. I've never seen you in an evening wear before. But this one is a bit loose on you.' The most unpleasant thing about Leslie was that he could never flatter.

'This is a borrowed one.'

'I see.' He gave a naughty smile, 'Should have borrowed a mini from Maria. I've never seen your legs.'

Next, he pressed his cheek on mine. A male touch of beard stubble on my cheek. A cologne intoxication in my smell. Over the square shoulder I saw Mukul waving hands at me, jubilantly. Next, he was doing somersaults and cartwheels all over the soft carpet. As unbridled as my love today. For Leslie.

After the music and dance stopped, it was decided to cut the cake. In Bengal one takes *Payas*. *Payas* is a Bengali sweet dish, a must for a birthday or any auspicious occasion. Rice boiled in sweetened creamy milk. But nowadays almost every educated Bengali gets a kick out of cutting a birthday cake. Tradition is out. This was anyway a Western affair. The birthday boy got ready. Girls were surrounding him. Madam Maria was clinging to his arm. I was at a distance talking with Dr Sen and Mukul. The candles on the pinkish strawberry cake were waiting to be lighted.

Leslie called me out, 'Hey Lucie, I've forgotten my lighter, will you get one?'

'I have it, here.' Madam Maria opened her purse. The light in Leslie's eyes were put out. He wanted me by his side, I understood. I went near the side table. Mukul also ran with me. Some long decorative candles were burning on the classy candlesticks. I took one burning candle from the table.

'Excuse me, Madam. Birthday candles we don't light with lighters.' I gave the burning candle to Mukul. He lit all the candles. Quivering flames. Blown off amidst lots of claps. Black faces of white wicks. The 'happy birthday' song. Some flashes of camera. Leslie cut the cake and without a warning, stuffed my mouth with the first slice of cake. My small mouth could allow a portion of it, while the soft cream smeared all over my lips and tip of my nose. A ripple of laughter among the guests. Leslie ate the other half of the slice, smiling sweetly. I turned to go out to wash my face. But a strong hand grabbed my wrist and a deep voice rang out, 'No. Not now. Be here. I have a very important announcement to make.' He handed me a paper napkin. I started wiping off the creamy mess. It was still sticky. Leslie started his announcement. I cut one big slice of cake and gave it to Mukul.

'Ladies and gentlemen, guys and gals, here is an important announcement. Today is my birthday, you all know. But you don't know another very important occasion I am celebrating today.'

I did not pay much attention to all his gimmicks. I cut a few more slices and started giving them to all the girls clustered around Leslie. The boys were at a distance, drinking. Munching snacks.

Leslie continued, 'Yes. A very important one. We are engaged.'

All of a sudden, all the blinking, drinking and clinking stopped. A vibrating vacuum. The blue chandelier of my childhood swayed wildly without the musical noise. I closed my eyes. This time to get plunged into the deep darkness to never come back again. Did I hear correctly? Yes, I did. Leslie repeated his words again. 'We are engaged.'

I stabbed the cake. My existence evaporated. A catatonic trance. For a few seconds, till I felt a familiar touch on my shoulder. Leslie had put his arm around me. I opened my eyes to get splashed by the aquamarine waves.

'We are engaged, friends, Lucie and me. Today is our formal engagement day too.'

For a few seconds, I stood dumbfounded. As if the words did not sink in. As if a bright flashlight fell straight on my eyes, blinding the vision. Then, I closed my eyes. This time to embrace my darling darkness. All my senses were lit up within. I turned into the sparkling, glittering chandelier, of my childhood hanging high and higher from a roofless eternity. A metallic touch on my fingertip brought me back to the earth. Leslie was about to put that blue diamond ring on my ring finger. I looked around. The girls looked like the lightless candles on the birthday cake. Colourful but fused. Confused were the boys. I saw Dr Sen's smiling face and Mukul's blank face. He was happily licking the cream from his small fingers, quite unaware about the shocking announcement. He didn't understand English. Leslie's ring hugged my finger. He brought his face nearer. I saw my aquamarine, deep and calm. But I did not allow him to kiss me. Made a sign to dissuade him. He understood my feelings. He was in India. He kissed my hand with the engagement ring on it. Mark clapped; the first to break an uneasy silence.

'A real bombshell, yea. You people are real smart. Anyway, congratulation.'

Others followed. A pile of congratulations. A few musical, a few prosaic and a few brittle. I looked at the blue stone. Remembered the sea. Remembered Goa. Remembered Mom. And I wanted to be alone. Alone with myself. Whenever I was very happy or very sad, I just wanted to be alone with myself With my God, or dream? Even Leslie would be redundant, perhaps.

Mark proposed a toast to us and one more bottle of champagne fizzed. I had to sip a little at everybody's insistence. Dinner was served. But it seemed the shocking news had filled up half the appetite. Even for me. Dr Sen was so wonderful. He offered his car to us. He would go back with the Gangulys. It was already ten. I asked Deepa to tell the superintendent that I would be back soon. Leslie told her, 'Say one hour. It is our engagement evening. That must be considered.'

'Don't forget the way to the hostel. Will you?' Deepa winked at me. Then she took me to a corner of the hall, away from the others and whispered, 'Hey Small Mouth. Have you kept it under wraps too long? Anyway, I'll deal with you later. Now listen, if you don't want to come tonight, I'll manage.' She showed her thumbs up to Leslie and winked at him.

They all went away leaving the three of us. Mukul started taking the gift packets to the car.

'Did you like it?' Leslie asked me. My eyes answered. 'Are you happy?' Again, my eyes outsmarted my lips. Yet the lips were more fortunate. They got pampered by my fiancé.

'I must claim my engagement kiss now.' Our lips got engaged in their most favourite activity.

Mukul sat in front of the car by the side of the driver. We were at the back. The just-engaged couple. He was restless. Playing with my forelocks. Rubbing his cheek against mine. 'Lessy, should I ask you something?'

'If you're going to ask me why I didn't ask you before, I can't answer. If you ask me, how I was so sure that you wouldn't say no, my reply would be I knew how you felt about me,' the conceited and overconfident voice replied.

'No. I want to know, are you going to break it like another decanter in your hand?'

His hands stopped playing with my forelocks. He stared at me for a few seconds. His eyes decanted love into mine.

Then, he gave a naughty smile, 'Who knows?' He kissed me on my forehead. To fill me with a feel of security. My finger touched his deep dimple. I kissed it fondly.

'I wish they were here. Our parents. I miss them. Don't you?' I said.

'To be very frank, no. You hardly allow me to think about others. You've changed me, you have spoilt me thoroughly.' He kept on fondling me.

'Did you tell them about me, about our relationship?'

'What can I tell them? You never allowed me to-' I covered his mouth with my hand. A comet in my sky and a Milky Way in my heart. I whispered, 'Let this night be ours, Lessy.'

'You mean it? Really? Really?' Feeling my body language he was elated, 'Oh Lucie, darling.' He kissed me on my neck. The goose bumps all over my body burst into twinkling stars in front of my eyes. I felt his body, the body of an engine juddering to life. So was mine.

His voice trembled, 'Yes, we must celebrate. This is our engagement night. Let's enjoy. Let us get crazy.'

He started rubbing his face against my neck and bare shoulder. When we reached Leslie's cottage, both of us were extremely· excited. We were expecting the exploration, the final revelation, the completeness of the relationship. We asked Mukul to bring the packets carefully. We almost ran towards the cottage. His door was not locked. The door was ajar. Leslie flung it open.

They were sitting inside. Mother and daughter. Meera and Leena. And Mrs Ganguly senior. A stormy wind died down abruptly. The moon withered in the sky to look like the dead face of a wilted flower. Leslie and I looked at each other. Two wounded looks. Leena's face was blank. Meera called, 'Well, come on in.' I did not like to step in. But Leslie almost dragged me in.

'Happy birthday and congratulations. Just now Mrs Ganguly informed me about your engagement,' Meera said with a pleasant smile on her face. 'Strange, you didn't invite us.' Now she sounded a bit sour.

'I'll throw another party . . .' Leslie sounded more uneasy than apologetic. I thanked her.

Leena smiled with some effort and said, We came to celebrate your birthday, to give you a surprise. Looks like we are the ones who got the shock. In any case, happy birthday and congratulations.' Her matte lips clipped her words. Her clay eyes looked cracked. She came near Leslie and unwrapped a small gift packet. Took out the gift. She tied it on Leslie's wrist. A gold watch. Lost its touch in a brass moment.

'Who are they?' Mukul asked with innocent curiosity. He had entered the room with quite a few gift packets in his hand. I helped him to stack them on the shelf and then holding his hand quickly went out of the room. Pretending to get more packets. In fact, it was getting suffocating for me there. Out of the room, Mukul came close to me and again asked, 'Who are they Didi?'

'They are your sahib's friends.' Will they stay here?'

'They will. You must behave nicely with them. I must go now.' We picked up the rest of the packets and went inside. All our expectations of unwrapping the packs, seeing the gifts and having fun, were dampened. The evening was full of shocks. Pleasant, unpleasant. Now, those stranger's hands would open the gifts and share gift-wrapped moments with Leslie. *And the greatest gift of my life? When will it be unwrapped? With music and melody?* With disappointment distorting my calm, I stacked the packets neatly on the shelf I looked at his bed, through the door of the living room. A dream buried. A curtain unraised. Mrs Ganguly bade us goodnight and went away.

'So, how was your party?' Meera asked.

'Wonderful,' Leslie said as he loosely spread himself on the sofa. 'You should have told me you were coming. You could have joined the party.' He hung the guitar around his neck and kept on plucking at the strings absent-mindedly, without creating music, making empty sounds.

I could have hung around his neck just like that; just this way those hands could play on my body, pluck my nerves. And the ninth symphony would have been created!

'Doesn't matter,' Meera said and then she looked at me, as I was going near the door to go out, 'Are you going now? So soon? Couldn't we talk for some time? We have not seen much of you.'

'I beg your pardon, madam. But I have to go. I stay in the hostel and can't be late.'

'Oh Leslie, you should have dropped her first at her hostel.' Leena's voice did not sound very normal. But I felt Meera was staring at me. The waning moon in her eyes. No live coals.

'Have you had dinner?' I asked Meera. She gave me a tired smile.

'Thank you. But our host forgot to ask us.' She looked at Leslie from the corner of her eyes. Leslie did not look ashamed.

He just lit a cigarette and asked, 'What would you like to have? I shall try and get something. It is pretty late and you can't expect something good at this hour.' Leslie was not looking at anybody, not even at me. He was feeling disgusted with himself. I realised. His face looked like a disintegrating graphic. I wished to run my fingers through his silky waves. His face would get back its live texture. He would close his eyes and then he would sink his face, the most perfect, the most handsome face in the world in my dove-feathered bosom. A ruffled restlessness, an aerial ecstasy.

'We've had some grub in a nearby open-air restaurant,' Meera informed him in a cold voice.

'Restaurant! My foot. A greasy spoon I'd say,' Leena said. Well. Our train was late. We reached around eight. When we reached here, nobody was in. Even the Gangulys had gone to your party. The servant could not tell us where the party was going on. Neither did he have the key of this cottage. We had to wait in Prateek's house till the Ganguly's came back. We watched TV. Got bored. Went out to have some snacks.'

'I had no idea you would be coming.' White rings of smoke puffed out of his cigarette. *He must be feeling lonely and empty like those puffs. Even with so many people around,* I thought.

'Are you sure you won't have anything?' I asked politely. 'No. Thank you.' Leena's matte lips wore a brittle smile. Well, goodnight then,' I said to them, looked at Leslie.

He did not look at me, took a big drag and threw the stub out through the window. Somewhere in the darkness.

'I shall just drop her and come back,' he said and without looking at me or holding my hand, went out of the room. Mukul was witnessing everything, clinging to me. He went with me to the car and sat with us.

'Where are we going?' Mukul whispered.

'I'm going back to my hostel. You'll come back with Sahib.'

'You were coming with us. You must come with us there.'

'Please Mukul. I can't stay there. You know.' His eyes made the night darker.

When the driver started the car, Leslie lit one more cigarette. He was burning inside, I felt. I took the cigarette from his lips and threw it out of the car window.

'You can't do this to you. Be sensible. Please.' He looked out of the window and shook his head in despair. Now, I ran my fingers through his hair and kissed him.

He rested his head on my shoulder and said, 'I am frustrated. We should have spent the night together. All to ourselves.'

'Don't be upset darling,' I said and pointed at the moon, 'Look, it has kept so many nights reserved for us. This is not the end of the world.' I tried to comfort him.

'I feel frustrated, Lucie.' His wild eyes looked tamed and tired.

'Me too,' I echoed back. 'but this isn't the end of the world.'

'Let us go to a hotel. Please. We must go to a hotel.' He got wild.

'Please Lessy. I can't do it. I can't.'

'Why not? Don't you love me? Don't you?'

'I do. But this is India.'

'So what? I give a damn for what people say. It is our life. It is our relationship. We should do things the way we want to do them.'

'Oh no, please. When you're in water you can't walk. You have to swim. And I love my Indian values.'

The driver announced that we had reached the hostel. We kissed each other goodnight. I saw Mukul had fallen asleep in the front seat. I kissed his forehead and went inside the hostel with a blank feeling. So much had happened in such a short time! An evening studded with engagement rings and ringing happiness. And the happiness stained by the matte lips.

Before going to the room I called mom. As it was quite late at night, the line was clear and I got Mom immediately.

'Hello, Lucie dear, how are you? How was your exam? It ended today I think? The theory part?'

'Mom, I've got engaged today.'

'What? What are you talking about? Will you repeat?' her worried voice rang out. I repeated the words.

'That foreigner boy?'

'Yes, Mom. To Leslie.'

'How could it get so serious? The other day you met Joy and decided to forget about him.' 'Can't explain, Mom.'

'You didn't feel it necessary to inform us?'

'I'm sorry, Mom. It all happened so suddenly. I shall tell you later.'

'Are you happy?'

I could not answer as I was not sure how to name my feeling. Happiness would be too small a word to describe it. Mom interpreted my silence in her own way and asked, 'Are you sure about the boy? About yourself? About your relationship? Do you know enough about him? About his family?' So many difficult questions she threw one after the other.

'I don't know Mom,' I could only express.

'Will you bring him here when you come home after your exam? Or do you want us to come to you? I want to see him. As early as possible. Are you planning to get married soon?'

'I've no idea, Mom. Lessy will tell me.'

'Dear Lucie. What has happened to you and your wit? I see this boy has got you under his thumb.'

I wanted to protest that, in fact, it was love which had got me under its thumb, but could not say so and Mom continued, 'This is not an ideal relationship. I want you to be sensible and act sensibly. Is he too overbearing? You can hardly be happy with such a person. You are too young to judge things.'

Mom sounded so very different. She was talking like a common Indian mother, deeply concerned about the daughter's future. Had I known this woman before? Would I grow up to be a worrying mother too?

The worried mother went on, 'Let us see him. Bring him here. Don't do anything in a hurry. You are only nineteen. Nobody gets married so soon nowadays. Well, love is a great thing. But mostly people don't understand what love is. What they think is love, is not love at all. They run for a mirage and discover hot sand. Get burnt. I don't want you to get hurt.'

Nomother wants her child to get hurt. But can they help it? Didn't Mom hurt me when she took me away from Darjeeling? Or when she sent me away to the hostel? Or when she burnt our house, my home?

Deepa woke me up early next morning. There was a call. The voice I heard, from beyond the other side of the world, it was Joy. His sixth sense had disturbed him.

'Hey Lucie, how are you? Is everything fine?' A pure snow-white shadow of childhood on the blue exuberant youth.

'Yes, fine.'

'I reached London this morning and called you. You were not there. They told me you had a party. Enjoying a lot and forgetting me? Here I am not able to sleep, you know? It is already one in the morning. I'm still wide awake, so I gave you a buzz.'

A block of icy guilt benumbed my senses. What should I answer? How I wanted to tell him about my engagement. We had shared so many emotions and moments together, in the shadow of Kanchenjunga and today he remained unaware about the Kanchenjunga moment of my plain life.

'I wish you could be here.'

'So do I. But you have to wait. Now most probably I'll be coming only after a year or so.'

'Alone?' I wanted some clutches to prop up my conscience. I heard a cheerful laughter of childhood.

'No, a band of blondes will accompany me. You wait and see.'

Joy's banters. So facile. So familiar. So dear. He enquired about my exam; narrated in brief: the situation at Darjeeling; said how much he missed me at the airport while going back, wished me luck and we hung up. A snow-clad sense. A hangover from childhood. I decided to write to him, as it would be much easier to explain things explicitly. Or could I be explicit?

The first two days of my practical exam went well. There was some freedom in fixing the schedule for the practicals. I selected a very tight schedule. So that I could finish all the indoor assignments, within three days and get some free days for Leslie. The lure of a seven-lobed leafed 'laurel' was now paler than the lyrical company of Leslie. In Shantiniketan there is no gold or silver medal. A leaf of Chhatimtree has seven lobes. One such green seven-lobed leaf is presented along with the black and white certificate. At the moment, I craved more for a cosy moment, under the *Chhatim* tree with Leslie than anything else. He had gone to a nearby village for two days with Meera and Leena. In the afternoon I was trying to do some extra work in the studio when Deepa rushed in and said, 'Lucie, he wants to meet you badly. That poor village boy.'

Mukul! Had I forgotten him in the flurry of events and emotions?

'What's the matter?'

'Don't know. He is looking for you a bit desperately.' Deepa sounded a bit disturbed. Her exam was just over and she was about to go home.

She would come back after two months to attend the next session. I· had tentatively decided to join the advanced diploma for another two years, which would endow me with sufficient knowledge in my field. However, 'I'm living only in the moment and for the moment' as Leslie would say.

Packing up for the day, I went back to the hostel. Mukul was sitting under the big mango tree. He came running. There was no light in his face.

'What's wrong?' I stroked his hair. Now, the frizzy crown had got back its original shape and exuberance.

'I won't stay there. They are not good people. Sahib's friends. And the landlords. They call me names. They say I am a bumpkin, a yokel. Call me names in English. I don't know the meaning, but I can make out. I won't stay there.'

'Did Sahib tell you anything?'

'Sahib says nothing to me. Sahib is out of the house most of the time. They ask me to do all the work. I don't mind. But I don't like the way they talk about me.'

'Just a few more days Mukul, then everything will be okay. These people will go away from our life.'

'They are insisting that I should go back home. Even Sahib tells me to go back home. There is no home for me. I won't go back there.'

'Mukul, do you know when your father will come back?' The poor boy had no idea. So, I called Mr Kundu, Dr Sen's assistant with whom I had gone to Mukul's village. He assured me to get the necessary information.

Leslie rang me up late in the evening.

'Missing you badly, Lucie. Haven't seen you for thirty-six hours. It's cruel.'

'Go back thirty-six days. You didn't even know me!'

'That life is now a stranger to me.'

'And those girlies? One is still with you.'

'Come on. You have to get used to the Western way of life. The sooner the better.'

'Leslie's way of life, you mean? Not dreamy, but oh so steamy!'

'Shut up. Are you free tomorrow evening?'

'Yea. For the next two days I'm free. But, Lessy, why is Mukul so upset? He metme today.'

'Leena and Meera are trying to convince· him to go back home. But he is not willing. You see Lucie, everyone is not a dreamer like you. They are down-to-earth people. I can't blame them either. And we shall leave the place in a couple of days, then he has to find out some place. So, it is better that he goes back home. His father may return in a couple of months, then his problems will be over.'

A person, who himself had never wanted a home right from his childhood, was advising another to go home. Why? Did he think the world was so different for two different persons?

I wanted to remind him about his childhood but said something else, 'I shall find out something for him. But till then please don't send him to his stepmother.' I wanted to add, 'For my sake, take care of him. You know how I feel about him.' But I did not.

'Can we talk about us for a change?' He sounded pretty annoyed. After a minute's pause he resumed, 'Come to my place tomorrow. Say around six. See you.' He made a kissing sound and I went to bed somewhat consoled.

After finishing the day's work at the studio I reached Leslie's cottage late, at around 6.30 p.m. Leena opened the door. I couldn't see anybody else. Not even Mukul.

'Mummy and Leslie have gone to Dr Bose. I can't tell when they will be back. You may wait if you like,' she chewed out the words very coldly.

'Thank you. I'll go. Where is Mukul?'

'That yokel you mean? Don't know.' She curled her matte lips. 'The whole day he roams around here and there. Comes home when it is time to go to bed.'

'He is a poor boy, recovering from a serious injury. If you could . . .' I stopped but my eyes implored. 'Can't you be more sympathetic with him?'

'This is not our house. Uncle and Aunty don't like such tramps in their house.' *Yet they housed Leslie. A few wads of notes make all the difference, notes make notables!* I thought bitterly.

Leena went on saying, 'We've heard about the boy from Leslie. You should have insisted that he stays in his own home. That would have been the only permanent solution. This way you are creating a problem for him. We've also tried our best to convince him to go back home. But because of you, he is now dreaming. He is not prepared to accept his real place in society.'

I didn't feel it necessary to reply to any of this snobbish nonsense.

'Why don't you come on in and have some coffee?' Leena suggested, 'I'm getting bored all alone. Aunty's family members have gone to attend some marriage party. There is no electricity so I can't even watch TV.'

In expectation of Leslie's return, I stepped inside. One emergency light was on. Leena poured some coffee from the flask and forced a conversation.

'Have you ever been to America?'

'No.'

'England?'

'No.'

'Any other foreign country?' I shook my head.

'I see. Leslie has visited almost half the world, you know?' I just nodded.

'Don't you feel insecure getting yourself involved with such a lady-killer?'

'No, but I'd be afraid of some killer lady,' I replied and my body language implied. 'I haven't met any such threat at the moment.'

Her ceramic eyes clashed with mine. We sipped coffee in silence. It was getting pretty dark outside. Because of the power failure, the road lights were off and the darkness outside was not a pleasant one.

'I must go. It's getting very dark. Thank you for the coffee.'

'I'm sorry, he is far too neglectful of his fiancée.'

'Don't worry, he is too good to make up for it.' I came out of the room and sped off on my cycle. I was frustrated with Leslie. I was worried about Mukul.

Leslie called me at my hostel around eight thirty. I was about to go to the dining hall. The lounge was not much crowded as half of the girls had already gone for dinner.

'I couldn't make it. Meera changed her programme suddenly. Let's go out for dinner.'

By now I was used to the Leslie way of doing things. But we have to find a way for settling dear Mukul.

VI

The Lost Shadow

WE WENT TO HAVE dinner at our favourite open-air restaurant. Amidst the huddled evergreen trees. With the wild erotic aroma of the mysterious Mahua flowers. The honey of the Mahua is as intoxicating as liqueur. We looked at each other with the Mahua flavour in our eyes. A passionate pastoral tune, of a tribal flute, filled the goblet of space. Delicious delights were served in the platter of the night sky. We were overwhelmed. And I could clearly feel his eyes were dreaming. His fork picked up a neat piece of dream and held it out to me.

'Let us go to Calcutta tomorrow and get married.'

I choked on a harmless piece of food. I coughed and he laughed. The duet was no music but a rapturous warm wind played on the keys of the *Ashok* leaves, Neem and *Krishnachura* leaves. The red dust danced in a whirl. The dry crimson earth smiled through its cracks. Sleepless white flowers echoed the serenade of the night moths. I realised I was not sleeping.

'I'm not kidding. We must make it tomorrow,' his voice came in floating with the summer wind.

'Was that on your mind when you called me?'

'Nope.'

Leslie and his instantaneous decisions! My eyes questioned, 'How tomorrow . . . ?'

'We'll go to a church and get married. Any problem?'

'My parents won't be able to come.'

'Doesn't matter. My parents can't come either.'

'Why such a hurry, Lessy? Are you afraid of losing interest in me, if it is later?'

He glanced at me with the warmth of the south wind in his eyes. The unbearably handsome face looked like a reflection in the still water. If I touched, it might be lost. Yet, I stretched my arm to touch his deep dimple. He held my hand and kissed it.

'I want to live with you. I want to sleep with you. After marriage, you will leave that goddamn hostel of yours and come and live with me, won't you?'

'Yes, yes, yes, yes,' every molecule in me chorused. Yet a niggling doubt pricked.

'Won't you take me with you to America?'

'No, I might take you to your dreamland, perhaps,' he smiled, without taking my words seriously. 'For a dreamland, you don't require any passport, any visa you know. By the way, do you have a passport?'

I had got my passport made last summer when I was in Goa. We were planning to go to our uncle, my mother's brother in Singapore. Leslie informed me that getting a visa would be easier for a girl married to an American citizen.

'So, we meet at the station tomorrow. The early morning train. Okay?'

'Meera and Leena? Are they coming with us?'

'Definitely not. Are you crazy? It is our marriage. I don't want a crowd.'

'In weddings, most people want crowds.'

'Do you?'

'My parents, my grandma, my granny. My very close friends.' I wanted even Joy to be there. Joy, fifteen years old, and his family. We had shared everything together always. Today's Joy would not fit here. With the child Joy, Mukul's face also floated up in my mind.

'Oh Lucie. Lucie. I've got very few days left in India.' His voice sounded as impatient as the hungry nestlings in the spring's nest. And the words pecked at my senses. 'You told me you would be free for the next two days. Let's make the best of it. Tell our parents tonight, if you like.'

But it was to be worse. I informed him about the change in the exam schedule. I had come to know about it in the morning. The guest examiner would be coming the day after next. So, that day and the day after, we would have our practical with him. There would hardly be any time on those two days. But he was thinking about tomorrow. 'Tomorrow, then. We'll come back in the evening.'

The high tide of the aquamarine, silenced all my arguments before they could be voiced. How do I take permission? How do I face the people and the university authorities for such an unconventional, unorthodox action? How do I answer my parents? How can I abruptly land on a new planet? Was my life ready to be launched? With Leslie it had always been blistering speed. If I could not keep up with it, I would be out of his luminous orbit. Swallowed by the black, wallowing in despair. No, my god was with me. My darling dreams. I touched Leslie's hand. Both of us felt a deep urge to grow out of our bodies and in the blind darkness, blend with each other. We could only hold each other's hands tightly and feel the wild dance of our nerves.

The dances went wild and wilder all night. I could not sleep. I did not call Mom as that would upset her and Father. Marriage. It was the last thing on my agenda. Till the other day. '*Yet tomorrow I shall be married!*' No *shehnai,* no party, no rustle of wedding gown, no bustle of people, no jingling jewellery, no flowery fireworks, no aroma of frying oil or smell of crisp gift wrappers, only *alpana* in the eyes, only *mehandi* in the heart, only the fragrance of love. Would it be enough? Indian marriages are always such a grand affair. It is the only adventure in the lacklustre life of a common Indian. In Bengal a traditional marriage ceremony continues for three days. The bride and groom are allowed to sleep together only on the third night of the ceremony. All the elaborate rites and rituals complete an Indian wedding. Like the fantail for a peacock. The excess is the essence of it! And here I would be married. A duet sung without an orchestra. My nerves, however, played an orchestra as I thought about the next night. Oh God! So much! So soon! After tossing about in the bed the whole night, I dozed off at dawn. There was no Deepa or Rani to wake me up. Deepa's exam was over and she had gone home. Rani was staying with her parents in the guest house, out of the campus. I dreamt about Draupadi. There was no Duhshasana, but Leslie's loving hand could not unwind my sari. It grew longer and longer. And still longer. And the dreaminess lingered, even after I opened my eyes. 'Has any man ever been able to unwind the drapery of a woman, with or without love? Has any human being been able to unwind the mystery of love? The more one unwinds, the longer it grows. Draupadi's sari. Dreams. And God.'

I jumped up from the bed. There was hardly any time to get ready, I would get late for the train. In a terrible hurry, I changed my clothes and rushed out of my room. I took my bicycle. There was no time to wait for a rickshaw. So the cycle had to be sacrificed. My cycle stumbled near the gate. Mukul was standing there. As pale as the dead dry leaves. His tears were frozen, it seemed. I got back on my feet. My elbow was bleeding. My hanky covered it. But I did not know how to cover this bare wound, standing in front of me.

In a trembling voice he told me that the Gangulys had asked him to get out. They did not want to see his face in their compound again. So, the last two days he had been on the road. He had tried for a job but did not get any. He could not meet me as I had been busy with my exam. Deepa was not there. Our regular gatekeeper was on leave, the substitute one did not know him. I looked at the boy, the shelter-less shadow, the homeless hollow. His frizzy hair had grown enough. The crest was formed. His glass-bead eyes were no more translucent. They were like a cracked mirror, where I could see the morning ray rebound to blind me for a few seconds.

Then I saw a broken world, a fractured sky and a fragmented land. A fissure growing deep inside. How helpless I felt. A small boy, a small body, a smaller demand. A shelter. And such a big world, an enormous universe is unable to provide one. He stepped into my life with blood and bruise. Gave me love and blossoms and I could not offer him anything. I just wanted to touch him with a magic wand and turn him into a little nothing or into smoke and keep him corked in a bottle. A bottle imp. Away from the unreality of the world. But I had to find a solution, somehow.

At that moment, I had to rush to the station. I carried Mukul with me. At the station, Leslie was waiting for me. The train was not. It was leaving the platform as we entered. Leslie was annoyed, and was dumbfounded when he saw Mukul with me.

'What is he doing here?'

'You people drove him out and you didn't even tell me!' 'Gosh! He went away two days ago on his own, Leena told me last night. She thought he had gone home.' 'You know very well that he will . . .'

'Come off it, Lucie. Enough of it. Shit! The only time I planned something . . . it goes all wrong!'

'We can take the next train, after two hours.'

'What about him?'

'Let me contact Doctor Uncle. He will help us.'

We went to the nearby PCO booth to make a call. But just like the train Dr Sen was also out of reach. He had gone to his village with his family, as his mother was seriously ill. My eyes pleaded with Leslie to take Mukul with us.

'Absurd, Lucie. We're going to get married!'

Yes, we were going to have a home of ours, a shelter of love yet this big world could not provide a small shelter for this little child!

Leslie's angry hand tore off the two tickets into pieces. Then, he flung down the magazine he was holding and hurled the mineral water bottle violently on the railway track. Next it may be his camcorder I feared, and handed him my bottle too. It met the same fate as that of the other. Quickly, I took out my sunglasses from the purse and held them out to him, 'Sorry, there is no glass. But sunglasses. Break them. There will be some music!'

His angry hand immediately snatched the glasses away from mine, but then, he smiled. I laughed. He laughed too. The morning sun laughed in the sky. Mukul laughed. A sort of infected laugh.

'Lessy, see that train is coming. From Calcutta. Let's get into it.'

Leslie's eyes threw a question, as he was too puzzled. 'We'll see the fair in the nearby village. Just two stations away from here. Come on.'

Holding his and Mukul's hand I dashed into the train. I myself felt that our roles were as if interchanged. Who was to know that such a wild girl was hidden inside me? Or was it a hidden urge to avoid a hasty marriage? Without my folks, without frolic or festive feasts. After all, deep inside I was a simple Indian girl. I did not want to let go of the one single opportunity to be in the limelight. To be seen and congratulated by hundreds of people. The common Indian or human psyche. In Bengal, they say, 'There are three occasions in your life—your birth, your death and your wedding, when you are seen by hundreds of people.' A human being can enjoy only one of them in full consciousness. Who would want to miss it? I wanted the whole world to see me by his side in a bride's dress. In my mind, I decided that I would go to Goa just after my practical exam, and get married there.

Both of us remained silent about our failed attempt to get married. We discussed every other thing except that. We enjoyed the fair. Its rustic air.

The carousel, the huge giant wheel. Mukul sat between us and when we reached the top, he threw his arms up in the air. 'Oh the sun is so very near.'

Yet it remained 'untouchable'. There had been a special well in the village, for the untouchables in the olden days. Upper castes would not take water from there. There was a temple. In Indian movies the hero and the heroine, who had families like the Montagues and Capulets, would go to the temple and exchange garlands in front of the idol. The hero would put *sindur* in the parting of her hair. And they would be married. There would be no one else in the temple. Af*ter* marriage, they would sing and dance around the trees. There would be nobody around them.

But in reality, there was hardly any place which was not crowded. The temple was crowded, the steps of the temples were crowded. The path to the temple was crowded with numerous hawkers selling flowers and incense and other titbits. Those films were the dreams of their makers. I never thought of making dreams come true. In fact, I never believed that there could be places like temples or churches or any other place which were exclusively meant for God. Does he not exist in each and every speck of dust, fill each and every inch of space? Then, why insult God by confining Him to some small territories? My god is in me. On the very earth where I stand. Even in dirt and filth. Who else could be so powerful as to be able to create anything? Even dirt and filth. Envy and violence. All we need to meet God, to feel Him, is an island of silence within ourselves.

With my own god surrounding my entity, I came back to Shantiniketan. In the late afternoon. Not married. Leslie came back with a lot of recordings in his camcorder. We went to the hospital to meet Mr Kundu, the office assistant of Dr Sen. He narrated a sad story. 'Mukul's father along with some others was taken to Saudi Arabia by some agency. They duped them after taking them there. He was not given the lucrative job, he had been promised. At present, he was working as a labourer there and trying to collect money to come back home. One man had come back as he had some money of his own. He had told the story to the others. There was very little hope of his coming back to India soon. So Mukul could not possibly go back home, I concluded decisively. Leslie accepted the fact, though a bit reluctantly.

However, he took Mukul with him and assured me that he would talk to the Gangulys and would definitely not permit them to throw him out on the road. We would settle him after my exams were over. I had to concentrate on my practicals for the next two days. A guest examiner will also come on the second day. So, I would not get any time to do anything for Mukul.

My concentration, during the session with the guest examiner, was not up to the mark. Only through instinctive reflexes I scraped through the morning session. During lunch, I tried to contact Leslie but he was not available. After a very busy outdoor session with our exacting guest examiner, I could come back to the hostel only around 10.30 p.m. I could not contact Leslie. There was a continuous busy tone. The phone must be out of order, I concluded as that was a common feature. I rang up Mom to tell her that we would be coming to Goa soon, to get married. One more day with the guest examiner, three more days of practical. One more dissertation.

'I've to oil it for the next few nights.' I told her. Mom listened and commented, 'Well after all, it is your life. You should know how best to live it.'

The night was dreamless. There were memories and thoughts of Mom, our home, our life in Darjeeling. *The antiques and the antics.* Antiques were lost in the flame. Antics were also not intact. Father was a subdued man after the Sheila Aunty episode; if not a changed one altogether. Sheila Aunty, however, had been separated from her husband, Ramesh Uncle a couple of years ago. Where she went and whom she selected this time, to get away from the selfish, fishy businessman I did not know. I had got only the news headlines the other day from mom and not the news story. Nobody was interested in the unhappy woman. Mom, Aunty, Joy, nobody. It would bring many unpleasant memories with it. However now I sympathise with that unfortunate lady, sincerely. Life treated her in a miserly fashion in spite of blessing her with a piggybank husband. A man and a woman. Their relationship. It had been a mystery at that time for me. And today I was all ready to get married to a man, to be a part of that mystery, that life had been writing and rewriting and yet not for setting any standard or for reaching any solution.

I had worked till late evening on the first day of our practical exams conducted by the guest examiner. So, the next day, i.e. on the last day with the guest examiner, all my assignments were finished a bit earlier than expected, around four thirty. The examiner was satisfied with my work. In the early morning that day, I could not contact Leslie on phone: I got a busy tone again. So this time, I decided to go over to his place and check out what was happening. It was a warm afternoon. The weather was getting· hotter and within a few days, summer would set in, in its full glory. Already a lot of red dust was blowing. Thy moisture in the air was vanishing fast. The tender mango blossoms were maturing into green and yellow mangoes. The smell of ripeness was in the air. The cottage door was locked from inside. I rang the bell.

Meera opened the door. Her eyes were a bit swollen, perhaps from a midday nap. She called me in. There was nobody inside, not even Mukul. A grim sense of foreboding was taking possession of me. She went inside to wash her face and the midday silence pierced my existence. Leena and Leslie were missing. Mukul seemed to have got lost from the scenario. And the phone on the table was left off the hook. So, this was the reason for the busy tone. Meera did not want to be disturbed in her sleep. I felt a bit embarrassed. Meera came back, well composed, and poised.

'I am sorry to disturb you at this odd hour. I was looking for Leslie.'

'He has gone to Puruliya. Didn't he tell you?'

Puruliya is a place near Shantiniketan, situated on the Chhotanagpur plateau. More red soil with a drier soul. He did not tell me indeed.

'The small boy Mukul, staying with Leslie, do you by any chance know where he may be . . .'

'Of course, I know. He has gone with Leslie. In fact, Leslie took all the trouble to take this boy there. I contacted some people I knew and I got the address of an orphanage, in Puruliya. Nearest place with a decent orphanage. So Leena and Leslie have taken him there. He can now have an address. He will have friends and security. And you two will get some relief, won't you?'

Meera's words sounded so unreal. Acid rain on the luxuriant greenery. The lost lamp of Aladdin. I stood there. A gibbering wreck. 'How could he do this! How could he!' Meera continued telling me something more, but nothing reached my ears as if the air between us had been pumped out in an instant and an unfathomable vacuum had suddenly spread. I just turned around and lugged my heavy feet to get out of the stifling place. Meera came very near and said in a louder voice, 'They are expected to be back this evening. Maybe, a bit late. Or tomorrow morning. I'll ask him to talk to you as soon as he comes.' I heard a door closing behind me. A door or a gate. From one gate to another. I could not just stop. I had to go on and on.

Coming back to the hostel I booked a call to Goa. Mom was out. Father received the call.

'Father please come here, come here, Father, just now. I need you.'

'What's the matter my child, you sound totally disturbed.'

'Yes, I am. But I can't explain. Will you please start immediately?'

'Oh darling. I'll just take the next flight to Calcutta. Don't worry. I'll be there.'

'Thank you Father. Please, bring Mom. Tell her I need her,' my voice was choking.

'I will. I'll definitely. But don't be so upset. Just wait for us. If anybody has hurt you I'll take care of it. He won't be spared.'

'No Father, it's okay. I just need you and Mom. I want to talk to you. I want to touch you,' I broke again and my eyes felt the presence of some strangers. Warm, wet, salty. 'We shall reach you by tomorrow evening. Just be patient till then.'

In spite of his advice I was terribly impatient. I did not go for dinner. Two glass-bead eyes and one orphan love were disturbing me, tearing me asunder. Yes, Lessy had made my love an orphan. He did not ask me, tell me, not even inform me before taking such a big decision. He just took me for granted as he did when he announced our engagement. I accepted it and I had allowed myself to be humiliated. And he went with Leena! Did she know anything about the boy? Was she the one who had got soaked in his blood? And yet he took her and not me, to the orphanage! And what about him? Did he never feel any love for that boy? Was it all through pity? Even after he stayed with him for so many days! What was it for me then? I feared to name it. And escaped from myself.

My god, this is the worst time in anybody's life, when you cannot face yourself: your god. You get afraid to look into his eyes, to plunge into yourself and dreams. But Mom was very supportive, when she rang up late. She promised to come with Father the next day. She did not blame me for not listening to her and for going on with an impossible relationship. She just assured me that even if I had made a mistake, nothing would be lost. 'Life is very long, and there is so much to see and know. Look forward to that.' Yet, I could not help looking backwards. All those feelings and all those stars. The aquamarine passion and the infiltrating desire. I could see them slip into the quicksand of time, struggling and sliding down, down and down. Into some deep nothingness.

To get out of this hollow feeling I escaped next day, very early in the morning. I went to the glass temple. It is made of exquisite stained glass. Panels of beautifully painted glasses fitted into the wooden frames. Glassy walls, a glassy ceiling, and a glossy cemented floor. It is a classy piece of architecture, which can be folded and unfolded like a tent. The colours of the panels make the space inside colourful. This was the prayer hall to pray to Jesus. Tagore believed in all religions and his ashram had accommodated it all. But it was not conventional. There was no pulpit, no altar, no pews nor chancel. Only the cross and Christ. His enormous presence in a normal size hall. One could go and feel the peace in the coloured silence. I sought for the same. Most of the time it would be empty. Today too, there was nobody. The guard allowed me in. Inside the vast empty hall, I blended in with the peaceful silence.

I was inside perhaps for a few minutes or a few hours. I couldn't make out the difference. I had left the watch at the hostel. Deliberately. Just as I used to, while going for an outdoor painting or sketching session. When I came out, I asked the guard what time it was. It was already time for the exam. I rushed towards the studio. I worked like one possessed and finished all the practical exercises, scheduled to be held during the next two days. I told my teachers that I was sick and had to finish and go back with my parents. They allowed me to work for the extra time. They took pity on my colourless face and soul. I had some quick grub at the canteen and worked till eight in the evening. Now, only one dissertation remained. I would have to finish it. That should be enough for my diploma.

As I was entering the hostel through the gate, I felt that touch on my shoulder. A familiarly unfamiliar touch. No goose bumps. No tremor. My limbs got stiff. Without looking at him I said,

'Yes, Leslie, what is it?'

He came in front of me. Erotically erect. Intoxicating enigma. My heart started pounding. I tried not to look at him. His charm would definitely disarm me.

'Where were you? From the morning I've been looking for you. Even at eight in the morning you were not in the hostel. The exam was supposed to be over at one. I came to your hostel. Nobody knew about you. Where were you?' he looked annoyed.

'I had to complete all my assignments. My parents are coming today.'

'Great.' He seemed to be happy. 'Should we go to receive them?'

I didn't know how they were coming from Calcutta. By rail or road. So, I said coldly,

'They will come here on their own. I shall wait.'

'Let's go for a cup of coffee?'

'No. I need some rest.' I started towards the hostel. He held my hand and stopped me.

'Why are you behaving so strangely? Because I went with Leena?' I didn't reply as I felt a dormant volcano awakening inside me. I wanted to be as calm as Mom in the windy nights.

He went on explaining, 'Listen, we took a night train, reached there in the morning. Got him admitted there and took a bus in the late evening. We reached after midnight. Meera told me you'd come.' I did not talk and kept on looking somewhere beyond the horizon. An uneasy silence for a few seconds. He didn't like it.

'Now, say something. For god's sake, why are you behaving this way? Why?'

'Don't ask me why,' I erupted. 'Just do me one favour. Give me the address of the orphanage where you have left Mukul.'

'I will. But didn't you like it? I thought that was the best arrangement for him. I thought you would thank me and Meera for finding out such an easy solution. You were always looking for some temporary place for him, at the hospital, in somebody's house. This will be a permanent place for him. I rather expected you would be overjoyed.'

'You didn't even think of asking me.' My volcano almost erupted. *Those women were everything for you that you listened to them? They don't even know Mukul. For them Mukul is nothing but a name with a human figure.* I couldn't spell out all this.

Leslie continued, 'You were busy with your exam. Meera and Leena suggested this would be the best solution and I agreed. It would be the best possible, safe and secure place for him.'

Under the brilliance and radiance, behind the oozing oomph and warmth suddenly, I felt the freezing touch of a polar heart. The bitter ice-cold coffee spilled.

'In fact, Meera took enough trouble to find out all about the orphanage. It was also difficult to locate the place. I don't know the geography of the place, nor the local dialect. Leena helped to locate the orphanage. Everything went absolutely okay. And here you are sulking!'

'Thanks for your concern. And for the great favour they have done.' Emotion welled up within me. I wanted to ask if Mukul had accepted the idea happily and if he had asked for me, but somehow, I could not. His feeling might be of no concern to them. They just wanted to get rid of him. Permanent settlement was just a permanent excuse.

Avoiding his eyes I said, 'Please, give me the address.'

'Let your exam be over, I'll take you there.'

'No. I'll go tomorrow and I'll bring him back.'

Nobody spoke for a few moments. Dry silence. Hung upside down like a cold brittle bat. The deep-sea voice echoed in the stagnant backwater.

'What will you do with him after that? Send him to the hospital? Has the doctor come back? How long will he shelter Mukul?' his angry tone hit me hard.

'He'll go to Goa. That's why I've called my parents.' I looked at his dumbstruck face for a couple of seconds, quickly turned away and entered the hostel compound. Leslie came behind me. With his long strides, he caught up with me very easily.

'Wait, wait a minute, will you?' he demanded in a perturbed voice. I had to stop. Some of the hostel girls were going out. They looked at us and smiled. By now, Leslie and our relationship was the talk of the town. One of them winked at me. I could not smile back. Leslie looked straight into my eyes. The aquamarine was very still.

'You mean he will go home with you?'

'Yes. I do. I wish I had thought about it earlier.'

'Are you serious?' His question got the answer in my eyes.

'Is he that important to you?'

I wanted to shout at the top of my voice. *Our meeting, our relationship, our moments together may not be that important for you. But it is for me. Yes, it is. And Mukul is always there on every page of our episode. He is the symbol of my love.* Helplessly, I managed to say, 'Please leave me alone. Please.'

I almost broke down but before being reduced to a complete wreck, I ran towards the hostel. The steps grew flat under my speeding feet and the long passage was covered in the twinkle of an eye. I entered my room and flopped on the bed. No, I did not cry. I panted hard. I just wanted to escape from myself As far as possible. From the vulnerable body, from the volatile mind. I didn't know how. I just stretched my hand and switched on the two-in-one. Increased the volume. The jazz razzmatazz overwhelmed my nerves. My body tossed on the bed, to its blistering tune. My nineteen-year-old body. Touched by an erotic dream. Caressed by a disastrous desire. I stopped when our room attendant entered and handed over a note to me. The address of the orphanage. Some directions on how to get there. In Leslie's handwriting. He called me too, just after a few minutes.

'Lucie, I can't help it if you're hurt. I thought you would accept it. It is the best possible solution. Come now, be sensible.'

'Thank you.' I couldn't talk more. There was an uneasy pause.

'Have you got the address? I gave it to your hostel attendant.'

'Yeah. Thank you.'

'When are you going? Let me come with you? You don't know the way.'

'Leena will be a better companion for you.'

'Lucie, I want to talk to you.'

Just that moment I saw Mom and Dad enter. Leslie was about to say something, when I stopped him.

'Excuse me Leslie. My parents have just reached. Goodnight.' I hung up. The communication was interrupted. I rushed to receive Mom and Father.

It took some time to explain the things to them. Mom asked all the questions. Father just stroked my hair. We started for the orphanage, after dinner. I explained to my parents the whole situation in brief, as far as my small mouth allowed it. We: did not get berths in the train, so we took a deluxe bus to Puruliya. It would be an overnight journey and we intended to return by the next evening. I had finished all my practical assignments already. So, I could go without any problem. One small dissertation, on the comparison of the modern art trends of East and West, was all that was left. I would prepare it and submit it. Due to so many pleasant and unpleasant happenings, I had not even started it yet. For the moment, I was only disturbed and concerned about Mukul. What he might have thought about me. How his small and sensitive heart must have suffered going into such a strange shelter. I had a strong feeling that he was uncomfortable there.

In the bus, Mom asked me, 'Suppose he likes the place. What will you do? *After* all, there may be boys of his age. He could make friends.'

My sixth sense says he won't. I know him, I thought. He needed the love of the morning dew. He needed camphor-scented affection. That would be the shelter for him, not any safe ceiling or a permanent address. And what did he think about me? How much had it hurt him to feel that I had sent him there? Didn't he ask me the last time when we had sent him to his native village? 'Why didn't you stop them, Didi? I told you I don't want to go.'

Mom repeated the question again.

'He will always prefer to come with me. Always,' I confirmed.

'Very well. So, he will go with us. And what about Leslie? Is he coming with us? Or has he changed his mind?' Mom's voice sounded more conclusive than curious.

'What do you mean, Eva? After we take the boy from the orphanage, all of us will go back to Goa together. We are going to have a wedding.' Father touched my hand. 'A little misunderstanding . . . You know . . . quite natural.'

'I hope it is a little. But better be sure. A man can always change his mind after spending two nights with a woman. That too, a white man.'

Mom's voice blackened the night. It had been grey confusion so far. I just thought that Leslie gave more importance to Leena and Meera's decision. He preferred to take Leena for taking Mukul to the orphanage, as I would not have allowed it. But Mom's wise eyes had seen the other side of the story. I was blind. I was always blind. Even when I saw the Noor Jahan bracelet on the wrist of Sheila Aunty.

'What are you insinuating, Eva? This is not the time to discuss all those things. Didn't she tell you they had been travelling by a night bus like us?'

'She did not see it herself. Moreover, why did her mother not accompany . . .'

'Cut the crap, Eva. You are making her miserable. Look at her face.' Father's words drew the attention of some of the co-passengers. But Mom remained composed. And her one look silenced Father. Her eyes had mirrored the burning shop of Darjeeling. The hungry tongues of a flame.

The, angry tongues of a flame. A face of Sheila Aunty burning. A face of Leena burning. My Darjeeling, my Shantiniketan all reduced to ashes.

'I love her, just as you do.' Mom's cold voice sounded, 'That's why I don't feel she should take a hasty decision about such an important thing of her life. Why don't they wait for some more time?'

Mom was talking from her own experience. Years ago, she and Father had felt a strong attraction for each other, even after they had been parted after her short holiday trip to Darjeeling. That's why the solemn highlands of Darjeeling and the undulating free waves of Goa had come together and made a home. Yet, my situation was different. I wanted to enjoy my womanhood by the side of Leslie.

It may last only as long a peg of wine does in a goblet. That will be my life. The rest will be only reminiscence. A few days' soft fleshy coating over a long-lasting scary skeleton.

I preferred a few days' ecstatic abode with my love, rather than an ever-lasting home, hanging heavy on my life. And it seemed, that one day was already over. My peg of wine was over. The glass had been smashed to smithereens. The pieces had been scattered in the night sky, winking at me. I could not sleep a wink the whole night.

We reached Puruliya early next morning. From the bus station we hired a taxi. The taxi driver knew the place. On the way, he took us to a good hotel where we freshened up and had breakfast. From there, it· was another one hour's journey. We reached the orphanage around ten in the morning. On the rugged plain of the Chhotanagpur plateau, stood a lifeless high-walled building. The paint-less decrepit bricks grimaced in pain. A weedy man, apparently the gatekeeper, opened the gate for us. Father and I entered. Mom preferred to stay outside. She sat on the worm-eaten wooden bench of a nearby tea stall, sipping a cold drink, not so cold.

We went inside. A skeleton of a tree at the entrance. An old three-storeyed skeleton-coloured building, holding so many pathetic childhood stories. A huge field all around. Only one goal post. A net with so many patches. A few swings. The only playing items. No garden, no flower, no softness anywhere around. We crossed the rocky barren ground and approached the building. The big doorway was gaping at us, hinting at the darkness locked inside. A man on the small porch, hit a gong. The doorway disgorged a few undernourished, underdeveloped unhappy urchins into the green-less open. I stopped and my eyes started searching for the terracotta body with the glass-bead eyes among the ragtag bunch of kids. I couldn't find him.

'Come on Lucie,' Father urged. He was already ahead of me. He stepped back to come near me. 'Is he among these boys?' he asked with some expectation. I shook my head and started moving forward with Father, looking ahead towards the building just to see if any other boy was coming out.

There was no boy. But to my utter surprise, I saw one familiar figure emerge from that darkness, as tall as my dream, as golden as my hope. My legs stopped on their own. Leslie came near us. Even under the broad sunlight, his golden complexion did not shine. His face was on eclipse. The always overflowing aquamarine was on an all-time low ebb. A pricking premonition. A thorny cactus sprang up inside.

'How come you are here, Leslie? Where is Mukul?'

All the water of the deep blue evaporated and a deep gorge gaped open.

'Tell me Leslie where is he?' I was getting anxious. Just behind him, there was another man. Apparently, one of the members of the management of the orphanage. His bald scalp was badly sunburnt. He inspected us with an opaque question in his eyes. Leslie did not look into my eyes. His voice sounded as dry as the rocky ground of Puruliya.

'Sorry, Lucie. I didn't fear this.' For the first time I heard him say sorry. Then, he shook his head in helpless despair. 'Shit. Why did he have to do this!'

'For heaven's sake, first tell me what has happened.'

'Mukul has run away. The police has been informed. He has still not been found.'

The words were shocking. Scorching. Leslie's sea-pearl face blurred before my eyes.

The bald-headed man said, 'I see. They are the relatives of that boy! Very strange. Very weird boy. Did not eat food, did not play with the others. Nobody knew how and when he slipped out. The police is looking for him.'

'Has he gone back to Shantiniketan?' Father asked.

'We intimated the police there. So far, no news.' A bald statement. The big bald sky. The big bald ground.

My small mouth could not speak. My big eyes could not react. Only my heart became hollow. A colourless blank. Not the darling darkness. The shimmering silence of a forlorn desert, devoured my senses. I turned around and started walking fast. Some faint voices knocked my ears. Maybe the orphan boys' clamour, maybe Leslie's and Father's call for me, maybe Mukul's call from the other side of the world.

'Didi, where are you?' Two glass beads rolled along the rough edge of life and fell off. Lost. I came out of the big gate. I was panting hard. Mom came up and I rested my head on her shoulder. My eyes were dry. But there was a shimmering blank inside.

Mom stroked my hair without a single word. The three figures soon came up.

'We must start for Shantiniketan, Father, immediately.'

A secret hope that he would come back to me, to search for his shelter as always, goaded me on. The bald man from the orphanage informed us that there was no bus before four hours and no train before the late evening.

'Why couldn't the police trace him out so far? He is but a small boy! How far can he go on his own?' Father asked.

'Well sir, to be frank, police these days are very busy with the tribal unrest. They have hardly any time to deal with anything else. They will take their own sweet time to look for a wretched boy. After all, they have to catch criminals and anti-socials first. There is no dearth of them in this area. You better go back and check at Shantiniketan. He might have reached there by. now.' Then, he cast a scornful glance towards Leslie. 'Why do you bring such nuts to our reputed place, Sahib? We get a bad name. The last thing we want is to, deal with the police. People say . . .' His nasal narration irritated me.

'Cut the crap and just tell us how we can start for Shantiniketan, immediately.' My singed tone surprised Leslie and he looked at me with disbelief in his eyes. The bald man took offence at my language and shouted angrily. Father took him away and said something apologetically. The tea-stall owner arranged a hired car for us and we left for Shantiniketan immediately. By car, it would be only a five-hour's journey.

Leslie sat quietly by the side of the driver. I sat between Mom and Father. There was an uneasy silence during most of the journey. Only the car recorder played a variety of music all through the way. *Rabindrasangeet*, *baul* folk songs, Hindi film songs, even a few Bon Jovi numbers. Every beat of my heart pleaded: *Come back Mukul, come back. Your shelter is waiting for you.*

He was not back in Shantiniketan. I looked for him in the hostel. The gatekeeper, the room attendant, the few students who were still in the hostel. They had not seen him. I went to the hospital. Dr Sen had gone to the District Hospital for some work. I enquired with everybody, the nurses, the staff who knew him well, the trees, the flowers, the red earth. Nobody could tell me anything about him. Just as suddenly as he had appeared from nowhere one fine day, with the same kind of suddenness, he seemed to have disappeared from our lives.

'Don't get upset. Maybe he will come back tomorrow or day after.' Leslie tried to comfort me. 'It takes time for a small boy to find the way. Let's wait.'

I went away from him without any word or any look. 'She is very upset. Let her alone; please,' Mom advised Leslie and he went off dragging his feet, on the rocky dead earth.

We sent Mr Kundu to Mukul's village too. This would be the last place where he could be found. Just a faint hope. Hope against hope. And just as expected, he was not found there. Mom decided to take me to the hotel where they were staying, as staying alone in the hostel room would mean more brooding and more bleeding. I preferred to be alone, with all my aches and bruises. But Mom came to my room, packed my Shantiniketan stuff and unpacked the memory box of Darjeeling. So many episodes, so many anecdotes. A joyride along the track of the toy train of Darjeeling. She tried to keep my mind as busy as her hands were. Father took us to the hotel and comforted me that Mukul would come back, within a day or two.

But by now, I had a strong feeling that I had lost Mukul. Yes, now I asked myself why would he come back to me or to Shantiniketan? Didn't he know that we had sent him to a heartless haven, away from the shelter of our love and affection? Why should he come back then, begging a morsel of our pity and compassion? No, he was not of that mould. He must have gone in search of a new loving shelter. He would probably never get it anywhere, in this big evanescent world. The boy who had ignited a flame of love, who had initiated the process of blending two hearts, was now lost to me forever. I could not hold back my tears. When Leslie rang up I did not speak to him. Father talked to him and informed him that Mukul had not gone to his stepmother's house.

Leslie wanted to talk to me and I rebelled, 'Tell him, I'll never talk to him. Never.'

Father asked Leslie to call tomorrow. He even tried to comfort me.

'Don't be angry with your fiancé, Lucie, he just tried to settle the boy safely.'

Why didn't he ask me then? Why not? Even once? Before taking such a big decision? These questions kept on gnawing at my mind, but I couldn't say anything. Why did he do it all at the instance of some people who did not know anything about the boy. Those who had no connection with him. Was it his keenness to settle him or eagerness to get rid of him? Did he never feel Mukul's helpless but hopeful pulse? How could he take it for granted that I would always say 'yes' to his every proposal? Even if it meant taking away the shelter of dreams from somebody? I couldn't accept it this time. He had taken away my real dream and left the unreality for me. How could I possibly live with that!

I was feeling empty. I was feeling betrayed. My small mouth had always been small. Now, it got sealed. I just couldn't speak. I couldn't eat anything either. I could not swallow even a glass of water that Mom asked me to have. I pushed it away. No greenery was left inside me. The barren, hardened laterite did not need watering. Mom did not insist. Father sat by my side and ran his short but strong fingers through my long hair. Touched my curly forelocks, his 'tender tendrils'. He tried to reason with me.

'Come on my child. Don't be so emotional. What did you expect of him? Did you think he would take that village boy of India to California? Along with you?'

That big expectation had faintly lurked in my consciousness somewhere. Father spelt it out for the first time. I would have loved Leslie to read it aloud. My secret thought. Perhaps, I expected too much and that too illogically. Father now explained it.

'Are you crazy? He is an American after all. How could he take him along with you? An American would wash away the last speck of Indian dust from the bar of Indian gold before he takes it to his country.' Father was philosophical. 'We get blinded by the resplendent West, and they take only the creamy substance of the east. Don't you see?'

No, I didn't see. That gold was as much a part of the land as the dust was. Moreover, Leslie was not a miner. He was a sea surfer. Would he break a pearl to get rid of its central grit? What would remain of the pearl then?

'It is quite natural. You can't blame him for this.' Father concluded.

I couldn't blame him more than I could blame myself for my exceptional expectation.

Mom took me to the library the next day. Work would keep me busy. I had to finish my dissertation too. I could not concentrate at all. Mom sat at a distance and started reading some magazines. This was the common study hall. I had taken some books on my card and was struggling with them. He came in. Handsome and charming as ever. Everybody's attention drifted away from their books. Even Mom put down the magazine and stared. I lowered my eyes.

Leslie came straight to me, 'I want to talk to you.' I did not answer.

'Don't behave foolishly. We must talk.' He bent over the table. I still looked down and remained silent.

His impatient voice rang, 'You must come with me.'

I looked at Mom nervously. Her eyes signalled me to go and avoid making a scene in front of the people. We came out to the garden. The garden around the library was as clean as a mirror. Gracefully mowed grass. Trimmed plants. Flowerbeds bedecked with cold colours. A few peaceful benches. Earlier, that had been our sitting place. We would come out of the wise world of books to get to the garden of wisdom trees, perhaps. Today, I felt worldly wise. We did not sit in the garden. Went out in the sun. Away from the library, to a less crowded corner. In the shade of a lonely *Chhatim* tree.

'Are you okay?' he asked as if to plumb the depth of my feelings. I didn't reply. He tried to hold my hand and I forcefully pulled it away.

'Do you think it was my fault? I never did mean any harm to him. Never. I meant to do good. You know that. How on earth, was I supposed to know he would run away? Run away from such a safe secure shelter? He is stupid, I would say.' Between every sentence he was giving a pause. Expecting me to speak. My silence was making him more and more impatient. Now he came very close· and grabbed my shoulders with both his hands. 'Look into my eyes. Just look.'

So far, I had been avoiding looking at him. Those warm blue waves, that killing curve, that deadly dimple. To look at him and not to love him was so very difficult. I tried to hate him. Closing my eyes. Shutting off my senses. His touch burned me. His warm breathing shook me. I slowly looked up. He was staring at me in silence. A smouldering wick. The black face of a lighted memory. Softly, he picked a teardrop from my eyelashes.

'This does not belong to you.' His killing curve straightened. Next moment, he stiffened and shook me by the shoulders.

'Very well. I'm going. I'm going to Puruliya again. I must find him. I must. I won't come back to you without him. No.'

His hands released my shoulders abruptly. Instinctively, I flung my arms around his neck and broke into sobs. He slowly pushed away my arms and whispered with the summer wind. 'You will but come to me. You have to.' With long strides, he walked away from me. Past the hanging roots of the ancient sad banyan tree, past the shrubs of gloomy bougainvillaea, past a crooked palm, past a cracked loneliness, a red silence, a blue dream. In my memory lane, I could still see him walking. His blonde hair jumping with the beat of his hasty stride. The golden nape of his neck, so alluring. His two long bare beautiful arms, swinging impatiently. And his dream body going farther and farther away from me.

After three days, when our train dragged its wheels and flanges along the heartless track at Bolpur railway station, I still perceived him walking away from me. Across the rugged, rocky, bleeding ground. A speck near the horizon, where the red wounded sun and the red pathetic earth were melting. Mukul had not come back. Meera and Leena had gone back. And Lessy never looked back. To a crimson memory, a dripping love, a swooping desire. On the rocky soil of Shantiniketan a saga of love had been written to be buried under the dust of time. It would remain there as young as ever. And I had to move on, away from the shelter of love.

I have to move on—I have to move on. I have to dreamwalk, maybe into a loveless nightmare.

BOOK-3

TO A REFUGE?

I

The Lonely Sea

'How long will you count waves?' Somebody asked me from behind as I was standing by the sea, the blue, billowing sea of Goa. I looked back to see my Granny. 'He is coming to India. Next Sunday. Does it mean anything to you?' Granny asked me while picking up an empty shell of an oyster. Cold and dead, half buried in the wet sand of the beach.

My granny, Rosana Fernandez. My mother's aunt, her mother's sister. Beautiful Granny, with lonely, blue eyes; a lonely spinster. Time has adorned her face with embroidery of wrinkles. Still she was beautiful. Granny's beautiful question rolled back with the retreating waves. Went back further away, near the horizon, to invade the sun, a rare, red existence in the abundance of the blue. I looked at the sinking grandeur. With a mind sinking in a deep nothingness. The waves were rolling out of nothing, rolling back to nothing. Near the earthy shore they were stretching their tentacles to grab something. Sand and sand castles. Granny was building some. Only to offer them to the waves pawing at the shore. To the awe of the unknown. Yes, we build everything in our lives; castle, home, nest, or road, only to offer them to that unknown. Every known thing to that one abstract unknown.

I looked at Granny. Her Dead Sea eyes. Heavy and drooping. The cold blue of the pupils spilled over into the white of the eyes. The poisoned blue poised for death. She was now sitting with her feet reaching out for the pawing waves. Sand on her hands, on her clothes and hair, and sadness on her puckered lips. I was standing by her side, facing the sea and with my back towards our hotel-cum-home 'Casa no Duna', i.e. 'a house on a sand hill'. A three-storeyed prosaic relief on a poetic panorama. The usual sunset scene at a beach in Goa. This was Bambolim Beach. Faces of the floating crowd. Tinges of floating colours. A plethora of floating sounds. Yet, Granny was lonely. I was lonely. A smell of loneliness floating in the languid breeze.

I sat down by her side. A wet touch at the bottom. A shivering sensation. She looked at me. From the other side of the world. From the other side of the sea, a message had come the other day. Joy would be coming to India for a month's break. A homeland vacation. To nestle against his familiar family circle. He would witness an ocean of changes in me. Two children, rolling down from the Kanchenjunga peak of childish innocence to the earthy plains to the sea level of sultry Goa. Into the sea of youth. A man and a woman. With an unfathomable distance in between. As Granny would say. My granny, Rosana Fernandez, now a museum meteorite and once a luminous meteor in the sky of youth.

<<< Rosana Fernandez in another era. Another sky with constant constellations and alien lonely stars. Rosana of Nerul village, floats alone in a small boat, along the long backwaters of the sea. A blue strip of calmness, away from the turbulent sea. A part and yet so much apart in nature. Rosana's lonely canoe floats. It floats along the river Sinquerim, river Mandovi too at times. Lazes at the confluence of the Mandovi and the sea. Turns back towards the land. The velvety Quegdevelim Beach waves an invitation, the lanky coconut trees with their swaying umbrella fronds beckon her towards the horizon, where the bottle green hillocks in the distance, reach for the blue beyond. Rosana's canoe lingers on along the sleepy bank, laced with serene green. As if an indelible dot in the picturesque landscape. No mother at home to call back or wait. Father is a busy doctor, with an MBBS degree, a rare species. that time. He has buried his bitterness and impatience in numerous needy patients. Rosana's body mirrors her mother. Rosana's mind remembers her mother. Always. Father married her when he was studying medicine in Bombay. Father's ancestors had been converted to Christianity by the great Saint Francis Xavier, people say. People also say he had been turned on by Rosana's mother's beautiful silvery hair. Shining and foaming like surf on the sea waves. They further say, she is just like her mother. Silvery hair. A white creeper-slim body. Transparent blue eyes. A pointed nose, vulnerably upturned. Father hates to look at her she knows, in order to evade the shadow of his dead love. She carries a ghost for her father. A ghost of a dead relationship he had with her mother. She deserted him

and fled back to her England with her English man. Father has been left with two growing girls, his ageing youth and a lot of old memories. Old and cold. Rosana has ever since been rowing. Rowing away from home, life and even herself.

Rowing along the rivers and backwaters of the water-fed Nerul. Sometimes alone, sometimes with Jose, a deaf and dumb boy of fourteen, their domestic help. His silent presence does not make much of a difference to Rosana, but it makes to the others. The busy fishermen on the banks, with their baskets full of mackerel and mussel. The women carrying water from the river. For them, Jose's presence is necessary. For Rosana it is redundant. She can move alone. On and on. On some days, when Jose cannot accompany her, her foreign looks give her one advantage. She can move alone. Otherwise, in Goa, a Goan girl or woman of a good family, does not move alone in ordinary circumstances. But her sea-foam hair, her blue eyes and her European features and complexion give people an impression that she is a foreigner, perhaps a Portuguese. So, she is secure in her boat and insecure in her abode.

Her sister Sabrina, is Father's favourite. Except for her extra-fair complexion, she is an Indian. Pitch-black hair. Long and wavy. Black-pearl eyes. Indian features with a faint foreign tinge. Even her name has an Indian touch. She is commonly called Rina by all. Rina is an Indian name. She married a Goan Christian. Valentino Pinto. Two sisters met him one day, on the way to their convent. Later, he used to wait everyday near the jujube tree. With the brown shadow of the church steeple on his body, to make it darker. Facing a lake of flickering water lilies, emitting an unknown smell of serenity. His eyes—kokum thirsty. Rosana thought it was for her. But Rosana and her cashew-nut body could serve only fatally intoxicating feni. Valentino wanted cool, cool kokum sherbet. Like any simple Indian. So, one day, when she discovered Sabrina missing from the school and rediscovered her in the shady palm grove, in the shade of Valentino, she covered herself with a beach aloofness. Now, Sabrina remains inside the house with a swelling family, a husband and children and in-laws while Rosana rows and rows away. 'Row, row, row the boat . . .' >>>

'My rowing days are over,' Granny told the young energetic boy in the motorboat.

The motorboat had just approached us with the driver, an acquaintance of Granny. A handsome Goan boy with an athletic built. Chocolate brown body. Black sunglasses. Spiky hair stood up as audaciously as his spirited youth. A rough and tough square face. And a soft touch. A swinging earring on his left ear. He had shouted at the top of his voice, to overpower the roar of the sea waves.

'Come ma'am, a free ride for you. Both of you. Your kin eh?' The boy had been looking at me, I thought, from the angle of his face. His eyes were hidden behind the black glasses.

'My rowing days are over,' Granny said more to the sea than to the boy. As if she was complaining to the sea. The sea had never missed her or her rowing. Then, she turned to me and asked, 'Are you interested?' I shook my head.

'Thank you Mauvin. Some other time, my boy,' Granny threw the watery words towards the sea. He waved his hand and his motor roared away, lacerating the swaying sea.

A motorbike roared in my memory. A vroom and a visor and a voice as deep as the sound of the soul of this sea. That voice had now made its voyage all over the world. Sailed to assail so many hearts with sweetness. Yes, Leslie's first music album had been out two months ago and it had been a success. Success for the critics and excess of excitement for women of all ages. Just the other day, I heard a classmate of Mom sigh, 'I wish I could be young.' He was now a celebrity. Yet, just as unpredictable as ever. He would not give up his privacy and avoid interviewers and reporters cleverly. I did not like the album in particular. I had liked him much more when he had been by my side with his musical aquamarine waves against the red backdrop. His voice had first called my name, 'Lucie', around six months ago. I heard it again. And now it was a duet.

'Lucie, Lucia,' Granny was looking at me, 'he wanted you in his boat. Not me. Now nobody wants me as his company, not even the boat.' Granny's voice crumbled like a sand castle.

<<< A sand castle crumbles under the feet of Rosana. In a hurry she has stepped on some child's creation. The child, a small chubby boy of five or six, looks up at her with wonder in his eyes. How a castle can be reduced to nothing within no time! Next he pouts, cries and goes into a tantrum. He takes handfuls of sand and throws them at Rosana. Tiny hands, the grains of sand do not even reach Rosana. She squats by the side of the

boy and gives him some chewing gum she always carries with her, on her rowing expeditions. They look colourful. Rosana rolls them on her palm. They look more colourful. Kaleidoscopic. The boy looks at them, allows Rosana to put one in his mouth. Rosana gives him some more in his hand. He is calm now. But Rosana is disturbed. Somebody has taken her canoe away.

It is Quegdevelim Beach. The confluence of the river Mandovi and the sea. This is one of the days when Jose is not with her. She stopped here to have some coconut water, to quench her thirst. From here, she had to turn back again. She was having coconut water, standing by the row of the fishing boats which emitted a slithery smell of fish and a decaying smell of the bright oil paint. Just then, an unknown male figure emerged from the clump of the shady coconut splendour along the beach, took her boat and paddled away. She was chasing him when she unknowingly trampled over the sand castle and had lost track of the man. Now she walks slowly, towards the sea. The man is rowing in the sea. It is low tide and her boat is moving away from her, swaying on the gentle waves. Soon, it becomes a speck in the blue, like a fading memory.

Rosana flops down hopelessly, on the wet sand. Her sky blue pupils dilate to accommodate the vast sea and to get back her only refuge from the world. Instead, diluted helplessness trickles down in tiny drops from the aching blue. Some fishermen, to whom she is as mysteriously familiar as the sea waves, come up and ask her about the boat. She does not want anybody's help. Just like the child, she grabs a handful of sand and throws it towards the sea. Half falls on the beach, half into the sea. Sand to sand, dust to dust, ashes to ashes. She gets nothing. She stands up with her light kitbag and a heavy existence.

'A Portuguese Fidalgo, miss.' One fisherman almost hisses out those words, as she asks him in pure Konkani. This is one of the last few days of Portuguese rule in Goa. It is not yet 19th December 1961. It is a summer afternoon of 1961. The Portuguese flag is still flapping on the Governor's house. Sad and shocked, Rosana gets up after a couple of minutes and plods along the sandy beach, with a blank mind trampling her small shadow all through. She hates to sit anchored on the beach, waiting for a presumptuous Portuguese. Yet, she waits. With expectation like the undulating wings of a ray. Time rolls with the waves. The shadows of the palm trees grow longer and darker. Rosana's canoe does not come back.

Rage crests inside while the outside looks crestfallen. She gets up, limps with time, with her fate. An old friend LuizinIho, calls her. His family was their neighbour once. Now, he is a successful fish businessman. They exchange a few words, talk about their childhood. Then, she quickly bids goodbye, before their conversation reaches the present from the past and gallops towards the future. She has nothing to talk about the present, an empty boat without pearls and coral, without even Luizinho's shrimps and prawns. And at present, that too is lost. The future for her is a bleak canvas. She now goes away from the sea, the golden beach, the missing boat and herself. Walks with the spire of the church of Our Lady of Remedies in her eyes. The long shadow, of the palatial house of the Bishop of Halicarnasso, grows even more mystic. She has to go back home. >>>

'Should we go home?' I asked Granny with some hesitation in my voice.

'You go dear, I would like to count a few more waves.' Granny was still lost somewhere. I knelt down by her side.

'Why don't you also come Granny? It is getting dark here. How will you count the waves? I need to talk to you.'

'About what? Joy's homecoming?'

'No. About Leslie.'

'Leslie! Have you heard from him?' She looked at me with the question quivering in her eyes. I shook my head and remained silent. A gust of wind blew, all of a sudden. Whirled away the sand, stirred the waves. The sea threw the white flying foamy scarf to cover the beach, only to let it slip off, the very next moment. Like the long scarf of Gene Kelley, in 'Singing in the Rain'. Singing in the rain. Dancing in the ray, the dying ray of the setting sun.

'I feel he is here. In India,' I said slowly, looking at his blue diamond ring, which now I wear on my middle finger. 'You feel!' Granny smiled. 'How do you exactly feel?' The wrinkles on her forehead and the crow's feet under her eyes emitted a sigh of time, lost time.

'Well Granny, today I received an envelope with a white paper inside. Milky white and absolutely blank. I guess . . .'

'It is from him,' Granny completed my sentence. Then, she got lost in thought. I saw or imagined a faint smile on her dry lips.

'Handwriting on the envelope?'

'The address is typewritten, but it is from somewhere in India. I could not make out the post mark on the stamp.'

'Don't you think of any other friend of yours who can play such a prank on you? I think there must be a dozen.'

I could not think of anybody, however. 'Let me see . . . Two of my classmates of Shantiniketan have continued writing to me. Both have left Shantiniketan now. One of them has got a job while the other has got married. I have lost touch with Deepa. She wrote to me a couple of times, but I did not reply . . .' Yes, I wanted to dismember my aching memory. No more looking back. No more plodding along memory lane that had petered out somewhere into eternity.

But could I really sever those feelings? Obliterate all those memories? I reflected. Every gust of runaway wind spreads the melancholy, Mahua smell. Every drop of the golden sun mirrors every moment of togetherness under the *Chhatim* tree. The breakers with their thorny crests turn into the blue cacti from the forlorn barrenness of Shantiniketan. Red barrenness, red agony. A love account has run into red. Each prism of red blood reflects each colour of love.

Every bit of me misses every bit of you.
Every atom crumbles in the world without you.

The world-less world. The lonely rainbow in the wet sky of Goa melts into a shapeless, formless jumble of colour. A smudge of pain. Permanent. Permeating.

I would regularly interact with Granny to learn how she had survived it all. A timepiece. Big size. Big golden numbers. Long shining pendulum. Only the hands are missing. And the whole existence is meaningless. I would always wonder at her, how she had kept all the broken fragments inside and carried those rattling piercing pieces for so many years.

Granny's agony rattled.

'So, she feels! Only the fools feel a lot. And women are the worst kind of fools. They feel a lot.' She almost mumbled these words and then looking into my eyes, she asked, 'Don't you think if he comes to India there would be some news about it? At least in some women's magazine?' Granny smiled with a bitter sweetness.

I saw the logic in her argument. Yet my dream, my god heard those footsteps on the soil of India.

'Ships come and ships go.' She shook her head seriously.

A remoteness sailed in her blue eyes. She was on another plane, at this moment. The next moment she sprang up, 'I want to see that letter.' The usual temperamental way of hers. Time and tide had waited for none, even Antonio de Rosario D'Mello had not waited for her, but the tide of time had wetted her wit to a spongy pulp.

We came back to our hotel-cum-home. Granny asked me to bring the letter to her place. She did not stay with us in the hotel building. There was a small cottage for her, a few yards away from the hotel building. A motionless museum of mutilated emotions. A lost world. I used to spend almost half the time with her. Two bedrooms. In the storeroom, a. very old, obsolete loom of Granny's great grandpa had been stored. People say he was a great craftsman. Granny used to often look at that decrepit machine. She used to spend most of the time in the larger bedroom, which was her studio also. It was a half-dark room, and always reminded me of our shop at Darjeeling. The whole room was full of life-size paintings, medium size portraits, big and small sketches and large well-framed photographs. Of two persons. Antonio and no, not Rosana, Granny's picture was nowhere. It was Angela, Antonio's daughter. A teenage girl, like myself in Darjeeling. A young dashing man and a cute little girl. Granny had captured their image from every possible angle. In fact Granny started painting only to keep them near her. She could not keep them in person and so kept them in their abstract form.

The man I thought was very dashing, I wouldn't say he was handsome. He was just wildly charming. He seemed to be popping out of the picture or photo with his vivacious charm. A splashing sea wave. The girl appeared serene. In one picture, a trickling teardrop had frozen on her cheeks, forever. Granny told me this was the last time she saw her. The teardrop was so unrealistically real. A white bubble, a shining pain. Another picture on the same topic was weird. A small face and a bigger teardrop, with a distorted reflection of barren thorny boughs. Granny kept on painting even now, in spite of her failing eyesight and trembling hand. She painted for herself and only for herself She never wanted to show them, to bring them out in the sunlight. It would be as if she was baring a bleeding wound. Had she done it, I am sure she would have been famous. But Granny did not want fame. Fame is as fleeting as Antonio. Or even worse. Granny stretched herself on the armchair and reached out a hand for my letter. For a moment she looked like a piece of taxidermy. I slowly touched her hand to feel the rhythm of her pulse, under her raisin-like skin. Dry desiccated rusty raisin, with a juicy grape-history.

'Granny, dear. You are very cold. Cover yourself. The letter is in my room. I'll go and bring it.'

I went out of the cottage and climbed the steps of our home with swift speed.

<<< Rosana climbs the stairs feverishly. She enters the room of her father. It is night. Mr Fernandez is writing a letter. The door is ajar. Rosana knocks on the door to draw the attention of the busy doctor.

'What's it, Rosy?' he asks without even looking up.

'Can I talk to you for a minute?' Rosana's whispering voice gives out a sigh. A restless rustle among the palm groves. The sea can hear it. Mr Fernandez closes the cap of his pen and puts down the specs he uses for reading and writing.

'Yes?' His two greying eyes get fixed on Rosana. He looks not at her but at some grey memory. Groomed in a grave. But the greying eyes fail to see the insecure inertia, so much in contrast with her mother. Rosana slowly comes in and closes the door. She goes near the dated figure.

'My canoe has been taken away by a Portuguese *patrao.*' Rosana pauses after relating a bare fact in an emotionless voice. She waits for her father's reaction.

'These white people! They only know how to take away. Have they ever given anybody anything?' A resentful voice resonates in the silence of the night. Rosana waits for it to fade out completely.

'I want it back. Please, do something.' Two blue pupils float up in a pool of helplessness.

'Who is the man? Do I know him?' Rosana shakes her head. The greying eyes grow impatient more because of an old wound, rather than a young helplessness.

'What do you expect of me? To know his whereabouts?'

'He is a big officer, sort of a nobleman. So it seems. Came here recently. This, I gathered from the conversation of the fishermen there. You are an eminent person, a doctor. You know so many people in the government, Father, why don't you . . .'

'Impossible, just impossible.' He stands up. 'A big officer. Maybe, a nobleman. I just can't do anything here. It is out of question. We are still not independent. I can't do anything. This is their usual way. You know cases, where they have even taken land and properties from the common Goan people.'

'Please, Father, I want my boat back. I don't have anything else.' The importunate soul faces the impatient mind. 'You can at least try.'

'I hardly get any time out from my patients. Moreover, I don't feel it will be of any use. They will start asking hundreds of questions, why you move alone in the boat, being a girl etc. etc. That won't be very pleasant for us. For my social position you know.'

'Father, please. I hardly ask you for anything.'

'This is not a request. This is . . . something of an imposition. I am sorry, Rosy.'

'Get me a new boat, then, will you?'

A wave of silence claws at the rocks of Dona Paula.

Mr Fernandez looks stunned for a few minutes. He starts pacing up and down, as if chased by the question. Rosana stands like a stationary rock. Repeats the question, after a few seconds.

'Give me a new boat Father, please.'

Greying eyes grow dark. Mr Fernandez comes very near to his daughter.

'It is a lot of money. I can't give you one right now. I'll have to think about it.'

'How long will it take?'

'I can't say.' His anger bursts on the blue eyes. He walks away towards the window. 'You should be ashamed of yourself asking me like this. Why don't you try to do something meaningful, instead of killing time by paddling. I sent you, you and your sister to the best girls' convent in Goa. What for? I wanted you to be educated, to help me, if not as a doctor, as a nurse at least. Rina married. At least, she is happy. And you . . . just squandering away your time. Valuable time. Always unhappy, making others unhappy. Isn't it time you settled down? I shall talk to your sister to finalise your marriage with the boy . . .'

Mr Fernandez hears a click behind him, turns around to see the door is ajar and the room is absolutely empty. >>>

I found my room entirely empty in the shadow-coloured loneliness as I entered it. Not that I expected somebody to be here, but I did not even find my own dreams. The windows were open and the curtains were pulled. The sultry sea was framed in the window and fragmented by the grill. The air smelt salty. I switched on the light. Somebody sprang up on the sofa. A face, no, not of my dream, not of childhood, not of my loneliness, not of my very own god. It had a chubby and complacent face like a fresh ripe red tomato on a flaunting green stalk, ready to be picked up.

'Bet, you can't tell who I am.' Her eyes fluttered. A twang of a rusty string. Somewhere I had seen her, but where? She seemed to enjoy my bewildered look thoroughly.

'Well, why don't you help me?' I asked a bit helplessly.

And just at the same moment a piece of Darjeeling cloud drifted into the Goan shed to shed some shrouded memories. I saw two tiny hands, two rosy cheeks under the five o'clock shadow of Joy. Yes, indeed, it was none other than Polly. So many times, I had carried her in my arms and today she was taller than I. When I had faced the home wreck at Darjeeling, I was fourteen and a half Polly would be about sixteen now. I saw not Polly, but a mirror in front of me and in that magic mirror I saw myself in Darjeeling. The scent of fog, the touch of chill, the sound of the Himalayan silence and an avalanche of myself.

'Lucie, are you home? Come and see who is here.'

The memory-mirror cracked and Mom came in. Polly was saying something, which I could not hear at all. She now went out and I heard a voice. From the voice, I knew her. The voice with a soft snowfall touch. Meena Aunty. She had not changed much. Only some silvery touch of time added to her natural grace. I had not seen her nor Polly since I had left Darjeeling, though they had come a couple of times to Goa to meet my parents. My father had been twice to Darjeeling to dispose of our property. Mom had never gone back even once, nor would she go, I believe. She had never grown roots in the hills of Darjeeling, and her sweet memories had got all charred by the fuming finale.

'When did you come, Aunty?' I asked as she came and hugged me.

'By the evening flight. We were looking for you before going to the airport. Where were you?' Mom asked. I could not remember when Mom had told me about their coming to Goa. I had grown a habit of listening to my own thoughts most of the time nowadays.

'I was with Granny.'

'Oh you were. Were you? You should give sometimes to yourself dear,' Mom said. I remembered Granny would be waiting for me and my mysterious letter. Mom asked me to go out with them.

'I'll come in a minute Mom, she'll be waiting for me. I've to give her something.'

'Viru will take it to her.' Viru was one of our hotel boys.

'This one I've to give her Mom. Excuse me for five minutes, please.' I looked at our Darjeeling darlings.

'Must be some of their artistic matter or materials!' Mom explained to them. She said to me, 'We'll be waiting for you in the balcony of our room.'

My parents' room was on the first floor, just above mine. Mom was going up with Meena Aunty while I felt a tug at my sleeves, 'I want to go with you.' Polly did not wait for my permission and waving at our mothers, accompanied me to Granny's cottage. Granny was not very easy with outsiders, so I hesitated at the door and knocked twice.

<<< Rosana knocks twice at a closed door. Sabrina opens the door. Sabrina, her sibling. The wife of Valentino. Valentino. Rosana's dead dream of yesterday. Sabrina's reality of today.

Rosana has avoided him, her dead dream. She hardly comes to their house, except, for some social occasions. Valentino has never known her feelings, neither Sabrina. Rosana has grown out of her feelings. Her boat has taken her away from that unreachable bank.

'Rosy! What a surprise! So, at last you've got some time for your sister. But why so late? It is already six.'

Rosana rushes past her into the house. The whole day today she has spent around the banks to get a glimpse of her boat. But it remained out of sight. She crossed the ferry to come to her sister at Taleigao. She pants hard as she goes inside and sits on the armchair.

'Something wrong? You look so terribly exhausted.' Sabrina is worried. Her black eyes shower white affection. Both very much Indian. Goan monsoon. Makes everything green. Rosana is in a blue funk. Sabrina's five-year-old daughter Eva comes in. She has broken her doll and wants to get it repaired.

'It can't be set right dear, I'll get you a new one. I shall ask your dad to bring one when he comes home.' Sabrina tries to convince her, but she wants just that doll to be mended. Rosana takes it and assures her that she will do it. She takes the child in her arm. The mad rush of blood inside her subsides. She kisses her. A bit fervently. Sabrina takes her away.

'Go and play.' She persuades her to leave the room. Then, turns towards Rosana, 'Why did you tell her a lie? This doll is beyond repair. She will throw a tantrum if you fail to keep your promise. I can't handle it.' She seems thoroughly annoyed.

'Who has made you a mother, I don't know. You don't understand a child's psychology.'

'What do you mean?'

'I mean I'll purchase one doll just like this one and deface it a bit, to give it that older look. Replace the new frock with the old one. She won't know the difference and will be very happy to get back her own doll.'

'That's a good idea. My god, Rosy, you have our mother's shrewd brain!'

'This is just common sense.' Rosana feels scandalised. 'Don't you people always compare me with her. I have nothing in common with her. Nothing.' Her voice sounded violent. 'She's got two husbands, maybe, by now many more. I don't have even one.'

'Calm down Rosy, I please. I'll bring some *kokum* sherbet for you. Just wait.'

'No. I need whisky.'

'Rosy dear, this is not the time . . .'

'Just go and bring one. I need to talk to you. Something serious.'

Sabrina brings the drinks and closes the door. Hers is a joint family. Just like most of the Goan families. She does not like them to hear the sisters' confidential conversation. Rosana swigs a big gulp. One more and one more. Then, the two sisters sit face to face.

'I want some money, Rina.'

'Money? How much? What for?'

'Not very much. Around 200 bucks to purchase a new boat.'

'New boat! My word. What has happened to the old one?'

'Gone. Gone. Taken away from me by some Portuguese Fidalgo.'

'How come? Taken by force?'

'He just stole it. They seem to think that the whole of Goa is their property and they can take anything, just like that.' She elaborated the incident to her sister, who sighed in despair, 'I wish we could be in India. Now, all the talks are going on to take us in India, Nehruji is trying so hard. But when will it actually happen dear?'

'Don't know. Maybe, not as long as that *grande ditador* Salazar is in command. But at the moment, I just think of today Rina, and I want a boat. Papa won't offend the Portuguese. Neither will he give me the money. I can get some seventy-five bucks by selling off my gold chain. I'd need around one hundred and fifty more.'

Rosana looks at Sabrina with expectation in her eyes.

Sabrina's pitch-black eyes hide themselves under the quivering eyelids. Time limps. Finally, Sabrina gathers enough strength to look up into her sister's eyes, 'Rosy, I'm sorry. We have just started our new restaurant. It needs a lot of money, dear. Just now it will be difficult. He has even taken some loan from his relatives. You know he is crazy about having his own hotel, one day. I can give you some fifty bucks I saved for buying a *foddo.'*

'Why don't you talk to Valentino?' Rosana suggests as a green malachite chain sways gently in front of her eyes.

'I don't think it will be of any use. Rather, I think Rosy, it is a boon in disguise. You can now forget paddling and meddling. Now, try and be a good girl. Marry and settle down. You know Valentino's friend, Vijay. You will be lucky to have him as your husband. He is a Hindu, so Papa will be happy at heart. You know papa became Christian to marry mom and he still . . . Anyway, Vijay works in the Vasco Iron Mines. He is from a good family, as far as I know. Lost his parents when he was a baby. His uncle has brought him up. He is crazy about you. I have told Papa about it. He wants to meet the boy soon.'

'Will he become a Christian?'

'He is ready to do that for you, but his family may not allow. They are freedom-fighters. His cousin was involved in the Daman uprising. Remember Vasudev Dhawalikar? You can also get converted to Hinduism. People are going back to Hinduism nowadays. You know such cases, don't you? You won't have any problems either. Vijay is all set to go to Bombay. Wants a better job. The Portuguese officials have been after his family since his cousin's death in the Daman uprising. Now, tell me one thing Rosy, hasn't Vijay expressed his feelings to you?'

Rosana recalls a weedy figure with a large cashew apple-shaped head and two big protruding iron-black eyes. Following her silently everywhere, to the beach, near the river bank, around her house at times. But very silent. No dash, no élan. They have spoken to each other only in some social gatherings or in the company of others like Sabrina or Valentino. She does not reply Sabrina's question. She questions, 'He is a Hindu boy, so Papa has to give dowry for my marriage, two thousand or three thousand. Hasn't he?'

'Yes, he will. Papa has saved money for that. Papa's clinic is more of a charitable institution. But he gets a good share from our grandpa's cashew plantation in Chimbel, you know.'

'Why can't he give money for my boat then?'

'That'd be a waste of money . . .' The words slip out of Sabrina's silly tongue. 'I mean you have had enough of paddling, now you should settle down. You are already twenty-five. It is time you had your family, husband, children . . .'

'Shut up,' Rosana shouts impatiently. She hates to look at the dull-black coal eyes of her sister. 'You want me to marry that stupid boy and get settled like the ore in the mine? You had your quota of joy, courting Valentino, eloping with him and for me you prescribe the darkness of an iron mine! You selfish crab.'

'But Rosy, you are so self-centred, you don't reach out to people. You live like a snail. If somebody shows interest in you, you avoid him. Vijay is reasonably good for you. You can't expect some prince for you. Here, only beauty does not matter. You are now overage for marriage. You don't have a good reputation because of all your silly· habits like moving alone in a boat. Most of all, you are from a broken home. You should feel lucky that Vijay has agreed to marry you. Papa can't carry your burden forever.'

The words are darker and heavier than cold iron and hotter than a burning piece on the anvil. Rosana darts towards the door, flings it open and slams it behind her. A singed soul. She now wants to cool off her burn. But where? She lugs her heavy mind along the lonely road of Santa Inez. A swaying palm grove sighs. A yellow ripe pumpkin-moon hangs from a trailing darkness. It is a full-moon night. The sea is on high tide. A staggering spirit steers a body at a high speed. Mad speed. To the sea. >>>

'To the sea? You want to go to the sea at night? There is nothing but roaring darkness,' Granny said to Polly after listening to her importunate demand. 'You'll get enough time tomorrow, young lady. And the next day . . . by the way how many days will you be here?'

'A few more days. Dada, my big brother is reaching Bombay day after tomorrow. From London, you know. We were there last summer. What a life! If you had ever been to a foreign country you would know.' Her superfluous snobbery disturbed Granny. With a scowl she asked, 'You are going to London now?'

'No, Dada is coming back from London. On vacation. He'll come here via Bombay. There'll be the engagement ceremony.' She winked at me mischievously.

'There's still enough time.'

'But I'll be going with my father to receive Dada at Bombay tomorrow. Bombay is a fantastic city. I would like to stay there for one day and do some shopping. Also it will be a great pleasure to see Dada, fresh from London.'

Polly's face got extra radiant as she mentioned him. She was proud of her successful sibling. But I saw agony on Granny's face. *Must be seeing the shadow of Angela, her own little angel*

She was a teenager too when she left her, I mused.

Polly was looking at the pictures on the wall. 'I've never come here before, have I?'

'Nobody comes here, except Lucia.'

'Is her name Lucia? We know her as Lucie.' Polly was a bit surprised.

'Lucia is the Portuguese name. I love to call her Lucia. Her mother named her Lucie. She has some fascination for French names. And Lucia's father is fond of Wordsworth's Lucy, isn't he?' She looked at me not to get the answer, but to recite a few lines from the poem. Then, she fell silent. Polly moved from one picture to another, passing black and white comments on each of them. Granny didn't listen. I went near her and said,

'Granny, I've brought it.'

'Oh the newspaper? Give me. Today I've not read the newspaper.'

'The letter, Granny,' I whispered and looked into her eyes. She had remembered it perfectly. I could read it in her transparent blue eyes.

'I've kept it in your drawer. See it later.' Granny got the drift and kept the secret intact. I didn't like to discuss it in front of a stranger. Polly was a stranger for me and would always be. She was so different. And so indifferent to the black happenings on the white summit of Nepal! As though nothing very unusual and shameful had ever happened in her life.

'Who are these two people? Why can't there be pictures of any other persons? Who are these two?' Polly was moving along the decorated wall.

'They are Granny's creation.' I answered, before Granny could say anything.

'You mean they are not real?' Polly looked surprised.

'For an artist his every creation is real,' Granny said and stared at Polly with narrowed eyes as if she was a piece of art. Or was she looking through a telescope, towards a bygone time and was peering at her Angela?

'Will you draw a picture of me, Grandma?' Polly's question splashed out of the blue against a shocked shell.

Nobody had ever asked or dared to ask Granny this, I believe. Did I hear a squeak at the hinge of a clam? Granny's eyes looked crystallised, a piece of taxidermy. I wanted to take advantage of the opportunity. This could be the best for the lady of Shalott, to break out of the reflection of her memory-mirror. To get out of the ever-stretching entangled lines of the two figures. Warp and woof Warp and woof. The ancient, obsolete loom of Granny's great grandpa loomed large. She could now knit some new neat lines. Of a stranger. A strange experience in her last twenty seven or twenty-eight years of life.

Granny stood up with an awkward jerk. An uneasy silence stretched its body on the bed of inertia. The air smelt lonely.

'I don't paint anymore.' The battered words came out of her mouth bitterly. Her face winced. The eyelashes wilted in lassitude.

'Can't you do it for my sake?' Polly was as obstinate as any teenager. 'Make me look my best. I'd hang it in my room and show off to my friends. I have many photographs. Every boy who gets friendly with me wants to take my photo. But I don't have a portrait. This would be great. To have a portrait of myself on my wall.' She went on, without paying heed to the obvious pain of the painter.

'Should I wear a swimsuit? Like that picture?' She pointed at one picture of Angela, in a shocking white swimsuit against the backdrop of blue towering waves. Every possible shade of blue had been used in the picture to sharpen the sparkling splash of the implausible white. Granny paced up to the picture, covered her eyes with two hands, probably blinded by the dazzling whiteness.

'Let me alone. Let me alone, kids. I want to be alone. Just alone,' she shouted. I grabbed Polly's hand and dragged her out of the room. Granny really needed to be alone at the moment. All alone.

'We shall talk to her tomorrow. She is in a bad mood today. Old age you know,' I whispered to Polly.

'Let's go to the sea.'

'Sea in the dark?'

'Yes, I'd love it.' She got bubbly. 'Let's race, who can reach there first.' And she flew past me. A child surged inside me. A Darjeeling snowball rolled. I rushed to catch up with her. I almost ran to reach an impoverished beach in dark tatters. There was no shimmering gold. Only our feet crunched on the scattered shells.

<<< The crunch of her footsteps on the shells makes Rosana conscious that she has reached the beach. Yes, she has. Without her refuge. Her cosy canoe. The roaring sea is flashing its teeth, sneering at her. She is twenty-five. Not married. Not tied to anybody with any emotion. Her life is the voice of death. A white face churns up her memory. A lingering jasmine perfume. Two butterfly-hands holding the paddles of a canoe and teaching her to row merrily, merrily, merrily. Two red-wine lips kissing her all over, leaving lipstick stains here and there. Five white lilac-fingers running through her hair, rested on a padded lap and a mellow mouth crooning a lullaby. Just eleven years. Just eleven years of her life could relish it all. Then, she had left her. Why didn't she take her with her? Sabrina was Father's favourite right from her birth. She was her mother's darling. Still, why did she leave her and take with her only baby Rita? Why? People here say that she was scared. Did not want to expose beautiful budding Rosana to her stepfather, much younger than Rosana's mother. But didn't she fear to leave her to a 'step-life'? More monstrous than a step-parent? She thought only about herself, although she taught her the gospel messages. She taught her to row merrily, merrily, merrily down the stream when life was but a dream. Her dreamboat is gone. Now, there is nothing but Rosana and the raging sea waves.

The sea is on a high tide. A blotch of a moon adulterates the darkness. Her last refuge. Rosana folds her hands. Unfolds her strength. Deflates a three-dimensional entity into a one-dimensional existence. Rosana throws her deflated self to float on the high tides without the refuge of her boat. The naked waves, the nude depth devour her. The girdling palm grove sighs out a lullaby for an eternal sleep:

Row, row, row the boat, gently down the stream. Merrily, merrily, merrily. Life is but a dream. >>>

'Life is but a dream.' A Hindi popular song was being played on my music system. Polly was half listening to it. She was with me in my room tonight. She was given a room. But she did not like to sleep alone in a hotel room. So, I had to give up my privacy temporarily. She was lying down on the bed and staring at me with a mischievous smile.

'If I were you I'd have married him just now and flown off to London happily. Why are you wasting time?' Her big ice-flake eyes exuded warm wisdom. My small mouth shrank smaller.

'Mummy wants to have the wedding now. But Daddy thinks only engagement now and marriage after Dada comes back permanently from London. In that case, you will lose the chance to stay in London. Don't you want to be there? I wouldn't have lost such an opportunity.'

Polly was talking like a mature practical woman. After all, she was a child of a successful business family. I had a close look at her. I could not find myself in her cool icy eyes. Her naughtiness was just like a rolling snowball. Moving but cool. Cool and cooler. A cool canned teenage. All the qualities intact, except a whirling freshness. Her cool eyes scrutinised my room, my cupboard, my bookcase. She pointed at the video cassettes kept on the TV side rack.

'Wow, you've a damn good collection. Let me see.' She went to the rack and started examining them. Behind the visible row one cassette was tucked away. She took it out. The vulnerable softness was taken out of the shell of a crustacean.

'Good God! "Killer" Leslie Fraser! Boy, doesn't your heart stop when you see him?'

My heart did stop indeed, at the utterance of his name. For a few seconds. Next, it started beating wildly and I just could not hear her babbling. But I could see her going to the rack. She inserted the cassette in the VCR. I didn't want to watch him with anybody else. I had always watched it alone. I could not see it with anybody else. It would be like sharing your night dream with somebody. You can share a bed, not a dream.

'Please Polly, not now,' I pleaded.

'Why not? I don't have it at home. Mummy doesn't like all these Western music albums. I saw it twice at one of my friend's house. Marvellous. Isn't he?' She switched on the VCR and got ready with the remote.

'Oh, I've forgotten my magazine in Mom's room. I'll go and pick it.' I wanted to go out of the room on some excuse.

'No,' she held my hand. 'Just sit down and see it. There he comes.'

I had my back towards the TV. Her exclamations and interjections pricked my ears.

I freed my hands and said, 'I have left some important papers at Granny's place. I'll go and fetch 'em.' I stepped out quickly and she shouted from behind, 'Come back soon. I can't sleep alone in a new place.'

I wanted to go to Granny's cottage. But as I was passing the corridor I saw Mom coming towards my suite.

'Lucie, you're here. The music is too loud. It is already ten. The customers will be disturbed.'

'It's Polly. What can I do? Why does she have to share a room with me? I don't like it.'

'She can't stay alone, so I thought this would be the best arrangement. Af*ter* all, it is for just a couple of days,' Mom said in a wise tone. 'Please, go and ask her to turn it down.'

'I can't. She won't listen. I asked her not to play it in the first place.'

'Well, I'll see. Come with me.' Mom hurried down the corridor. I didn't go with her but kept waiting there.

After a few minutes, she came back. She was looking grave. *Didn't she listen to you?* I wondered, as hardly ever did Mom fail in doing things. If she knew that she would fail, she did not attempt it.

'I want to talk to you,' she said without answering my question.

She must have succeeded in her mission but it is something else, I thought and I was disturbed. I followed Mom out of the hotel, into the back garden. We went near the boundary wall. Tall trees were crowded along the wall waving their leaves in the soft breeze. Far away, somewhere in the dark sea, the searchlight of the lighthouse was flashing off and on.

'When did you buy that cassette? You never told me?' Her eyes as sharp as the pine needles pierced my heart. Bleeding. I could not answer.

'You told me you're trying to forget him. I believed you.' She waited for me to answer. The pine trees murmured, pining for the bygone days. I could not even mumble.

'You know very well, you have to marry Joy. It is now all fixed. It is best for all of us.' I grew as silent as the surrounding plants.

'Don't you remember your Darjeeling days? So happy you were with Joy.' Mom started telling me some interesting anecdotes from frozen memory. Half of the words did not enter my ear. Today, Mom was telling about all that happiness. Yet she had not hesitated a bit while leaving Darjeeling and Joy. Joy's sad and helpless face on the last day at Darjeeling, still lingered in my memory.

'He still loves you so much. You will make a perfect couple.' I could clearly hear these words.

'But Mom, what's wrong if I watch his album?'

'There's nothing wrong in watching his album. But something is seriously wrong, when you watch it hiding from others. Why didn't you tell me? Why did you hide it from us? I'd never have objected.'

'I thought you would and so . . .' my voice trailed off as I looked at her searchlight eyes, stripping my soul to the buff. The wet leaves shed two drops of dew.

A shrill voice rang through the silence of the night. Polly had come out on the verandah, looking for me. Mom held me in her arms and planted a sympathetic kiss on my forehead and whispered, 'I love you, dear. I'm with you.' I rushed back to my musical room with my whimsical roommate. The music had, however, stopped. She came in from the verandah, as I entered and lay down quietly on the bed. I was going to switch off the light but she stopped me.

'I always sleep with the light on. Don't switch it off.'

'The night lamp will be on.' I assured her, although I was used to sleeping in the darkness without any night lamp. Darkness was my darling. In the light you see, in the darkness you feel.

'No, no, one of the tube lights must be on. I hate darkness.'

Just one night. I would have to get along with these things. Polly rolled over on the bed and giggled.

'It's difficult to sleep without any blanket or quilt. I can't sleep without that. I always miss it. On top of that, this sound of the sea. How do you sleep? You must be pretty used to it.'

She was forcing a conversation and I could not respond. 'Your pillows smell great. Do you spray perfume on them?' I nodded to her query.

'Good idea. I'll also do it at home.' She sank her face in the pillow to smell the scent and I could not help blurting out, 'Peek-a-boo, peek-a-boo.'

She sprang up on the bed, pretty amused. We laughed. Our Darjeeling days came swaying back to us. For a moment I could not hear the roar of the sea, although the sea was at a high tide.

<<< The sea is at a high tide. The waves are on a high. The mad wild body of water plunders the body of Rosana, the body, the consciousness, the life. A crab digs up a void. The palm fronds pant hard. The seabed sinks deeper. The water churns up turbulence. Rosana has submitted herself unconditionally. To the lacerating lust of the sea. A violent, terrible

transit from the conscious to the unconscious. A complete surrender to be torn asunder. The roaring sea wraps up a heart-rending story.

One solitary figure emerges from the palm grove. The long scarf flies. The strong legs sprint. An expert kingfisher dive. A war with wild water. With obscuring darkness. With rapacious rip tide. Miramar Beach murmurs a prayer. Finally, a slug existence comes out of the water, sheltered in two shell-arms. The man puts her down on the wet beach. Turns her over, flat on the stomach, pumps her body. Once, twice, three times, four times . . . To the beat of the waves, to the beat of life. He rolls the lifeless body again on to its back. An inflatable beach ball. He leans over her.

The moonlight and the light darkness have painted her face with all grace. The sea and the beach have adorned· her with glistening silica atoms, on her eyelashes, on her cheekbones, on the tip of her upturned nose. The motionless figure arouses a nameless emotion in him. He rips open the drapes around her body. He eyes the white-beach body, lays his head on the two white sand dunes. A quicksand as if pulls him down passionately. No, he has come out of it. For the time being. And this time, no, he is not kissing the deflated lips, perhaps he is trying to blow some life-air into her paralysed lungs. He is probably trying some artificial respiration. The wet cold body is oozing out fire. The darkness is burning.

Without darkness my eyes were burning. I was unable to sleep. All of a sudden the phone rang. So late? I looked at the clock, it was eleven. Perhaps, Meena Aunty wanted to talk to Polly. I picked up the receiver. Said, 'Hello.' There was no response. But some breathing whispered into my ears. Was it my imagination? I said, 'hello' again. Again, all quiet. A disturbing silence which was almost speaking to me. After a third hello I put down the receiver.

'Who was it?' Polly was inquisitive. 'Nobody spoke.' I shook my head.

'I got it.' She snapped her fingers. 'Must be Dada. Many times, these calls get one way; one person can hear while the other cannot. When we call him or he calls us it happens often. He will call again, you'll see.'

The phone really rang again just as she finished. I picked it up and again the same distant and disturbing presence puzzled me. It was not any one-way snag, I could clearly hear the soft breathing. A faint tap too, perhaps.

'I can't hear you. Will you, please, speak loudly?' I said impatiently. And this time I heard a clear sound. The blank caller just hung up. The click was loud and clear.

'Bad luck.' Polly's tut-tut was loud and teasing. She yawned and covered herself with a light bed sheet. 'Good night.' She turned her face to the wall. Within a few minutes, she was fast asleep. I switched off the light. The deep darkness got filled with that soft breathing sound. It grew much louder than the roar of the sea. >>>

The roaring sea rapped loudly on the side of our boat. Polly had taken me out to the sea and we were rowing along. No, Granny was not with us. Her rowing days were over. She would now be rowing only through the waves of memories. Rowing or wallowing. I looked at her solitary figure from our boat. On a crowded, secure golden beach she looked obscure, brassed off, with an infinite insecurity. Polly was bubbly like the waves. She was listening to Mauvin Gonsalves, the rower and the owner of the boat. He had a few rowing boats and speedboats. This was his business. To provide boating services to the tourists. In fact, it was their family business. His father had been doing it for ages. His brother also helped him apart from doing his part-time job as a tourist guide. Mauvin had been to Kuwait and had worked there for a few years. He had come back just recently, a couple of months ago. He was explaining things to Polly like a tourist guide. His English was pretty good. She was throwing hundreds of questions towards him about Goa, about the sea, or seasons. Her tomato face looked more juicy and shiny under the bright sun.

'You don't talk much miss.' Mauvin tried to attract my attention. My answer was a semi-smile.

He didn't quite like it and said again, 'This boat is meant for old people. You should come with me on my speedboat. That would be fun. Look at that.' He pointed at a speedboat flying past us with a long white surfy trail.

But Polly almost yelled, 'Oh no. I'm not going in that. My head will reel. I'll fall down.'

'I'll drive miss and I won't allow you to fall. You'll wear a life jacket. I'm a great swimmer. Nothing to worry at all. You just tell me.'

Polly gazed at the speedboats moving at a great speed, cutting through the liquid sea waves. Then, she glanced at the solid rippling waves of the muscles of the two strong tanned arms, paddling hard. I saw her looking straight at the hairy chest of Mauvin, half bare under his unbuttoned sleeveless denim jacket.

'Would you like to . . . ?' Polly turned towards me.

'You go. I've done it many times.' I assured her.

After a few minutes, I saw them speeding through the blue in a speedboat and watched its long white foamy wake. She was holding his waist very tight and both of them were laughing in a carefree way. A sixteen-year-old bubble and a twenty-five plus ripple. Under the bright sun of a cloudless day, they were looking marvellous. I stood on the white sand. Waves came and washed my feet now and then. The beach was full of tourists, Indian and foreign. Some of the foreigners were lying on their stomach, in swimsuits under parasols and were being massaged by the local boys.

'Where is that sassy brat?' somebody asked from behind and without looking back I knew it was Granny. She came up and stood by my side. I just pointed at them, without saying anything. She smiled sweetly and the haggard lines around her eyes deepened. We stood for some time, in silence. Both with our own loneliness, own memories and helplessness.

'What did you decide about painting a portrait of hers?' I asked Granny whose remote eyes were fixed on those two closely glued, glowing figures. Granny did not reply immediately.

She narrowed her blue eyes and gloom spilled.

'Why do you think I should? There's nothing spectacular about the girl. She countered without looking at me.

'You'll make her spectacular. Your brush will. After all, there is all success and radiance about her. Your brush will smile for a change.'

'Radiance blinds me as does love. A blind person cannot paint,' Granny sounded obstinate.

The radiant pair came back to the shore in high spirits.

'It was really great fun. Oh, I enjoyed it so much.' She flopped down on the sunny sand and rolled all over. Mauvin left the boat and came near us. His conch-white teeth flashed.

'Miss. This is not enough. Let's go for some water sport. Surfing? Waterskiing? That'd be still more fun.' Will you do it with me? I don't enjoy it alone.'

'Of course miss. I will, with pleasure. Come on.' They ran away, hand in hand, towards the part of the beach where water sports facilities were available.

'Come back before lunch,' I shouted after them.

But they came back much later. After many rounds of waterskiing and swimming.

Around 5 p.m. I finished my painting. I used to take orders and supply paintings to the hotels and rich families. One such order was completed. I was worried about Polly and went out to look for her, as she was getting late. I was a bit absent-minded, and in the corridor I just walked into somebody. Something fell down near my feet. A key ring, with a bunch of keys. I picked it up and handed it over with a 'sorry'. He was a customer at our hotel. A foreigner. He whistled and breezed past me, twirling the key ring around his finger.

Just then I saw Mom and Meena Aunty and between them was Polly, almost flaked out. She was literally carried in by Mom and Meena Aunty. Her tomato face looked like a grilled delicacy. But she was in pain. Long exposure under the bright sun had made her sick. She had a terrible headache. She had not eaten a proper lunch, but some junk seafood, offered by Mauvin from some beachside food joint. She started vomiting too. Mom called our physician and he gave her some medicine. Polly was crying and cursing. Cursing the hot sun, the beach, the food and of course, Mauvin.

'What kept you so long at the beach? I told you to come back before lunch,' I asked.

'I should have.' She was tossing on the bed with a splitting headache, even after having popped a couple of strong painkillers.

'This girl. She never knows when to stop.' Meena Aunty grumbled, 'If she likes something, she goes beyond the limit, to the extreme. She always overdoes things. Unnecessarily. Doesn't listen to anybody.'

'Aunty we should let her alone. She needs some sleep,' I said and started drawing all the curtains of my room.

'No, don't make it dark,' Polly clamoured. I remembered last night and how she wanted to sleep with the light on. I pulled the curtains and made signs to others to go out as I did not want Aunty to go on with some indulgent criticisms of hers. But as we were approaching the doorway Polly shouted again, 'No, no, don't go. Don't leave me alone. I get bored. Be with me. Mummy, stroke my hair, oh Mummy.'

Meena Aunty sat by her side and ran her fingers through Polly's hair.

'Doesn't she sleep alone, even now?' Mom asked Meena Aunty.

'Manasi shares the room with her.' Manasi was Ramesh Uncle's daughter who had been left behind by her mother. 'Sometimes, whenever she insists, I too have to be with her, till she falls asleep. Then only can I come to our room. Many a time, I fall asleep before she does and spend the night in her room.'

Naresh Uncle came in to check if she would be okay within an hour as their flight for Bombay would start at nine.

'I can't go,' Polly said firmly. Meena Aunty also said that in this condition she would not be able to go.

'Let's postpone,' Polly urged, her face winced in pain. 'Can't we go tomorrow?'

'No.' Naresh Uncle was firm enough. 'Joyee will reach Bombay before us, in that case. That's absurd.'

'He can wait, can't he?' Polly was stubborn as usual. But Naresh Uncle did not wait for her. It was decided that instead of Polly, Father would accompany Naresh Uncle to Bombay to receive Joy. They would come back with Joy the same day as without Polly, shopping at Bombay would not be necessary. It was the most sensible decision. However, we held it back from Polly. She would throw a tantrum, Meena Aunty feared. So, the two adults started for the airport when a strong tranquilliser was injected into Polly's arm to give her relief from pain. It started working on Polly and soon, she closed her eyes in a deep slumber.

II

Row The Boat

WHEN ROSANA OPENS her eyes, she is confused. A white unknown ceiling with aluminous chandelier, greets her eyes. It does not look like a chandelier though. Just a hanging hazy halo. Without any outline. A smudge of a damp, drab brightness. A spongy lump of luminosity, dipped in deadly quiet and dripping dead silence all over. *Is this death?* Rosana wonders. Slowly, she looks around her. It looks like a huge earthly room with mortal details. *Is it death? Is this the colour of death?* Her eyes stagger over the pale yellow curtain with brown flowery exuberance, over the dull brown carpet and the huge white walls. Is death nothing but a replica of life on earth? Is it capable of giving refuge to the immortal desire then? Rosana's eyes start blinking. With every blink the outlines get sharper. She discovers herself in a huge four-walled room, heavily decorated with mahogany magnificence. A faint current passes through her numb limbs and senses.

'How are you feeling?' It is as if silence is echoed in the words. The voice of death? It sounded like Portuguese. She strains her ears. And her eyes sense a visual wave. A Series of animated sequences, frames of movements, one following the other in a slow motion.

'How're you feeling?' The voice speaks in Portuguese again and an image emerges in front of her eyes. A close-up of a face. Two straight eyebrows, one sharp-pointed but a little-dented-in-the-middle nose, two deeply set slate eyes, with her miniature face inlaid in them. A man is leaning over her. A man she can't recognise from her past life.

'You are sweating. I must switch on the fan,' he continues with his perfect Portuguese.

A fan! Rosana sits up on the bed. Shocked and shattered. A live, mortal room leaps up in front of her eyes with details, with bold and cold outlines.

'Back to square one!' Rosana sighs deeply. 'Back to square one.' The deep sigh spirals through the silence and gets lost under the growing whirr of the fan.

'What?' The man turns back, the switchboard behind his auburn head looks a pathetic black. He starts in Portuguese again.

'What did you say? I couldn't follow you.' He comes near the bed. Looks into her eyes, with questions inscribed on the slate. Rosana looks on but does not speak. A dashing Portuguese figure with crew-cut hair, a long and strong body, a square face with a slim moustache.

He looks at Rosana's dazed face and shoots another question. 'Feeling okay now?' Rosana nods. A robotic nod. 'Want to go home now?'

'No, I don't.' Rosana replies violently in her imported Portuguese with a Goan accent.

'I see. You're not a Portuguese, are you?' Rosana shakes her fair head, very slowly.

'Strange!' He raises his straight eyebrows with a curve. Then he speaks in English, 'Who are you then?' The question is direct, as he looks directly at her.

'I am a Goan,' she replies in a low voice.

'Impossible.' He comes nearer, looks at her sharply, shakes his head in disbelief 'You just can't be a native Goan.' He keeps on looking at her extra-white skin, her fair hair, her facial features and her clear blue eyes. Nowhere does he find any *feni*-fed, *kokum-brown* shade. He waits for her correct reply. She is silent. He grows impatient.

'You mustn't hold back anything from me. You know who I am? I'm a military officer. So, you better tell me the truth. I'll try to help you.'

She does not answer but opens her eyes wide and fixes them on his eyes. An aloof blue wave touches him coldly. 'What's your name?'

'Rosana. Rosana Fernandez.'

'Well Rosana, I've saved your life.' He utters the words with some extra pride but is shocked to get no response from· the other side. Only the eyelids roll down like tiny shutters, to conceal the transparent blue and the long brown frond-like eyelashes cast a beige shadow on the pale cheeks.

'Do you understand that I saved your life?' He notices only a faint nod from Rosana.

'Strange! You didn't even thank me.'

The turbulent undercurrent, flowing below the transparent calm, suddenly surges high.

'No, I can't. I just can't thank somebody for prolonging my misery. I won't.'

Her two blue ripples of eyes overflow. Rosana covers her face with her hands and uncovers her weakness. Breaks into tears. She is back to mortality. She is back to insecurity. She is back to the most abstract phenomenon under the sham concreteness called life. Tears trickle through the chinks of her fingers. Roll along the hands, forearms, down to the elbow-points and drip on the bed. The man is touched. He promptly goes close to her, holds her head against his wide chest and tries to console her. He strokes her silvery hair, her bare arms, half-bare back and all her body.

'Come on. Be a brave girl. Tell me what is it?' he repeats the question again and again. Slowly and gradually she stops sobbing. Then, she feels the touch. A male touch, male and melting. A sudden shudder and she tears herself away from him. He sits by her side. His body glows brighter than the midday sun. It is a heat wave. Yet, she wraps the linen thoroughly around her body. He comes closer. Rosana moves back to the edge of the bed. He slides still closer. His stormy breathing makes her breathless.

'You are so beautiful,' the stranger whispers. His whole loud appearance, strangely enough, gets softened to a fluffy whisper. His strong square fingers run along the highs and lows of her face, with a soft brush touch. His moustache does not prick as he kisses her on the cheeks, rubs his face against her neck. He kisses her all over her body, kisses her mouth again and again. Rosana drops on the bed, a pulpy mess, a palpitating bundle of nerves. She does not comprehend what is happening to her. Yet, as he attempts to strip her, Rosana resists.

'No, please no.' She can't hear her own voice.

He struggles with the folds of linen. He can't succeed. 'Don't be stupid. I have already seen your body. Who do you think changed your clothes? Washed your body clean? Now, let me love it. Let me.'

Rosana imagines her bedraggled body on the bed, placed there by two rugged hands. A deep flush makes her more attractive, more vulnerable.

'Oh God. I'm going to take you. Now.' He crushingly hugs her.

She struggles hard to free herself, 'No, please. Have mercy on me. No I don't want. I don't.'

'But you wanted death.' He loosens the hug with those stiff words. She gets stiff. The silence stiffens. Rosana looks at the face leaning over hers. It speaks again.

'You were going to die. Do you think it is going to be worse than that?'

No, Rosana does not think so. Rosana cannot think so. Rosana flings herself towards the stranger and holds him tightly. An unconditional surrender to the stormy waves. For the second time in one evening. And this time not to be saved by any strange saviour. The night around them melts away. >>>

The night was not old. Polly was sleeping. A strong dose of painkillers and tranquillisers was working on her. The fever was down. I looked at the clock. It was ten. The phone rang. Quickly, I picked it up. Polly was not to be awakened. Nobody spoke. I sensed the presence, I felt the breathing. As soon as I hung up, it rang again. And again that same vibrating silence. I kept the receiver off the hook and sneaked out of the room. I had to talk to Granny. It was a hectic day, I wanted a private night. I crept along the garden, avoiding the gravelled path. The gardenias on the hedge were exuding a Milky Way mist, spreading a nostalgic fragrance. Far away in the black corner of the garden, a few fireflies were perforating the darkness at random.

'Life is too small to dream to your fill. Why do you come to life? Because you can dream, A dream has no past, present or future. Those who dream to make it true, they don't dream, they desire and drool.'

When I approached Granny's cottage I saw her pacing up and down on the verandah. She stopped on seeing me. Her lips parted as though to say something, but she shook her head and went inside. I followed her. The sound of some loud band floated in the air. A racy Goan tune. Goa always celebrates with music, with dance. With natural grandeur. The gregarious waves followed each other out in the dark. A piece of music of their own. The same over the ages, and yet so refreshing. Granny's heart was out of tune. She went to the room where her heirloom was kept. Warp and woof. Warp and woof. Musicalsound. Monotonous.

I went near the table. A newspaper. There was a small headline underlined with a painting brush, by Granny. She even wrote with a brush. You wouldn't find a ball pen anywhere in her cottage. Bank cheques she used to sign with her cartoon-drawing pen. The blue brush highlighted a few black words: SINGING SENSATION ON A CHARITY MISSION.

The news story said that Leslie Fraser, the latest singing sensation, had come to India and donated a large sum to an orphanage *'Amar Ghar'* in Puruliya in West Bengal. He had freely sung songs for the children. But refused to say anything about his schedule in India. In my mind, I read the headlines as EXOTIC EXPIATION. A large sum paid to the poor orphans in expiation of the wrong done to one of them. *Where are you Mukul? Have you found your shelter to protect your dreams? Or your refuge is still elusive?*

My heart longed for a time machine. My dream, my time machine. To go back into the past. To rewrite the history. To recreate the music. Bit by bit. The terracotta face of Mukul. The enchanted, black-bead eyes reflecting my red bindi. The aquamarine waves. The resonant laughter. The spread of the migratory wings. The red, rocky, barren expansion. A blue mood. A green touch. A white hospital bed. A white smell of scorching heat. Orange heat and vermillion dust. The coloured moon of Holi. The disco loured face of Leena. An aching weed. An interrupted tune. A flowering feeling. Bit by bit. Bit by bit.

Every bit of me recalls every bit of you. My sky expands in the wings of you. Oh where are you!

Just a few days. A few moments. Yet, it seemed I had lived my whole life during those Mahua moments and the rest was only its lingering aroma. Leslie must never have felt any regrets. He wanted the depth and not the length. I remember when we had spoken about the deep agony I had felt at famous skater's sudden, untimely death at the age of 28. I had even wished to die, if God could give back his life in exchange for mine.

'It was the most perfect death I would say.' Leslie had put it very plainly. 'With the skating boots on, and by the side of his love. After a fairy-tale-like life. Could anything be better than that? Only because his life was shortened, you don't like it. But his was a real fairy tale. Never go by the length of it, Lucie. Plunge into the depth. That is life.' An epiphany. And that was love for him. Now, I faintly felt, maybe he was right.

'You were right.' Granny's voice dropped in the still backwaters of the dream. The calm reflection broke. Circles in the water. Bigger and bigger, still bigger. Granny sipped at a glass *of feni,* the alcoholic drink made of cashew nuts.

'He is in India, . . . sent the blank letter. Hmmm . . .'

And now it is blank calls, I thought as my mind went blank for some time. Then, I flung open the French windows and descried a moving dot of light along the horizon. A ship. A sailor. A journey. An anchorage. Slip anchor. Granny sipped the f*eni,* I got the intoxication. I got the toxic torment.

He is in India and all he does is give me blank papers and calls! Where did he call me from a few minutes ago? And why did he? Is it all blank for him? Why did he bother to send them then?

Granny gazed at my face through *the feni.*

'Generous sea . . . returns what it takes away. My boat is lost. My caravel is sunk.'

Granny laughed. A long high sound. Sounded more like a wail. She took out the blank letter and tore it into pieces. Let them fly in the air. The white pieces floated in the air for some time and then fell on the floor, on the table, on her fair hair, on my arms, everywhere, like the words without melody. I saw the face of agony. I heard the voice of the ultimate void. I took away the glass of *feni* from her hand. She did not allow me to hold her close.

'Go and find him. Go now.' She almost commanded. In a military fashion. Then, dropped on the chair. She whispered, 'Don't lose him.'

She took up the Bible. Held it close to her breast. Eyes closed. In the darkness she was looking for a refuge. The refuge that light cannot show.

<<< For a refuge. For a refuge, Rosana's body writhes. For a refuge, Rosana's body clutches the body of the stranger. A heavyweight body writhes heavily on her, yet it is just weightless. It turns her own body light and lighter, almost bodiless. Shapeless. Watery. A swaying wave. An oar in the water. Glides deep and deeper. Strokes . . . ,—fast and faster.

Dip and splash.
Dip and splash.
Dip and splash.

Her boat is in motion. Her refuge. Her freedom. She feels free from her body. It is all body. And no body. It is just a violently pleasant spasm to wrench away from the body. And it is all happening to Rosana. A tryst with death, an encounter with desire, a climb on the peeks of passion. Is this called life? Rosana gets it only when she hugs death?

The stranger hugs and kisses her lightly when all the paddling is over. The canoe is ashore. Only a quiver lingers.

'May I know your name?'

'Don't you know me much better than that?' he sneers.

'How should I call you?'

'That's a valid question. Call me Antonio.'

So, Antonio is the name of her present. She does not want to think of the past and does not wish to go into the future.

'Now, I'll ask you something. Why did you want to die? I want to know.'

'I thought death would be better than this life. My life. That's why.'

'Was it a heartbreak? Some guy deserted you? Tell me your story.' His eager eyes get fixed on Rosana. She does not understand why this man wants to row across the whole length of Rosana in one night, explore her geography, excavate her history. His longing glance, however persuades her. She strokes his hairy chest and tells a bit about her mother, her father. Finally, about her boat and the impudent Portuguese Fidalgo. He listens in silence, without interrupting her narration. Rosana cannot speak much. Her eyes hurt. Her body loosens.

'Can I sleep now? I'm so sleepy.' Rosana's heavy eyelids droop.

When they open wide again, broad daylight kisses her all over. A familiar smell; a very, very familiar smell hugs her senses. Rosana feels heavy, Rosana feels warm and Rosana feels at home. Home! Where is her home? The last night swings open out of the blue. The blue spreads above her, from horizon to horizon. Rosana springs up on her bed. It is not a bed. It is a canoe. Rosana scrutinises. It is her canoe. Yes, it is her lost canoe. Her oars with R F inscribed on them. Her cushioned seat. Even her small basket with the titbits. And the canoe is on the beach. At the lonely corner of the beach where she lost it, at the confluence of the Mandavi and the sea. At a distance, two fishermen throw curious glances at her. It must be early morning. Very few people are on the beach. There is no sign of the white man or of the multicoloured night. As if they never existed. As if some time machine took her there and brought her back to this time. Otherwise, how is she now here? In her canoe? Yes, her canoe is back with her. Without any trouble or effort. Yet, she does not feel so happy as she should be. The lost canoe is found. Some fond something is lost. Rosana steps out of her canoe. It is too small to accommodate her new self anymore. It is lost to her forever. >>>

'You've never lost him. No, I don't think so.' Granny made the statement. Her fit of agony was over.

We were sitting in the dark. There was a power failure. A small candle was burning and beckoning insects. Numerous variety of insects that the warm Goan climate has created and nursed. Some of them were buzzing around the flame. Granny repeated her buzzing words as she would do if she believed them strongly.

'You've never lost him. No, I don't think so.' Her dewy eyelashes glistened in the candlelight. She was having a cup of black coffee I had prepared for both of us.

'Let him come. Let him come. I'll see how far it is true.' My wish rushed in with a gust of wind which almost blew the flame off I got up and closed the French windows. Through the glass I could see the trees swaying violently. The moon was blotted out. The storm clouds were gathering.

'Granny, I fear a storm.' I closed the storm windows of her cottage. Then came and sat by her side.

'There will be a storm.' Granny paused. Her words dived into nothingness, like the insects into the flame. She turned to me.

'Why are you getting engaged to this boy?'

Granny's sharp glance pierced my senses. Through and through. Her blue eyes got turbid. Our enormous black shadows on the wall quivered in silence. Like two flailing wings of a wounded bat. The question wounded me. Didn't I ask myself the same question over and over again before coming out with a yowling 'yes'. Just a few days ago. After he became a common name. I could not expect anything uncommon to happen after that. He had never written to me, although he knew my address in Goa. Even when he was not famous. Now his e-mail address was well known and Internet services had just started in Goa, to unite e-strangers. Not to reunite e-stranged lovers? With a deluge of fan mail in his Inbox every day, how would he find out my message? Even if he found it, why would he answer? His epiphany was long over. His deciduous memory must have shed my love, with an autumn-smile. His spring-smiles had been flashed in the papers and magazines with various beauties and I had transferred his blue-diamond-smile from my ring finger to the second finger, seconding Mom's proposal to marry Joy. Mom considered the marriage as the refuge. From the void, named Leslie. From the reality devoid of dreams. I could not refuse her.

'Will you refuse him if he also comes?' Not a difficult question, but absurd. Hypothetical.

'I want him to come back in my dreams. I want my dreams to come back, Granny.'

Her eyes examined me, as if through a microscope. If she could read my mind she would know that it was saying, *I don't want to drag my dream into reality. Both will be spoilt. I'll have nothing. I know the life which has forgotten to dream. Here in front of me. That Dead Sea heaviness, those features, pieces of taxidermy. I don't want to push my god, my very own god into the territory of others, to have him fragmented. I won't allow that one solitary super abstraction to be decimated and reduced to ritual concrete. Moulded concrete models. Repetition, one after another and another, when God wants them to be different individuals like their own thumbprints. I love my god with my own thumbprint.*

Perhaps, Granny deciphered my emotion. She heaved a sigh and stretched herself on the old· spacious teak armchair. Just then with a click the power came on.

'What a relief! I can work now,' she said more to herself than to me. Next, she put on her glasses and took up the palette and a brush. This was her way of saying bye. I wished her goodnight and slipped out.

'Let the door be open,' Granny said without looking at me.

'The weather is stormy. The wind is blowing hard. You'll catch a cold,' I insisted.

'Never mind. The cold has never caught me. I am too cold for that.' She coolly leant over her work. I had to obey her.

Through the open door I saw the two hands of the clock meeting on the number twelve. It was midnight. But Granny would keep on working. For her the difference between day or night hardly existed. Someday she would be awake the whole night and sleep the whole morning. She did not have an office job to attend to or any social obligations to meet.

Strong stormy winds hailed me as I went out. I heard the groan of the struggling trees. The hissing of the waves. I ran towards the main hotel building with my hair and frock flying rebelliously. As I tapped on the sliding glass door, our night watchman who was watching TV, came up and opened the door. Many a time I used to come late from Granny's cottage, he knew. He wished me goodnight sweetly.

The door of my room was closed but not locked. I slowly entered without making any noise, lest Polly should wake up. All the windows were open, even the French windows. The curtains were flying madly. I rushed towards the windows and struggled to close them. One by one, I managed to close them. My verandah was strewn with big leaves from the young jackfruit tree and the cute pinnate leaves of the tamarind tree. Both the trees were shaking violently and their boughs were bowing down. I shut the French windows and turned back to see if Polly was okay, in spite of all the noise. The bed was empty. There was nobody on the bed.

'She was alone and must have gone to her parents' room,' I concluded. I felt guilty, decided to apologise to them in the morning. This was not the right time to do it. I slipped into my night gown when I heard a knock on the door. It was Mom.

'So you're back so late! Went to Granny? How is Polly feeling now?' Mom queried.

'Sorry Mom. Polly has gone to Aunty it seems.'

'Absurd. That room is locked. Meena and I are sharing our suite.' Mom was worried.

'What do you mean?'

'Around eleven when the lights went off, I came here to see if everything was okay. I couldn't find either of you. I thought both of you had gone out, maybe, to your granny. Didn't she go with you?'

'No Mom. I left at around ten. She was fast asleep then. After that, I don't know.'

'Ten thirty Meena came to take her to their room as today your father and Naresh-da have gone to Bombay. She saw her sleeping like a log. She tried to wake her up but she was under the effect of painkillers and tranquillisers. So she let her sleep here. We decided to share our suite.

Their suite is kept locked. We were remembering our Darjeeling days. And planning for your future. Yours and Joy's.'

Mom's eyes showered happiness even in this unhappy situation. Mom would be always so cool. She went on with her narration. 'Meena fell asleep after some time. Before the power failure. I couldn't find you then. So now again, I came to make sure you people were back. The weather is getting pretty bad. Oh God, where can she be?'

'Let's go around the hotel. She is mischievous. Maybe she is strolling around.'

'She can't stroll alone. She is not that adventurous. Her wildness is not without purpose. Hope, she has not gone to the beach,' Mom said glancing remotely

A chilly wind crept through my spine. Could it be that Mom was thinking the same as I was? I remembered the water scooter, her arms holding Mauvin's waist tightly. Their white teeth flashing, hair flying and brushing each other's face. Polly was quite brave and uninhibited like many rich girls. I remembered the unhappy incident, which had caused Naresh Uncle's heart attack. Would she repeat the same thing, even in a strange place? How could Mauvin dare to do such a thing? He was a very familiar character here, in our hotel. He was friendly with all our hotel staff. Why did he do such a thing to us? But Meena Aunty could not wake her up even at ten thirty. She was sick. Too sick to go fooling around. I looked at Mom. She was engrossed in thought. I gave her a slight nudge to ask her what to do.

'I'm going to the beach, just to take a look. You see around the hotel. Don't wake up Meena. And don't you tell anybody about this now. Okay?' Mom rushed towards the door. I could not stop her. She would not be afraid of some simple sea storm. I changed and stepped out of my suite.

<<< Rosana steps into the house of her father late in the morning. Nobody is there to ask her,. 'Where were you? Why didn't you come home last night?'

Her father is not home. Must have gone to his dispensary. He must not have even noticed if she was back at night or not. Jose, the small deaf and dumb boy who does daily chores for them, and gives her company in the canoe, is pulling water from the well. She can hear the squeak of the pulley. The banana trees wave their shining green leaves and welcomes her. The pale green guava tree is in blossom. Rosana rushes into her room. With a new body. A body of gooseflesh. Rosana pants hard. Her eyes fall on the long mirror of the dressing table.

This is not her frock. A white lacy, flouncy thing. Surf white. The surf, strained off from the blue. Deposited lifeless on the beach. This is not her dress, and this is not her body either. Lips are swollen. Love bites on her neck, shoulders, cheeks. She looks at her arms. A few scratches. She touches her face as if with the hand of that man. How did he feel? Why was he so intoxicated? This small thin cashew-nut body, how much *feni* did it ooze last night? An alluring flavour of *dudhshiri* floats in the air. A seductive tune of *mando* spreads in nature. Rosana looks at her. Rosana wonders. Next, she hates it. She unbuttons the dress in a rage and tears it off from her body. A small petal-like thing falls off from her bra. It touches her feet. Rosana picks it up. A small chit. She unfolds it slowly. An oyster shell opened ajar. Six words: SIX THIRTY AT DONA PAULA, ANTONIO. A seagull spreads her wings over the blue. The areca grove showers white softness. Rosana flings herself on the bed.

'He is so strange. Oh God, life is so strange!' Rosana laughs and cries at the same time.

Dona Paula, an area belonging to the Portuguese nobles. The place,—connected with the legend of two longing lovers. A Portuguese lady and a Goan lad, of the sixteenth century. This is the blue burial depth of that evergreen love. The landscape covers a large escarpment with a bay and two small picturesque beaches. An islet linked to the mainland by a bridge and a quay. Surf trimmed unruly waves beat against the jagged rocks jutting out over the bay. Here is a riot of blue, watery, ethereal, with some evanescent white lace and a solid sombre touch of black brown. The setting sun adds a melancholy crimson to the scene. The air whispers pathos. Lady Dona still wails they say, for her brawny ingenuous Goan lover. Rosana closes her eyes and feels the touch of the damp air. For her it is not wailing today, it is lulling. A boat approaches along the Zuari River. Rosana goes to the farthest point of the quay. The boat stops. A hand is held out. Rosana steps into the boat. It is her boat. Now, it is not her refuge from the world. Now, it is her world.

The boat goes away from the quay. From the mouth of the river towards its origin. From the turbulence towards the quiet. Rosana looks at those slate eyes. They are also fixed on hers. They don't talk. They don't listen either. They don't move. Only two arms operate mechanically. Dip and splash. Dip and splash. The oars rip the waves, the waves rap on the side of the boat. The long wake froths frivolously. Away and further away from the limitless expanse of the sea. To the limited extent of a peaceful stream. With a setting sun on their horizon. When the land recedes farther away, Antonio stops paddling. Let his paddle trail in the water. Comes nearer to Rosana and kisses her. A sea-deep kiss. And long, very long. Till it is dark and the stars sparkle, not only in the sky but in their senses too. The boat floats along the calm. They hold each other closely and the water dreams.

'So it was you who stole my boat, wasn't it?' Rosana talks after a long time.

'I didn't steal it. I just took it for a ride . . . for rowing . . . I mean.'

'Don't take me for a ride. Will you?' Rosana smiles. He smiles too. Time smiles in silence.

'Are you really a big military officer?' She gets a big nod from her companion.

'How long have you been in Goa?'

'Just one week,' he says in a confused tone. 'It seems a long period though.'

'You feel homesick?'

'No, never.' He almost spits out the words with a jerk.

Then says with a watery melody, 'I'm fine here, now that I have found you.'

He slowly paddles the boat towards the lonely part of the bank. Marshy bank, reedy grass and drifting mangroves. All are dark and mysterious. Oozing a melodious silence. Antonio secures the boat with a rope to a nearby tree with its boughs drooping tenderly over the river. The moon is yet to rise to weaken the darkness. In the darkness, they don't see each other. They feel. Violently intense feeling. The boat rocks. The waves coil, the bank shudders.

Dip and splash. Dip and splash.

In the blind moments of time, they blend with each other. The moon rises in the sky, ripens with the night as they get lost in each other. >>>

'She is lost, my God!' I could not conceal my anxiety, as we could not find Polly anywhere around the hotel or the beach. Mom came back from the beach heavily drenched. While coming back from the beach, Mom had even checked Granny's place. She was not there. The storm had subsided now but rain had started. Goan rain. Sea pouring on the sea. After changing her clothes and pouring herself a glass of brandy, Mom decided to ring up Mauvin. She had a strong doubt just as I had. The excuse would be if one of our hotel boys had taken shelter in his place, which was not very far from our house. Mom is always so brilliant when it comes to the presence of mind. She rang up and came to know that nobody had turned up. Mauvin's father received the call. He was sleepy but confirmed that Mauvin was very much in the house, in fact, sleeping in the same room with him. We sat speechless gazing at each other as it poured and roared in the sleepless darkness.

Next, Mom asked our watchman. He said almost all the tourists were back by ten. Only one family, that had gone out for the Dudhsagar Falls, set against the majestic hilly backdrop of the Castle Rock, had come back after the power failure. The foreigner who was staying in our hotel, at present, had gone out once or twice, but, had finally come back much before I returned from Granny's place. It would have been around ten thirty he guessed, when the strong winds had started blowing. He had not seen anybody going out or coming in after that. He had come to my room and kept a lantern on the corner table as soon as the light had gone off.

'Why ma'am, something wrong?' he asked with curiosity. Mom shook her head while still pondering over things deeply. We peeped through the door of Mom's room and felt a bit relieved to see Meena Aunty fast asleep. The air· conditioner was already off. Mom reduced the speed of the fan and dimmed the night lamp. She closed the door without a sound. Then, we went to my room. My eyes were aching. Mom still looked calm. But I could feel her pulse. It must be such a terrible feeling for her.

'It's puzzling. It's just puzzling. A girl, half-sick, completely under the influence of strong tranquilliser, just vanishes into the air! Impossible. Just impossible.' She bit her finger impatiently. This would be very damaging for her and for the beautiful relationship these two families had shared over all these years. It seemed, for the first time Mom was unable to diagnose the situation. She was getting vexed with herself.

'Oh Lucie, if only you could have stayed with her!' Her voice spattered despair and her sea-anemone eyes shrank in guilt. I put my arms around her. The branches of the young jackfruit tree rattled against my windowpane. The strong wind was howling again.

'Mauvin is at home. But did somebody from Darjeeling follow her? She does have a bad history. Gone astray at such an early age.' She shook her head in despair, 'They should have controlled her in time.'

'Could she run away with somebody? Like she did, the last spring when uncle got a heart attack?' the words gushed out of my small mouth.

'In that case, she must have shammed illness and avoided going to Bombay. Possible. But the doctor was convinced, so was I. It sounds so incredible. She is but a kid.'

'It beats me too. Something has happened, Mom. We better inform the police before it is too late,' I told Mom, whose mind I presume, was diving deep where the raindrop could not reach and the writhing sea anemone was trying hard to stick to some solid, rational rock. A Darjeeling snowball rumbled down my heart. The rain got heavy, the darkness got heavier and our minds were the heaviest. Mom's mind still roved around and so did her eyes. An ejaculation ensued soon.

'Somebody was here. Look here.'

<<< 'Look here. It is all for you,' says Antonio pointing at the jewellery shining and sneering. At least, Rosana thinks so. They are as usual floating in her—their boat—along. the reach of the Mandovi River. Near the Chorao islet. In semi-darkness. Away from the crowd. Lost in their own world.

'Why this?' Rosana asks.

'I love to adorn you. Your beautiful body.'

'But I don't like it.'

'You don't like the design?'

'I don't like jewellery. These are meant for showing off. I hate to be in a crowd and I hate to show off.'

'But I love to see you adorned with this jewellery. I'll bring even more.'

'Why? Are you sort of paying me?' Rosana's clear blue eyes harden like sapphires.

'Nonsense. How could you say so? After so many days and after so much intimacy don't you understand how much I care for you, how much I love you?' Rosana sees the moon in Antonio's slate eyes.

'Love? You never meet me in the daylight, in front of others. We only meet at lonely beaches, paddle about along the river, or go to some lonely island of some lagoon. Do you really love me?'

A tired breeze cuddles the restless ripples softly. The trees arch further to touch the water. A small cloud hesitates to cover the moon. Antonio hands over the oars to Rosana and lies down resting his head on her lap.

'I know your feelings. But I am helpless you know. I am a military officer. There are limitations for me. If I were a normal Portuguese man, a businessman, a doctor, something like that, it would have been easier for me. How I wish I were not what I am.'

'I love you just the way you are. You may leave your job someday and we may have a bright tomorrow, can't we?' Rosana's dream draws the picture of a doubtless dawn.

'Yes, we can. But first tell me, if you don't like jewellery, what would you like? I want to give you something you want.'

'Give me a houseboat.'

'Houseboat? What's that?'

'A boat as well as a house. A floating house. You find them in Kashmir, a place in North India. I have read about it. Sister Margarita told me too. She went there on a tour. Why don't you go and see and get one for me?'

'May Antonio de Oliveira Salazar allow me to do so.' Antonio smiles. 'Can't you ask for something a little more easily available?'

'Yes. I can. A child. Your child. I want to have your child. My sister has children. My friends have children. I want a child.'

Antonio sits up. A sharp pain spirals inside the coconut trunk. The flowering shaft is sliced. Pain is dripping. Drip drop. Drip drop. Rosana goes on.

'I'll be a mother and I'll never leave my child. Not the way my mother did.'

'You have to wait for that, sweetheart, I need some time.' Antonio strokes her cashew-nut body. Coconut sap ferments. Toddy froths. The air spreads a sad intoxication. Rosana looks up at the stars to see the light of the time of her motherhood. Is it some light years away?

Rosana's clandestine adventure first gets exposed to Sabrina. When she comes to meet Father, her wise and wide eyes fall on the love bites on Rosana's lotus-stem neck. Two rainbow patches. Sabrina can read the colourful story.

In Rosana's room, she whispers, 'Who is it Rosy? Do I know him?'

Rosana closes her eyes as if the world would get blind with her.

'Tell me Rosy. I won't tell Papa. Jose informed me that nowadays, you do not take him on your rowing trips. One day Valentino told me that he saw you from a distance near Reis Magos, with a man in the boat. I told him it must be Jose. Now, I know he did not make a mistake. Tell me dear, who is it?'

Rosana has never wanted to part with her sweet secret. She does not open her eyes because she feels as if she has been stripped. Sabrina persuades her.

'You never had any secrets from me, nor did I. Didn't I tell you when I fell in love with Valentino? You were the only person who knew about our eloping. Papa did not approve of Valentino as he is not well educated. But I'll see that in your case, it does not happen. I'll convince Papa to marry you to him.'

'Will you?' Rosana's heart surges. The dancing lamps in a dark night of Shigmo. 'Really?'

'Who is he?'

'The man who gave me back my boat.'

'Yes, you said that one day mysteriously a man brought back your boat. You didn't say anything in detail. That man must have had a name. Why are you hesitating? Is he an illiterate fisherman?'

'No, a Portuguese military officer.'

A wild gale blows out the dancing lamps of Shigmo. 'What!' For a few moments the words do not sink in. Sabrina blinks blankly.

'Will you go back on your words now?' Rosana wants to know with a note of disappointment.

'Are you serious? With a Portuguese military officer? You remember Joao, you know how mercilessly they beat him, j ailed him. You know they killed our dear Uncle Dharwadkar, when he took part in the non-violent Satyagraha and you are involved with a Portuguese military officer,!'

Joao is Sabrina's brother-in-law. A member of the Azad Gomantak Party. He was jailed for bombing a police station although he was actually not involved in that. He is still rotting in jail. Uncle Dharwadkar was Rosana's neighbour and was killed in the police firing on the *Satyagrahis* of 1955. In Sabrina's eyes, Antonio is nothing but an animated rifle. Sabrina's eyes reproach Rosana.

'Shame on you, Rosana. Shame on you.'

'But he is a loving man, just as loving as your Valentino.' Sabrina does not realise that.

'Forget him, Rosana. Forget him. Come back before it is too late. He will never marry you. Never.'

'He will. He loves me.'

Rosana goes out for her regular rendezvous.

Soon Mr Fernandez learns about it from some well-wisher of his, who does not want his family to be involved in a scandal. He does not pay heed to it. Slowly, rumours mushroom. Mr Fernandez first asks Sabrina about the fact. Sabrina weeps as she cannot tell a lie to her father and only pleads, 'Just get her married to a boy. Any boy. Would you, Papa? Immediately? She is possessed.'

Unfortunately, the marriage medicine does not grow in the vast green fields of Goa, nor can it be fished out in *ramppons*. So, Mr Fernandez enters Rosana's small room where one afternoon she is trying to· weave something on the antiquated heirloom. *Woof Warp. Woof Warp. Today. Tomorrow. Today's Rosana. Tomorrow's mother. Reality and dreams. Dreams and reality.* Rosana always mixes them up. Takes one for the other. Rosana loses both. The threads get all tangled in the out-of-order antique piece.

'Rosana, don't step out of the house from today. If it's urgent I'll send Jose or Samson (his middle-aged assistant) with you.' The stern and serious voice of Mr Fernandez echoes. The woof, the warp tangle and break.

'You can't ground me like that.' Mr Fernandez hears the voice of a British pride. A pestle on a mortar. Kokum is crushed. The salty tang hangs in the air. Rosana stands up. 'You can't ground me like that, Papa, I am an adult.'

'But you don't behave like one.' The greying eyes droop in shame. 'You should know what you are doing.'

'I do know what I am doing. I'm doing nothing wrong. Nothing.'

The clear blue eyes get clearer. Rosana looks straight at her father without a whit of shame.

Mr Fernandez recalls those words of her mother, 'I'm doing nothing wrong. Nothing. To stay with you without love would be wrong. We are not in love any more. We should not be together.'

'For the sake of the children. Please. For my sake. I'm still very much in love with you. Please, stay with us.'

'I'm sorry. I can't. I can't do injustice to myself'

'I, me and myself . . . all you white people can do, is to think about yourself. Can't you bloody well look beyond yourself and do things for others? You see our women, they would die but they would not leave their family, their children. They would suffer poverty, a drunkard husband, his torture . . . you have seen it for yourself.'

'Go and marry one of them? I have no objection. But let me tell you if a person is not happy with herself, she cannot make others happy. It is impossible. A blind man to tell you the colour! My foot! All this big talk of sacrifice—what utter rot! All of them are frustrated, bloodless creatures. They pass it on to their children, weakness, wallowing in self-pity, lack of self-esteem and confidence. That's why foreigners ruled over you for years.'

A dark slap to shut up a white arrogance. Mr Fernandez comes back to the present and to Rosana, with her clear blue eyes reflecting all those noxious, blue memories. His stern face softens.

'Just think of our name and prestige. This Portuguese officer will never marry you. You don't know these settlers well. They prey on naive girls like you, wherever they go. Forget him. I'll marry you off. Just listen to me, my dear child. Think of your poor papa just for once.'

Rosana feels it difficult to defy the helpless tone. The shell of the crustacean has fallen off. The sloppy sluggish lump inside lies bare. Tears well up in Rosana's eyes.

'Papa. Let's wait for some time. He just needs a little time.'

Time, however, does not give any chance to Rosana. Rosana goes to meet Antonio, with Papa's permission to call him over to meet him. One of their usual meeting places. The calm greenish blue backwaters, arching and whispering palms, the boat waltzing on slow ripples. The setting sun in a pool of colour. A soothing shadow, a placid pleasure. Antonio is already near the boat. Rosana rushes into his arms., Antonio's kiss is just moistening and not flooding. His eyes do not close tightly, but blink as his quivering eyelashes tickle her cheeks.

'Something wrong?' Rosana's clear blue eyes reflect a black premonition.

'Everything is wrong.' Antonio moves away from her and stares at the beyond. The long scarf around his neck flies, strong shoulders droop, long arms dangle. A ship or a wreck? A small bubble grows larger inside Rosana. Large and larger gapes the void encased in the bubble.

'I have to leave Goa and you,' Antonio says still staring at the sea. The bubble breaks. Noiselessly. The emptiness, the pain-coloured emptiness stretches all over. Rosana props herself against a leaning palm. Tears stream down her cheeks.

'Yes Rosana, I'm leaving Goa. Within a couple of days. This is the order of my government.'

'Can't you take me with you?' Rosana sobs. Antonio looks back at her. He shakes his head.

'I can't. I just can't. I'm not going to Lisboa, I'm going to Africa to fight for our Great Salazar.'

'Why, is he not content with his own country?'

'That's also a part of his country, like Goa.' A colonial coolness overshadows the passionate warmth. 'It is my duty. I have to go.' His nasal drawl noiselessly drills holes in her heart. Her senses ache. *Boom and flash. Boom and flash.* A war-ridden sky spreads over.

'Newspapers say very long fights are on there. Won't it end?' she speaks in agony.

'Hopefully I'll try to do so with my men.'

'And you'll come back then? To me? This one colony of yours and only yours you've won without any fighting? Or don't you value anything which you get without a fight?'

Antonio sails to Rosana and she gets anchored. Two assuring arms.

'I love you, Rosana. I don't want to leave you. I don't.' Fervently Antonio kisses her all over. Rosana's heart pounds, Rosana's existence throbs.

Dip and splash. Dip and splash.

'Just pray to God I survive the war to see you again.'

'You will. You will. You have to. You have to come back to me. We belong together. You can't go anywhere else without me. Not even to death. No, you can't.'

For the first time they go inside a church together. The Se Cathedral. Also known as the St Catherine's Cathedral Church. Although the church is open for all but traditionally, the whites and browns do not take the same pew. The evening prayer was just over. The enormous hall is empty. The wide nave welcomes them. They kneel down. They look up at the cross. It is said that the miraculous apparition of Christ took place on this one. Their eyes rest on the majestic Chapel of the Blessed Sacrament. The grand quiet soothes their restless soul. With kindled spirits they glow like two altar candles. The blue grows calm, the slate gets solid.

'I want to walk down the aisle.'

'You will, dear.' Antonio holds her hand.

'With you.'

'Yes. Darling. Let's pray for it.' They stare at each other and their eyes talk loud as dumb moments watch in silence. >>>

We stared at each other. Thunderstruck. Mom and I. Her finger pointed at a small cigarette holder, near the French window. A delicate piece. A non-delicate mystery. Some third person had been in the room. The window was not bolted. Mom swiftly opened the French window and went out on the verandah. I followed her. The strong wind had slowed down but the rain was still pouring. The bloated body of the water-soaked darkness depressed me thoroughly. Mom held away the swaying branches of the young jackfruit tree. She leaned over the railing. And we discovered. The big footsteps near the verandah on the wet ground. No smaller steps of Polly's size were there. Rainwater might have washed them off or it might be . . . Both Mom and I said in a panic stricken whisper, 'Kidnapped?'

No clap of thunder followed the words.

The frogs croaked monotonously out in the field, the silence wailed with the stridulating crickets, the window shutters creaked in the wind. Mom seemed to be sure that she had cracked the problem as usual. At least, the problem of how Polly vanished. Mom dragged me in immediately. Her cold eyes were fixed on me.

'So you left her to be kidnapped.' A conch-shell face stared at me. A cold slobbery snail inched along my senses. An inky silence wrapped up everything around.

A sharp sound severed the heavy silence all of a sudden. My telephone rang. Automatically, my eyes rose to see the time. It was two in the morning. Mom picked up the receiver with a tinge of hope quivering in her eyes. It might be Polly, talking from wherever she was. She picked up the phone before I could. 'Hello,' she said twice. 'Hello, just speak out what is your demand,' she shouted the third time and fourth and then banged the phone down. She stood there almost out of breath for a few seconds.

'Was it the kidnapper?' the words spiralled out of my mouth.

'I thought so.' Mom shook her head in despair. 'But no, it was a blank call. Why the hell will a kidnapper make a blank call! Oh blast, time is hard on us.' She sank in the sofa helplessly and my mind sank in me. In a complete blank. The blank call. Didn't I link it with some blank space in my life? A sharp secluded pain knocked against the eggshell to see the light of day. I wanted to express my doubts about the blank call to Mom, but the words remained retracted in the scallop cover. Pulsating.

With a little hesitation, I said after a few moments, 'Mom, it may still be a case of eloping . . . I mean . . .'

'I don't think so.' She was thinking about kidnap only. 'Anyway we cannot rule it out completely.'

She made me feel a bit relieved.

'I wish Mummy were here. She knows the police officers so well!' Mom sighed.

My grandma, was with her son and his· family at the moment, travelling all over the world. She had gone to her son, two months ago. A doctor in Singapore. I also could not help thinking how hard the episode had hit Mom. She was visibly upset. A blue wave flattened and discoloured. This incident would deal a blow to the deep-rooted relationship with Joy's family. It would also mean a bad name to our hotel, dissuading the tourists. Disturbing the business. I went near Mom. I always felt warmth from the limpid flames of her eyes. Today, they looked like the black cores of the tongues of flame of the flickering candles; empty, lightless. I stroked her head. Mom held my hand. We felt each other in silence. I recalled the night when we discovered the mystery about the Noor Jahan bracelet and held each other in such poignant agony.

Mom shook off the inertia soon and got up. 'I must go to the railway station. You go to the airport in the morning. There is no domestic flight before tomorrow morning.'

'You don't go. Meena Aunty mustn't know . . . send Viru,' I suggested.

'Maybe, you are right. We can depend on Viru. He'll call us if he finds them. I'll go to the police now.' 'Wait Mom. Let's try our best before involving the. police. In case it is not a kidnap?'

'But how?'

'Ring up the hotels.'

'You mean they might be hiding in some hotel and we must ring up to find out if any girl of her age has come to stay this night, late night. We could do that. Good idea. They are mostly known to us. We can pretend some friend was supposed to come here but did not arrive. Weather is bad and we are worried about them. Well Lucie, you start. I'll go and talk to Viru.'

I started looking up in the directory and for the next one hour or so my telephone remained busy. Mom too joined me in the meantime. But there was little success. She might have changed her name. But in most of the places no such young girl checked in during the night after eleven. In one place one teenage girl did come at night, but with a family. Parents and all. Two hotels did receive one young couple each, late night, but they were not sure about the age of the girls. In some hotels only watchmen were awake and they could not give any information. When our endless endeavour finally came to an end, it was almost five in the morning. I sent Mom to her room asking her to take care of Meena Aunty.

'I'll start for the hotels in half an hour. Send somebody to the airport,' I said.

'Why Viru did not call? I was expecting his call.' 'Our phone was continuously busy, Mom.'

'Yes, and I asked him to call here only. He may ring up now. You will let me know as soon as he calls, won't you?' Mom departed, after getting an assuring nod from me.

I stretched myself on the bed not for sleeping but for looking back and looking deep inside me. Huge waves of memory. Stronger waves of emotion. I went surfing. On my dream board. The waves were turbulent. The waves were rough. Strangers and familiar faces. I went surfing. Real and unreal. I went surfing. My god showed me the way. My very own god. Not accessed through any scriptures of any religion. For some result. I just felt him within myself. That feeling is the result. Nothing else. I can't tell how long I was in the half-conscious state named sleep, a mechanical sound slapped me back to consciousness. The telephone was ringing. Yes, it was.

'It is him. It's him.' My conscious self gushed out of me to receive the call.

III

A Broken Sky

'IT IS HIM.' Rosana looks expectantly as she sees any foreigner with crew-cut auburn hair from behind. In the shops, on the roads, and on the beaches. No, she does not row any more. There is no more *Dip and splash* for her. *Time and space. Slit and slash. Slit and slash.*

She is cut off from her Antonio, and her own self. She does not recognise the old Rosana. She just sits quietly at a lonely corner of the river bank, or the beach. She looks for the face and doodles on the sand. Face of Antonio, profile of Antonio, soul of Antonio. She repeats the lines from his letters, which she gets off and on. He is busy fighting. He remembers her. He misses her. He misses Goa. The colours and the calm. Afternoon siesta, before-noon water sports. But he does not say when he will return. When his one colonial duty would be over and another colossal task will start. A colossal task of marrying a girl from a colony he rules. He knows he may have to leave his job. Or they may have to wait till Goa gets independence. And Rosana has to leave her father. A Father whose black blunder with a white girl still hurts, will never accept her choice. But that is so far off. Seems to be a few light years away. When can it happen to her or will it happen at all? Rosana's fingers plough furrows in the sand. She has been ploughing a lonely furrow, how long she can't remember.

Unfortunately, in spite of all the deep, daring '*Dip and splash*' she is not pregnant, much though she wanted to be. So desperately. Even at the cost of society's fury. Antonio could be hers because of the child and through the child. His blood could run through her stream, mingling and jingling with it wildly. She wants a result. A result of her love, a reality for her dream. She wants a refuge in her own womb. She can't go back to her mother's. Her own fertile womb is a woman's greatest refuge. Not her mother's womb. Along with the embryo, her own entity is enclosed by the safe, secure, sheltering fluid. A morsel of life, an embryo is her mortal refuge for immortality. A dream,—breeding reality.

Rosana envies her sister Sabrina. Sitting pretty with two beautiful children. A fertile womb. Valentino is not half as passionate as Antonio. Rosana of today thanks God that Valentino did not choose her. She would never have known the depth of passion. The taste of ecstasy. Still, why is she deprived of motherhood? Rosana does not get the. answer. At home she draws the sketches of Antonio. Tipping her love for Antonio onto papers and touching him through Imagery. *Tip and touch. Tip and touch.*

This is the start of her artist's life. An artist for artist's own sake. She never wants to show them to anybody. A secret passion like her secret love. She dares to send one such to Antonio. along with her letter. An overwhelming reaction from him amazes her.

'Darling. Your work is brilliant. You are a genius. Pursue it. Do some with colour. And do send a portrait of yours. During a campaign I have lost the only snap of yours I brought with me.'

She cannot draw, however, anything but Antonio. At his instance, she goes to sister Margarita, her teacher in her school days. A good artist. She sells the jewellery given by Antonio. To meet the expense of painting materials.

Margarita is a kind woman, she does not charge her, as she wants to help all hapless souls. But the cost of painting materials is high. So, Antonio's mementoes are sold. One by one. Finally, she sells her canoe. No more rowing refuge for her. Now, it is sailing through the colours. Her strokes and brush. Her strokes and brush.

Rosana picks up the art of oil painting very fast. Within a couple of months. With her limitation to paint only one person. Even when she paints the dream of their reunion, her face remains veiled or she is shown from the back facing her beloved, who is in fierce focus.

With this brush she resists everything. Father's advice, Sabrina's advocacy and Vijay Naik's advance for marriage. She has no time for anybody. Just no time. Yet, time and space never favours her. *Slit and slash. Slit and slash.*

Rosana bleeds. The first oil painting, a small portrait of Antonio sent to his regular address comes back to her as the addressee not available. Maybe, he is coming back. Rosana's mind floats in a dream-jacket. The red cashew flowers spread the blooming blue scent all over. With time they faint, they fall. The kidney-shaped fruits dangle. Urrak soaks through the soul. *Feni* froths. A cashew-nut body gets roasted. As deserted. No news from Antonio. For months and months. Sand dunes shift from one beach to the other. The large universe expands a little larger. Rosana's blue depth looks for Antonio. 'Where is he? Where is he?' >>>

'Not here. She is not here.' Viru was on the phone, no blank calls any more. Viru said, 'I've checked everywhere in Margao station. She is not there. One passenger train was going to Vasco. I boarded that and reached here some time ago. She is not here either. What shall I do now?'

'Come back.'

By now, I was getting ready to face the worse. Enquiries of the police, crowding of the reporters, curiosity of the customers. And a desolate and deserted looking Meena Aunty. 'What would be Joy's reaction if before his arrival, she does not come back?' The first faint ray of the sun penetrated the overcast sky. It was still more than half dark. The rain had stopped but the weather was damp, heavy and gloomy. All the leaves of our garden were still dripping. I started preparing for the difficult day ahead. If I had to move from one hotel to another in the morning it would take a long time. Mom would be calling the police by then. Poor Mom. She had saved a home wreck. This time it would possibly wreck her business. A kidnap in a hotel. Who would come to stay in a place with this reputation? And the relationship with Joy's family? Mom's call came as I was thinking about her, and I informed her that Viru had not found her.

As I hung up, a cautious knock on the door startled me.

Who could be so early? I was not in the habit of taking bed tea. Even that would come not before seven at this time of the year. The soft rap sounded again. This could not be the rap made by some of our employees. An unearthly excitement ran through my spine. In a second, a series of possible events invaded my mind. Could it be Mom? Or Polly? She might have gone out with somebody. A friend from Darjeeling, who had followed her here. For a carefree night. For a forbidden pleasure. Or that face, I had been dying to see. Come to Goa and to me. To his reverie-refuge. Was I going to see his halo of a face after so many light years? I was dreaming even in this dreary situation. I lost my strength to move. A sparrow with soaked wings. The knocking grew a bit impatient. So did my heart. I wanted to go to the dressing table. The night I had spent almost sleepless. My eyelids were abnormally heavy and I could guess the eyes would be pretty reddish. My clothes were shabby, last evening's casual wear. A skirt and a blouse. But I had hardly any time for make-up.

I dragged myself somehow, towards the door. With a heart-stopping squeak, the door opened. It was an anticlimax. Who was this man? An alien? The person standing outside with a bit hesitant look, I had never seen before. He was a foreigner. With a robust body and a, robotic stern face. Dark brown hair and hazel eyes. My hand felt a strong. urge to scratch off the unknown mask and discover that familiar one. I controlled myself

'May I come in?' a mechanical male voice sounded. A heavy voice with a digital sound effect. No, it could not be him.

'No, you may not. I'm sorry.' Indian custom does not allow a male stranger to come inside a woman's room at this dark hour. He looked a bit puzzled at my apparent rudeness. I corrected myself.

'Well, tell me what can I do for you?' I asked and my eyes definitely suggested, 'You can very well tell me standing there.'

His hazel eyes hesitated a bit. He started twirling a key chain round his finger. And instantly inside me, a faceless memory flashed. I had a collision with this man in the corridor yesterday. I remembered the twirling of the key and the white skin of the half-bare arm. He was a customer of our hotel. At the moment we had only one foreigner. So, it must be him, I concluded.

'Yes?' I repeated again, this time with the professional polish of a host.

'You have to come with me. Now.' His tone was quite unpolished.

'What do you mean?'

'I mean you want Miss Polly back?'

What a question! I wanted to ask him how he knew her. Who he was. Why he had taken Polly away. Finally I could only throw a simple question, 'Do you know where she is?'

'Yes. You have to come with me.'

For a moment my mind darted forward and my body was going to follow it. Then a sixth sense restrained me. 'Why can't you bring her here? Why do I have to go?'

'I'll explain things on the way. There's nothing to worry about. She is absolutely okay.'

'Who are you? Why did you kidnap her?'

'Oh shit! It's no kidnap. It's a mistake. A big mistake. But will you hurry, Lucie?'

'How on earth do you know my name?' I was bewildered and gazed at my mysterious guest.

<<< Jose holds out the mysterious envelope to Rosana. But the moment she takes it in her hand, she feels it. The familiar handwriting fascinates her. The brush drops down from her loosened grip. Smacks the floor with deep crimson. Rosana tears the envelope and finds a note inside.

'I am back. See you later. Antonio.'

Antonio is back. Her Antonio is back. And she does not know. She is not informed! Rosana dips her present in a deep expectation and a splash of dream colours a rosy future.

The scenario in Goa, is however, not at all rosy at the moment. It is December 1961. The carefree air is heavy with mistrust. The exuberant colours are mixed with pale suspicion. India is knocking at the gate of Goa. The basking beaches of Goa are shuddering at the advent of war ships. Already in October, one Indian ship has entered in the Portuguese sea boundary. Sabrina's one brother-in-law has been deported to Africa by the Portuguese government because he had taken part in the freedom struggle. Now, her three other brothers-in-law are working with the Azad Gomantak Party. The rich green palm fronds, the life-green coconut crowns are counting days when they will sway alongside an Indian tricolour. As free as them. As natural. Rosana's mind counts days for only Antonio. For her he is not a Portuguese. She is not a Goan. He is a part of her sky, she is a part of his sea.

Rosana quickly gets dressed and rushes out of the house. It was only three at noon. The siesta time for Goans in a normal situation. But now the political turmoil is brewing. She takes Jose with her, in order to avoid the curious eyes of the clustering groups of people and the patrolling police at every corner. She walks madly to the house where she first met Antonio. Jose has to run to keep pace with her. This is the place where she was reborn, in the body of a woman. Earlier to that she had just been a living being. Within these four· walls is sealed that night, which is deeper than the sea and wider than the sky. Now, this afternoon, after about seven months, the house wears a different look. Rosana has to stop at a fair distance: The whole area is cordoned off by the soldiers. White and black. Portuguese and African. A lot of soldiers and ammunition have been unloaded on the peaceful beaches of Goa. From Portugal, from Africa. They have come all the way, not to smell the ravishing aroma of the baby dawn hanging on the branches of kokum and cashew nuts. They have come to smell the gunpowder. They have come to shell Goan resistance whereas, in the shell called Goa, the world has manifested all the rainbow colours. Rosana feels pity for them.

Rosana takes out the letter from her pocket. Posted in Panjim. She watches the note carefully. At the corner of the paper an ornamental M is printed. Rosana's mind works out a solution. Could it be Hotel Mandovi? The spectacular extravaganza by the river Mandovi. Started some five years ago and the best place for the foreigners on a short visit to Goa. There is every possibility that he is on an unofficial tour and has put up at the hotel. Rosana moves along the bank of the Mandovi and not along the water. No more rowing for her. No more *Dip and splash*? Her stiletto collects dust. She asks Jose to catch the return ferry to Nerul and enters the hotel alone. The gateman hesitates a bit before pulling the door open for her. Her white skin, fair hair and the blue eyes are enough for her to be taken her for a foreigner, a European, notwithstanding her not so expensive dress. Rosana goes to the reception and inquires about Antonio. The receptionist looks up in the register and with a damp delicate smile says, 'There is nobody by that name staying here at the moment, miss.'

'Are you sure?' Hope floats on Rosana's blue eyes and the words do not sink in.

'Yes miss, I'm very much sure. Nobody by that name has checked in or out in the last two days, miss. Any other help . . . ?'

Rosana looks at the slit of a mouth-hole darned by lip-gloss, and desires to scratch outits dull drab dulcet tones. She controls herself and just manages to mutter, 'Never mind.'

Rosana steps towards the door. Just then, some noise and a scream. A small girl of five or so, comes rushing down the stairs like a shot of a gun. Her golden brown hair flying. Her eyes fluttering and shedding tears. She tumbles while turning down from the half landing and she rolls over the steps. Rosana rushes madly towards the steps and saves a crash landing. The sweet flaccid lump lands safely in her arms. She holds her tightly. The baby sinks her face in her breast and breaks into sobs. An elderly lady, who has been running after the child and calling her to come back, comes down.

'Thank you very much. God bless you. You have saved her. She could have been fatally injured. Now dear baby, come to me. Don't be so stubborn, dear. It will harm you.' She tries to take her back from Rosana's arm. She exudes panic. Her dry fingers dig in her soft skin. The child resists. She kicks wildly in the air and clings to Rosana.

'I won't go to you. I won't,' she sobs out. 'Take me to Mummy. Mummy, where are you?' She starts crying. Bitterly.

A few hotel assistants come near them. The lady gets embarrassed. Her sagging chin sags further. She swallows a lump. She blinks fast.

'Has she gone wild again?' One of the assistants shows some sympathy for the helpless lady. Another asks, 'Where is her father? When will he come?'

The lady nods meekly and her pale brown autumn-leave eyes dangle helplessly. Rosana strokes the silky hair and tries to console her.

'Don't cry dear. You'll go to Mummy soon.' She assures her, although she notices with annoyance that. the lady makes signs to her to say no such thing. But the words work on the child. She lifts her face and confronts her. A small cherubic face appears close to her eyes. Very close. A European face. White tear tracks on the pink cheeks, a red running nose, pouting lips and wet eyes. The eyes. The pale grey shade. The strong lines of the eyebrows. Reminds her of someone she found and lost somewhere. She can't remember at the moment. The pale grey wet eyes look into hers, very directly.

'Will you take me to my mummy? Will you? Do you know where she is?'

As Rosana gropes for a convincing answer in her mind, the lady with autumn-coloured eyes speaks out, 'Well' dear, your mother herself will come here. Don't worry. Just wait. She will.'

A few hotel assistants come near them. The lady gets embarrassed. Her sagging chin sags further. She swallows a lump. She blinks fast.

'Has she gone wild again?' One of the assistants shows some sympathy for the helpless lady. Another asks, 'Where is her father? When will he come?'

The lady nods meekly and her pale brown autumn-leave eyes dangle helplessly. Rosana strokes the silky hair and tries to console her.

'Don't cry dear. You'll go to Mummy soon.' She assures her, although she notices with annoyance that, the lady makes signs to her to say no such thing. But the words work on the child. She lifts her face and confronts her. A small cherubic face appears close to her eyes. Very close. A European face. White tear tracks on the pink cheeks, a red running nose, pouting lips and wet eyes. The eyes. The pale grey shade. The strong lines of the eyebrows. Reminds her of someone she found and lost somewhere. She can't remember at the moment. The pale grey wet eyes look into hers, very directly.

'Will you take me to my mummy? Will you? Do you know where she is?'

As Rosana gropes for a convincing answer in her mind, the lady with autumn-coloured eyes speaks out, 'Well' dear, your mother herself will come here. Don't worry. Just wait. She will.'

'No, she won't. They've taken her. She is gone. You take me to her. Take me now.'

She kicks about impatiently. Rosana tries to comfort her, 'I'll take you dear. Let's go out. To the beach. There you see. The river. It is flowing to the sea. The sea, very big vast blue sea. And there is a beach. Very beautiful. We shall go and wait there. There across the sea a ship will sail. A very big caravel. With seven sails. Square and lateen. All up and filled with air. The ship will come towards us and from that your mother will come to be with you. To take you.'

'Will she?' the child is excited and Rosana sees in her eyes, a dream sailing with erect masts and radiant sails. The child is now pacified but she gets impatient to go to the beach. They were speaking in Portuguese so far. Now, Rosana suggests to the lady in English to bring some food and some sleeping pills and follow her to the beach. The baby does not understand English but the lady goes up and brings a basket. They start for the Miramar Beach. Rosana has not come here for this. Yet, where is she going now? >>>

'We are now going to Leslie,' the man grinned.

The sound of Leslie's name sent a sudden sharp electric wave through my existence. Then, the shock numbed my senses for a few seconds. If only from the name I could erect that fantasy figure! Every bit of it. *Every bit of me is for every bit of you.*

'Quick, please.' The stranger's voice shook me.

'Wh . . . where is he?' A bit of me could not be controlled.

'A few miles away. Sent me to pick you up. I made a mistake and took her,' he grinned.

So that was it. It was all for me. It was possible. How could I not get it earlier? Those blank calls were a definite cue. It was possible only for him. Leslie and his queer way of doing things! Ending up in a mess, so often. Those daring arms. Those undaunted hands. Those aquamarine eyes. Oh! I had not seen him for aeons. Not touched those blond streams of hair. Those satin lips with killing curves and that deep dimple.

Every bit of me is for every bit of you.
And so love is born,
And life moves on till tomorrow's dream.

My thought was kidnapped and although I could see the man's lips moving, I could not hear anything. Maybe, he was elaborating the events and explaining the reasons. Everything was meaningless. Now that he was here. Now that he was waiting for me. Now that I was going to meet him. The smoke of red dry dust suddenly rushed into a damp dumb dawn.

'Come on,' he almost shouted, 'Leslie is waiting for us.'

I gathered myself and picked up my purse. Then stopped at the doorway and asked the man,

'But how should we go?'

'I have my hired car.' In Goa it was common for the tourists to hire a two or four-wheeler during their stay in Goa. Hiring vehicles to the tourists was a big business here. 'No. Not your car. My scooter. I'll take my scooter.' I wanted to take control of the events as usual. 'Well. Give me the key. And come quick.'

'I'll drive it. You may take your car or sit on the pillion.' He looked at me for a few seconds. Smiled half-heartedly and we rushed.

'Which hotel?' I enquired as we were starting.

'No hotel. It is Lino's bungalow. Lino Mascarenhas, the singer. A good hideout for Leslie from the crazy fans,' he informed me in a matter-of-fact tone.

Goan pop king, Lino Mascarenhas, was then riding high in the Indian music scenario. It was natural that Lino, the owner of the huge architectural extravaganza, should shelter a fellow singer. In any five-star hotel he would be exposed. Lino's house is somewhere between crowded Calangute Beach and colourful Anjuna Beach. A prohibited place for common people. A celebrity never allows common people to approach the boundary of his larger-than-life entity, although it is the common people who increase their boundary of fame. Today, I would get a chance to be admitted into that no-admission area.

The sky was overcast. The first ray of the sun was seeping through the cloud. The air was cool. The sea was pampering the beach with white caresses that could be seen through the darkish veil of the cloudy dawn. Trees were still dripping. My love journey started. With a third person behind me and a fourth person in front of him, perhaps. A miserable humour hammered my mind. I steered like a water scooter. Glided like a skater. The roads were mostly empty. Road lights were still on and looking down at their distorted reflection on the wet road. We passed a few fishermen carrying their *ramppons* going towards the beach. I had never driven so fast before. Something was goading me on. I was Leslie-possessed. I was dying to see him, to talk to him. To touch him. The man behind me shouted something, most probably imploring me to slow down. But I was riding on a dream, towards a dream.

Reality touched me in the form of cold drops of water. A sizzling desire. A frenzied ride. In a hurry we had forgotten to bring our raincoats. However, I could not stop for that. I hailed the drops like a tree and just barrelled on. Over the long Mandovi bridge. Along the highway of Porvorim. Overtaking a couple of trucks. The rain was getting heavy and heavier. The drops were dancing on my body. Blurring my vision. The hazy white spire of the Saligao Church indicated that we were nearing our destination. 'Roll on the reunion,' I prayed. And the very next moment, my wheels rolled over the side of the road. I tried my best to control the machine. But it skidded, throwing us off the seats. We slid down the slope. The scooter dashed against a roadside tree, fell and stopped there.

Fortunately for us, because of incessant heavy rain, the ground by the side of the road was soft like dough and muddy. We did not get hurt. We got covered with mud. We looked at each other in annoyed amusement.

'Let's take shelter somewhere. It's pouring,' he pleaded. 'No. We are very near. Come on. Help me lift the scooter. If it's okay we'll carry on.'

The scooter started without any problem. 'Will he see me after so many days bedraggled and grungy?' I got worried. My companion pleaded with me not to drive so fast. But I was not myself My love was calling me. My scooter barrelled along the road. The next thing I knew, with a screech it stopped at the formidable gate of the famous Lino's residence. Next stopped my heart. In suspense? In happiness?

<<< Happiness flashes in the eyes of the child as they reach the beach. Rosana makes her busy in counting the waves, searching for the beautiful shells, and building sand castles. She gets busy and excited. Now, Rosana turns towards the lady with the autumn-coloured eyes.

'What's the matter, if I may ask?'

'Thank you very much, miss, I feel so relieved. It is so difficult to manage such a capricious child. Right from the time we have come here she has been troublesome. Always asking for her mother. Wanting to go back home . . .'

Rosana stops her whining and asks, 'I understand. But may I know who are you?'

'Yes, miss. Certainly. You know magic. For the first time I see her so happy. Look at her, how she is cleaning that empty shell. Oh yes, what did you ask? Yes, I am Philomena D'Souza. Her governess. Well, I am not the real governess. The original one has refused to come here. She is my niece. I expressed my willingness to come to India. I am very fond of travelling and seeing new countries. I have already-'

Rosana has to stop her from elaborating, as she is least interested in the geographical names and details of some countries.

'Very good. But where is her mother? Why does she want to go back home? Has her mother deserted her?' Rosana asks eagerly as her own soul writhes in pain. The lady lowers her eyes and hesitates. Rosana stares at her confused and wavering countenance, then says, 'Very well. I'd better take your leave. I have my own engagements. Take care of the baby. Elaborate on the ship story and if she is getting wild, give her the sleeping pill, dissolved in her milk or juice. Goodbye.'

Rosana stands up. Philomena stands up too. She fights her doubts. Then overcomes them and says, 'Wait a minute, miss. Please. I feel very confused. I am not an expert in babysitting, you see. But you are a natural one.'

'Watch your mouth, my dear lady. I am not a babysitter.' Goan tradition as well as Indian tradition looks down on babysitting as a job. The babysitters were no better than the maidservants. 'But you are certainly not efficient in babysitting.'

'Yes, miss. I agree. But you see I am a spinster. Maybe, you are married with children and so taming a child is so natu . . .'

'Shut up. Will you? I am not married either.' Rosana casts a glance at the frisky figure of the child and cools down. 'I just love children.'

'So nice of you, miss, so nice of you. Please, help me a little longer. Till she falls asleep. I'll tell you her story. A sad one.' Her autumn eyes darken. She continues, 'But one thing is disturbing me. I am supposed to keep it all a secret. Won't it be treachery? It's a family matter. They believed me when they appointed me.'

'Don't worry dear. Don't tell me anything if you don't want to. I don't want you to betray anybody. But you can always tell me a story without mentioning any names.' Philomena likes the idea.

So, for the next half an hour or so, Rosana roams along the lanes of Lisbon. The story begins where the others usually end. A man marries a very beautiful woman. Definitely they don't live happily ever after. Then, there would be no story. They have problems within a few months of their marriage. The woman is insecure. The Second World War broke up her family. She was brought up by her not-so-sympathetic uncle and aunt. She is extremely possessive. She is jealous of anybody the man shows a little interest in. She makes a scene every now and then. The man gasps for space. He is an officer in the army and so goes on assignments to various Portuguese colonies. When he comes back on leave, they both swear to be happy with each other. A few days of ecstasy. Then, they are at it again. Pride and prejudice, jealousy and arrogance, insecurity and incompatibility. He escapes again to his foreign assignment. In the meanwhile a baby daughter is born to them. And quiet flows the Tagus.

He takes his wife and child to Mozambique. Things seem to look up a bit. Her possessiveness subsides and his wildness wilts considerably. Then arrives the daughter of his boss. The man gets friendly with her.

And suddenly it is night. They grope for each other.· They cannot reach each other. The woman tries to run away from her home back to Portugal. All alone. Mozambique was already in political turmoil. She gets into trouble. She gets raped. The man is devastated. They come back to Portugal. She develops psychological problems. Her condition deteriorates. Finally, the man has to get her admitted into a mental asylum. What will happen to the tender child? He takes her along with him, to give her to some of her relatives who will look after her.

'And that's why we are here,' Philomena says. 'He preferred not to keep her with his parents or brothers. He believes the relative here is the best person to look after her. After we hand over this child to her, we shall go back to Portugal again. But this is a beautiful place. Tell· me dear, are you away from Portugal for a very . . . long time? Your accent is a bit different.'

'I'm not a Portuguese. I am a Goan.' Rosana throws these words on her bewildered face. The autumn leaves crinkle up.

Rosana adds further, 'You should not worry any more. Look there.' She points at the golden child sleeping peacefully on the golden sand. >>>

She was sleeping on the sofa, under the golden light of a decorative chandelier. Or so I thought, when I entered the living room of the cottage by the side of the big bungalow of Lino. Her tomato face was as fresh as ever. Not wilted as I was expecting. Rather a brighter tinge was added to it. I stood near the doorway unwilling to go inside and spoil the ravishing rug with my muddy shoes and wet clothes. My companion had already asked to be excused. He had gone to change just after ushering me into the room. It was a great relief to see Polly sound and safe. I looked around myself. A telephone was kept at the corner just a couple of steps away from the doorway. I went out of the door, took off my shoes, wrung out my frock, then re-entered and rang up Mom.

'Mom, I've found her.'

'Where, where are you speaking from? Is she all right?' Mom asked impatiently.

'Don't worry. She is okay.' I assured her.

'Is she with you? Where did she go? Who kidnapped her?' Mom sounded anxious.

'Tell you all in detail later. If Aunty is not awake don't tell her anything.'

'She is sleeping. I'll tell her you were out for the morning walk with her and got held up because of the rain. But will you be allowed to come back safely?'

'There is absolutely no problem. We are coming back right now, Mom.'

'No, we are not.'

I turned to see Polly near me. She burst into a peal of laughter. Definitely at the poor sight of my bedraggled figure. I hung up as I started sneezing badly. Controlling myself soon I said,

'Let's go Polly. We must leave without delay,' I said looking around the room and then glancing through the doorway across the porch out at the garden and beyond where the heavy downpour had filled up the space in between the earth and the sky like an undulating white semi-transparent screen. I expected to see a face with green exuberance of the rain forest and blue lavishness of Goa. I saw black and white rainwater instead.

'Where to go?' Polly's tomato face blinked blank.

'Home. Everybody is worried about you,' I said impatiently and then added, 'only I wish we could get raincoats.' Again, my eyes searched for the face in vain.

'You've already told them I was okay. What is the hurry?' She went back and stretched herself on the sofa comfortably. I was filled with amazement at seeing her careless attitude. She gave me a side glance and with a hint of a salty smile at the corner of her lips, asked almost maliciously, 'And will you go without seeing him?'

A surged up wave froze abruptly. An inanimate, immobile feeling.

'What are you talking about?' I asked after a few still seconds.

'You know very well Lucie-*di*, what I'm talking about. You never told us you have a boyfriend called Leslie. Does my poor dada know it?'

'He is my friend.'

'A friend does not kidnap a friend, does he?' Her tomato face was overripe.

'Listen Polly, we can talk about it all when we get back home.'

'I'm not going back home now.' Her defiant note was emphatic.

My body was shivering all over in the soaked clothes. My mind shuddered looking at her stubborn peanut eyes. But where is he? Won't he appear in front of me? Won't he? My hope trembled with my drenched body.

'Are you joking, Polly? Be serious and come with me.'

'Who the hell is joking, darling. I'm serious. I'm not coming now unless I'm promised what I want. He has not promised me so far. I've asked only . . .'

I could not hear her as a fresh fit of sneezing seized me. The cold wind was blowing hard accompanying the rain. A chilly feeling cut across my mind. What was this saucy tomato up to? I could not help feeling a bit amused at the thought of a kidnapped asking for ransom from a kidnapper. Just then, a sound behind me made me almost jump.

No, it was not him. It was that customer of our hotel. He had changed and was looking fresh. Two was no company here, so three did not make a crowd. Rather I felt relieved. I wanted to shout at him, 'Where is Leslie? Where is he? Why doesn't he come running to see me, to touch me? Call him this moment.' Instead, I just managed to ask, 'Can you arrange a car or raincoats for us?' He threw a pitiful glance towards me.

'I'm sorry, you need a change. Come with me.' As I was following him, Polly also got up and started with us.

'You may wait here, Polly,' the man said in an authoritative voice. However, it created hardly any impact on her.

'I'll come too. She must be going to meet him?'

'Of course, she is.'

'I'll go with her.'

'No, you won't. He does not want to meet you.'

'I don't believe you. I'll go.'

Deep inside me a green desire was sprouting. An impatient gale was gathering momentum. I decided to intervene. 'Will you excuse us? I want to talk to her alone. Will you Mr . . .'

'Call me Bill. First, you need a change. You'll catch a cold.'

'Thanks. But we are used to rain. I wish to take her back. Her mother is waiting. I only need two raincoats,' I insisted.

'Very well, as you wish.' He shrugged his square shoulders and went out as I looked very calmly at the saucy youth. 'Polly, will you please tell me what have you asked him?'

'I've asked him to take me to the States and allow me to move around with his troupe all over the world. Bill, his secretary was telling me he would have an all-Europe tour for the next two months. It would be marvellous and I'll be famous.'

'What did he say?'

'He laughed it off. He thought I was a kid. I am not. But thanks Lucie-*di*, only because of you I could see him. Live. Oh God. It is just incredible. On the screen, he is gorgeous. In real life, it is killing. I could not breathe for quite some time. I thought I was still sleeping. I had to pinch myself hard to believe that it was all real. And you won't believe this, he was so taken aback when we entered the room. He looked at me and asked Bill "Who is she?"'

'How did you come here, do you remember?'

'Not very clearly. I was sleeping heavily in your room you know. I don't know how he carried me into the car. In fact, I got up when the car swerved sharply. It was a near thing, Bill said. A truck was rushing madly and wanted to overtake us on a turning. I was sleeping on the back seat and fell down from the seat. I got up. I did not understand anything. The effect of the drugs was still working. I sat up and for a few minutes could not feel anything. I thought we were in Bombay. Then, very slowly, I understood that I was alone with a driver. It was so puzzling. I asked that man where we were going. He told me, "Wait and see." I waited and within five minutes we reached this palace. It is like a palace. Isn't it? He was waiting for us. He was so upset when he knew it was a mistake. He abused Bill badly. Poor Bill, tried to explain the things. The power failure. The insufficient lantern light . . . but he wouldn't listen. He banged down the piano lid and stormed off.'

'When did you ask him to promise then? Did he come back again?'

'No. While going out, he ordered Bill to take me back immediately. Bill asked me to go and I refused. I wanted to know what it was all about, although I could get a hint from their conversation. But they were speaking very fast as they were excited. I could not follow everything. I understood that I had been mistaken for somebody else. They never used any force, so I never felt I was kidnapped. Of course, Bill told me it was never meant to be a kidnap. He was sent to bring you with him. He knew your room, did not know you well. Saw a girl was sleeping. It was dark and only a small lantern was lighting the big room. He wanted to wake me up, but as I was fast asleep he rang up Leslie and he ordered him to carry her down.'

I was visualising the whole thing in front of my eyes. My limbs yearned to see that man again who would never do anything in a straightforward way. Our engagement, Mukul's admission to the orphanage, and now this kidnapping. He is still incorrigible, I thought with a sigh.

'What does he actually want to do with you?' Polly asked me.

'I don't know. But what you want to do . . . Beats me.'

'Naturally, I want to make the best of the present situation.' A very calculated and cold brain answered me. I could not but stare at this teenaged arrogance.

'Polly, look I'm very cold. Let's go back and then we shall talk about this with Mom and Aunty.'

'No way.' The haughty head deprecated the idea vehemently with a vigorous shake. 'I won't go without signing a contract with him. Now that you are here, it is better. You are an adult and can be my guardian.'

'You can't force anybody like this.'

'Can't I?' Her slanted look gave me a start. After a few seconds' meaningful pause, she resumed, 'I am kidnapped. I am a minor. I can always level the worst possible charge against him.'

An iceberg hit the Titanic. But I could not hit her, she held my wrist in a strong grip before that. Next, she pushed it away scornfully.

'I think you better change your clothes and call your boyfriend. We will settle the matter amicably. Once I am with him, I shall know how to win him.'

Her conceit confounded me and I found myself speechless for some time. Then, I tried to reason with her. 'Dear, you have gone crazy. You are an innocent little girl, your lie will be detected easily.'

'I am not a virgin any more. You must be aware of that. It is now twenty first century. You can't expect a sixteen-year-old intelligent girl to remain a virgin. I'm not an unattractive girl by any standard. He should accept my proposal. Otherwise, there would be a great scandal for him. I'm going to win either way. Going to hit the headlines. Don't you see?'

The saucy tomato with a tangy tongue and a brazen insolence.

'You can't do this. This is immoral.'

'That word is no more in our dictionary Lucie-di. What kind of morality did you adopt when you were two-timing my dada? I don't blame you, of course. That is the spirit of our times.

We must know how to make the most of a situation. I've a golden opportunity, It'd be foolish to lose it.' She fluttered her eyes. Not starry, but tarry. An image of a fabricated future stuck on them. She came near.

'Lucie-di. You are shivering. Please, change your clothes. Come on.' She held my hand. A singed sensation. I ran away madly, out into the garden. Sad daylight entwined with mad rain, caught me in its web. I groped for my motorbike. I tumbled against something. Two strong arms held me. The world swooned in front of my eyes. Yet, I could feel his touch, I could perceive what was going to happen.

<<< *Whatever is going to happen will be for the better*, Rosana thinks. She has been at the Dona Paula jetty waiting for the last two hours. Looking at the surf-trimmed waves. Dream-trimmed dreariness. The giant clam with hinged sky and sea has just concealed the crimson, soft, vulnerable body of the sun. Rosana does not have a shell. Rosana stands still with each wave of darkness beating on her. Each shred of expectation draping her and each passing moment stripping off the drapes. *Rip and rush. Rip and rush.*

As it darkens, Rosana cannot see things. An embracing wind shakes her. She shivers, buries her head in between her knees. A blue silence groans around her. A slug of a crescent moon creeps above. A pathetic tune of *mando* saddens the sky.

Antonio has sent a hand-written note to her this morning. Asking her to meet him at this place at seven in the evening. Seven in the evening in Goa is very calm. Roads become almost empty. No woman of a good family moves alone in the evening. Nowadays, military patrols are at every nook and corner of the state. They can arrest any woman for any suspicious action. Earlier, she used to move in the boat. Darkness used to disguise her. Today, she took the ferry to come across. She has actually come long ago, much before the sunset, when doubtful eyes do not rove. Now, she is hiding behind a big rock. This is more or less a desolate place, with a dripping nostalgia for Lady Dona and her lover. Some soft noise. Rosana peeps and she knows he is here. She slowly stands up.

'I'm sorry. I'm late.' The words dive deep into the blue, hitting the seabed. Hit and crash. All· the pain of separation crashes down to oblivion. Rosana looks up. A purple spasm. A splicer silence. A dovetail union. Two pairs of sea-licked lips. The spire of the Chapel of Our Lady of Cabo aspired still higher. A crowning green exuberance of palm fronds, after a tall total barrenness. Rosana's silvery hair splashes against the rocky refuge. Or is it the ultimate refuge?

'Where were you?' 'Why didn't you write so long?' 'Did you forget me?' All those obvious questions. Like the salt in the sea or in the tear. Antonio clasps her violently as if she is the fleeting tide or the evanescent time. Time and tide wait for none. She has been waiting for him. So long. Antonio does not speak. His slate eyes answer. His arms assure. His lips reply. And her reveries reverberate through his soul. The Oddavel Beach squeaks as the two solid waves roll along the rejoicing ripples. *Dip and splash. Dip and splash.* The darkness sparkle.

'We need to talk. Come with me,' Antonio's voice wavers as the wavy bay palpitates. The listless islet languishes.

'Tell me now. Have you come to take me with you?' Rosana queries in a whispering voice.

'Our Great Salazar has sent me here to fight the impending war with India. But that is not the only reason. I have come to give you what you wanted.'

'I knew it.' Rosana closes her eyes. A perishing pleasure. A spongy 'full-fill-ness'. But may be a shell-stiff ignorance! Rosana resists Antonio's effort to stand up.

'Can't we celebrate a little more?' Rosana's silvery hair covers the bronze body.

'We don't have much time, I'm afraid.' As if the frail time speaks in Antonio's voice.

Yes, time is the commodity Rosana is not aware of at the moment. *Time. A shapeless, sizeless, characterless, intangible, uncontrollable, malignant enigma. Time may be a great healer, or stealer, even a fair leveller. But it can never provide a shelter. It can never be a refuge. We grope for taking refuge not in time, but away from time. And we fail. Miserably. There is no shell of time, no sale of time, time solely sails.* The sailing time and the sound of shelling shake Rosana up. Antonio gets disturbed.

Somewhere in coral-coloured darkness some Goans and some Portuguese soldiers fight, face to face. Here they walk side by side. A Portuguese man, a Goan woman. From the beach to the quay. From the quay to the narrow path. Then, they roll not on the waves, but the wheels. Not towards the sheltering starry horizon, but towards the three-star luxury.

The hotel Mandavi. The carpeted cosiness. The cushioned caresses and the pushbutton hospitality. Rosana goes out on the balcony, overlooking the river. Antonio orders drinks over the phone and calls Rosana.

'Come inside Rosana, We have to talk.'

'You come out. Get some blue in your eyes. They have witnessed enough red I believe, and are going to get some more.'

'You have already enough blue in your eyes, dear. Do come In.'

The waiter comes in before Rosana does. Vermouth is served. Antonio drinks eagerly. Rosana holds the goblet in her hand. She is not thirsty. Antonio drinks heavily and blinks heavily. Rosana cannot decipher what is written on the slate. An uneasy silence. ferments.

'What is it?' Rosana asks as she takes away the vermouth from Antonio's eager mouth.

'I love you Rosana, I love you very, very much.' Vermouth spills.

'Yes? I know that dear.' Rosana's goblet reflects the enchanting chandelier. Antonio stands up, paces up and down. Restlessly. Helplessly.

'What's eating you?' Rosana goes near him. A brownish body. Two brawny arms. A squeezing hug. Countless crushing kisses.

'I want you Rosana, I want you more than anything in my life. I cannot live without you.'

'Neither can I. I am yours. We are one, dear. I curse him who has created us separately.' Rosana reciprocates. Her clear blue eyes darken. 'Something wrong dear? Has your country not allowed you to marry me? What if you leave your job? You are not made for war. You are not meant to be a patriotic mercenary killer. You kill me. Kill me with your love. Destroy me with your desire.'

Rosana's flying sea-gull eyebrows spread and soar. The sky is stooping, the sea is surging. Antonio rubs his face violently against her neck, shoulder, cheeks. Something is rubbed off. What? Rosana holds his face in her hands. Looks straight into the eyes. A pair of blank slates. Everything is rubbed out. Wiped clean. Even her own reflection. Rosana gets scared. Steps back. Antonio reaches out for her and opens his mouth, when the door clicks. Rosana turns around.

The door is flung open and a small golden wave comes splashing. Standing at the doorway is Philomena D'Souza. She goes out and closes the door.

'Papa, Papa. Mummy is coming. Mummy's coming you know?' Rosana stares at the kid. At the dream, she has injected into her. Antonio kisses the child and chews out the bitter words.

'I can't marry you Rosana, I can't. I'm sorry.' Split and smash. Split and smash. 'Forgive me Rosana. Forgive me. I am helpless.' The slate cracks.

'Why are you crying Papa, Mummy is coming. In the ship.' The child comforts.

Rosana stands deluged with memories and reveries. And there was the sudden resurgence of the refugee in her. 'You've betrayed me. You've deceived me. You too . . .

'No dear, listen to me.' Antonio holds her hand. A hard shell touch. A spiky tiger-conch. Rosana withdraws her bruised hand. Bruised self Rushes towards the door. Antonio quickly holds her by the shoulder from behind with his strong arms.

'Stop, Rosana, stop. Just see, I have come to give you what you wanted from me. Yes, I have.' >>>

IV

Towards Tomorrow

The two strong arms, carrying my half-fainted self will now take me where I have always wanted to go. To home. To the ultimate refuge. He will, I believe. He will not make the same mistake as he did with the terracotta stranger boy. With my eyes closed and my consciousness enclosed by his, I shall absorb his dripping repentance. The hourglass turning up and down. Up and down. Each grain of sand asking the other,

'Why couldn't you forgive my mistake?'

'Why couldn't you forget your ego?'

'Didn't you miss me as much as I did?'

'Didn't you feel me close to you as much as I did?'

And each falling on the other. Each echoing the other. Hourglass to year-glass. Half-year glass. At last, I shall hear his sea-deep voice.

'Lucie, your Lessy is here. Open your eyes.'

I shall not. I shall love to drift into my darling darkness relishing his mesmerizing touch. Revelling in revealing sensations. A huge wave surging from the Mariana's depth. A contralto convulsion. To a soprano elation. The spreading sea floor. A minute of history. A minute—the history.

'Open your eyes, and let me see the world.' His crooning tone will pop out like a pop-up page of history. This was the first line of one of his songs in the album.

'Not yet. Have you seen my curls?'

'They are drenched.'

'My cheeks?'

'They are covered with mud.'

'My dollops of lips?'

'For heaven's sake, Lucie, let me see those dark grape eyes. That would be the only clean spot, I believe.'

Leslie dear, with his usual humorous touch. I shall shrink in his arms. Oh yes. As always, I shall appear before him in an awful state, bedraggled, mud-covered, shivering. My nimble fingers will grope over his face. That pinnacle of a nose. Those passionate eyebrows. That satin sensation. Next, I shall try to feel that deep dimple, as deep as human consciousness, or even deeper, as the subconscious.

'Where? Where is it?' I shall scream and open my eyes to find a bristly beard covering his chin.

Then, I shall remember the singer Leslie with a beard. A flat finesse without the dimple dimension. Yet, I will find it through that bushy and brushy excess. Fullness in the emptiness of a hollow. A bird's nest.

'I can still see it. Wanted to hide it?'

'Not from you. Kept secure for your eyes only.' He will bend and kiss my eyes. The muddy frills along the maddening thrill.

'How can he talk in my language? How can he act like my dream?' I shall wonder.

'You're kidding. Must be your producer's prudence?' I shall tease.

His aquamarine waves will sluice over my doubtful mind. His spirit,—in spate.

'No producer in the world can prod me into doing such a thing, you know.' Speaking in my language! 'This is exclusively yours.' He will smile. That killing curve for which so many hearts crave. A little blunted by a slim moustache.

'Wanted to kidnap me, why?'

'Why didn't you come to meet me on your own. There was news published in the newspapers all over. Didn't you see it? Tell me the truth.'

I shall nod faintly, 'Yes, Granny showed it to me.'

'Yet, you did not come and were getting ready to marry somebody else? May I ask why? You don't love him at all.' *One has to live one's life. Wearing Joy-cut overcoat. With a Leslie dream-lining. Nearer to the body, closer to the heart. But the world sees the 'over-coat' adorning the body.*

'Answer me, don't you stare so abstractedly. You were just going to have a cold-storage life in that cold hilly place. You are not meant for that. Not for sure. I won't allow it. So, I got you kidnapped. But I should have gone myself It would not have been such a mess then. Bill does not know you so well. He has only seen your photos. Made a mistake. Bullshit.'

'Lessy is messy.' I shall tease him pinching his nose.

'This time I won't mess up again and take you with me. Do you understand, you headstrong gal.'

'I think you are going to take me.' Polly will come out and speak out her mind. Standing just near the doorway. Both of us will glower at her.

'She is nuts, Lucie. Wonder how her brother would be.' Leslie will burst out angrily.

'Oh no, please.' Both of us will utter spontaneously and eagerly and Polly will continue, 'Don't drag him in this. He is too good. She does not deserve him. A two-timer filth. But Dada is just mad about her. Childhood love, my parents say. So, let her go back to her own place. And I will go with you.'

'I don't get you. Is it your interest or your dada's interest you are working for?' Leslie will make queries.

'For both, I may say.'

'She is crazy. Absolutely crazy. How old is she? I don't think she is eighteen.'

'No, she is sixteen.' I'll reply and think. *She is sixteen, going on seventeen and you are not eighteen but more than that. That is why it is so dangerous.*

'Jesus Christ, this is a doozy! How these small girls are acting big nowadays.'

Yes, satellite-wise, remote-sensing. The whole world is at the door at the press of a button. The whole world is so unrealistically real for them. Reality without a dream. A prescribed prayer to God—nothing but daily routine. Just like eating, sleeping or making love. Following a few structured strictures. Dreams have no structure and no stricture. A dream can't be routed through a routine. Neither a routine can be channelled to reach a dream. How can God be a routine?

'Lucie-*di*, I think you are going to catch a nasty cold. Go and change first, then we can talk.'

'Talk about what? Listen girl, take this one cool. I don't know you and I'm not going to take you anywhere not even to hell. Now, just get out of my sight.' This voice of Leslie will have no music.

'And again you're talking to me like that. You can't talk to me in that tone. Nobody has ever talked to me in that tone. Even though you are the great singer.' Polly will almost break off and the coddled child in her will start shedding no crocodile tears. She will scream in a steaming temper, 'Why did you kidnap me, if you didn't know me. Now that I have seen you I can't give you up. I won't. I always get what I want. I do.'

'But I won't give in to a stinker's demand. I'll turn your water off I won't take you with me. Go back to your place and hide your ass from me. You understand.'

Before my saying anything, he will lift me in his arms, carry me upstairs. Through the rain. To somewhere, over the rainbow? One more door opening in front of me.

<<< Rosana cannot open the door. She takes away her hand from the latch. Turns back. To face a faceless facet. Antonio looks into her eyes. The Goan blue, the clear blue, but without its coolness. Antonio cannot stare on. He turns towards the small child, holds her in his arms and says, 'You wanted my child. Didn't you? Here she is. All for you. I have come to give you my child Angela. She is yours. Take her and take care of her.'

The Goan green loses its freshness. The sea regurgitates the age-old sedated sedentary dregs. The palm fronds hiss out. Rosana had a dream in her mind. Rosana prayed to God to help realise her dream. Rosana wanted his child, he has given her his child. A de-crystallised dream. A rude blow. A crude joke.

The whole story told by Philomena in the morning swings in her mind. A mentally ill wife. A homesick child from a sick home. And so he seeks her help. Rosana bites her lips and turns back to go out. But this time, another hand stops her. A small hand. A fleecy touch. It is the child.

'Has the caravel reached the shore?' she asks her, looking up. Her pale grey eyeballs half hidden under the upper eyelids like a blinking doll.

'Has the caravel brought my mummy?' she repeats. her innocent question.

Nobody answers. Some stray dogs of the night bark at a long distance. Antonio stares at Rosana. Tries to figure out something.

'Was it you in the morning?' a semi-doubtful query. 'Her governess told me about the incident in the morning. So, it was you. Wasn't it?'

'Yes, I came here. I thought you were staying at this hotel.'

'I'm in my official residence. But they are staying here. I didn't want them to be among guns and rifles.' He stops for a moment, then gratitude floats in his eyes. 'I knew you could do it. Only you could do it. Only you can help her. I'm so sure about that. Obrigado.'

'And you are damn sure that I'll definitely accept your proposal?'

'No, I'm not. But I hope you will. I beg of you.'

'Tell me, has Mummy reached?' The girl does not understand the adult language, tugs at her skirt. 'Tell me. Tell me. Tell me.' She scratches on her stocking-covered leg, rips the stocking. But it is no Christmas stocking. No Santa Claus has kept a gift in the form of her mummy in it. Only a bit of pink skin and a reddish line. The mark of her nail track.

Antonio takes her away, shakes her violently, tells her off.

'Behave yourself: Angela, you've torn her stocking. You have hurt her,' he shouts. And Rosana reflects with a ripped smile. A child's china doll hand. A stocking ripped. A man's grapnel hand. A heart ripped. A dream dashed.

Rip and dash. Rip and dash.

Who says life is small? It is too long. Her love story: prehistoric. Her desires: fossilised. Rosana takes the crying child in her arms, rocks her and tries to console her.

'Your mummy is here. Very much here. Only she is playing hide and seek with you. Just hide and seek.'

Rosana's eyes cannot hide the tears and cannot seek a refuge. The child stops crying, looks at her. An adult face with a child's insecure innocence. A mother's face smeared with tears. Smothered in agony.

'You are crying? Why? Grown-ups do not cry. Papa tells Mummy. But Mummy cries. Every day. Mummy does not play. Mummy break things. Broke my doll.'

'My doll is broken too. I shall give you a very big doll. Very big. Unbreakable,' Rosana speaks through her tears.

'Give it to me. Now. Just now. I'll have it.' She kicks her legs about. Rosana smoothes out her expression, smothers her pain. They go to the shop in the hotel and purchase a big blinking doll for her. Angela feels better. Antonio deposits her with Philomena and takes Rosana a bit forcibly, to the hotel room.

'Rosana, dear, if you knew how much I'm suffering . . .'

'I know your story. I have heard it from Philomena. She didn't tell your name though. Wanted to keep it a secret like a loyal employee.'

She gives out a sigh here. 'You're very lucky, Antonio. You've got a loyal employee, a loyal wife, a loyal lover.' She is still choking.

'What are you driving at? Do you mean to say I am disloyal to all? Am I? I was very loyal to my wife. I was. I was never a Casanova. No, I was not. I wanted a normal home with a charming wife and sweet children. But she . . .' He pauses to dredge up the old memories. 'I made a wrong choice. We are incompatible. Just like that. I have never done anything wrong to her knowingly. I had no serious affairs with anyone. Absolutely nothing. Believe me.'

'And what was it with me?'

'Oh dear, I was talking about the days before I met you.' Antonio comes nearer and holds her hands, in spite of her resistance. He takes a deep breath. 'With you it was love. Only love. But that was not betraying her. The worst had already happened, if you know the story correctly. She was under treatment. Could not tolerate my sight. She was shifted to her cousin's place at the doctor's advice. I escaped to Goa. And I found you. My true love. You know that, feel that pretty well, don't you?'

Two grey slate eyes in front of Rosana. Her reflection smudged. Her relationship smuggled. Rosana shakes her silvery head.

'No. I don't know. I don't believe. Why didn't you tell me you were married? Love does not lie. Least of all true love.' Rosana's dry voice was such a contrast to her wet eyes.

'I didn't lie. You never asked me if I was married.'

'I asked who were there at your home. You said only your mother and her sister.'

'I told you the truth. She was living with her cousin's family. With my daughter. She was not at my home. I was never at home with her. Never.'

His fondling finger slowly plucks a teardrop, hanging from her long eyelashes. She does not say anything and he continues, 'I come home to you. I love you and only you. But god damn it, I can't marry you. Not now. I just can't.' Grudgingly, he kicks the chair standing nearby. Then, helplessly sinks in the sofa.

'I'd have been the happiest person if I could. But now it is impossible. Had she not been ill I'd have divorced her. But now it'd be inhuman. My authorities, my society nobody will approve of it.' He breaks off and sighs. 'Should have come to Goa earlier.'

'Don't you have anybody to look after your child after your wife has been admitted to an asylum? Your mother? Her cousin?' A polar coolness touches Antonio.

'What do you. mean? Of course there are so many people who can look after her. In fact, her cousin does not have any child even after ten years of marriage. She agreed to take care of Matilda, only in the hope that she will get her child. She was cursing me when I took Angela away from her.' He sits up. A bold voice vibrates in passion, 'Don't you ever think Rosana, I'm asking you to keep the child for my convenience. I'm asking because you wanted my child for you. Because I know you are the best person to bring her up. Because I want a part of me to be with you, always. *Para sempre.*'

'para sempre para sempre para sempre para sempre' the air croons the *cancao de amor.*

Antonio stretches out his arms, his *amor.* The golden beach of sun-soaked Goa. No anchoring harbour. Yet Rosana reposes herself in the *'Casa no Duna'.* Her latest refuge. Or is it a refuge at all? >>>

Time is never a refuge. I will know that in time. Leslie will know. Even Polly will know. Time, the age, her age, her minority—on her side at the moment. Her mom and my mom will have to come to the house of Lino. To rescue Leslie from her. The kidnapper from the kidnapped.

A mildewed afternoon. With the colour of a mild beer. No sun, no rain too. Only a rain-flavoured nature. Outdoors and indoors. I shall be indoors with a body pain, cold and fever. Lying on Leslie's bed. Alone. He will be sitting by my side. On a sedan. Untroubled, unworried. Just like the body of his guitar. The visibly motionless wooden board behind the violently vibrating strings. He will be strumming a love tune on the guitar. Polly will be half lying on a sofa, staring at Leslie and his every minute movement. A kingfisher fledgling.

Mom and Meena Aunty will enter into the room behind Bill. Aunty will rush to Polly and hug her. Mom will come and touch my forehead.

'Come on girls, let us go.' Mom will urge.

'But Aunty, what are you going to do against this man? When will you complain to the police?' Polly will shout.

'It's not a case of kidnap. It's a case of mistaken identity.' Bill will say with all eagerness. I shall nod my hot, heavy head, confirming his statement.

'He molested me and violated my honour. What about that?' Polly will start crying.

Mom's searing eyes will get a cold answer from my burning soul.

'It's a damn lie, Mom. Don't believe her.' I shall try to sit up and Leslie will come and force me down on the bed.

'Stay there. It's my order. Don't exert yourself. Let them do whatever they want. I don't give a toss about it.'

An eddy in the aquamarine. The crumpled satin. The recoiling rapier. He will kick the small centre table and leave the room strumming away on the guitar. The overturned table. A fallen ashtray and a smoke of ash. The ashen face of Meena Aunty. The line of her mouth askew. Her eyes frozen with utter bewilderment.

'It's all wrong, Aunty. He has not even touched her.' I shall put my words as clear and transparent as the cashew *feni*. Strong. Effective.

Mom will hold my hand. An assured touch. But Polly will scream, throwing back her head indignantly, 'How can she be so sure when she was not here?'

'Because you told me Polly. Didn't you?'

'This is a lie, Lucie-di. You can't do this to me to save your boyfriend. You can't betray me like that.' A cacophonic cry. The frozen confusion will melt into frenzied convulsions. Meena Aunty. Heartbroken, betrayed. Mom will try to console her.

'Don't touch me. Don't you dare touch me at all.' A wild protest from a tamed mother. 'I wish I could die before facing such an embarrassment,' Mom will mutter.

With Lino outstation, his house will become full of non-musical musings and acting.

An oppressive opera.

I shall pull myself together and get up. Putting my arms around Mom I shall try to push her. 'Let's go Mom, please let's go from here.'

Mom will hold me and we shall step forward, while a deep voice will pull us backward.

'You can't go. You mustn't. You know very well who I wanted to bring here. So you must stay here. I won't allow you to go. Not this time.'

I shall glance back to see the glint of passion in his eyes, the gleam of possession in his arms, held out. Leslie the glamorous, at the top of the staircase. What a relief! A glade in the entangled forest of emotional trauma.

He has not changed, I shall think, and Mom will drag me forward and further away. I shall hear the speedy tramping down the steps. A strong hand with throbbing blue veins, will hold Mom's hand, 'What are you doing? She is not okay, the doctor has advised her bed rest. Look she is so hot and shivering. How can you take her like that?'

'Because I am her mother. And I am taking her home.'

'She is home. With me.'

They will stand, face to face. Two tongues of fire licking each other. One cannot burn the other.

'The last time I did not insist as I had a sense of guilt. Today I have none.'

'What is that, then?' Mom will point at the collapsing figure of Meena Aunty, against the cool column and Polly standing by her side.

Next, with his long majestic stride he will reach Meena Aunty, stoop a little and speak in a clear tone, 'I never apologise. But that girl's story has taken you in. You must believe me. Ask anybody in this cottage and in that house if you like. There is just nothing between us. She is a stranger for me. A total stranger. I have not even kissed her. My secretary made a mistake and brought her, instead of Lucie. Lucie is my fiancée.'

A flailing batfish in the deep dead sea. A slashing tail of a stingray, splitting the waves. Meena Aunty's eyes will stab me. The wounded, the paralysed look. A few moments of brewing silence. Darjeeling tea aroma will not follow. Meena Aunty will silently hold Polly's hand and go out of the room. Even Polly will not be able to resist. A dear satellite lost in the space. Snatched away from the sphere of love. The moonless sky of the earth.

I shall run madly. After her, across the porch, along the gravel way, trampling on sad gloomy wet gravel, to the door of our car with Meena Aunty's hand on its handle. I shall touch it. As cold as the body of a snail. My voice steaming.

'Give me one chance to explain. Just one chance, Aunty.'

<<< Time gives Rosana no chance to settle down. Cruel time. Has taken away Antonio from her. Far away. Time has not given her a chance to meet Antonio before his marriage. It would have been another story then. A story this world does not want to read. It is afraid of perfect things. Whirling with immanent imperfection. An imperfect dawn with pale light grins at her. It may rain any moment. The small drops from the faraway sky will touch her, but Antonio won't. A deep sigh rips her ribs. The All India Radio has just started. Vande Mataram is floating in the air. Now, they are in India. Independent India. The Portuguese are gone. They have left behind destroyed roads, demolished bridges, damaged economy. Shelled airfields. A shattered Goa. Antonio is gone. Left behind a shattered Rosana. He fought the war as bravely as he fought the battle of his own life. It is possible that he was one of the 500 soldiers who fought the last fight at Marmagoa. The last fight of the Portuguese before their surrender, very late in the evening, of 19th December 1961. She is not very sure of anything about him. She has not heard anything from him, in these four months after Independence.

There is no relation between the two countries. No communication between the two souls. Or is it still there? Still Rosana hears the voice of Antonio inside her. Father and Sabrina say he is killed in the war, or he would have communicated. They also tell her a story that a snap of a Goan girl was found in the pocket of a dead Portuguese soldier, in the fight in Marmagoa. They say that may have been Antonio. But Rosana does not believe them. Rosana believes he is alive. Alive and out of her reach. The destroyed Banastarim Bridge despairs. A shattered Albuquerque sinks deeper in the sea.

'Avoi!' a small bundle of softness leaps in her arms. This is the only thing for which she can live now. Angelina. Antonio's daughter. Like most of the Goan girls she has got luxuriant hair. Only the colour differs. The golden beach at the glorious sunset. Rosana kisses the colour. Sinks in the sunny waves. Angela hugs her and goes out to the garden. She will play with the flowers and the butterflies. And the small puppies her dachshund has given birth to yesterday. As happy as the spreading wings of a seagull. Rosana happily gazes at her.

She has taught her to call Avoi, which means mother in Konkani language. Angela thinks it is her name. Every time she calls her Avoi, Rosana's seabed touches the sky. Her next few hours remain busy in washing and cleaning Angela, feeding her, dressing her up. Then, she teaches her painting. Angela learns less, plays more. She dips her finger in colours and creates patterns on Rosana's cheeks and foreheads. They have great fun.

'How long will you play with her? After all, she is not yours.' Rosana turns back to see Sabrina has come. With Eva. The elder brother of Eva has been sent to Bombay for higher studies. Rosana's father wants him to be well educated and a doctor like him. Sabrina allows Eva to go out and play with Angela.

'Why did you say so? She is mine. Antonio has given her to me.' Rosana answers as she wipes her colourful face. Deep inside her red blood turns cool white.

'I think it is high time you had your own. By your age I had both of them. My parents-in-law now want a third one. Valentino is not ready.' Sabrina is in a mood to advise. 'Moreover, people's tongues are clacking a lot about this girl.'

Rosana is well aware of that. In the neighbourhood, nobody plays with Angela. Young children come out to play for one or two days but their parents do not permit them afterwards. She has only Rosana and Jose as her playmates. Even in Sabrina's house, she is not welcome. Sabrina's in-laws do not like it. Once, Rosana took her there and faced a lot of embarrassing questions. She has stopped going to Sabrina's house since. Sabrina comes here with Eva and Angela gets a playmate for a few hours. But Sabrina does not like her. For her, she is nothing but a stranger.

'Why don't you send her to some convent in Bombay? She will get some good education and you will be able to start your own life again,' Sabrina suggests seriously.

'She will be with me. That's why Anton has given her to me.' Rosana makes herself clear.

Sabrina sneers, 'Do you know why he has given her to you? So that you cannot marry anybody else.' She bitterly mutters then, 'Selfish brute.'

Rosana protests against her language. Yet, this is the truth. Rosana knows. She has accepted it. Love has to be selfish. A part of Antonio will always be with her. Always. He did say that. Rosana will make her a part of hers too. Rosana can foresee that with Antonio's slate eyes, Angela is blinking heavily, like Rosana. With Antonio's wide mouth, she is smiling shyly, like Rosana. Her Portuguese rifle body is shooting Rosana's sexy bullets in a killing spree. Rosana wants to bring her up just like that. But the world does not. Not even her own sister Sabrina, who has always been so close.

'You must seriously think about your future, Rosy. I have a man in mind. Felix,' Sabrina continues her grey counselling. A grey mind in a green body. Sometimes, Rosana wonders how she had a sea-blue love affair with Valentino. Now it is the cold backwaters, stagnant, a swamp of mangroves. The stagnant swamp's voice states, 'Felix is a widower, with one child. He is our caste too.'

'Christians don't have caste.'

'Goan Christians do have, you know.' The mangroves thicken, 'You won't miss Angela. You'll get a child. A six year-old boy. You can have your own too. I know you are very fond of children.'

'I don't want to marry anybody. I will have nothing to give him. You know I have already given my everything to Antonio.'

'Shhh. Don't you speak so loudly, dear. You should be ashamed of yourself for losing your virginity before marriage. That is a sin. You did not even confess. I always pray for you. May God have mercy on you Rosy.'

'Mercy! Sin! To leave your young children—isn't it a sin? Who has been punished for that? Don't dredge up old resentments. I am happy with Angela. She loves me, I am bringing her up. I don't want anything else.'

'It's a pity, you manage children so well, and you don't have any.'

'I do have. Angela is mine. Mine. I don't want anybody else.'

Angela is the angel, sent to her by God, she feels. And so, in spite of all the criticism and gossip of the society, Rosana pulls on. Every day she opens their letter box, her Pandora's box. But Antonio's message does not come.

Goa starts a new journey along the path of the damaged geography and dilapidated economy. Construction. Creation. Renovation and self-discovery. Or rediscovery. Rosana raises a life. Creates Angela's mind. Her imagination, her dreams. Angela paints, Angela speaks in English, Angela loves Goa. Goa grows. Village administration starts. Mr Fernandez calls Rosana one day. His face wears a grave expression.

'We have to do something about the girl. We can't keep her anymore.' His tone frightens Rosana.

'What do you mean Papa, she is a mere innocent child.

People may say bad things about me, why about her? She is a legitimate child of a good family.'

'People don't think so Rosana, neither do you have any proof about it.' Mr Fernandez diagnoses the situation calmly.

'I know that, you know that. I am not bothered by what people say.'

'Me neither. Although the way people talk about you hurts me, hinting at your character, doubting her parentage. They drag your name in it. But I see you are happy with this doll. So, I keep my eyes closed. My ears shut. But recently, I've heard that if we cannot provide specific information about her, local authority may order us to send her back to Portugal. Somebody has complained, it seems. The Portuguese have left behind as many foes as friends,' Mr Fernandez says in a matter of fact tone.

In a moment, Rosana no more gravitates towards the land of Goa. As if she is moving on the moon. Weightless. Unattached. Mr Fernandez feels deep pity as he looks at her bloodless face. A colourless large sea bubble, about to burst. He takes her in his arms. The touch of fatherly arms, a new thing for Rosana. The touch of helpless tears, a new experience for a father.

'We shall find some way out. Don't worry.' He comforts her.

But the way, that he finally suggests, is nothing more than Sabrina's sadistic suggestion about sending her away to a Bombay convent. Father and daughter both try to convince Rosana in turn, that this is the only possible solution with a satisfactory, if not happy, end for all. Angela will get a satisfactory life. and education, Rosana will get a satisfactory husband, her family members will get a satisfactory reputation. Life will be waxen smooth, or so they think. Rosana thinks about a foreign land where Angela is not with her, about a foreign element called husband who will be implanted in her life, as redundant as a tumour. Rosana makes up her mind. >>>

'Have you made up your mind?' Granny will ask while dabbing my face with the soaked sponge. Granny, the nursing assistant of her doctor father, not with a nursing degree, but with a caring heart. And the art of nursing she learned from none other than her father himself. A hollow heart, in need of nursing, got over the illness by nursing others. She did it for almost twenty years, until her father died. After his death, the house with the health centre was sold off, at the insistence of Sabrina and Valentino. With the money, they started their hotel. Granny came to stay with them. She used to get a portion of the income from the cashew orchard her father had inherited. Her uncles allowed it to her out of pity. To provide an economic spine to a lonely spinster.

'Have you made up your mind?' Granny will repeat her question as usual. 'I think you are awake for quite some time now.'

'No Granny. Not yet. I'll wake up to dreams,' my heart will say. And my aching head and burning body will suffer in silence. I shall remember the scenes in Lino's house, one by one.

'Where are they? All of them?'

Granny will not answer. She will put the thermometer in my mouth. I shall look around my room. To search for somebody. One calendar on the wall struggling with the strong wind. The pale face of the greenish white money plant. The cloisonné flower vase,—empty.

'It is still very high.' Granny will dip the tip of the thermometer in water. One tiny bubble will float up. 'I should call the doctor again. Your temperature is not going down.'

'Will you call Mom?'

'I am a trained nurse. Your mother can't help you the way I can. If you don't want me I'm leaving. Have your mom and all the others in the world,' Granny groaned bitterly.

'Sorry Granny, if I've hurt you. Please don't go away. I want to talk to Mom about something.'

'She has gone to Hotel Sea View.' Noticing my questioning eyes Granny continued, 'Your family friends have shifted there. She has gone to them.'

So Meena Aunty and Polly have left our home. Home-cum-hotel. They left their old house and moved to a place twelve kilo metres away. We left Darjeeling and came to a place a thousand kilometres away. Hotel Sea View is just a few metres away from our hotel. But this time the distance is the greatest. I don't feel we shall be able to cover the distance even if we walk for a whole lifetime.

And the distance between Leslie and me? I shall hear a knock on the door.

And there he will come in. His face covered with a broad-brimmed Panama hat. Made of straw, by some local Goan craftsman. Almost the whole face is hidden. But my eyes will dip into that deep dimple. A bird's nest. The refuge of my dreams. The mystery of reality. Bill will close the door from outside. He will wait outside to prevent any unwanted visitor. The tall upright body nearing my bed. The Panama hat will be flung away at the corner table of my room. The beard and moustache gone. A well-shaven face. The face with the enormous pull for the female galaxy. So near to me.

'How are you feeling now?' my hands in a warm grasp.

My eyes washed by a warm aquamarine wave. 'Okay.'

'You are burning.' his questioning eyes on Granny.

'This is my granny. My mother's aunt. My friend, philosopher, guide.' A little nod at each other. Wonder woven in Leslie's eyes.

'She is not one of you people, she just looks so. She is an Indian,' I shall explain to him.

'I don't think you would like my presence here, young man. But I can't leave the room now. I used to be a nurse and now I am doing the job of a nurse. She needs me more than she needs you at the moment. You have to bear with my presence.' A straightforward statement transparently delivered. Impressed Leslie, embarrassed me.

'Oh Granny, I'm fine.'

'Your temperature has already told me how fine you really are.'

'Granny used to work as a nurse with her father, a doctor . . .' my small mouth will shrink like mercury in ice.

'When will she be okay?' a direct question to Granny from Leslie.

'Well, I'm not a doctor. But hopefully within three days.' Granny will raise her eyebrows, 'Her temperature is still a hundred and two. She is not well.' A series of sneezes will confirm her statement.

'Three days, you said?'

'Let's hope so.',

'How long will you be here, Lessy?' My cold-choked voice won't sound emotional. But he will catch the undertone.

'How long do you want me to be here?'

'Oh, that hardly matters.'

'You know that's all that matters.'

'You must have so many engagements. Shows, interviews.'

'I am not available for interviews. Shows, we'll take care of But when are you going to be okay? Why did you fall sick?'

'Why did you try to kidnap me?'

'Why didn't you contact me when I came to India?'

'How do I know you still remember me? You didn't contact me either. You knew my address.'

'Even people who don't know me try to contact me.'

'I won't do that, you know.' My aversion to ambition—well known to him.

'So, I kidnapped you.'

'Why didn't you come directly?'

'That's not my way, you know. Hah! To show up after such a long time without a real big show! I wanted to shock you.' He will laugh, that resounding laughter.

A shudder in my heart, a shiver in Granny's body.

'You will get a big enough shock when that rotten Polly drags you to the court.' Granny will speak out here.

'Will they really go? You think so, Lucie?'

'Possible. They have left our hotel,' I shall say.

'Good. They will not try to marry their son to you anymore. An easy solution.'

'But you never know about the son. Dear young man.' Granny's voice—a bit alarming. 'I don't think he will give up so easily. It's his childhood love.' After a meaningful pause, Granny will say, 'You have to face him.'

'I think Lucie has to face him.'

'Both of you, no doubt. You should be ready for that.' And just then some noise at the door. A few indistinct words. A click of the latch. Bill's head will peep in, 'A guy wants to come in. His name is Joy. Should I allow?'

<<< 'Should I allow you to go to Bombay? With Angela? Don't ask me such a stupid question. You are out of your mind.'

Mr Fernandez tells off Rosana. His specs slide down his long nose. His nostril flares. But Rosana sticks to her decision, with the stubborn claw of a crab. If Angela has to be sent to Bombay, she will go with her, stay in Bombay with her.

'But where? Where will you stay? You've never been out of Goa!' Mr Fernandez tries to reason with her. 'Life in Bombay is tough, very tough.

More so for a single woman.' Rosana has heard about that. Life is no widespread beach there, it is a narrow alley. Yet, she will go there. Away from the cloudy eyes of her relatives. Clacking tongues of the neighbours. Complicated claws of the law.

She slowly answers, 'I am just following your advice Papa, yours and Sabrina's. Sending Angela to Bombay. Only I added myself to it. Because as of today, I can't think of my life without her.'

Sabrina tries to bring her to her senses.

'Today, you think you can't live without Angela. Get married. You will forget her. Your husband will see to it that you forget everything else but him.'

'I think I'll be more miserable. Every moment spent with that man, will remind me of every moment I spent with Antonio. Every ecstatic moment.' Rosana reminisces about those evanescent evenings with everlasting feelings.

'You will be lost in a city like Bombay. Don't go. Don't leave us.' Sabrina's wet words just draw a few tears from Rosana, but she does not change her decision.

Rosana contacts sister Margarita. A distant relative of hers, Sister Gabriela is a nun and a teacher in a Bombay convent. Sister Gabriela promises to help Rosana. So one fine morning, when the busy fishermen of Goa are pulling out their *ramppons,* full of writhing fish, Rosana starts for Bombay with young Angela. From India. To India. The steamer breaks the wave. She wonders where was the dividing line between India and Portugal, earlier. It seems so incredible to see no Portuguese ship along the coast, with its green and red flag flying high. A couple of Indian Navy ships are visible. The emerald coastline of Goa vanishes into the blue. There she has left her home, her childhood, her youth and abundance. Now., she is sailing to a new life. From the excess to the paucity. From the known to the unknown. Rosana gets the same feeling she had in her veins, before plunging into the sea, that fateful night. Will there be Antonio to save her again?

As a saviour for the present, comes Sister Gabriella. Rosana drags her existence along the traffic-infested road. Angela's sleeping face slides down from her sheltering shoulder. Nothing but the sea is common between Goa and Bombay. Even the sea looks so squeezed. Between Nariman point and Malabar Hill The beaches are pale. The sea is grey. Rosana does not find any colour in Bombay. A black-and-white city. Crowded and crumpled.

A black-and-yellow taxi. To a small flat. By the standards of Bombay, it is spacious. One hall, two bedrooms, one balcony. No garden, no trellis, no earth-smelling terracotta tiles, no seashell windows, no gracious gables and here she has to stay! How long? Till the end of the jetty called life? And a death caravel comes to take her away from it all? For a few moments, Rosana resents her decision. Rowing has been over for her. But not growing with the life-coloured green exuberance. Or throwing herself to blend with the blue expanse. Shimmering with the golden beaches. Waiting with the dark brown rocks. Blushing with the russet terrain of Vasco. The smell of the surf, the shade of the jujube trees, the innocence of white lilies, the whisper of palms, the loneliness of lagoons, the completeness of the lush islands, the mystic shadow of the Western Ghats, all start ringing in her memory. The bells in the Se Cathedral. The lamps in the tower Deepmal. The illuminated tune of a ringing *mando.*

'Why are you crying, *Avoi*?' Two tiny hands touch her tears. Turn them into sparkling crystals. Rosana remembers her mission. Not missing Goa, but growing with this young heart. She kisses Angela. A kiss as colourful as her Goa. As musical as her Goa's breath. And they start their new life with Sister Gabriella. Her institution takes care of orphans. Angela gets admission as an orphan. There is no other legal way. With a battered heart, Rosana has to accept it. She accepts a job too, in the institution. The job of a lady peon. She is not 'class ten passed' and cannot be a teacher. However, Sister Gabriella inspires her to study and pass the school final exam.

Rosana's time passes as fast as life does in Bombay. With her modest job, mobile daughter, immobile study. And a monumental agony called Antonio. Rosana now tries to believe that Antonio is dead. Antonio will never come back. Her monumental agony slowly takes the shape of Goa's Deepmal, illuminated by the lamps of memory. No more fire. Soft soothing flames. Then, Rosana misses herself more than she misses Antonio. She is now a new person. A prudent worker. A responsible mother. Those days of pining and craving for something unknown are over. Those undulating pangs of her restive soul to see and touch the romance are straightened, folded and ironed, stored with mothballs.

Folded into a cocoon. For her it is going the opposite way. From a butterfly to a cocoon. The butterfly is flying in her garden now. Angela. Colourful. Playful. With her, Rosana makes a small trip to childhood, everyday. Feels a fleeting sensation of growing up.

In the process, Rosana passes the school final exam, as a private candidate. She writes to her father, knowing that at least this one achievement of hers will make him happy. She has never made him happy. Who has she made happy? Antonio? She has a doubt about it. Angela? Maybe, yes. She has completely forgotten her past. She knows that her father was killed in the Goan war and she was saved by Rosana. Her memory about her mother is very feeble and foul-smelling. Smell of blood. *Her mother is breaking her dolls, a piece of broken china hits her, mother comes to take it out. Mother's hand smeared with blood.* Her wound smeared with blood. Angela does not want to remember those days smeared with blood. To go back to those days. She goes ahead with her new life.

She has just entered her teens. Thirteen years and three months. Rosana counts on the invisible abacus of time, seven years and six months. She has been with her that long. Or is, it short? Life has gone at the speed of light, with the brightness of light with this lightning kid of hers. Antonio would have been so happy, had he seen her. So graceful, so smart. So loving.

'Aren't you packing up, *Avoi*?' She enters the room. A fresh smell from the just-bloomed rose.

'Have you finished yours?' Rosana asks.

'You have to do for both of us. I'm no good at packing you know.' She smiles.

'Well, let me pack for you. But this time I'm not going.' Rosana gets up to fetch the suitcase.

'What do you mean? You are not going?' Angela looks at her with disbelief in her eyes. The same disbelief she saw in the eyes of Antonio, when she told him she was a Goan and not a Portuguese. His every expression is distinctly etched in her memory.

Every year, during the summer vacations of May and June, they go on a trip to some nearby place of interest in India. Mother, daughter and Sister Gabriella. Anywhere other than Goa. Rosana does not want to go back there. She gets letters from Father and Sabrina occasionally. Once a year or so. They have not forgotten her, neither forgiven. Father was happy at the news of her success in the school final exam. At the same time, he resented that she was not utilising it for a better cause.

Sabrina is flying high. Valentino has opened a restaurant and is earning well. Particularly because of the American hippies who are now crowding Goan beaches. They just enquire about her, never ask her to come back. They and their good reputation. So no more Goa for her.

Aurangabad is the place chosen this year for travel. Aurangabad famous for the ancient Ajanta and Ellora caves. 'I've already told Sister that I won't go this time. I am trying hard to appear for next year's pre-university exam. This is the time to concentrate. The vacation time. You people go ahead and enjoy,' Rosana says.

'I'm not going without you.' Angela shakes her head.

'No dear, you must go. Sister is looking forward to it so much! She will be upset. If both of us don't go, she won't· go alone. You will like it. You paint so well. There are those ancient paintings. They are marvellous.'

'I know, but I won't enjoy anything without you. Please Avoi, for my sake you have to go. Your study is not going to be affected just because of a short trip, for a week or two.' She tries to convince Rosana.

'Now you are a grown-up girl, sometimes you should travel without me.'

'I won't go if you don't.' Angela sounds quite stubborn. Then, she comes and hugs her. The life. The refuge. The ultimate gain. To cling to something, who clings only to you.

Just then Sister Gabriella comes in. Her calm aged face is disturbed. Her deep meditation-coloured eyes are watery, colourless. She is somewhat breathless. She sits on the sofa, covering her face with two bony hands.

'Anything wrong, sister?' Rosana gets worried. Sister Gabriella is always so well composed. *Her emotions are well controlled, like Bombay traffic on a highway. Systematic traffic lights at all crossroads.* But today, it seems like the lights are suddenly off Rosana goes near her and touches her drooping shoulder. She looks up. *A cross without the memory of Jesus.* She shakes her head in despair.

'This year we are not going anywhere.' She announces in a trembling voice. Although Sister Gabriella is fifty-six, her voice has always been clear and authoritative.

'Why sister? Do you also have some work like Avoi?' Angela asks her with curious eyes.

'No, because your Avoi's father is coming here tomorrow.'

A seagull moment swoops and seizes a piece of memory. Rosana's boat in the middle of the inert mangroves. Rosana's boat doesn't budge. Stays static. >>>

V

And . . . The Rainbow

A STATIC IMMOBILE MOMENT. Joy's arrival. Leslie's presence. Fever in the air. Mist in the sky. The white straight strokes of rain—framed in the window. The water festival of nature. Unaware of a fragile moment. To be handled carefully. Or a shower of slivers of glass. As much white, as straight. Like rain. But piercing.

Joy will enter the room. The Himalayan snow-white heart, the aromatic Darjeeling air.

'Did you have to fall sick just today? The airport looked so empty!' His happy-valley smile. His sunrise eyes. *He is coming straight from the airport. Nobody must have told him anything.* I shall realise.

'Where are the elders?' I shall try to grin. The grinding will be on, inside.

'Don't know. I came with uncle in one car. The others are in the other one. They fell far behind. An old driver. Uncle drove very fast. He is just coming.' He will come near the bed, as jovial as ever, 'Boy, you are looking great. Eyes are red, cheeks are white, nose is swollen, lips are dry. I should think twice about my proposal.'

'You had better . . .' A grave voice will send a tremor through the ribs of the air.

Joy will turn his face. A choking surprise. For a few moments Joy's eyes will forget to blink.

'By Jove! If I am not mistaken he is the latest singing sensation Leslie Fraser. Am I correct?' He will look at me and then at him and again at me for confirmation.

'You are very much correct, my dear.' Granny will say from behind him.

'Oh, you must be Granny, aren't you? Pardon me, I did not see you. You are just as dear as Lucie told me.' Then looking at Leslie he will say again, 'But I don't understand how he is here. You know him, Lucie? Your friend?'

'I'm . . . .' I'll have to stop Leslie.

'Lessy, this is my childhood friend, Joy, I told you about.'

'Hey, but you never told me you had a celebrity friend like him? We spoke even last Friday! Since when have you started keeping things up your sleeve?'

'He was not a celebrity when I met him in Shantiniketan.'

'Yeah, and she made one out of me.' Leslie's humour.

'He is kidding, Joy.'

'Good gracious. This is a real surprise you reserved for me.' Joy's eyes will be still filled with disbelief.

'I think the real surprise-' Leslie's words will be interrupted by Father's entrance into the room. Fortunately.

'How are you feeling, Lucie dear?'

'I'm okay, Father,' with a sneeze I shall blurt out, 'but are they okay? Meena Aunty? Polly?' A benign blink in Father's eyes. An assuring touch.

'I'm going to them. You don't have to worry about anything. You talk to Joy. He has come a long way. Your mom is there. Aunty Rosana will look after you. I've called our doctor too, to come and check you once more, before going to bed. You mustn't come out of the blanket. There is a nip of cold in the air. And it's still raining. You'll get worse. Take care. We'll be back soon.'

'Father.' A stealthy tug at his sleeves, and my eyes will say, 'Nothing should get worse, Father. Do all the things that are right for me. Will you?'A pearl-warm pat on my hand and a lighthouse look. Father will slowly give a half-nod of recognition towards Leslie. Next, he will say,

'I want you to come with me. They are waiting.'

'I'll come later.'

'It's better if you come now.' Father's voice will be very firm and bold.

'Please Lessy, listen to Father.'

A hesitant gesture. A wavering look from me to Joy. And my assurance:

'I'll be waiting for you.'

<<< 'I was waiting for you to come back to Goa. Why didn't you?'

Rosana cannot answer her father's question.

Tears bring the memory of the torrential blue-flavoured rain of Goa. The musty melancholy. A gigantic swing swings her back to the calm, long reflections of palms and coconut trees in the solitary Sinquerim. To the dripping coconut sap, and its 'miss you' smell. To the crab's subtle claw prints on the smooth wet sand. To the broken shells with the watery history of a pearl-less oyster. Nothing is lost. Not a single grain of sand. The smell of the oil paint of her boat, the whisper of the fronds, the touch of the morning cool wind, the flavour of the rice and kokum-rich fish curry. Nothing has slipped from the mind. Nothing. Although she has always thought that these are deciduous memories, gone with the wind. Swept by the waves. Dissolved in the dreams. To touch them she has to wake up to dreams.

Now, she is not dreaming. She is holding her father's flat, hard palm, looking at him through a gossamer web of tears. Angela comes and wipes off her cheeks. It is sunset. The sunset of Bombay. A dull twilight filters through the window.

'Avoi. Don't cry. I feel like crying if you 'Cry.' She pouts. 'Leave them alone, my dear 'child.' Sister Gabriella intervenes. 'She has met her father after a very long time. Let us go out and get some crisp snacks.'

'She should be happy as her father has met her after so many years. She should smile.' Angela's young mind does not quite make out the subtle difference between smiles and tears.

Mr Fernandez speaks to make it clear, 'Maybe you will feel the same way if you meet your father after all these years.' His voice sounds like a dying gale, a fading coda. Rosana's heart leaps. Why does father say so, when he believes him to be dead long ago?

Angela's mind gropes in the past, for a feeling called Father. Gabriella takes Angela away from the house. Rosana sees her father the way he was, when she last saw him. That same mellow maturity in his eyes, that old bitter droop at one corner of his upper lip, that palm-erect structure, untouched by age or agony. Only the last words he uttered were so very different. And the tone in which he said it!

Mr Fernandez feels the creeping curiosity in Rosana's eyes. He hugs her and kisses her hair. Rosana closes her eyes. To let this closeness sink in. She has never been so close to him so far.

A few years' distance has brought them so close.

'Rosy, you were right. He is alive.'

The lively words open her eyes. And then over the square shoulder she catches sight of it. A forgotten tune. A distorted memory. An incomplete fable. An undreamed dream.

A seagull spreads its wings from the sunrise to the sunset. Rosana's reverie vibrates. A new home. Home sweet home. The ultimate refuge of this life. With him, she and Angela. The dead sun gets resurrected in her eyes. Rosana frees herself from her father's hug and rushes. To blend into a blind bliss. But her blind world tumbles. A civilised hand holds out. For a civil handshake. A linear smile.

A few fish-smelling words, 'Nice to see you after a long time.'

He stands there. A frozen shadow. Every line of his body frigidly straight. Every dot . . . grains of sand. Rosana avoids a gritty grasp. Perhaps, a sea of time passes before she catches on to the truth . . .

So Antonio is not dead, Antonio is a stranger!

Rosana does not know this man who comes stealthily behind her father. Waits quietly with folded arms. Shouldn't those arms be held out to fold her in them? Shouldn't those perpendicular lines of his body be bending to sweep her away? Shouldn't he march into the room much ahead of her father and take possession of what is his own? Shouldn't his straight-line smile be an undulating wave? Shouldn't those half-closed clams of eyes bloom wide to shower every fragrance on her? What a reunion after seven and a half years! And the dream Rosana used to have in the first couple of years after his disappearance! Rosana has always wanted to turn his dream into reality and reality has turned her away.

In Rosana's dream he was fighting wars in Mozambique, Angola, carrying her memory along with his rifle. But in reality where was he all those years? Why didn't he contact her before? Why has he come with her father and not alone? Rosana wants all these answers. From somewhere beyond time, from the palette of Goa, colours flow. She looks around to see Father has gone. She slowly advances. To touch Antonio. To bring life into a golden statue by an anti-Midas touch. Touch of life, love, passion. But before she fingers even a dot, he speaks. Perhaps, in Greek language.

'Where is Angela? Will you please call her? I want to see . . .'

Yes, it must be Greek, as it takes quite some time for Rosana to realise what he is saying or asking about. Rosana looks around to make sure that there is nobody else in the room. So, he has addressed nobody but her. After an era of separation, in the privacy of a room he has nothing else to say to her!'

Indeed, Antonio is not dead, he is just another stranger.

Rosana's eyes cannot bear the sight. Her fingers get clenched in a fist. She wants to punch the air, punch her fate. Deep inside she hears the echo from the past. *Dip and splash. Dip and splash.* And she still struggles. Lifts her earthly face up, very near to his.

'Anton, I am still waiting for you. Can't you see?'

A pair of dead stars stare at her from the remotest corner of the universe. A sagging darkness throws its arms around her. A hug without a touch. A kiss without any taste. A deep pang bubbles up inside her. *Dip and splash. Dip and splash.* No. The oar is muffled. A muffled pain.

A knock on the door brings Rosana back to herself Sister Gabriella and Angela come in. Sister goes inside. Rosana introduces Antonio to Angela. 'Come and meet your father, Angel.'

'My father! My father! *Avoi,* he was killed in the Goan war they say.' Angela is shell-shocked.

'I never said so. I never believed so. He was missing.'

'Now he has come back.' Rosana says and as Antonio's eyes look for his future in Angela and

Angela's eyes search for her past, she goes out, silently.

In the kitchen, Sister Gabriella is preparing tea. Evening tea with snacks. Mr Fernandez is watching the sea of traffic from the narrow balcony. From them she comes to know about the missing part of Antonio's life. He fought battles in Africa. Got thoroughly fed up with a battle-strewn life. Then, he escaped to America. Settled down there. Now, he has come to India as an American tourist. His first stop was Goa. Mr Fernandez has brought him here.

If he has come to India to see her, why is he in the mask of a stranger then? Rosana' cannot figure him out. Rosana's heart flickers like a dying star. Something is disturbing her. Something she cannot name. As if Antonio has worn his personality inside out. But why?

Rosana wants to go out there. Near him and confront him. To ask him straight, 'Why are you behaving like another Antonio?' She does not have to. As she approaches the door of the kitchen, Angela rushes in. Angela flings her arms around her. Her face is crimson. Tears streaming down her cheek. She breaks into sobs on her shoulder, 'I won't go *Avoi,* I won't go with him. I won't leave you.'

The face of Antonio at a distance. The mask of Antonio. Rosana does not know the man. >>>

'How do you know him, Lucie? Tell me.' Joy will get impatient. 'Answer me. How and when did you meet him? I just can't absorb it. How on earth is he in your bedroom?'

With room in my bed. Room in my heart. And Joy does not know that.

'That is a long story. A very long story. Life is full of stories. Stories and stories. I can tell you some. Very interesting.' Granny will go on with her words, knitting her words.

'Tell me this one, Lucie. Will you?'

'It was in Shantiniketan. He was working there.'

'With you?' Joy's usual way of interrogating me and my small mouth to get the most out of them. 'He is not a painter!'

'And have you brought the painting I asked you to get for me?' My desperate effort to change the channel. But how long?

'Yeah. It is there. In the car. But . . .'

'Won't you show me? I'll tell you all. Later.'

The obedient child will go out and Granny will call some boy to help him.

A shiver will run through my body and soul. *What is happening in that hotel with Lessy and the others? Who will protect him there? Or does he need any protection? Will Polly leave him in peace? Will everything be the same again as it was between us and Meena Aunty and their family?*

'No, it won't be,' my answer to myself. And the very next moment, a terrific effort to go to the door and reach the scenario.

'What are you doing?' Granny's arms will hold my teetering frame. 'Back to the bed. Back to the bed.' She will pull me along.

'Granny, my presence there is necessary. Absolutely necessary.'

'No, it is not. You can't stop anything. Nobody can stop anything. *Que sera, sera.*' Fatalist Granny will fasten her eyes on the remote nowhere. And her arms fastening around my shaking frame. I shall lie down again. Granny's lips still forming those words, without sound, *'Que sera, sera. Que sera, sera.'*

'And I know what will happen.' I shall be able to visualise it all. The train of incidents. No, Polly will not be polite enough to accept the truth. Her dream has to be fulfilled. For all like her an unfulfilled dream is a waste. Meaningless. They drool over dreams, devour them, digest them and defecate. What a dream they dream! She will force her parents to lodge an FIR. Mom will be discreet enough to send a specialist doctor, with the help of our physician, to check Polly and give a report. In the hope that in the long run that will save the day for Lessy. Otherwise, they will possibly turn it out to be a hopeless case. Polly will not be ready initially, but her parents, and specially Joy will insist in order to know the truth. On the way to the truth, lie a lot of lies. Statutory rape charges against Lessy. Lessy on bail. Lessy in the dock. No room in the court. Even outside, the waiting fans will bustle. Polly will get what she wanted. Front-page, cover-page.

'Cover yourself with this mink coat. Feel the softness.' Joy's Pandora's box,—bringing out one thing after another. The painting, the dresses, the richness. His moving lips, Granny's moving lips. The Judge's moving lips. All juxtaposed. Black and white headlines running through Joy's watery face.

'Rape of a minor. Lessy Fraser faces serious charges. Career at stake.'

'This time no woman. Lessy Fraser is after a minor girl.'

'And so he is at it again. But this time caught.'

Distorted, refracted, corrugated words. Wriggling lines of Polly's face. Tomato face. Overripe and rotten. Festering fluid. Hundreds of camera's flash on them. Meena Aunty's face never to be seen in the court. Mom in the witness box. Father in the witness box. Witless face of witty Naresh Uncle in the witness box.

A box of exquisite glass menagerie. Joy's deft hand handling them. Displaying each piece carefully to Granny and me. The iridescent radiance of the pieces, of the box. Joy in the dull witness box.

'Polly is your sister?'

'Yes.'

'Did she tell you about her traumatic experience inflicted on her by this man?'

'Not directly. Others told me.'

'Who are these others?'

'For example, my mother.'

'You didn't talk to her about this?'

'I did. Asked her if it was true.'

'What did she say?'

'She just nodded.'

'So, you believe that this man has . . .'

'No, I don't believe he has done anything wrong.'

'Why not? Do you have any proof, evidence?'

'No. But he cannot. Because Lucie loves him. Lucie cannot love such a man. I know that.'

A new name for the first time uttered in the court. All the efforts of Mom and Father and myself and even Leslie to keep me out of it all, will be in vain. All of a sudden, a lot of questions. A deluge of episodes involving Leslie and me. I will be exposed. Fortunately, not in the box or in front of the camera. Not in exaggerated colours. Just through black and white blabbers. Just the very next day, Polly's family will withdraw the case. Because of a renegade Joy's statement or the imminent tabling of the doctor's report on Polly's condition. Or because of the saturation coverage given to the indecent incident, or the overdose of the media attention and a final realisation of the meaninglessness of it all by Polly! The masses. A massive feeling, of reaching the masses, rooted deep in these hearts. To be accepted by the masses, to accept the god of the masses. The superpower, the omniscient God knows you, yet only his inferior children can make you superior in this life! Her god is not my god. My own god, whom I reach in my own way. Touch in my own way. Not through any religious scriptures to feel him vicariously.

My god will show me Leslie's face. In the newspapers. Now vindicated. A fragile smile on his cut-glass lips. Cutlass lips. The phrase 'Racily with Leslie' will race along the road of history. My history will knock on the door. Leslie will come in. The glass menageries will lose their radiance. Joy's hand will lose its deftness. A beautiful piece will slip out of his hand. And what a surprise! Leslie's hand will catch it with a sharp reflex. I shall remember the day when he tossed his camcorder most mercilessly or the day when he dropped the goblet most casually to· drive home the message of transience.

Yes, by now he must have realised that the urge to make transient permanent is called love.

Two transient faces will look at me with the permanent emotion that nature nurtures perpetually.

<<< Antonio's face is devoid of any emotion as he faces Rosana.

'So you have come to take her away from me.' Rosana's. inside bursts in pain, as she confronts the slippery slate eyes. She does not see any past remembrance written on them. Any episode from the history of their rapturous moments together. Any chapter of scriptures of their commitment to each other, 'I love you.' And suddenly Rosana gets a strange feeling that Antonio's death might not have been so painful. Antonio avoids Rosana's eyes. That strong vivacious voice sounds old and shaky. His lips tremble as he says with difficulty, 'Rosana, it is not so, try to understand . . .'

'There is nothing to understand. Just nothing.' The agony breaks into angry pieces. Rosana's pain becomes violent. After seven years of pallid patience her heart is in the grip of violent impatience. Her whole existence shakes uncontrollably as she almost bursts, 'You can't take her away from me, she won't go with you. She never will.'

'I'm not taking her away from you. She is yours, she will always remain yours,' but if you just understand . . .' He breaks off. And with a great difficulty ferrets out two words from his mind, 'It's Matilda.'

So that insane shadow is still following this man! Turning him into a shadow. Without any words, Rosana opens her questioning eyes wide. Antonio mumbles as if a heavy burden of guilt has squashed his heart and mind.

'Matilda is now okay. She was sent for her treatment to America even before I went there. The treatment there did wonders for her. Now that she is okay and remembers things quite well, she is desperate to get her child back. Her doctors have advised to have the child with us. Otherwise, there may be a relapse.' Antonio's plangent voice chokes in pain.

'You must try and understand. I know it is very selfish of me to ask for this, but I am helpless. Just helpless.'

The last few words whirled in the air like weightless feathers. But fell heavily on Rosana's mind. This man is begging of her. Who will she beg of? In this big, big world who will show her charity? For the first time, she feels a strong wish to change her place with the sick woman.

'I wish I could be her!' A deep sigh shakes her ribs.

'No, you should not, you must not.' Antonio's soul squeaks. An old Antonio's soul comes out of its shadowy countenance and holds Rosana in his arms.

'You are not Matilda. You can't be Matilda. I don't love her. I just pity her. I've loved you and still love you. Always. *Para sempre*,' he says, fixing his soul-searching eyes on her. His warm breath touches her impulsively, so does his question, 'You know the difference between love and pity, don't you?'

'I know, because I love you and pity myself:' Rosana says with a remoteness in her voice, as if she is talking from under the deep water. Words are coming up and breaking like silent bubbles. The next moment she wrenches herself away from his hug and her sore heart bleeds through the words, 'But I don't like to pity myself I want to love myself: like all the others. And I want to hate you. You and your pity. Your Matilda and her sickness. I hate it all. I won't give what's mine. I won't let you take Angela away from me. I have brought her up, given her so many years of my life. She is mine. She is mine,' Rosana shouts madly.

Her mad outburst invites the other people into the room. Angela, Mr Fernandez and Sister Gabriella. Angela holds her in a tight embrace. Mr Fernandez strokes her hair, tries to console her. Rosana still behaves like a mad tornado. She points at Angela and screams, 'Ask her, just ask her who does she want to stay with. Just ask her.'

'I'll be with you. I'll never go anywhere, leaving you behind Avoi.' Tears well up in Angela's eyes. Sister Gabriella remains very calm amidst all these disturbances and takes charge of the situation. She goes to Antonio and in a pleasing authoritative voice instructs him, 'It is better for you to go now, Mr Antonio. You heard what they have said. Now think over and decide. We'll meet tomorrow.'

Antonio hangs down his head and goes to the doorway.

There he turns back, 'Rosana, you can come with us. You too.' Too! This is one word too many for Rosana to tolerate. She gets furious. 'I don't want to go with you and be your kept woman. I won't do that. Take it from me, you sick man, and go back to your sick wife. Angela will never grow up to be as sick as you are.'

Slit and slash. Slit and slash. The deep ravine gapes wide.

And wider. The face of reality with a defaced dream. Mr Fernandez takes Antonio out. Sister Gabriella puts her arms around Angela and takes her to the other room. She knows Rosana would prefer to be alone now and cry her heart out. Nobody should see her and take pity on her. She will face herself alone. Face to face with her true self. >>>

Two faces. I shall not see mine. Or maybe I shall. In the depth of the aquamarine. In the height of the Kanchenjunga. They will be sitting side by side. By my side. Granny will be gone. With her agony, with her sense of decency. She will leave us in my bedroom, to decide our lives for ourselves. After giving me necessary medicine. A friendly room, protecting us from the torrential rain and mad storm. A friendly room. With three friends, two strangers. Or all strangers! I shall love to fall in love with a stranger all over again! How? The strong stormy winds will blow across the sea. Mad nature and the intoxicated sea. Inebriated waves. Incessant rain. The green smell of wet grass. The mad smell of rain. The sad smell of damp darkness. A burning body. With fever, with desire. Eyes blind with confusion. Moments dumb. Minds limping.

'I want to get your autograph. The book is not with me at the moment. But you are in the city tomorrow, aren't you?' Joy will know how to break the ice. Joy from the snow land.

'Depends on her.' A factual voice without music.

The first blow of the monsoon. The first fall of snow.

Joy's snowy eyes will fix on me, putting me in a fix. The blue-winged space fluttering in the clutches of time. The air wounded. The moisture burning. Two leaves and a bud. Two leaves and a bud. And a Happy Valley villa. And a dream. And the reality.

'Joyee, do you remember the snowman we used to make on our trips to the Himalayas, white snowman? Every winter. Do you make them in London?' I shall try to take him back to our childhood. The common ground on which both of us had trod.

'You are crazy. We are grown-ups now. But I see little children do. I remember those days. You wait and you will also get many chances to see, when we'll be in Darjeeling.'

'I missed it so much always, in Shantiniketan, in Goa,' I shall say listening to the crazy orchestra of rain and storm.

'Did you miss it more than you missed me? I shall be furious.' Joy laughed. Alone.

'She did not miss you any more than she missed her childhood.' Leslie will quip. Not very wisely though. But how long shall I avoid the zero hour?

'Do you want to tell me something Lucie, which you should have told me? Much earlier?'

No Darjeeling mist in Joy's voice. As moist as Goan air. 'I think it is time for the music. Don't you want to listen to live music from me? Free of charge?' Leslie will try to make up for his unwise remark. He will now stand up shaking out the unfamiliar inertia. He will open the door and get his guitar from Bill.

'Maybe, some other time, Lessy Fraser. I want to talk to Lucie.' Joy will sound unusually cool.

'She is sick, can't you see? This is not the right time to talk. Let's have some music.' Leslie's hand on the strings.

Joy will stand up, and go near him. Face to face. 'Are you serious about Lucie?' Joy's tone—absurdly serious.

'Why do you ask? Don't you see?' No hesitation in Leslie's voice.

'No, I don't. You have the reputation of dealing with relationships as you would with throwaway glasses.'

'Bullshit. Some throwaway journalist's throwaway gossip. Don't swallow it.'

'Will you marry her?'

'She will marry me, only me.'

'No. She is going to marry me. Ask her family. Tomorrow is our engagement.'

'We are already engaged. Look at that ring of hers.'

'Let us ask her.'

Two pairs of eyes waiting for an answer.

<<< A question without an answer. Antonio is standing there just like that.

'I' m going back, Rosana. May God bless you.' Like the soft raps of dry leaves, his words hit her.

Antonio is going. Going away from her life. He won't come back again. Never. He is taking away with him not only the man Antonio, but also all the memories associated with him. They will never frequent her memory, the way they used to. The colour is crippled, the tune is mutilated. The dream is demolished. Rosana will never dream again. For

Rosana, dreams are a hazy estimation of the future. They should come true or they are meaningless. So, Rosana will never dream again. She will look at Angela, the lively connection to a decaying sickness. And she should be happy. Happy or satisfied.

Rosana and Antonio stand facing each other. Like two trees. In their own spheres. The roots in the deep, were tangled long-long ago. That ancient bondage throbs and sobs. In the dead veins. They don't touch each other. The space between them kisses their depth. After a long time Antonio advances, his fingers reach for Rosana's face. Rosana retreats.

Antonio wants to touch her with his words, 'I have loved only you Rosana. Only you. Always.' Sweet words. Too sweet, perhaps. Too sticky, like chewing gums. To beguile her? Rosana strengthens her mind. She does not react to the words. Looks somewhere far away. Antonio speaks again.

'I have one last request. A small one. Please, don't say no. Let her see Angela just once before we leave. Just once.'

The words squelch along the sodden past. The wet and soft memory. Rosana cannot say no. At the same moment, a deep fear of losing Angela also gnaws at her heart.

'Well. Let her see Angela.' She almost gasps with pain, 'But once she sees Angela she may not be ready to leave her behind.'

'I have made up a story that Angela will need some time to get her passport, visa et al'

'Angela does have a passport. Me too.'

'Hardly matters. I told her that Angela would follow us after some time. I have bought some time. For the rest, I can only pray to God.' Antonio heaves a sigh which shakes Rosana to the core. *Hit and smash. Hit and smash.* All are broken. All dreams. All hopes. Expectations. Squashed flat. In a ruin of her own passion.

Rosana does not take the chance of sending Angela alone with Antonio. She herself accompanies them to the hotel where Antonio is staying with his wife. All three sit very silent in the taxi. The Bombay traffic roars around. The Goan memory sings aloud. But they don't speak. The three with their own doubts and hesitation. The mobile taxi carries the immobile heaviness. Rosana's grip tightens around Angela's wrist. A great insecurity grasps her. What if Angela opts for going back with her mother? She is her mother after all. Her flesh and blood. Rosahas no right, no way to stop her. She has given everything to Angela that a mother gives. But she is not Angela's own flesh and blood. And flesh and blood are very real. Very raw. They are the strongest bond. But Rosana cannot afford to lose Angela. What is there in her life but for Angela? She will not give away her Angela.

'Just remember I sacrificed my life for you. My life, my Goa, my everything.' She will tell her. She will remind her of all the best memories they shared together. Rosana rehearses her dialogue. What will be more effective? Maybe, nothing. Maybe, the only words which can stop her would be, 'If you go with her I'll kill myself Angel.' And she will say those ultimate words to stop her. She has to.

With a screech, the taxi stops near the hotel. Rosana's heart stops. She is going to face a defaced past and a faceless future. Rosana does not allow Antonio to hold Angela's hand. She puts her arm around Angela and holds her tightly. Rosana longs to bring out twenty hands of the mythological Ravana and hold every part of Angela, her hand, her mind, her wish, her emotion. A demonic possessiveness possesses her. She follows Antonio like a robot. Angela's confused eyes look for an answer. Antonio knocks at the door of a suite. The dark polish on the door darkens, in front of Rosana's eyes. The door opens with a click.

Rosana is waiting at the door. Angela has gone inside with her father. Rosana counts every breath of hers. The rose-red carpet of the hotel corridor rolls out in front of her eyes. She is living every second, without any past or future. Angela comes out of the room. Two teardrops dangling at the corners of her eyes. What do they mean? Do they reflect Matilda's flat face or Rosana's glassy one? Rosana cannot see. She feels blinded for the moment.

A warm touch wakes her up. Angela is holding her. 'Won't you come in, *Avoi*? Come with me. Let us say goodbye to them.'

Rosana cannot believe her ears, for a few moments. She looks blankly at Angela. A mirror without reflection. She wants to make sure. 'Are you coming back with me? Angel, are you?'

Angela is shaken by the question. Her wet eyes lowered. 'Yes *Avoi* . . .' she pauses for a few seconds, then raising her eyes she asks, 'why are you asking me? Haven't we already decided about it?'

Yes, they had. But Rosana had doubts that, after seeing her own mother, Angela might change her mind. She has not. Rosana madly takes Angela in her arms. Kisses her on her hair, forehead, cheeks, neck and everywhere. It is a relief A great relief Angela will be with her. The mother in her will be with herself. She will remain a woman. May not be as a wife or lover, but as a mother. The woman in Rosana feels elated.

Antonio comes out. The door gets wide open. Rosana cannot but see the frail figure behind him. A long pale face. Two dim eyes. Two wooden lips. A sand castle. Matilda advances towards Angela. Puts her watery hands around her. Kisses her on the places where Rosana planted her kisses just a few minutes before. She embraces Angela just as madly as Rosana embraced her. And strangely enough Rosana feels she is in front of a mirror. There stands herself: sobbing on the shoulder of Angela. A helpless face. A hapless existence. A life without life. Looking for a life in the ·child. Rosana sees herself juxtaposed on Matilda. A woman in distress. The woman in distress. Since the beginning of the human civilisation, perhaps.

'Can't she stay with us tonight?' her sad wooden lips move to utter the words. The pallor of her eyes implore in silence.

'Let her go now. She will come and join us in America soon.' Antonio puts his assuring hand on her back. And she is assured. Her eyes get a brighter hue. The beguiled woman. The vulnerable woman. *Beat and squash. Beat and squash.*

Here Rosana is standing, tricking another Rosana in a different attire. Rosana feels a deep hatred for herself. Antonio vanishes in front of her eyes. It is only one Rosana against another. Antonio will remain the same with or without Angela. But not Rosana. This one or that one. A mother. A mother longs for her child. Rosana has been a mother for the last seven years. But Matilda has never got her own child's company for so many years. Poor woman. Can she trick her? Rosana retreats towards the door. The words flow automatically from her mouth, 'Let her stay here tonight with you. Let her.'

The next moment, Rosana sees herself flying down the stairs of the hotel. She madly rushes across the lounge, then out of the door. She does not know where to go, she' only knows she has to rush. She has given away everything. And now she wants to escape from that hollow nothingness called Rosana. Where, she does not know. Just skip this life. Skip and rush. Skip and rush. Somewhere beyond the reach of joy or sorrow. Away. Far away.

Thud. Rosana collides with somebody. He holds Rosana strongly. The face Rosana knows. Has seen somewhere. It takes a few seconds for Rosana to recognise the man. Her father.

'Rosy I knew, you would need me. That's why I came from Goa and that's why I've followed you here.' He takes her in his arms and Rosana breaks into sobs on his shoulder. Mr Fernandez takes her inside the taxi, waiting for him.

'We shall go back to Goa. Tonight.' He holds Rosana close to her. The child with the face of her mother, has got the fate of her father. She is now so close to him. His story is rewritten in her life. His hurt is renewed in her. Nobody offered him a balm for his shredded self. But he will change the lifeline of Rosana. He wipes away Rosana's tears.

'Don't cry my child. Snap out of it, dear. You have lost one child. I'll give you hundreds of children. You will look after them. You will give life to them. You will learn nursing. Help people. You will forget. All these tears you will forget.'

Mr Fernandez and his old ideological values. Rosana does not understand his language. The stale night with the cold stars, closes in around her like a coffined void. Her journey of life starts with stagnation of death. With no Angela, with no Antonio. >>>

'No,' I shall say 'no'. Clear and emphatic. The word will echo deep inside the cavern of my consciousness. No. No. No. The two faces will look at me with twilight in their eyes.

The no is meant for which one of them? They won't be able to figure it out. They will look at each other. The same confusion, the same curiosity will spill out of their eyes.

A splitting pain. A fatal haemorrhage. A silent fall of a soft toy from the height of the sky. A silent destruction. All within me. I shall say to myself, 'My life will start its journey along a new path. From this point. A poignant point. Those two faces. So very dear to me. The most difficult question of my life. The answer is not difficult. The answer, known to me for ages. But how to pronounce it? That is the most difficult part. A Happy Valley villa, a turbulent sea. I shall find my refuge in one of them. Or they will find it in me, one of them. One of them. How can I hurt the other? It is cruel. I can't do it. I can't see the soft snow melting. The fragrance of childhood in the Tibetan incense holder. Antique smell. Antiques are expensive. Valuable. An invaluable enigma. Interlaced with my simplicity.

The life-loom has produced a wonder. Warp and woof. Warp and woof. Who can unravel it? Neither he. Nor me. But I cannot reveal it. Like all big truths it will remain a secret. Who says truth is light and truth can never be concealed? The truth of furiously battling mute roots is hardly unearthed. The truth of a foetus's consciousness? Or the truth of the conscious mind entering the door of death? Or the truth of dreams? The truth of God?'

'No. Not now. Not now. Don't ask me now.'

'Why not? Now is the time for you to say. I must hear it now. Right now. Now or never. I've come to take you. So spell it out and let's get out of here. Quick.' Leslie will be impatient.

If only he knows how difficult it is to spell it out. To kill one with a word. To bulldoze the Happy Valley heart. I can't do it. I won't do it. I shall live with my dream, I shall live with my god. 'Sorrrry,' I shall say. A Russian 'r' will reverberate. 'Forrrgive me. Both of you.'

I shall close my eyes in order to avoid meeting theirs. 'Are you kidding, Lucie?' Joy's voice will sound so strange.

'Look into my eyes and answer.' Leslie's music will echo. 'You heard me. Please, let me alone. Please.' My heart will sob.

Leslie will shake me hard, grabbing my shoulders, 'Look at me. Just look into my eyes. You can't do this again. No, you can't. You know you love me. Just dare to accept it. Open your eyes. Open your eyes.'

Wake up and smell the love.

Before it is too late, before it is dark.

This song of his will echo in my ears. But my darling darkness in front of my tightly closed eyes will see him clearly. The warm aquamarine. The killing curve. The deadly dimple. The blinding blond.

I shall hear Leslie smashing his guitar. The door will slam shut. Joy will touch his lips on my forehead. A drop of melted snow. A bindi of childhood, the loveliest. A soft exit. My eyes will open to a deep nothingness. 'If only I could wake up to a dream!'

'How could you say goodbye to both of them?' Granny will be furious with me.

'I can't see him hurt.'

'Don't you think he is hurt now? Don't you think *he* is hurt too?'

'Not that way. It won't have the sting of defeat.'

'Aren't you hurt?'

'Oh Granny, please.' My sore heart will cry.

'You foolish girl. You have made the greatest mistake of your life. Mistake. Yes, mistake. Mistake. Do you hear me? Mistake.' Granny's regular way of irregular talking. And her eyes will cast a guilty glance towards the past. 'Why do they make mistakes? Why did I make mistakes? I did, I did indeed. Why did I?' She will mutter on and get lost in the shadow of the past, or in the mist of time. After some time, she will shake her head with a violent zeal, as if throwing away all confusion, 'I won't allow you to do this. I won't. You cannot escape like that. I escaped. You won't. I won't allow you to. Why to escape? You cannot escape yourself. You cannot escape life. No escape. There is no escape. There is no scope to escape. Life takes it all.' Granny will cover her face with her hands. Then, she will sit by my side and try to hold me up.

'The fever is low now. It's better. But anyway, you must go and stop him.'

My questioning eyes will make her speak, 'I saw him. I talked to him. He has broken his guitar, next he will break himself Bit by bit. He will marry. Once, twice, maybe three times. But they will break him further rather than make him. He will take them like drugs. And be destroyed. He will destroy his own self, his charm, which is out of the world. Maybe, when he dies at the age of fifty his marvellous body will be as old and decayed as that of a seventy year old man. It will be beyond recognition. Will you allow that to happen?'

Granny's face will grow very pale. 'I allowed him to sink in sickness. And I nursed the sickness of all others. That is sick. All we need is just to lean on each other at the right moment.'

Yes. Granny will make me feel. The ego. The misunderstanding. One's advances, the other's hesitation. Out of tune. Only one simultaneous muscular jerk is needed for both the wings and then it is an unbridled flight. But simultaneous action. Just before taking off, the momentary wavering of one wing would mean nothing but a fall. I shall want to let my love fly free, high and higher.

'Shall I call him?' I shall ask Granny.

'How can you? He is flying to Bombay this evening. Barely one hour from now.'

'Then? Even if we start now, we can't catch him up.'

His mobile number will not be known to us. Granny will suggest we leave a message at the airport for him. We shall do that.

'Mr Leslie Fraser, Lucie is coming to see you. Please don't go.'

Yet, Granny will not be hundred per cent satisfied.

'You can't just count on that. Knowing the way our people work. They may forget to announce. He may not hear. He may be hiding in some nearby place to avoid the crowds. So, we have to do something else. Something else. Yes, something else.'

'What Granny?' My sick brain will not be able to produce any idea, but Granny will stand up.

'We have to reach there, within the hour.'

'Impossible!'

'No, we shall row. Row, row, row the boat gently down the stream. By water, it will hardly take twenty minutes.'

She will immediately call Mauvin. For a boat. For three. Granny will have to accompany me. To take care of my sickness. Granny will ask him to take a small motorized rowing boat.

'But Grandma, the weather is terrible. The sea is so rough. The wind is strong. The waves are sky high. I won't advise . . . .'

'You'd say nothing. Just row for us. Aren't you a jolly brave young man? Or a coward?' Granny's words will goad him. Her tempting proposal too.

'I shall pay you in dollars. Hundred dollars. Will you take us? You have to take us.'

'Make it two Grandma. The sea is real rough. It is raining. The wind is very strong. And it is so dark!'

Granny will agree and three of us will start. To love. Love which Granny lost and which I must not lose. The journey will begin. Row, row, row the boat, gently, no, strongly down the stream.

Rosana Fernandez is lying on the seashore. After her last journey. A journey by boat. She is lying on the shore. Face down. Arms spread. The storm has subsided. The rain has stopped. The clouds have dispersed. Rosana is lying all alone on the beach. The sea is caressing her body with every splashing wave of passion. She is still. Her flyaway silky silvery hair is dull and solid. Rosana Fernandez lies motionless. Or it is not Rosana Fernandez? She has escaped somewhere. This is the body of Rosana Fernandez, that sea has deposited on the shore. Like an oyster shell. Along with some broken planks of the boat.

Mauvin's skilled hand will save me out of the clutches of a turbulent sea. Wretched weather. Wrecked dinghy. Granny will be lost. In the sea. Her final refuge.

Rosana Fernandez, the real Rosana Fernandez is now rowing her boat, somewhere beyond the depth of the sea. Here the sea splashes on her body. Water adorns it. Brittle water. Breaks into pieces. Rustles over her like wasted dead autumn leaves. Yellow with the wilted moon on it. The water turns her into water.

A watery body, a flowing body in the arms of Leslie. My body. In spate. Every bit for every bit. Every wave for every wave. At last. *Dip and splash. Dip and splash.*

A man and a woman. As far as reality and dreams. As near too. As real. Together, it makes life. Antonio's life. Rosana's life. Rosana's soul takes a dip in the deep. Where is Antonio? Row for him. *Dip and splash. Dip and splash.*

My watery body will deepen. The oar in the water. The churning. *Dip and splash. Dip and splash.* Reality takes a dip. Dreams splash. Life rows for a refuge. From eternity to eternity.